HALF PAST THE
DEAD OF NIGHT

HALF PAST THE DEAD OF NIGHT

Cleo Baldon

iUniverse LLC
Bloomington

HALF PAST THE DEAD OF NIGHT

This is a work of fiction. All of the characters, names, incidents, organizations, and dialogue in this novel are either the products of the author's imagination or are used fictitiously.

iUniverse books may be ordered through booksellers or by contacting:

iUniverse LLC
1663 Liberty Drive
Bloomington, IN 47403
www.iuniverse.com
1-800-Authors (1-800-288-4677)

Because of the dynamic nature of the Internet, any web addresses or links contained in this book may have changed since publication and may no longer be valid. The views expressed in this work are solely those of the author and do not necessarily reflect the views of the publisher, and the publisher hereby disclaims any responsibility for them.

Any people depicted in stock imagery provided by Thinkstock are models, and such images are being used for illustrative purposes only. Certain stock imagery © Thinkstock.

ISBN: 978-1-4917-1042-5 (sc)
ISBN: 978-1-4917-1043-2 (hc)
ISBN: 978-1-4917-1044-9 (e)

Library of Congress Control Number: 2013922295

Printed in the United States of America.

iUniverse rev. date: 03/21/2014

To my Wonderful Husband
and Spell Check

Acknowledgments

Dear friend and mentor, coach and council Marilee Zdenek
Son and Hollywood Hi graduate Dirk Baldon
F Bomb and other current language consultant John Latimer
Dear friend and reader who didn't like Ula, Gloria Wineberger

Chapter 1

It was half past the dead of night, and the ever-present purr of the city had not yet begun to dial up to the roar it would become. No individual sound had yet detached itself: no dog barked; no rescue vehicle screamed down the boulevard. Even the night birds were still during this time between.

The sequin net of lights thrown over the city from Malibu to LAX did little to dilute the black of the moonless night.

The first sound of impending day would be the crash of bottles against a wire rack, and the image of a milkman delivering to Chateau Marmont would pop up in J.'s mind. It could not be a milkman, of course, couldn't have been for seventy years or so. The milkman's shoes would have been whitened every night, his pants newly washed behind the porthole door in the Bendix and dried all day in the sun on a line out by the incinerator. The pants would have had a button fly, and he would have worn a shirt to match—no T-shirt yet, and the cap would not have been a baseball cap, either backward or forward, but a pork pie thing with a covered button on the top, also not long from the Bendix.

When the milk went to cardboard carton at the store, the man would have gone to work for Lockheed or maybe joined the Navy. Maybe he came back and bought a bungalow with his severance pay, and he could be slowly walking the neighborhood every morning now, on VA and Medicare.

J. never knew what the bottle sound was. It must have been some kind of equipment, set to go off automatically on a timer, but nothing but the milkman fit.

The second harbinger of a new day was just as reliable. It was the three-syllable bird who, like a windshield wiper, said what you wanted him to say. This one was screeching, "Up to bat, up to bat!" The two-syllable harbinger of day soon flew in with a "nit-nit." As J. waited for the single-sound forager to join in, he chose this wakeful time to contemplate the final decision that must be made later today. He was all but sure whom the opposition would choose for their candidate, and he set that image behind one of two podiums on the back of his eyelids and tested each of his party's possibilities in turn. The person needed to be smooth, smart, unflustered, and of a ready wit; have good hair and clothes that fit properly (especially around the neck); and be able to look presidential enough for a TV series and possibly say something of moral value. He rejected each of them in turn and had to start over.

Predawn sounds began now, a little thicker texture added to the basic sounds. A car started up, the bottle delivery rattled, an early flight from the far-off airport added an almost imperceptible purr and blinking lights, a pool filter started, and a familiar barking began, a little dog bark, sounding ankle-high. There was a faint white hiss of a sprinkler going on. Someone hummed, taking early room service to one of the cottages, and two lights—three floors apart and on opposites ends of Chateau Marmont—flashed on in turn as though triggered, one by the other: New York actors staying at the Marmont, rising for early makeup call. Dial up the sound and cue the day.

Light began to seep into his room, and J. could make out his white robe and a door trim, and then the furniture began to materialize. Daylight was coming, and this was his time to push dark thinking back into the dark and go back to sleep. He hit the remote to close both sets of curtains, plumped the pillow with his fist, and turned onto his side.

When he awoke, it was to the smell of coffee. Angela, whom his mother had called her house angel, must have let herself in some time ago and progressed to the kitchen. It was later than he'd planned to wake. He reversed the curtains, letting in a brilliant February Tuesday.

The season was recognizable for there were still only those white fluffy trees in bloom as far as he could see, which was clear to the ocean, though today there was no Catalina. *They must have sailed it away,* he thought with amusement—this is what he had believed when he was a little boy.

He retrieved another remote and turned the television on to the morning news, which was covering little besides voting and a high-rise fire that was pretty much under control.

Moving to the bathroom, he showered great quantities of water upon himself in celebration that the retiled shower was no longer in danger of leaking into a downstairs hall. Soon he was dressed in black briefs, a black tank, black socks, newish Levi's, and a knobby crew neck in a color he had heard called "oyster." Looking about for shoes, he took off the socks and shoved his bare feet into the Bruno Maglis that he spotted partially under the bed.

As a matter of principle, he chose to take the stairs two at a time rather than the elevator, though from childhood, he had liked its sound and the way it raised its floor to be exactly flush with the tile floor of the entry hall above. He yelled a "good morning" into the quiet house.

He drank half the cup of coffee Angela had just left him on the breakfast room table and scooped up the sample ballot and script along with the *Times* in its plastic cover, which indicated the possibility of rain or the sale of an ad on it. He yelled his goodbye in the direction of a vacuum cleaner sound. In the garage he put down the top and hit the door opener and then rolled his BMW out into the narrow, hillside street. Usually, he would have walked to the voting precinct, but in the family-room polling place of many years three blocks up the hill, the floor was getting redone, probably stone this time. His precinct had been combined with another one and set up for the day in an unused ballroom on the third floor of a hotel on Sunset. This was good; the parking was easy.

When J. arrived, the cheerful lady whose floor was being redone was at a round table, looking desolate and lost in the dimness of the partially lit vastness. The voting booths were spotlighted. Behind the short curtain of the other party's booth he saw the shortest of skirts and the greatest legs of the century, bare, with feet enclosed in the crisscrossed straps of high-heeled sandals. The shoes were red with tiny brass buckles. He wished for a moment that he had not gone five days without trimming his beard but then was glad that he had not after all pulled on the black watch cap that suited his mood.

His precinct lady was running an arthritic finger down the page, looking for his name. She'd had no need to ask for it because they had been together for many elections—though maybe not really together, for he suspected she was very liberal, judging by some serious tie-dye and various book titles in her family room.

He needed to know who belonged to those legs and was thinking about how to negotiate for the information when the other precinct worker sitting at the table ran her pink-polished nail down a list in another book. Trained in detail, he was able to see, upside down, a name before the book was hastily closed to protect the voter's privacy. Too late—he had seen the name.

Just then the curtain of the booth was pushed aside by a huge red handbag, followed by a pretty blond, supported on those legs, those legs.

Wearing a broad smile, as though she had elected a presidential candidate for her party all by herself, she handed over her sheathed ballot and stalked toward the elevator.

"I shall return," J. said, dropping his unused ballot on the table.

"Be sure you do, Douglas," said the woman who was of an age to remember Douglas McArthur leaving the Philippines.

He took long strides, calling "Mary Ellen, Mary Ellen!" as he pursued the woman. "Mary Ellen?" he said one final time as he stepped up beside her, just as she reached for the elevator button with her left hand.

She wore no wedding ring on her finger, nor was there any tan line to indicate one had been there. She had the kind of skin that cosmetic companies try to tell women comes from their bottles, and the only artistry was eyeliner and lashes.

She replied in chimes, "I'm sorry, I don't go by that name enough to recognize that it is I someone is calling."

All that and proper grammar! "Well then, Ms. Higgens . . ."

"No, I didn't mean that, just that I go by my initials, M. E. Did I forget something?"

"Yes, you did. It was I."

Of course it was a line, but it was good enough that she smiled. They stepped into the elevator together, which felt to J. like a symbol of commitment. The two floors were interval enough for him to suggest to her that she had done a noble day's work and must be hungry.

"Do you have a favorite place in our neighborhood for brunch?" he pursued, implying a certain safety because they were neighbors. "I can bring you back to your car."

"I walked," she admitted.

"Well then, I can take you home, wherever that is. I, like some other people I know, go by my initial. It's J. for Jared— Jared Dunkin at your command, ma'am. We could go to Clafoutis, or to Cravings if the stairs are a bit much for those heels."

Her laugh sounded like chimes. "I have acquired a certain skill," she replied.

Good, she was a little defensive, he thought, and so would show him the stair trick.

He prayed she would not evaporate while he brought his car to the front door. He might have left it with the valet had he known how seamlessly he would like it back.

As he pulled up, he hid his sample ballot and pulled the half-marked-up script and newspaper over to clear the seat. She was still there, waiting.

She laughed as she smoothly opened the door, and he felt a little defensive—was she laughing at his car?

"Same as mine," she said. "Different color."

He coasted the Beamer down the driveway apron, craned around to judge the fast flow of late-morning traffic on the Sunset Strip, and joined it adroitly after a Hummer limo. He had several blocks to get into the left lane at Sunset Plaza. When the wind began to whip her hair around her face, she set her bag on the floor and held her hair with both hands.

"I hope you can take a long lunch hour," he said.

"Yes, I'm the boss—how about you?" she asked and then looked at the script lying beside her. "You a director? Writer? Actor?"

"No."

"Want to be?"

"No."

"Then what do you do or want to do?"

"I want to criticize."

They had come to the break in the median strip of cute plantings and set-in pots of seasonal flowers. J. made a sharp left and rolled down the steep driveway to the parking lot a floor below the street. It wasn't lunchtime yet, so they had their choice of spaces. He chose one with an empty to the right. She established their relationship by waiting for him to come around and open her door. So she was looking at it as a date, he decided—good.

As he stood at her door, he had the opportunity to look down at the part in her hair; it was natural or a very good and recent job of honey with California girl streaks. It was that thick handful kind of hair.

She swung her legs around and ignored his proffered hand, but he was still close enough to catch the scent of her.

"Mm, Ingénue," he said.

"Yes, how do you know that?"

"Family predecessors in the studio makeup business."

They walked toward the stairs leading up to the street, and she stopped at the bottom. "By the way, how did you know my name?"

"I distracted the precinct commander and read upside down."

Her laugh sounded like chimes again.

She navigated the stairs very well. Three risers and a landing, followed by another three risers and a landing, and she never touched the handrail. When they emerged on Sunset and turned left, he noted the sound of her heels clicking.

They threaded through the table-choked sidewalk in front of Chen's, only about half-full as yet, and came to a halt where the chairs were of a different manufacture and the awnings a different color.

A tiny, dark woman all in black greeted them with an open smile. Clutching menus to her, she said, "Oh, Mr. Dunkin and Ms. Higgen, his regular table or yours?"

"Let's have a neutral one, inside, up in the back," he requested. J. was chagrined to realize he'd mispronounced her name at the elevator. "I thought it was 'Higgens' in the usual Irish way."

"It's Higgen in the unusual Irish way. And the M. E. is pronounced Emmy."

Once inside, they followed the hostess up the two steps, where she swiveled the table so that Emmy could sit on the banquette. They both commented on the new chairs, substantial enough that J. did not fear collapsing one, as he had with the skinny iron ones before them.

They were hardly seated when the black-clad waiter appeared with a drink in either hand. "I didn't know you knew each other."

J. solemnly said, "Not in the carnal sense, but I'm working on it." He noticed Emmy's slight discomfort and felt encouraged by it.

He watched her sip from her glass and said, "I would have to guess the server knows you never drink anything else. What is it?"

"Lillet."

"May I taste it?" He was more interested in the intimate gesture of putting his mouth where hers had been than curious about the drink.

She took it back from his hand, touching his fingers slightly.

"So, of what are you boss?" he asked.

"I have a showroom called Stuff, and my website is named M. E. Stuff. I do a lot of studio rentals and collectables and interior designer's accessories."

"Like what?"

"Well, right now I have a uniform from the Winkie Guards."

"Blue, isn't it?"

"Wow! How'd you know that?"

"Addicted to *Gone with the Wizard* and others."

"You are? How I love films!"

"Favorite?"

"I think it would be an obscure picture called *The War Lord* with Charlton Heston and a stone tower strewn with fur rugs."

"You stumped me right out of the gate," he said. "Speaking of collectables—do you know whether anyone collects old milk bottles? Do you remember what the covers looked like?" He told her about that early morning milk delivery.

"We will find out. I think you owe me some personal information now . . . what do you do with that marked-up script?"

"Jared Damon Dunkin, script supervisor, ma'am. I'm the guy who prevents the heroine from pulling her left earlobe in the close-up and the right in the long shot. I save motion pictures from themselves. They also pay me for historical research for accuracy that they can choose to ignore."

"What, do you have one of those useless degrees in history, like mine in art history? Where did you go to school, and what is your favorite movie, if you are allowed to have one?"

"Gardner Street, LeConte, Hollywood High."

"Where did you go when you got out of our hood?" she pursued.

"From no tuition to high tuition: USC for history and then two more years to try to decide what to do with it."

"Your master's—that's great!"

"Yeah, I could teach."

"Not bad."

"I could barely hold still in class. Couldn't see a lifetime of it. How about you?"

"My father was pretty thrilled that I went from Buckley tuition to the state university system: UCLA. But he couldn't understand what I would ever do with four years of art history. Now he knows."

The waiter appeared, and J. suggested another Lillet, but the waiter, with the aloofness of knowing her better than he did, said that she never had a second but that he would bring him his usual second scotch. And what did he want to order today? the waiter asked after noting that he knew J.'s companion would have her usual quiche, though it was earlier than Ms. Higgen had ever appeared for lunch.

"So are you any relation to the Damon Higgen that I was named after?"

"Not *that*, but *whom* you were named after—or more accurately, after whom you were named. What lady in your family was in love with Old Rascal Damon? I know *for sure* that somebody was." She hit "for sure" with a Valley girl accent, poking some fun at Damon's fans.

There was a slight tired edge to her voice, as though this had come up far more than once. "Kin?" he guessed.

"Yeah, father's father."

Thinking of celebrity bios he had read, he asked, "Did you know him?"

"Tall man, white coat, cigar. My father was from an early wife. Number three, I think it was. And you didn't answer favorite movie. I'll bet it wasn't one of his."

"I'm sitting here trying to think of an endearing, funny, perceptive choice with historically accurate and attractive accessories, some Turner classic with a beautiful mistake not immediately discernable to all. Have you heard that *Lord of the Rings* has a New Zealand fence post that didn't get edited out?"

"You mean you didn't see it? You must have blinked into a handful of popcorn."

What a nice opportunity this was to lay out some bait. "The Directors Guild screenings don't have popcorn, cell phones, hissing, booing, or even—except very seldomly—applause."

He studied her as he spoke. What a nice face she had, and she was not a self-absorbed beauty. He considered that she might even care what others think. He was trying to figure out whom she looked like—a little like Rossellini, but that one was a great beauty. Emmy had that flattened nose bridge that he thought of as Irish, but without the freckles he would expect. The eyelids above her blue eyes retreated into her eye sockets like all descendents of cold climates. He liked the slight irregularity of teeth. Her hands were good, with strong thumbs and nails she had left natural. He was guessing she did this to prove that she really could grow her own that long. Under the leather jacket and turtleneck sweater, he couldn't tell if she had the breasts to tape up to her chin in a bare dress when he took her to some award ceremony or other (to which he had never yet been invited). It should be a shimmery dress, slit to the hip to show at least one of those legs, those legs.

She had a nice full mouth and wore lipstick so pale it was hardly visible. He would guess Ingénue's Tangiers. She stretched it into a smile with a look of square corners, a smile of great appreciation.

"You belong to the Directors Guild?" she asked.

"Yes, script supervisors do."

Her quiche and his omelet arrived with a flourish from the waiter, and J. chugged the second drink and ordered coffee, all the time trying to decide whether now was the best time to ask her to the screening tonight.

"So did old Damon come through with any tuition?"

"I don't think so. No, he was way too fertile. He could have started a school of his own kids."

"Then you have aunts and uncles?"

"Yeah, four each, and two sisters who have apparently inherited that fertility. It's a bunch at Thanksgiving. How about you?"

"Well, I took my grandmother and her boyfriend to a restaurant this Thanksgiving. There's no one else left."

"That sounds like a sad story."

"Yeah, instant orphan, but I inherited a lot of real estate and an Eames lounge chair."

"You know they come up at auctions now like antiques. Don't tell me you have the rosewood one!"

"It would have pleased my mother if it could be regarded as antique because it was the only thing in the house that wasn't. I hope you'll think she had a good eye. It was always out for some wonderful old piece of furniture. Me, I'm modern. I want to lead a modern life. They gave me two Mies Barcelona chairs when I moved into my condo," he said, giving out information to get some in return. He noticed that Emmy had nice use of a fork; some women didn't.

The waiter hovered. He filled her coffee cup, and she thanked him prettily. "You do develop an eye for objects hardly even seen across crowded rooms, like junk stores. I confess," she said, in what seemed like a promise of personal information, "that I once sat at a notary's table in her dimly lit house and just knew that table was Stickley, and when I heard that she died, I went over and made an offer on it. It is a great one. Stuff that came out of a bungalow goes back to the bungalow." She pushed aside the salad, a great heap on the plate beside the quiche.

Noting the gesture he recited, "Eat the greens / They really are a treat / They make long ears / And great big feet."

The chimes came again in reply. "Greens aren't breakfast food—didn't your father tell you that, Thumper?"

"Very good! You must win at movie trivia."

"Last time I played was on a ship, and I got all but one: 'what movie tough guy posed for baby food ads when he was an infant?'"

"We should go away together and finish the game because I know it was Humphrey Bogart."

She smoothly ignored the mention of going away together, choosing instead to pursue Bogart. "Is he a favorite of yours? Did you know he was distantly related to Princess Di? I like him because he brought us Bacall, and I don't buy anything to wear without thinking whether she would like it."

"All right, if we can't go away together, would you like to go to the screening at the Directors Guild tonight?"

That seemed to please her, but she asked what was being shown.

"I have no idea. Movies are an art form for which I do not want to have read a review or seen an ad. I want to sit down front, right in the picture, and not know what it is until the red curtain parts, and the screen lights with the title. I've seen a lot of junk, but that's the price I pay."

"Do other people go along with you on this madness? Have you ever been married? And if so, is that why she left you?"

Now they were playing for the information they both had wanted as early as the elevator. He chose not to capitulate without a skirmish.

"The Guild sends a monthly magazine with a schedule of screenings. In my day planner, I scribble 'DGA' at the bottom of a day with a screening. If it's something I know I want to see, I underline it and then don't peek back. The schedule only tells who directed anyway, as though that were all that was important. And maybe it is. I go when I can and see it fresh. I've seen a lot of movies by myself lately." There, that sounded provocative and available. Would her reply be about the films or the woman who had left him lonely?

She was good; she was quick. She asked, "Was it a wife who left you to see movies alone?"

"No, we were posslqs."

"Oh, did your mother read Jack Smith to know that useful Jack-invented word?"

"I read the wordsmith myself." And then just because he wanted to use the word "sex," he recited, "Persons of the opposite sex, sharing living quarters."

Not quite ready to talk about that, she reverted to Hollywood High instead. "Your school—it always looked like more fun than I was having, not that I didn't like Buckley, and I did appreciate all those languages I had to learn, useful if I ever get to travel."

He filed that away to think about what travel he could offer her, with a lovely little hotel. He took up the topic of languages. "Well, we had languages. It was said that there were seventy-two languages spoken at Hollywood High. I hung out with speakers of three or four of them, the whitest face in the crowd. With my black Irish hair I could get by from the back, if I turned up my collar and kept my hands in my pockets."

She laughed, obviously visualizing, and he continued.

"We knew about Buckley. We used to say that there were these two Buckley kids talking at lunch and one said to the other, 'I heard your mother got married again; who's the guy?' . . . 'Oh, him, he's okay. We had him last year.'"

"Yeah, like Hollywood High was full of traditional families. We always heard it was two kids from Beverly Hills High who had that conversation."

She supposed she'd thought he was Irish too. It was, after all, the biggest ancestral group in the country by now. He was an interesting guy. If she were sketching him, she would start with a strong shoulder line. Everything about him seemed to hang from those straight-out-of-the-neck shoulders. When he moved them, the rest of his body followed. His face must have been intended for gorgeousness, but the sculptor got a little too much clay above the eyebrows and on the sides of the nose, which looked as though it was meant to be aquiline, but wasn't. It was hard to tell about the mouth under the beard, untrimmed and looking like five days of carelessness. His utter sureness of himself was pretty attractive. He seemed like the kind of man who would tell

13

you that you could go along, but you'd have to carry your own suitcase.

It seemed safe to stay with Hollywood High, and she attempted to pronounce it as he did, "Hahwood." And did he ever see his buds from there?

"Sure, a lot of us are somewhere in the industry. Tonight at the screening, one of them, an out-of-work-from-the-strike associate director, will be there with his blond mop posslq. But let's not go out with them afterward. I'd rather just talk to you."

She didn't remember accepting the invitation to just any movie, but why not? Maybe it was an underlined one.

"Instead of taking you home to get your car, why don't I take you to your showroom, and then I can pick you up for the seven o'clock screening, and we can eat afterward and then I can take you home?"

"Because I feel apprehensive without my getaway car."

"I'll be gentle."

She did look apprehensive then, but hid it quickly.

"I'll be there about five. Is that when you close? Then I can see the Winkie costume."

"And look for milk bottles."

Emmy adroitly slipped out her credit card and suggested splitting the bill.

"No, this is a date. This is our first date, and I am so well funded now." Surely she had seen the ugly ass Bruno Maglis and the Rolex.

When they returned to the car, the parking spot beside his was no longer empty, so getting her into the car was more intimate, and he was able to pull out her seatbelt and lean across her to fasten it. She did not retreat at all—very good!

As they drove up the driveway to the Strip, she dug into her big red handbag, brought out a scarf, and tied it under her chin. Nice pattern, a kind of art deco with a dash of red.

"What? No sunglasses?"

"I don't do sunglasses—or umbrellas."

"That's not entirely Hollywood. Aren't you a native? Where did you live as a cute little virgin?" He knew this was a hard-to-field question—protesting it would not be smooth, and answering it would be self-incriminating.

His admiration was great when she said, "Surely you are not saying I was a Hollywood virgin, locally defined as an ugly six-year-old." Then she returned to the question.

"We lived just below Sunset on the Kentucky Fried Chicken street, where a tall apartment building looked into our backyard. Then we moved to a bigger house on the upper side of Sunset, same street. My father saw the sale sign out when he was walking the dog, and he was getting pretty prosperous by then."

J. thought she might want him to ask what her father did or does, so he asked.

"He makes buttons." Her tone suggested she had played with this answer before and was ready with more information, so he didn't ask. He asked only where they were going, and she directed him down Crescent Heights and then to a left turn on Beverly. "You don't fall far from the tree, do you? Where do you live?" She would have to tell him, for he would be taking her back there after the screening.

"Even closer to the tree, three blocks from old home. I own a Craftsman bungalow, with all its old glass doorknobs intact."

Was there apprehension in her voice? In a reassuring tone he responded, "Don't worry, I won't seduce you there; we'll go to my house for that. It has its original doorknobs too."

Bless her, she laughed and finally asked what pictures he had worked on and saved from disaster. What a good opportunity to tell her that he had them all on discs in his bedroom, ready to slip into his player.

She was directing him down a driveway now, behind her business, to a small parking space. He could see a very attractive courtyard entry. She got out of the car, not waiting for him, and set those beautiful legs in march to the door. She called over her shoulder that she'd see him later.

"Okay, I have to go back and vote."

He retraced his journey and paused in the sun-drenched parking lot of the polling place hotel to pull out his cell phone. She answered right away.

"Grandsweety, I just found her," he said. "The best legs in town, an Irish girl who uses Ingénue, Mary Ellen Higgen. She goes by Emmy, for her initials, and as you probably can guess, her grandfather was Damon Higgen. I was feeling so dark, bleak, and down. I went to vote and there she was! Mood change!"

There was a pause, and then his grandmother said, "Oh, ah! She's not for you. I'm serious, not for you. Just don't impregnate her on the first date, you know. You never do that anyway, and you never did get to that Italian lawyer lady bitch, even knowing how much I wanted those dark-eyed great-grandbabies. You're all so lucky now with contraceptive choices. We just didn't know what to do, you know."

"Grandlady dear, you skipped a generation here. In all of history, my parents' generation was the only one to have sexual freedom, in the time between the pill and AIDS. There is no casual sex now. You can get worse things than pregnant, you know. You poor thing, you couldn't even get a safe abortion, and besides, you had to walk to school in the snow."

"I did, you know—I had the prettiest little black suede boots with a white fur trim one year, but it was only three blocks."

"You did have condoms, you know. I know because a guy landing on the beach on D-day would put a condom over the rifle muzzle to keep it dry."

She protested how he could know that.

"Do you want me to get my PhD in history before you just believe me? I don't know if they shot through them or rolled them off. They wouldn't be much use for their intended purpose afterward anyway."

"Your education has really paid off for you to know that, or was it in a movie?"

"Well, so you didn't get Italian grandbabies, but my cousin's got you a grandbaby now—and in wedlock. I guess I'll never see him. Is he cute as hell?"

"No, he looks too much like you."

"Dark and handsome. I doubt he's tall yet."

"No, they call it long in babies."

"Oh, is that how he looks like me?"

"Naughty boy, it means he was twenty-one inches long, and he weighed seven pounds and twelve ounces at birth, and I do adore him. So what about the legs girl? She must be black Irish, spawn of Damon."

"No, she's blond, and there she was in the wrong voting booth. We're going to a screening tonight, and I don't know how we'll talk about the primaries because she starts off so wrong."

"She is wrong for you, dear. Just don't take her out again. I'm serious. She is not for you. You were down, you saw her, and then you were up. A story as old as history."

"Grandcritic, now who's naughty? Well, little Miss South Dakota who knows everything, Norwegian isn't the only thing you can be to be in the pageant. Irish is not that bad—you married one and had those blue-eyed babies."

A moment later, they said their goodbyes because he still had to vote and do some work on the script, and of course, he had to shave a day or so off his beard.

At the end of the day, he didn't change his clothes because she couldn't do that at her showroom, but he put on a sport coat, the so-casual vicuña one his mother had brought him from Argentina.

He went around to the Whole Foods parking lot and picked up the three orders of fried wontons that he had phoned in to the Thai place. He then drove down La Brea to come out in front of her showroom and found street parking because it was early for restaurant patrons.

The show windows were lit, and a display of iridescent glass glowed. "Wow," he said, pushing open the door as its buzzer sounded.

"You like carnival glass and American art glass?" she called out from the back. He looked up and saw her slipping into a short satin trench coat.

He looked back to the items on display. How he longed to take home to his mother the black-footed, shimmering, jade-colored martini glasses—and the satin lady.

Emmy invited him to look around and introduced him to her assistant, who was just turning off a computer at a back desk; the young man registered the Bruno Maglis with undisguised envy.

The music was still on, and a last customer was pulling out a credit card and cooing over how perfect her purchase was. J. thought he recognized her from a passing TV screen image.

There was a radio on, with someone speculating about the candidates, but there were no conclusions yet. Iowa and New Hampshire were long over, and how important could this be? Very, he concluded.

He wandered. Lighted cabinets, shimmering screens, fabrics, changing floor surfaces and colors, ancient objects, and modern ones. And throughout a scent that he thought he could identify as patchouli. He kept feeling blown away.

Emmy caught up with him in front of the Winkie Guard uniform.

"Is that how you remember it?"

"It's smaller, but so was I. And what's this?"

In the case on shelves were letters and a studio contract, which upon looking closer he saw was signed by Ray Bolger. He said the only appropriate word: "Wow!"

They nibbled wontons over a glass counter with a display of consigned art deco jewelry glittering on black velvet, and again he could only say, "Wow!" J. felt gratitude that his mother had talked ceaselessly about objects, about stuff.

At the Directors Guild Theater they arrived early enough to have parking luck, directly opposite the elevator.

He thought for the hundredth time about how forlorn and ugly the parking floors were, before visitors encountered the ground floor opulence that some committee thought was great (but that always reminded him of director taste, the alpaca cardigan golf sweater). The ugly parking was a puzzle to him because almost everyone saw it first, so for whom was the lobby?

"I love being here," she said, "but who did this carpet that clashes with the floor color?"

He said a few hellos on their way to the red plush seats in the fourth row.

"There will be friends coming down who will stand in front of us to talk, mostly to check you out," he predicted. And so it was, one just back from scouting locations in Death Valley; another just promised assistant director for a soap, if the writers ever settled the strike; another at "momentary leisure." And then there was the handsome bearded friend with a blond big-haired woman who fortunately didn't even suggest going out together after the screening.

As the lights dimmed, J. whispered, "It's an underlined movie."

"I know what it is," she whispered back. "I called the Guild screening hotline."

Chapter 2

"I don't leave until the end of the credits," J. said as the music swelled. "I wait to see the disclaimer that no animals were hurt in the filming of this picture."

They did not speak again until they were in the lobby passing the huge marble columns, almost to the elevator. He asked what she thought and whether the film deserved its underline.

"You first," she countered.

"Well, I saw the crew only twice, once reflected in a store window and once in a hub cap."

*   *   *

It is a nice face, she thought, *with that stubble beard reduced and tidied. A straight guy who can be wowed by beautiful objects and even seems to know something about them. The way he throws himself into the booth, the shoulders followed by the rest of him, like the abandon of a kid. He must be midthirties. Nice hands, but let's not think of that. The jacket is a wild thing, the kind that should be kept in the family for a generation at least— maybe it has been.*

"What to drink? I doubt they have Lillet. This is no fancy spot, but the parking is reliable, they stay open late, and they make their own mashed potatoes from potatoes—and it's quiet so we can talk."

"Unusual to be able to talk in a restaurant. Don't they know that here? Didn't it used to be browner than beige and called Theodor's? The glass cabinet with the custard pies, by the front desk, is still the same, just new pies."

An indifferent waiter appeared; he neither told them his name nor vowed to be their waiter tonight. He took the order for J.'s scotch and Emmy's Tanqueray on the rocks, to be delivered from the glassed-in, darkened bar next to the entry.

She was pleased that he ordered for her and that he asked for an order of fried zucchini without asking whether she liked it.

The car radio had reported the finalists in the two party primaries, and her sigh had told him her disappointment. He'd held back his elation for the win of his candidate.

"It could still go your way. There's a convention and an election ahead, though you better not count us out."

It was much safer to talk about the film now than the election.

"So what was it about the movie that didn't work?" he asked. "When did you know you were bored?"

"I didn't know right away. The beginning was so beautiful and moody. Then I kept looking at you, but you were rapt."

"I was deep in wonder that that much production value didn't have a plausible story. To tell a story is what it's for, and they didn't, and these are good people. What was it for you, or . . . was it good for you?" He changed his tone to a seductive one for that question.

"Not as advertised, not 'best of the year.'" She let her voice go coy and batted her eyelashes as though she were answering a question about sexual performance.

He liked her better all the time. "But really there was something terribly lacking. What did you think it was?"

She responded in seriousness, "I didn't like the jerky montages. That style didn't seem the right pace, and worse, there wasn't a believable woman in the whole thing."

21

"I think you've got it. What about the things, the stuff? I thought the bar cart by the fire was straight out of an old movie, and they weren't trying to make that reference." He shook his glass for the ice sound and staged a mannered toast.

"Right, I didn't think of it, having seen that so many times. Whoever put that tray together with fresh ice and the right number of glasses?"

"The set designer, of course, the same one who clears a parking space for the arriving hero," he explained.

"Movies with you are fun."

"Then shall you sleep with me tonight?"

After only a fleeting faint change of expression, she replied, "I don't think the word 'shall' works in second-person question at all. It expresses simple futurity in first person. It expresses determination of futurity, however, in second and third person. You might say, 'Will you?' and then I would say, 'I shall not' to express simple futurity—or 'I will not,' to express determination."

"Is this anything like no?"

"Yes," she said, smiling prettily.

"If it's yes, shall we go now?"

"No, no, we will not. Or with 'we' as first person, will it be 'shall not'?"

"Does this have anything to do with what is is?"

"What I want to know is," she said, "do you get slapped often?"

"Actually not, but once at a wedding, I got a full margarita thrown in my face."

"The salt must have stung."

"Garden wedding. Had on my sunglasses."

But now he needed to return to a safe topic. "All that academic knowledge, and you are completely into stuff. Your showroom is terrific. How did you do all that? You have a bloody fortune in stuff."

"I'm blessed in being very organized and in the work being computerized, and the fabrics and samples are supplied by the manufacturers. A lot of stuff is samples, and a lot is on consignment. My customers are all comeback people—a lot of interior designers who take stuff on consignment for their clients to see. They mostly do the room and take back anything the client won't buy. I must say that most of them are awfully good, with not a lot of returns, but when their clients reject any stuff, we always cheerfully restock it.

"Some come in for gifts and some to buy for themselves. Sharon Stone bought herself a lot of tumblers with the initials 'E B' etched on them, Ethel Barrymore. She has great taste for color and offbeat things. She asks where did we—she and I of the dirt-poor Irish—get our taste? A movie buff, she wanted to know just anything about my grandfather."

"Do you like her?"

"Yeah, I really do. She had a cat with very big eyes named Miss Davis. Did you see her in *Casino*, working the room? She got the Golden Globe for it, and I thought she would get the Oscar, but Susan Sarandon did. I wrote her a note that said, 'For Sharon I'm carin', but Susan I'm choosin'.' She called and thought I'd come up with it, not knowing it was from the mouth of David Wayne, in *Brigadoon*, wasn't it?"

"*Finian's Rainbow*, Fred Astaire. It's such a great place, this. How did you get started?"

"Oh, and Frank Sinatra sang it a lot. About the showroom, in the beginning I had the good fortune to become a partner to a guy who is now nothing but a brass memorial plaque under a tree on Santa Monica Boulevard across from Koontz Hardware. If he could see us now, putting digital photos of stuff on the website . . . I don't tell everybody this, but I have a guy who goes to garage sales."

"Really! Does he pick up old paper? I don't tell everybody this, but I collect autographs."

"Oh, it's hard for me to see you sitting still over albums. What's your best one?"

"I would have to say a signed studio portrait of Clark Gable. I bought it from a vendor on Venice Beach."

"And is that your best movie moment, 'Frankly, my dear'?"

"I also like 'Stella!' What's yours?"

"Omar Sharif on a camel, materializing out of the horizon. You?"

"The horse's head on the bed."

"Paul Henreid lighting two cigarettes at once."

"Better was 'of all the gin joints . . . '"

"Gin was mother's milk to her."

"What we have here is a failure to communicate."

"I have a new favorite. Last night I watched a very-late-night *Hello, Dolly!* I loved it when a young and infinitely graceful Walter Matthau turned his back to the camera and danced with Streisand."

"I don't think I ever saw any of that, except for the set that was the street scene left up as the entry to Fox. I always felt I should be in a vintage car to go to a screening there." He thought it good for her to know that he went to screenings on studio lots as well as at the Directors Guild.

A second drink arrived, and they paused to order, for her a Monte Cristo and for him a hot turkey sandwich for the mashed potatoes.

She returned to films. "The bacon and tomato sandwich without the bacon and tomato was a great one from *Five Easy Pieces.*"

"Yes, I would have known that, though I'm not sure of the sandwich filling. I thought it was chicken salad, but I did know it was on toast. The director lived right down the hill from us, and his son shattered the night with his drums. His father built him a soundproof room, but you can't keep drums out of a neighbor's stomach."

She laughed. "Celebrity hazard. Can you present without identifying the film?"

"Maybe the rule should be that you have to know if challenged."

"Then I challenge you because the two cigarettes weren't from *Casablanca.*"

"So what were they from?"

"I'm not sure. How about 'I'm ready for my close-up, Mr. DeMille'?"

"*Sunset Boulevard*. Great one. How about 'You know how to whistle, don't you?'"

"Whistle while you work."

"The green corridor with Dorothy and friends reflected in the floor."

"How about in *Terminator*, when the floor bulges up and forms into a silver man?"

"Oh, yes." He recalled it fondly. "That picture got the Oscar for special effects. I know the guy who did it."

"Patton standing in front of the flag."

"I should have thought of that first. How did you come by that one? It's the original man's picture."

"My father would like to play it every night. What about the little kid calling Shane? Or is using its name against the rules? If so, delete *Patton*."

"How about Tradition?" he said as they clinked another toast.

"Anything from Fiddler. Vanessa Redgrave in ermine, arriving at Camelot in the snow. White on white."

"Danny Kaye. 'The chalice from the palace has the brew that's true.'"

"Get it?"

"Got it!"

"Good!"

"Go ahead, make my day."

"I'll have what she's having."

"Now?"

His question hung in the room, and they both exploded in laughter as they visualized Meg Ryan acting an orgasm, while Emmy was near blushing at what "make my day" had inspired.

"You are really good at movies. I wonder how long before I'd stump you, no pun intended."

The sandwiches finished, he ordered the coffee and Baileys Irish Cream as a buffer before he took her home.

"My great-great-grandfather probably drank poteen from an illegal still in the mountains, beside a turf fire," J. said, "but my grandfather sipped his Baileys by his log fire, laid and started by the housekeeper, in a huge fireplace, outlined in Batchelder tile."

"Oh, you do know your objects. Have you ever been out to Batchelder's house in Malibu, every surface tiled?"

"Yes, it's rented out for weddings. That's where I got the margarita in the face."

"I can't think of a nicer place to dry off. But say more about your grandfather. It sounds as though he wore an ascot and had a mustache. What did he do in old Hollywood?"

"Right on the mustache, but I remember him most in a white tennis sweater. He was head of makeup at the studio and invented some cosmetics. His grandmother wouldn't understand what that was all about as she washed her freckles in cold spring water.

"My own grandmother was much younger than he. Her family is from Norway. She was Miss South Dakota, third runner-up for Miss America. She will never let you forget it or that she made six movies, one with your grandfather, actually. I think it was she who gave me his name for seconds. I will take you to meet her. She is now my entire family."

"This is part of the sad story that you are yet to tell me? You didn't mention our connection before. Was this a 'failure to communicate'?"

"Yes, but it's time to take you home to your bungalow with its full set of glass doorknobs, where we will have our first kiss on the porch. They all have porches, don't they?"

Such was his intention, but that first kiss happened instead moments later, in the car before they even pulled out of the parking lot of the Silver Spoon.

The subsequent kiss on the porch was much deeper, and she was much more responsive, even with a small moan, but she wouldn't let him in, even to prove the full complement of glass knobs in which he professed to disbelieve.

"There's a screening tomorrow night at seven," he noted.

She smiled the smile he was already calling, to himself, her secret grin and said, "Yes I know. I think it's underlined. Pick me up here at my house. Six o'clock?"

When he got home, he called the cell phone number printed on her business card. "How about a game of memorable movie objects? The moth-eaten old Maltese falcon."

"The shower curtain in *Psycho*."

"Excalibur."

"Rosebud."

"The kitchen table, Lana Turner and John Garfield thereupon."

"This was a setup. Goodnight."

* * *

He awoke in the blackest of the night, as he always did. There was rain splattering on the balcony tiles, but now it was somehow pleasant, could have even been called cozy. Where was she in this darkest moment? Did she sleep on her side? Which side? Was she wearing a nightgown or nothing? Under a down quilt? Please, no pajamas, those legs, those legs!

* * *

Through the leaded window, from the porch, J. could see a fire in a coal grate. The doorbell was a turning one, like a key, and he set the night to buzzing—a 1912ish buzz. Accuracy gone mad!

As she opened the door, he pushed the flowers in front of him and asked, "Do you have a Craftsman vase? My Hollywood High friend in the flower business said these would be appropriate to Craftsman. Now everyone knows about you. Did you sweep the kitchen table clear?"

"No, John, I'm not Lana. I was busy being the set decorator, and how nice to finish it off with these beautiful flowers."

By the fireplace was a bar cart, elaborately set with an ice bucket, tongs, napkins, glasses, candles, tiny square pâté sandwiches, and more bottles than possibly necessary. J. gave her the rewarding, expected laugh. He made a great business of selecting a scotch. He could see that some of the bottles were new enough to suggest purchase today, to complete this theatrical set. All were opened.

"So great, and so little time to play this scene."

They stood close for a toast, and a kiss concluded it. When it became impassioned, Emmy pulled back and stammered, "Cut!"

"I long to kiss you on the navel."

"Big deal!"

"From the inside?"

She gave a little lurch. It was good that she was fighting to control the situation, even if she wouldn't be able to.

"Oh! I've never had a boyfriend who talks dirty. My girlfriends say it's terrific."

He lifted his glass in admiration. "Drink—it's time to get to the movie. Turn off lights and fire and set the burglar alarm. You won't be home tonight. I'm going to ravish you at my house, in the entry hall."

"You can't if I say no."

On the porch a few minutes later, J. looked back at the door. "Is that an authentic, period LED alarm light?"

"A girl has to make some compromises."

At the curb, shining under the streetlight, was an old Packard, yellow. That it was in brilliant condition was clear even in this lighting.

"Oh my God, look what's on the street," Emmy said. "Gorgeous!"

He took her hand to cross the bricked parking strip as though to look at it closer and then opened the door for her.

"You're kidding. This is yours, or borrowed? It's fabulous, fabulous! Where do you keep it? Talk about it!"

"I have four parking spaces. Full. I'll have to get rid of one car to make room for your car."

The car glided into traffic as though it were not the great lumbering hulk it seemed. It smelled of new leather and restoration. J. drove downhill on the empty street that turned onto Sunset, and the Packard got two thumbs up gestures within a block—and more yet as they descended into the Guild parking entrance. The attendant escorted them into an oversize spot.

Waiting for the elevator, she said, "I'm too awed to speak." But she did until the lights went down.

In front of the Palm after the film was over, J. attempted to provide the valet attendant with some car-starting instructions, but the man said aloofly, "We're professionals," and slapped the ticket into J.'s hand like a nurse giving a scalpel to a doctor.

"You'll get a good potato here," Emmy said, establishing that she'd been here before and, what's more, that she was already learning his particular tastes.

"New York, charred rare?"

"Yes!"

After going to a neighborhood hangout the night before, he'd decided this was a good place to take her, because it looked like one but wasn't. The noise level was enough to mask conversation without drowning it. There was sure to be a celebrity or two in the big, straight, wooden booths, and everybody would look to see if you were one as you passed by. There were a few places left like that.

"Now about the movie . . ." J. said.

"I think I liked it better than you did. You probably weren't able to justify the depth of the woman's anguish and loss. I failed to believe, though, that she would live in that apartment without doing anything to fix it up."

"Actually I did get the anguish and loss, and I believe that she would eat chocolates until noon and not give a damn if the place went to pieces around her."

Abruptly, in a complete change of subject, he said loudly, "Let's go home and play *The Unsinkable Molly Brown.*" The woman who had just slid out of the booth across from them tittered as she passed by.

"Well," said Emmy, "I suppose she was a totally different kind of woman."

"I guess you didn't realize that was Debbie Reynolds who just went out."

"No! I always liked her. Remember *Singing in the Rain*, and they had to teach her to dance—or was it sing?"

"*Molly* was all I could think of on such short notice."

"*Molly* was much the better than *Singing* because she was totally it, all grown-up, not the ingénue anymore." Emmy went digging in yet another oversize bag, Prada-style, or maybe Prada itself. She handed J. a manila clasp envelope. "I have something for you. I thought I remembered it, but I wasn't sure."

He opened it curiously. "Wow, awesome! Gable and your grandfather!" The two men were shaking hands on a tennis court. "Where did you get it? Your guy at a garage sale?"

"No, on that tennis court actually. When Granddad died, we each got to choose something of his, before the estate sale. I chose a Feininger painting and a wonderful, very old, worn rug that no one else had coveted. Everyone coveted it later, though, when they saw that it was silk and beautiful in my room. My dad and I went up to his house in the station wagon to pick up stuff, and there was this pile on the tennis court, meant to be burned or thrown out. No fool was I, even then. We scooped up albums, posters, brochures, letters, and books signed by the authors. Treasures, just in time. I own most of it still. I sell something from time to time, the duplicates. Most of it is still at my house."

"What a story. That's how things get so valuable—so much is thrown out by the unknowing or gets burned up in house fires. An early governor of Massachusetts had a ton of Colonial American documents that were destroyed that way."

"The executer of the will was something else. He said he would take the wine cellar off our hands so we wouldn't have to bother with it. My dad was no fool either, and he said, 'Thanks anyway.' He put one of the bottles in a KCET auction, and it went for three hundred dollars. I still have one bottle from the year I was born."

"So Gable was at your grandfather's house playing tennis. Do you suppose my grandmother was ever there? I'll ask her."

"Do you suppose Loretta Young was ever there? Gossip circa then was that she and Gable were an item and had a daughter who didn't know he was her father."

"It wasn't just gossip. That daughter wrote a book. She didn't know until she was a teenager. Until the book, all her friends knew who her father was and thought that she didn't. Affairs were very secret then. Careers could be ruined. Then they had behavior obligations in their contracts, morality clauses."

They had begun their second drinks when the steaks arrived. *She eats with gusto—admirable and sexy*, he noted. *Rare is a good sign.* She didn't retreat from his foot-to-foot contact either.

"We will Google your grandmother for a picture so I can see if I have any photos of her in my albums. Is she your paternal grandmother?"

J. nodded.

"So I guess she'd be Dunkin now, but what was her name then?"

"I will look with you. Your assistant big on Google?"

"He protects me. It was his gaydar out for you, though. He says you are straight, but he wants your shoes."

"Actually, you already have a picture of my grandmother, probably in that huge bag—her profile is on any Ingénue product."

"Oh, so that's the cosmetics line your grandfather was fooling with! You must be very rich."

"Well, I couldn't endow an entire hospital, a wing maybe. I'll probably lose most of it. My cousins are suing me."

"I could have told you not to take the best rug."

What a woman—able to tell when he had reached the end of the information he was ready to give. J. suddenly realized that he had neglected to tell her how beautiful she looked and how amazing was the many-colored sweater she was wearing, and he corrected the oversight.

"From Peru, hand-knit by women who must be the greatest craftsmen in the modern world, undoubtedly descended from the men who built Machu Picchu without mortar."

"Have you been there? I have. I will take you there. There's a little hotel that guarantees ecstasy in the altitude."

"Is sex all you think about?"

"Did I say sex? I said altitude. The alternate answer, however, is yes. Tell me you don't have any other commitments ahead."

"I've been celibate a while."

"How long?"

Emmy looked at her watch. "Well, what time is it?"

They hadn't laughed for a few minutes, but now they did.

"Tell me about the almost-wife that got away. What happened?"

"She was a lawyer, a trial lawyer. The more she trialed, the more she liked to fight. I don't. I'm not very good at it. Besides, she didn't like movies all that much. In fact, she refused to watch *Casablanca* one more time, this year. Now, what would you like for dessert?"

"I'll just have a cappuccino. I really don't eat dessert."

"You will tonight. I told them it was our anniversary to be sure to get a good table."

When they finished and stepped out of the restaurant, the car was waiting for them.

"How do they do that?" Emmy asked as J. held the door for her and shut it.

"They always keep it next to the front unless it's trumped by a Lamborghini or an older Packard," he said as he opened his own door and slid inside. "My father said that once at the Hotel Bel-Air, Mayor Bradley was still waving his ticket when my father drove off in this car, which had been waiting, parked by the gate. Besides, I think the waiter communicates with the valet someway."

32

He turned right out of the lot and then right on Doheny, to occasional choruses of car appreciation.

"Where is your condo anyway?" she asked.

"At the west end of the strip, the Sierra Towers."

"Oh my God, that's so public!"

They rode in silence, and then she said, "Maybe you should take me home. I think I forgot to feed the cat."

"What happened to the worldly woman I just had dinner with, who was playing footsie with me? I wondered about a cat when I saw a full bowl with a two-day supply of food at your house."

"How did you see that? His bowl is in the kitchen."

"But I see everything; it's my profession. And the door was open. Nice kitchen. Where was the cat anyway?"

"He was pouting. He's jealous. You're lucky he didn't come out of hiding and scratch you."

When they reached the Strip, he turned right, away from the Sierra Towers, and wished he could watch her face. "Sierra's rented out," he said with a smile.

The strip was crowded for a Wednesday night, the traffic slow. He thought of stopping somewhere for a nightcap to regain the mood, but he did not. When he was opposite the big square bulk of towers and terraces that was the Chateau Marmont, where the opposing traffic always cheated the centerline of the turn out, he pulled the big Packard to his waiting stop. He hoped, as he always did, that he would not be plowed into during this left turn.

"My goodness. That was close."

"The daily terror," he said. "I'm half up the hill, the mezzanine, and this curvy little street is about the only way home." He negotiated his way among the disputing limos, the paparazzi, and a late emergency plumbing-repair service truck.

"I wonder who's staying here with the cameras waiting," he said. "They have a pretty garden terrace—nice place for a drink."

"Yeah, but the parking is nonexistent or the valet pricey," she said, establishing that she had been here.

When they arrived, the garage door opened smoothly; he was never sure it would.

"My goodness. This is a great old Spanish colonial—with really thick walls!" Emmy said. "It's a mansion of a thing."

"No, not a mansion. To be a mansion, it has to have his and hers powder rooms and a tiled ballroom for an entry hall." As they passed through a thick, carved door, he said, "This is my entry hall, but it's not going to happen here after all. I need a warmer place to take off that beautiful sweater, a story below this one. I shall have you there."

She shuddered, ever so slightly. He could tell the juices were draining out of her sensible, protective brain, but she must have known that she was swimming with a shark.

"Is that shall or will?" she teased.

"Okay, I might."

"Not if I say no, you can't."

He moved her toward the elevator. He pressed her against the nailhead-studded, leather-upholstered panels for a soft kiss as he activated the descent. He doubted she saw the stenciling on the leather.

A moment later, they exited into a dimly lit hall that was warmer than the upstairs room.

"Wow!" she said. "The floor glows, and I can't see where the light comes from."

"Shouldn't that be 'from where the light comes'? It's from the quirky mind of my mother, who never got to complete the remodel. The floor is warm too, heated by solar collection from under the terrace. Kick off your shoes and see how nice that is."

She did and then left them where they fell—pumps this time, he noted. Very good, he thought; she had already partly undressed and had done it herself.

J. opened the door at the end of the hall for her. "It's a special night. It can never again be the first night we sleep together."

"We can't if I say no."

He followed her into the room and pushed buttons on a panel next to the door. A remote started a fire with a whoosh in a small fireplace. There was a whirr of motor, and a great expanse of curtain drew back to reveal the sparkling lights of the city, from Hollywood to LAX and on to the dark curve of the Santa Monica Bay.

She took in a quick breath and said quietly, "Amazing!" It was the most proper use of the word that J. had heard in years.

Soft music came on then: Stevie Nicks. She went to the window, compelled as everyone always was to identify landmarks—the urban towers of downtown Los Angeles, then Century City to the west, the ruby and diamond bracelet of the come-and-go of traffic on the 405 freeway farther out, and above, the planes blinking their way in and out of LAX.

"Awesome," she said again. "It's like we're on a darkened stage, with the curtain opened to the house lights, courtesy of the Department of Water and Power."

"Look toward your house, out this way, past Greenblatt's parking lot."

"I think I can see the school almost at the base of the hill, where the lights begin to climb."

Ice rattled in the bucket as J. poured two drinks, the firelight playing off the Steuben glasses. "Come, only the beautiful and the privileged may sit on my Mies chairs. They were designed for the king and queen of Spain, visiting the German Pavilion in Barcelona, you know."

"Yeah, we had a chapter on early modern furniture. I bet you didn't know that Lauritz Melchior, representing German opera, came to the Barcelona Pavilion to sing for them."

"You're right, I didn't. You're too smart for the room."

"Smart enough to know that you must have brought the glass coffee table from your condo, 'cause it's way Miesian. And how did you know my other favorite was Maker's Mark?" she asked as she sipped her drink.

"Almost empty bottle in the kitchen."

"How did you know it wasn't drunk by others?"

"You must have no one but me on your kitchen table."

He wasn't sure whether she had seen the other side of the room, still curtained from the view, to know that it was his bedroom. By now he was guiding her across the warm floor to where a quilt was turned down on his bed, while exploring her back for her bra hooks.

"Victoria's Secret, front closure," she muttered.

"I'm going to make wild and tender love to you, unless you say no. Is it no?"

"No."

Gently, what he said he would, he did.

"God, you're wonderful!"

"God, *you* are wonderful!"

*   *   *

The next night, they were at her house, the following night at his.

"I can't see you Saturday night—buds and tickets to the game."

"I can't see you next Tuesday—girlfriends at a shower."

"But that's our anniversary. It will be an entire week since we met. We're due at Clafoutis."

"Why are you laughing? I'm clear for lunch. It's evening for the shower. It's a baby shower. They don't last all that long."

"You can call me from the car when you leave. Then on Sunday we could spend the day at your house and look at the tennis court stuff. Is it easy to get to?"

"Of course, I'm organized and neat."

"I'm not."

"I know."

"I'll bring provisions when I come to you late Saturday night."

"Like what?"

"File folders, magnifying glass, Sharpie markers, frozen pizza, condoms, my gray terry robe, and the *New York Times.*"

"You're on."
"As often as possible."

*   *   *

J., in his robe, made a credible breakfast for Emmy, who looked content with his care as she sat at the table in her red Vera Wang robe. J. read the calendar section of the *Times*, and M. finished the funnies before she rose to clear the dishes. The cat chose this moment to come out of hiding. He jumped onto the kitchen table in a graceful arc that took him higher than his landing surface, on which he came down gracefully, pinning it like a gymnast.

J. did not see the tail lashing; Emmy did. "Be careful," she warned, turning back to the kitchen sink.

"I know cats; he will get to like me. He's already coming to me."

He was a beautiful thing, a perfect Siamese with crooked tail and aqua eyes. He walked across the table, and sat before J., who reached out and picked him up.

Just seconds later, J. wailed. "Please help me get the claw out of my lip!" he cried out in a muffled voice.

The blood coursed down through the morning stubble on his face. The cat's claw was buried, stuck in his upper lip, and they stared at each other, J. holding him clutched to his chest while the cat snarled his feline equivalent of "help."

Emmy did, of course, help, with great care and some alcohol follow-up. "Poor baby," she said when it was done, suppressing any inclination to laugh.

"Him or me?"
"Should that be 'he or I'?"
"He wasn't pouting; he was seething," J. said.
"I might have done the same."

*   *   *

37

In spite of it not being modern, J. thought Emmy's the best dining room he had ever seen because except for two windows and two doors, it was completely lined in bookshelves, full. He told her so.

"Well, this house is not the smallest Craftsman bungalow, which I think of as size one. I think it's a size two, and this room is just big enough. I've been looking at a size four up on Gower. Twelve feet wide is pretty standard for a dining room. You have to allow three and a half feet for the table width, plus two feet for the two shelves, which leaves you with three feet and three inches on either side for the chairs and to pass behind them. I chose books instead of a buffet. That four on Gower is pretty nice, the dining room a little wider."

"Well, Gower is still in your hometown, if anyone knows where Hollywood really is, or *if* it is."

"I've been doing very well, and I think I can afford a size four now, and that's the best view of the Hollywood sign—and close to that good Denny's breakfast. But I liked yours better," she hastened to add.

"Have you ever wondered how far east you can go and still use Hollywood on your return address? I found my mother's letter paper in her desk, and different batches of it sometimes said Los Angeles or sometimes Hollywood. Watch it, though—it's a funny time for real estate. No one knows, with the strike freezing the industry, and projects in progress that never come back after a strike, the mortgage meltdown and talk of recession, and then there's the election. What if your candidate wins and changes everything?"

"What if yours does and doesn't?"

To contain her files and memorabilia, Emmy had made wooden boxes like slip cases with leather tabs pegged on by brass nailheads, and each tab had a number gold-tooled onto it. A leather book listed the numbers and content. He was thinking seriously about his own collection that he had not shown her yet.

He could understand why she had asked him not to strew things about and get them mixed up. The loose papers seemed to be in chronological order, as were the albums. They were beautiful old leather things in fair condition, no leather rot yet, better than anything for sale now. The paper was heavy, decal-edged, the photos all mounted with photo corners. Opening the first one was like the suspense of waiting for a film to start.

Emmy selected an album from a run of camel-colored albums and opened it to the middle at the dining table in front of J. There were black-and-white snapshots of a party on a terrace beside a pool. A very young Elizabeth Taylor was dancing with a boy with a familiar face, but J. couldn't place him. In a flourishing hand, the label said, "Some of the new players at a birthday party."

"I'm Harrison Ford with the lost ark."

"Let me see your lip. You're not still bleeding, are you?"

"Grandmamma is older than this; her ingénue time was earlier." They leafed backward to J.'s grunts of happy discoveries. "If we get married, they will say I did it for your collection."

"Maybe I want yours."

"Mine is always there for you."

When they returned to the album, a few pages brought them to another party. "Hey, look at this—it must have been an Easter egg roll," J. said. "There's my grandfather, and the teenage boys are my father and uncle!"

"Isn't this funny—that much smaller boy in the short pants and long socks is my father standing with my grandfather."

"If I put a blue sticky back on the page, may I take out this photo of my grandmother to show her? She'll be fascinated. I've never seen this one, but it looks like she has. It's signed, 'To my dear friend Damon.'" It was a large studio photo in which his grandmother was striking a glamour pose in a white satin dress and white fur chubby.

"You didn't tell me who she was right away until you admitted that the packaging profile was your grandmother. You know Ula Brenholm was terrific, not obscure like you made her sound. I've probably seen all her movies. I have the one with my Higgen hero. Shall we watch it tonight?"

"She must have loved that photo. It's so early fifties, isn't it? The peplum dress. Is that what you call it, peplum?

"Yes. It's funny how everybody from the same time looks alike. How do you change faces to go in and out of fashion? You see it in portraits in the whole long history of art."

"Let's do some more archeology," he said, "and then I'll send for a pizza if we can come to an amicable decision on what kind."

"I thought frozen pizza was one of your supplies."

"Hate it. I'll call Raffallo's."

"That's really in my neighborhood. They could toss it over."

"Maybe you shouldn't move to the size four on Gower."

Chapter 3

J. pulled out his cell phone and pressed a programmed number. "Gloria, I'd like to order a delivery . . . yes, credit card . . . mushroom and sausage." He gave her Emmy's address. "Yes, yes, about a week. Yes, she is. Thank you. We'll leave the porch light on." He turned back to Emmy and said, "Let's take a fast look at the clipping files."

"There aren't a lot. My father took most. I hope he didn't get neat and throw them out, or my mother either. She's a thrower-outer, but she always saved our report cards."

"Oh, I love old reviews and old gossip," he said. "Look at this one—your grandparents on a ship. See the date, it must have been the first you could travel after World War II."

"I wonder how he could afford to be out of town when the younger leading men were coming back from the war. Do you realize how much art was looted and how much is still missing? I was just reading an article about a special detail of American soldiers who managed to get stuff back where it came from. The few remaining veterans were interviewed. My heroes all."

"Some papers didn't get back, and they're in my collection. Don't let your heroes frisk me," J. said.

"Well, I've shown you mine; show me yours."

"Gladly, my dear."

Just then the doorbell rang. It was the first time J. had heard it from inside the house, a raucous rasp of a thing. They ate their pizza quickly.

* * *

He really was a gorgeous man, there in her bed. Chest hair was a great thing. Clothed he was great too, and even in that black underwear, or maybe especially. He said he periodically bought a batch of black tanks and briefs, and when any of it started looking shabby or grayed, he pitched them all and got another batch of same. He had certainly learned to cope as a bachelor.

"I wonder why chest hair doesn't grow like the beard hair so close above it, so fast, or like head hair at still another rate."

"Perhaps you would care to research the question further, madam."

"You feel so good—when do you work out?"

"I haven't since election day."

Later when the movie was on, they watched their respective relatives with great attention.

"Ah, what a flirt was my grandmother the Ingénue!" J. exclaimed. "Look at that trick with the slowly raised, shiny eyelids. She still does that, by the way. And look at the hand gestures. She should have had some daughters too, to pass on such art."

"Look at him. What a good body late in his career. He looks as though he could still swing from a vine or fight a duel."

"I'd like you to meet, you and the Ingénue, as we call her. Is Saturday good for you? She likes to go out Saturday. She sings an old song, 'Saturday Night Is the Loneliest Night of the Week.' I hope the photo doesn't make her even lonelier. It must be from about the time she met my grandfather. She and he moved a long time ago to that first big condo on Wilshire, huge rooms, big as a house. She loved it, the doorman, the pool, and no need to deal personally with a plumber, handyman, or trash man. When my grandfather died, she moved to the currently popular building and had that condo done up. She's a condo junkie. She thinks she's making money buying the next new one before it's finished.

"She's waiting now for the one that looks like Bullocks Wilshire. She can have anything she wants, you know. Some of the best personal fortunes are in cosmetics."

"So you're rich too, but not flaunting it, working and camping in the corner of that big house, and you, you poor thing, don't even have a pair of pajamas."

"But I have a fabulous new woman with a movie star grandfather, and she went to brunch with me without knowing I was rich. I can only hope she won't mind when I lose it."

"What are you? A secret gambler? That's all right; I'm still working."

"Great, no one's ever offered to keep me before."

"I almost could, you know. Why would you lose it?"

"My cousins are filing a wrongful death suit against the estate for the death of their father, my father's brother."

"What do you mean? What happened?"

"My father's grandfather came out from the New York stage and started and owned the company that was then called Movie Magic, while he still worked in the studio. In fact he worked the studio—to finance most of our house as a movie set.

"His son, my grandfather, worked in the business and studio makeup and contributed his wife, the Ingénue, as new company name and advertising icon. One of their sons, my father, got his degree in business management, and my uncle, their other son, got his in chemical engineering. Those two inherited the company and took it big, and they sold it big. All the world's toys were there for them. Unfortunately, one of the toys was a super airplane; both brothers had flown in Vietnam. Nobody knows exactly what happened, but on their last trip in the plane, they went down, their wives—my mother and aunt—with them."

"Oh my God, how terrible! How can you bear it?"

"At first I didn't think I could."

"I remember hearing about that on the news, but I didn't know the names. It must have been more than a year ago now, right? I was there when my father clipped the obituary. He seemed very upset. It sounded as though he knew them. Maybe from way back, 'cause I knew all their friends."

"Well, remember that photo, the Damon Higgen connection."

"Isn't it funny the way we always say both names of stars as though there were no space between the words? Like DamonHiggen, ClarkGable, GretaGarbo. And you would think Humphrey was a sissy name if it weren't connected to Bogart." She ran on because it was obvious he needed to get hold of his usual cool. She rubbed his arm, as though trying to erase something.

"I have my mother's wedding ring. Somebody found it, blackened, and had it polished for me. I didn't know if it should stay with her or not, but I remembered that she had her mother's, so it should be all right to keep it. I have that ring—her mother's—too. I don't know what happened to the engagement ring. Someday someone will find the stone by the road, the modest diamond of their youth. The plane went down on a freeway off-ramp and skidded into a tree-growing farm.

"You would have liked my mother. The best thing about her was how much she liked my father—and me too and my brother."

"You have a brother?"

"Had. Poor bastard, born irrevocably messed up. Nothing was too much for her to do for him, and he never even made eye contact with her. No 'Rain Man,' no nothin', my older brother. He finally died in my last year of high school, releasing all that care money for USC tuition for me. Guilty is a mild word for how I felt."

"None of it was your fault. I'm just grateful they had the guts to go for you, for a second child."

"I guess you can understand why I don't want to make any babies."

"Oh."

And that was Sunday.

On Monday Emmy went to the showroom and cried a little over her computer keyboard, sent out for lunch—a turkey sandwich, roast turkey, not loaf—and cried again. She told her assistant she was getting a cold, but he looked doubtful. He suspected it was about this new man in her life. He handed her the duplicate key she had asked him to have made, and she put it in the front of a filing cabinet where it couldn't be seen or found.

J. called late in the afternoon when passing cars had that going-home sound that reminded her how much she didn't like dusk. "Hi," she said, "This must be the distinguished archeologist Jared Dunkin."

"We missed a screening last night," he said, "and there isn't another until Friday. There is also one on Saturday, so let's take my grandmother out Thursday instead. I've asked her. I've ordered Thai for tonight from near my house, and we'll pick it up on the way. I really want you to see my autograph collection. Maybe even look at the house. That will leave you without a car for tomorrow, but you can take mine. As you know, I have backup vehicles."

Then he rang off, maybe not wanting to hear any protests.

*　　*　　*

Emmy loved sweet and sour pork, even the smell of it in the car.

The housekeeper or someone had set them up in a paneled room off the entry hall, with an enormous TV screen. "One of the best toys they left behind," J. said. "They also left a boat in the marina, a house and pool in the desert, the house they stayed in while she did the desert house, and a house in Doheny Hills that they were moving into while she redid this house. I don't know how much she planned to do here."

They sat side by side on a velvet sofa; the takeout cartons, napkins, and plastic-wrapped fortune cookies strewn on a coffee table before them.

"You are telling me that this is the *before* of a remodel? I thought it was the after."

"They were already just starting the demolishing when the contractor heard on the morning news that he had lost a client the hard way. Later I had him come by to put back some tile so I could use my bathroom. The "hers" of the his-and-hers bathrooms is in bad shape. You probably didn't notice it was there once you had your toothbrush in my medicine cabinet."

"Why are you here? How can you stand the combined grief and nostalgia? I drove by my childhood home the other day. Someone has kept it up well, repainted it a good color and trimmed the trees. There stood the double entry doors wide open and also doors in the back of the house. I could see through to the bright, sunny backyard where we played. I felt a wave of need for my parents and sisters, and they're just a phone call away, usually. My parents are on a long vacation trip. In London by now, I think.

"The only great grief I've ever had was the death of my partner. I still keep wanting to talk to him, like today when I thought I could authenticate a signature on a painting, just in from a garage sale. A California plein air painter, I think. It looks like Chouinard. That would be fabulous.

"Anyway, after he died, his sisters came to town and wouldn't admit he'd died of AIDS. They were ready to hold a going-out-of-business sale when they found out that I was the heir. They sold his house, though, a beautiful little remodeled-with-lattice in West Hollywood. I'm not sure they understood it and may have sold it short to get back home."

J. forked the last two sweet and sour pork chunks and put them on her plate like consolation. "Bet they wouldn't understand this one either. Described by one magazine as hacienda and by someone else as reminiscent of the most authentic Mexican bed and breakfast. The most recent whole house redo was a long time ago, by Gladys Belzer, Loretta Young's mother."

"Yes, mother of three great beauties. She was a legend, wasn't she? I like the old, wood chests and hand-done iron—really good stuff. My partner sold to her. He said when he went shopping in Europe, he brought back things that he knew she would buy."

"Did you ever go?"

"No, I've been holding down that store since I got my first car, in high school. It was he who sent me for art history."

"Talk to me about stuff here. Some things have been changed. Do you like the big ottoman instead of a coffee table, with a tray when you need it?"

"Yes and no. I like toys on the coffee table."

"I like scotch on the coffee table and sometimes coffee. Let's go look at the house and then come back for that."

"I can smell it. What do you have? A smart pot? An iPot?"

"I've heard of an eye cup."

"That's very good. I wish I'd thought of that one too. I went to a book signing of a book about houses, the tech stuff. The author declared there's even an iIron. I shouted out, 'I don't.' I loved getting a big laugh."

"There's an acting gene in there somewhere."

They went up the three steps into the infamous entry hall. He opened the front door, and they stepped out onto the big, high-walled entry patio where a carved stone fountain was still sputtering because he had just turned it on. It was only now beginning to spill over its rough-edged bowl.

"You didn't know this was here, did you, always coming in from the garage?"

Soft light from lanterns positioned all around, along with seemingly magic light from unknown sources, made yellow-orange and scarlet bougainvillea glow out of the dark. The flames of candles quivered in glass cylinders on glass tables. Feathery palm fronds swept protectively over the whole. The floor was made of irregular tiles, giving back soft reflections.

"Oooh," said Emmy. "I've never seen better. I've never seen as good!"

"Typical Hollywood Hills Spanish. Did you know the realtors are calling us Sunset Hills now, anything from Sunset Plaza to Laurel Canyon? I see it's cold for you; come back inside. We'll look at the dining room and then the billiard room-slash-den, where my collection is."

"It's a night room," he said, switching on the lights to the dining room.

And it was, painted terra cotta, even on the ceiling, except for a great oval of bright white in which an iron chandelier of branches and tendrils and leaves was centered. Sconces surrounded the room.

"Wow, this is a definite 'after'; there's hardly anything I would change except the buffet chest. There's better around, heavier with more age and wear. It's a great room. It feels as though it's seen a lot of wonderful dinner parties."

"Yes."

"Now please the fabled collection."

"Okay, walk with me. This, the den, is a better day room, though each room in these thick old houses has its magic brief time on any sunny day, when it glows. My desk can overglow in the late afternoon, and I have to close the curtain to work. Here, come sit at my desk.

"In a way it's a child's collection. When I was little, I was allowed to go to the studio sometimes with my father, for early morning makeup call, and he picked up mostly New York actors staying at Chateau Marmont. Can you picture this cheery little alpha kid, popping out of the backseat, shoving a pen at a poor guy who hadn't even had his coffee yet?"

"How could anyone refuse?"

"After a while I began to specialize. Here, look."

He popped open an album before her. It felt very intimate for her to be at his desk at the side of the big room. It was a huge old partner's desk polished by many hands. In the showroom, she would have priced it high. It was English, probably from Jones/Hutchinson, chosen by Gladys Belzer. He might need a better chair.

There on the left page of the album was a letter written and signed by Gordon of Khartoum. On the right was a letter from Charlton Heston, and she could see rapidly enough that it was about playing Gordon in the movie.

"Evil Knievel and George Hamilton, Moss Hart and George Hamilton, General Bradley and Carl Malden, Abraham Lincoln and Raymond Massey, and on and on," said J. as he flipped the pages.

"How totally fabulous is this! I will keep my eyes ever open—and my garage sale guy on the lookout too. I have a Ray Bolger, but I don't have a scarecrow."

J. was overjoyed that she got it. Ignoring that his quiet housekeeper had set up coffee and dessert in front of the big screen still on in the living room, he propelled Emmy toward the elevator.

Later, in that stillest, darkest time of night when he usually awoke, he did. Emmy awoke to see him standing by the bed, a silhouette against the slightest of window light.

He let out an almost primitive howl. "Dear God, I'm thirty-seven years old, and I've been in circulation for more than twenty years, and I've never felt this way before. I'm in love!"

From the pillow came a faint answer: "Me too."

He climbed in beside her, and she slipped into his arms.

"Shouldn't that have been 'I too'?" he asked. "Don't go back to sleep. It's almost time for the milkman's delivery."

And there it was, that sound. "Yes," she said. "He's an old wino now, and that's the sound of his empty bottles rolling in the market cart stolen from Ralph's."

"Go to sleep. I'll wait up for the night birds," he said. But soothed by her regular breathing and those legs beside him in his bed, he did not.

When he awoke again, she stood fully ready to leave. She must have had this other sweater in that big bag.

"You poor darling," she said, "you'll have to go back to work too when and if they sign the writers' contract." She pressed the duplicate key to her house into his hand and said she would meet him there after the shower. He could take anything out of the files or albums if he put the sticky in its place, and there was a copy machine in the laundry room. "Look out for the cat. His name's Thaibok."

"Wait, I have to ask: when did you know?"

"By the elevator."

"First one or second one?"

"First."

"I too."

*   *   *

It was eleven thirty before J. heard Emmy's key in the lock, which he had to assume was authentic to the house, judging the difficulty it had given him when he'd arrived at four. He had made a mental note to get some WD-40.

He sat among strewn papers and abandoned food containers. The room was blue with sticky back notes.

"These are signed photos that should be in my collection," he said as she entered. "I'll buy at current value, and you can nest-egg it away or buy Stickley. Come look. There's some Ula, the movie star ones, and everybody else. Here's a Judy Garland to put with your Ray Bolger."

"I'll bet there's no one there that the actors played."

"Whom they played. Sweet darlin', here's a Churchill."

"Do you suppose that could have been when Granddaddy and his then-wife took that ship to Europe right after the war? On the back it says, 'To an Irish star from America.' This is fabulous. I missed that important face when I went through before. Is it worth a lot?"

"It's a good one, and a lot of actors have played him. I've looked at this clipping again, and it refers to their trip as a true second honeymoon. Here is another one that deepens the mystery or solves it: 'Mrs. Damon Higgen, back from Reno, Mrs. Damon Higgen no more.'"

"I guess she divorced him. They all did. He must have been playing around. I never heard this story among the stories. The date is a bit before my father was born, and that wasn't his mother, who also divorced old star."

"Here," he said, "is a story I never heard. 'Annulled: Marriage of young stars Ula Brenholm and Todd Mikelsen.' No date and no other information. Very interesting. I can't wait to ask her. Get me a copy of this, and then let's pack it in and celebrate our Tuesday anniversary. I have something for you."

"You always do!"

"Now who's talking dirty?"

He produced a palm-size box, professionally wrapped. She opened the box to find a diamond tennis bracelet. The chunky E-shaped links culminated in a clasp with a large encrusted letter M—ME.

"I don't deserve this, so soon," she said. "How did you ever find this? It is flat-out gorgeous. Oh my, oh my. Oh my!"

"My cousins can't take that away, but mind that you keep your sleeve over it if you see them coming."

"I didn't get you a present."

"Yes, you did: sanity and adoration."

"Mine for you or yours for me?"

"God willing, it's both."

*   *   *

Breakfast was coffee and toast, a heavy, nutty, and wholesome toast that J. failed to understand. He commented that his mother had always made his lunch sandwiches with such and that all he'd ever wanted was white Wonder Bread like the rest of the kids.

"And now you're all grown-up and can have most anything you want."

"Yeah, most anything, except the ambitious drive of poverty. You can't buy poverty."

"How come? There seems to be a bit of it around and maybe more if we really do go into a recession."

"There won't be one if my candidate gets in."

"There won't be one if *my* candidate gets in."

"I guess there won't be one then. And what are you going to do in the great prosperity?"

"I'll still shop at Loehmann's," she said.

"And what would you do if you were rich?"

"I would never buy seedlings or saplings, just specimen trees. I would have a bearing, specimen avocado craned over my house into my backyard and probably shop for dinner more at Bristol Farms."

Just before noon, she called him. "I am rich. I sold the Winkie Guard uniform and the papers. It was the Judy Garland that sealed the deal. They asked if I knew where the red slippers were."

At one o'clock he called her. "We've been invited to a back-to-work party tonight. Strike's over—the writers signed."

"Good, our hometown will go again! But what is this 'we' stuff? They don't know me."

"Yes, they do now. I've told them that you're blond and hot and good in bed. What else would they need to know? It's a potluck. I'm calling home and having Angela make a vat of chili."

"My lady is at my house today. I'll just have her screw the cleaning and do a kettle of my mother's mother's potato salad. This is great news about the strike! I know how much you wanted that for all of you."

* * *

The smells of the day, unusually warm for February, had lasted into the evening. Down the block someone had mowed a lawn. Camellias and azaleas were luminous in the streetlights of these blocks below Sunset. Emmy had always assigned these streets of houses a vintage date of 1929 and noted that they must all be of the same floor plan but made to look different from each other. This one was Spanish in style, painted white and surrounded in palm trees. The hedge at the street was of white azaleas blooming so close together as to seem a white box. Beautiful!

The furnishings were a sparse, midcentury style with several red Eames lounge chairs in good condition and a Bertoia wire chair with new white linen cushions.

The mood was joyous, the hospitality was warm and welcoming, the hors d'oeuvres were plentiful, and the host proudly announced that the bar was still stocked even after the weeks out of work. Hastily made red paper hearts were pinned around in honor of Valentine's Day on the morrow.

Patio furniture had been shoved off a large covered patio. There was a bearded man in a gray watch cap serving as disc jockey, and his music was beginning to duel with that from another party next door.

Emmy had begun to feel as though she were under surveillance and questioning and was glad of a chance to go outside and dance. She drew J. with her. She warmed to the music, and presently he found something about her that he had not known. She was a wild and uninhibited dancer. Others joined them and began chanting, "Get a room! Get a room!"

"I'm so glad you're a good dancer," she purred to him.

"Our relationship is backward. It usually starts with dancing."

Exhausted, they found themselves sitting on barstools, backs to the bar. A man around J.'s age sat on a big sofa facing them. Emmy had already identified him as an old friend to J., maybe as far back as grammar school. He was a dark, good-looking man with a slight, almost imperceptible accent. He might have been one of the ninety-two languages at Hollywood High. He asked, "Who do you think you are, critics Ebert and Kelly? If I know you, J., and I do, you have seen almost everything that's up for best director, to vote honestly. Now you have only eleven days until the Oscars to see the rest. What did you hate?"

J. pulled on his scotch before he took the bait. "My vote would be against *There Will Be Catsup*. I don't get it as a classic. No story arc, no growth of character, no rosebud, and for acting, I liked James Dean in *Giant* better."

"It was a series of well-made dots with no line connecting them," said Emmy, giving it a thumbs-down.

"For actress?" asked the friend.

Emmy darted in with her answer: *La Vie en Rose*. She was Piaf, inhabiting her, everything acting is supposed to be."

"I'd have said Julie Christy, not since *Doctor Zhivago*!"

"What about *No Country for Twelve Angry Old Men*?"

And so it went with everyone gathered around, a lot of them with futures pinned on winners.

"It's not up for anything except nonsense of the year, but I know you like science fiction, so what about the monster that ate New York?" asked a man in a red sweater.

"I loved the handheld amateur camera," said Emmy, "and how it came to be used, and the end of what was to be her 'beautiful day.'"

J. conceded with a nod but said, "But I have three questions: Where did it come from? What size was it anyway—a size-shifter? And where did it go? Did you see the old 1960s film of the monster that ate Copenhagen? Miserable production, shoestring budget, but it made story sense—reconstituted itself like a starfish when a prehistoric frozen piece was found. It got huge and stayed the same size. When the army shattered it to bits, we saw a claw at the bottom of the harbor beginning to twitch. It answers my three questions."

"You've always asked three questions, J., or your single famous one, 'what's the story?'"

"Hey, back to work just in time for Oscar. Do you think there are any involved writers who haven't made notes for presenters' speeches?" asked the hostess, who had finally left the kitchen.

"Where were the bumper stickers to say 'I'd rather be writing'?" asked someone who was probably a writer.

"It's not been my favorite year for film except for *Elizabeth: The Golden Age*," said J. "Good points for historical accuracy. My favorite lady in all of history actually did ride up and down in armor, encouraging her troops with her hair blowing in the wind. There has to be an Elizabeth film every few years."

"My favorite would be Eleanor of Aquitaine," said Emmy, "but I can think of only two films about her. It doth not a marathon make."

"Elizabeth doth a weekend make," said another party guest.

"Let's," said someone else.

"I've got Judi Dench in *Shakespeare in Love*," chimed in another.

"I have Bette Davis."

"Should it start with Anne Boleyn? *Anne of a Thousand Days*. I think I remember a little Elizabeth in a white dress."

"We see her as a newborn in that one too."

"I have a really big screen and the one with Jean Simmons as a young Elizabeth," said J. "There will be chili, and there will be milkshakes."

"I drink your milkshake."

And just like that, it was scheduled and subscribed to, with a secretary and a director.

"If the country is invaded, we will go as a unit," declared a petite blond in very tight jeans.

Later in the car he said, "Now that you have seen my friends, you know who I am. My father used to say that, which his father always said at birthday parties where he didn't know the other guests: 'Show me your friends, and I'll tell you who you are.'"

"Which one was the host tonight?"

"It was hard to tell, wasn't it? We're all the same age save for some younger wives. And everyone goes in and out of everyone's kitchen and bar. He was the very tall blond guy in the red sweater who said your potato salad was the best he ever ate."

"A discerning fellow of great taste."

"His wife was the one in the kitchen a lot. She has a great business. Her family are nurserymen, and they started her out while she was still at Le Conte—that's middle school—sending mail-ordered jade trees in little pots to the cold Midwest. There's a running hedge of them on Selma, and she slipped 'em from there, but they are in her backyard now, and she's still doing it. If you noticed, their house is the last before the boulevard, so they have a side alley that the garage opens onto. It's shipping and receiving, and he has to park his new Mini Cooper beside it."

"That's why that white hedge is so good—it's professional. What does he do?"

"Studio electrician, but like any good, red-blooded Hollywood citizen, he's working on a screenplay. She could pay the household bills now if he gets really serious."

"Who was the friend from way back with the questions?"

"That's Ray, from kindergarten at Gardner Street. My grandfather nagged him through his MBA. He's marketing director at Ingénue now. You should see him in a suit and tie."

"How come you didn't go into the family business?"

"They didn't make films."

"For one of the partygoers, you were the focus of attention—the one in the leather pants, with the stylized black hair and the blazing bright lipstick. I think you have been with her, and she wishes it were still so."

He did not commit the error of saying anything.

She let it go and said, "Introduce me to your grandmother, though I'm a little frightened."

*　　*　　*

Emmy selected a lovely small brooch of fretwork and opals from the 1920s, from her stock, and wrapped it carefully with silver cord from her trim line, not the wrapping counter. It looked so pretty that she fastened tiny silver tassels to the knotted ends and taped a candy heart near the bow.

She called J. and left him the message letting him know that his wonderfully proper Valentine roses and candy had arrived.

She was walking around the showroom trying to think of what would be an appropriate gift for him when he called back.

His grandmother had asked them to join her at her dining table instead of going out.

Chapter 4

He came for her in the Packard, saying it was to hold up the Ingénue's status with her doorman. He was wearing a suit, an awfully good-looking one with hand stitching, a detail Emmy could always see across a crowded room, with a silk turtleneck sweater. There was a heart-stopping moment when he nuzzled her, smelling wonderful, newly showered and shaved and kissing hungrily.

He seemed truly pleased with the silver hip flask dimpled from the hammer of a fine craftsman and engraved "D. H."

"Was it really his? I guess this means you are not going to let me go, because I would take it with me forever. Did you know that it's marked by Porter Blanchard? He was the greatest. He taught his son-in-law Alan Adler, another great silversmith whose shop was on the strip right where a car would hit it if it went out of control on Sunset Plaza—and one did once."

"That would be where Chin Chin is now?"

*   *   *

The doorman said how pleased he was to see them and opened his telephone to announce them. "Your grandson is here, the one with a Packard and a beautiful girl."

Emmy had never been in this building before but had thought it the best of the balconied cliffs that lined this canyon section of Wilshire, just out of Westwood. She found the hall very well done, mirrored and Venetian-plastered. Indents for doors gave it individual privacy, and her high heels wobbled slightly in the deep carpet.

A young woman opened the door, red hair in a ponytail, wearing a black velvet shirt and Levi's. After a fast greeting, she scurried for the kitchen.

Behind her a beautiful creature rose from a pool of light and glided upstage toward them. She was every bit a movie star.

"Jared, my dearest love in all the world. And Mary Ellen, you are a lovely woman. I was acquainted with your grandfather, you know."

"Yes, I do know. You made a picture together. J. screened it again for me."

J. had disappeared to find a home for the load of red roses he'd brought for his grandmother.

"My J., such a dear boy—when he was little, he was uncontrollable all over everything, my monkey boy. There is something I've always wondered about him: is he good in bed?"

Emmy knew this was a test, that she was supposed to be flustered, and so she asked her own question. "What did the Italian lady lawyer answer when you asked her that?"

"Well, she said yes, and that he hangs from the chandelier by his tail."

"Well, she wasn't all bad. The only thing I've learned about her so far is from a leftover height and weight chart tucked in with the appliance warranties and manuals in the kitchen."

The older woman's face had a strange quality of coming to a peak in the front, from hairline to chin, and when she laughed broadly, as she did now, her mouth opened larger than might be expected from the neat small lips. This reminded Emmy of a snake or a cat, with a large mouth for large prey. Not that she thought her a snake or a cat—well, maybe a cat, an expensive Persian brushed and groomed to take best in show.

J. came into the room and looked gratified, even relieved, that they were laughing together. Both J. and Emmy were pleased when she liked the pretty package and then the broach too. It did seem perfectly suited to the delicate older beauty she had become.

Over drinks she asked Emmy about her business—she knew about it, and her most recent designer had bought a Tony Duquette mirror from her. "It's in the powder room there, dear, when you need to use it." She continued, "With all those beautiful things that pass through your life, what more would you have if you were rich?"

"Sometimes I think I'm almost there, and then they change the definition. I think I would build a dear little shingle-and-stone Craftsman guesthouse in the backyard for my housekeeper and her boyfriend so I could have her full-time. That includes her green corn tamales. When I can, I will expand my showroom, buy the building next door. I have first refusal on it now. I have thought to lease out a small brunch and tearoom on the center court so that I could have food smells and the tinkle of spoon on cup. I could expand for more serious antiques. I would like to take on the real challenge of making an upstairs so accessible that people would actually go up there, like an open glass elevator, wide but not deep.

"I'd also give more to AIDS research. I was thinking I'd like to devise some beautiful cases for movie costumes and offer them as decorative accessories. Do you think there would be a market for them?"

"Oh, yes, wouldn't it be wonderful to have the cantaloupe seed wedding dress from *Camelot*? And very early, Joan Crawford did the Charleston on a table in a beaded dress I have never, ever forgotten, and you know I would love to have it."

Ha, she's hooked her too, J. thought.

"Really, my dear, have you been to the new wing of the museum to see the Eli Broad collection yet? There are a lot of bleached white animal skeletons on glass shelves in the most beautiful glass cases ever, with chrome frames and remarkable hinges. Actually, that was the only thing I liked. You could hinge a thin case, you know, to the wall and swing it out like an opening door, to see from both sides."

"I'll go tomorrow, the last day for members," Emmy said, though she hadn't planned to use the tickets she had phoned to reserve.

Over the salad, Ula Dunkin talked about her lovely days in the movies. And wasn't Damon Higgen a splendid figure of a man, and wasn't he lucky to be beyond military age and still young enough to be a spectacular leading man with those flashing blue eyes? "Paul Newman, at my same age, now has them still. He's always Hud to me. And do you remember Sinatra? We loved him so in high school when he was a skinny, little blue-eyed thing. The last time I talked to him was when he was master of ceremonies for the Rose Parade. I rode on a float that year, you know. Damon was gone by then. He left a nice body of work. I can only hope you have seen it all.

"I wish I could have seen him on the stage in Ireland, before he came over. It's really a good thing he didn't have to be in the service. He had such ambivalent feelings about fighting on the side of the English.

"Then there was that Englishman. No, no, O'Toole, Peter O'Toole, must be Irish too. Those glowing blue eyes in *Arabia*!"

Emmy contributed that she rather favored the liquid brown eyes of Omar Sharif, whom she quite adored in *Lawrence of Arabia*.

"It's so nice to talk about men! So tell me, dear, what is your other heritage? Your skin is so lovely, it could be Scandinavian."

"My mother's family is English, from way back. It must be the Ingénue cosmetics. I carry your portrait in my bag at all times . . ."

"Foolish dear, it's not in the bottle; it's in the genes and that cold, rainy, northern climate. We last well too. Eva Marie Saint lives near here. I really don't know her heritage, but you should see how beautiful she still is, and *On the Waterfront* was a long time ago, and I guess *Exodus* was too. Blue-eyed Newman again, if you remember. When you get a good deal older, you will find the compensation that you won't have to shave your legs, and the hair on your arms and armpits disappears too, and then you won't get pregnant or get your period, that foolish design.

"Did you ever want to be an actress, dear?"

Emmy explained that she'd had a brief career, a commercial when she was three. "I was absolutely adorable, and then I retired. In school for the plays, I always wanted to be on 'em, not in 'em. I got pretty good at backdrops."

With the arrival of the salmon, Ula Dunkin switched topics to talk about her current life. Emmy remarked on what beautiful rooms she had.

"I'm a nomad," she said. "I keep the components of my rooms small enough to be portable. The screens can move about to be room backgrounds."

Emmy noted that she had a wonderful issue of Coco Chanel's suede and nailhead sofa.

"Yes, it's moved about for years. It even used to be in the Hollywood house before Jared's parents bought it from us. Do you like how his mother redid some of the rooms? She was a beautiful woman, you know. Her skin was flawless. My son met her when she was working at a cosmetic counter in Paris while he was stationed briefly in Germany. I thought she developed a fine taste."

"It's a beautiful house. I think I like it better than J. does."

"I like the freedom of condominiums. I'm due to move very soon. The new building is nearly finished. J. says it looks like Bullocks Wilshire. I wish you could have seen that when it was a store and its tearoom was the very center of life."

"I have actually had the privilege of going to a tea there," said Emmy. "I guess the law school still maintains some elegant rooms as they were. It was a tribute for Jodi Greenwald, who founded and headed the interior design program at UCLA. We have an entirely different set of celebrities than you movie people do. I had spoken at some of her events where I was more than pleased to tell students the importance of accessories."

The Ingénue gave Emmy her full attention. "Well, speaking is certainly theater, as we notice in the current elections. That gave you a nice chance to pre-sell to future interior designers. You must be doing very well. Things of your selection sell quickly, and you own the building?"

"Yes, I do, and I've entered the monopoly game with buying some houses."

J. thought it might be time for a little rescue before his grandmother asked Emmy for a copy of her financial statement.

"Emmy is like the little white-haired shopkeeper who was hit in the crosswalk in front of his Fairfax store. While they waited for the 911 guys, a passerby put a blanket over him, and another one got a pillow out of her car and tucked it under his head. The passerby asked, 'Are you comfortable?' He opened his eyes and answered, 'I make a good living.'"

"All right, Jared, I guess she does . . . I suppose you have noticed, they have taken my Robinsons away from me now, and I have to go all the way to Neiman Marcus. I still drive in the daytime, but not at night if I can help it. There is a driver and car on call at the new building. I shall miss the doorman here, though. I think he is in love with me. We go walking some mornings now, Blaine and I, and I think that if we didn't get back in the usual time, he would come looking for us.

"Jared, I want to talk to you about something. Did you see in the paper the other morning the article about a new building in Century City? It's called the Green Blade, very, very tall and slender—you know, with views from all the flats—and hung with vines growing on the way up, hydroponically, I would guess. I really want to reserve a unit in it. Could you find out about it for me? See if they are selling smaller rooms lower in the building for guests or help, like the Sierra Towers does. I'll need a two-or three-bedroom so Marina can be with me all the time, in case I should fall, or something." She turned to Emmy and remarked, "Jared calls Marina 'Marinara' for her red hair."

Dessert was crème brûlée in heart-shaped dishes, and Emmy was very impressed, not least by having cupboard enough to give space to once-a-year dishes. It was served with some very heavy spoons that didn't match the dinner service. She was sure they were vintage George Jensen, and she longed to look, but didn't. While they ate, the red-haired woman was fussing with something on the coffee table.

As they went into the living room, she snapped on a spotlight that blazed over a tray, on which was arranged a giant heart made of M&M's surrounded by a band of gummy bears, to the delight of all four of these grown children, including the red-haired lady who had done it.

With the Baileys and coffee arriving on the table, J. disappeared.

"He goes to my bathroom," his grandmother explained. "I think he can't stand the Tony Duquette mirror in the powder room. What a darling he is. He thinks he is my favorite; I never should have let him know.

"But he is really not for you, you know. He doesn't want children because of his ruined brother, and you will be so frustrated because you will. The little slimy thing that moved out of the swamp of its own volition and evolved through a million years to become you will be cut off with you. You will suffer and grow cross with my Jared the younger."

He reappeared, large envelope in hand, and drew out the 8 × 10 glossy he'd found in Emmy's things. "Look what I found, Granddarling. Was it an Easter party?"

"Oh!" she said, seeming troubled a little, Emmy thought. "Where ever did you get that? From one of your autograph dealers? But no, it isn't signed. If I look hard at it, I could probably tell you the year, you know, by the clothes and such. Oh, oh, oh, my poor dead boys. They went to that same Easter egg hunt every year, for fathers and children. So I couldn't go. I think this must have been in a movie magazine. Where did you get it?"

"From the collection of Ms. M. E. Higgen. And other stuff too. Why do families not tell each other things? I never knew you had been married to someone before Granddad, if ever so briefly, considering it was annulled."

"Oh, Jared, so long ago. Why did you have to find all that? There are no other witnesses to the fight left. I thought you'd never have to hear it from anyone. Your grandfather was such a muscular man, so movie-star good-looking he was, in that white tennis sweater. I shall never forget. I had thought he was married, but he wasn't anymore. He was on the way to making a fortune. He had the intention of courting me. And the studio thought they had to marry me off to that boy, Todd Mikelsen."

"Does 'have to' mean what it usually does? Are you saying you were already pregnant? What? What's my name, Mikelsen?"

"Oh no, dear, that wasn't even his name. You're not going to out me now, are you, now that I've gotten a great part for the first time in years? That part is what I wanted to tell you about tonight. Is this woman going to come between us?"

*　　*　　*

"The doorman actually whistled for the valet. If you think it's hard to sleep now, think of that, living here. There would be a lot of whistling in the early evening, then more further apart into the night, and then another one just after you got to sleep." Emmy did a credible imitation using the two-finger shrill whistle that her father had taught her. J. was inspired to launch into the Anvil Chorus, using "pum, pum, pum" for words. With Emmy's whistle appropriately interspersed, they got all the way to the Santa Monica intersection before they had to talk.

When they were past that difficult left turn, J. said, "You go first. When did you know that you wished you had dipped the broach pin in the vessel with the pestle? What did you say to her after Marina suggested it was time for us to leave and not hurt her? You put your arm around her, which is the right thing to do with a sobbing actress, but what did you say?"

"I said, 'You cheat, lady—you're wearing Chanel No. 19, not Ingénue.' She actually laughed and then said, 'It's so hard to find anymore.' Then I said, 'J. loves you so much; he would never do or say anything to hurt you. It's not really very important who a person's grandfather was. We never talked about yours, and we are not going to talk about his either.'"

"Maybe you are not, but I'm going to find out. What we have here is a major failure to communicate."

"She has lost a husband and two sons, two daughters-in-law, and before that a grandson. What do you want of her?"

Three blocks of silence. "Did she see the bracelet? What did she say?"

"'Hmm, Em.'"

*　　*　　*

"Hello, it's Emmy Higgen calling to thank you for the elegant dinner party last night . . . Yes, we went to the museum today. I persuaded J. it was his civic duty to see the remodeling . . . No, not really, maybe the lamp post regiment and certainly the daylight on the top floor, but the plaza is blank and sad . . . Yes, all too much like the cathedral downtown. When we left, there was a man moving the Bertoia wire chairs around, and he said he was just trying to make it look better . . . Oh yes, I loved the elevator. Did you notice the floors? A wonderful expanse of wood, but the boards are cupped and the seams sprung in places already. They are going to have falls in there.

"The museum, oh, you are so right about those skeletons. I always have to pick a favorite, and I just loved the turtle, up at eye level so you could look down his nose to the end of his tail through that intricate sculpture of his body.

"And then there are the cases! They are exquisite, perfect. I'm starting to think about costumes in shallow cases made like those. I was looking at a recent auction catalog, and there was a maroon silk smoking jacket and black pants. 'CG' was embroidered on the jacket pocket, custom-made for Clark Gable. Wouldn't it be wonderful to have that in a case in your bedroom? . . . Yes, I'm sure he was welcome in many . . . Pricey, yes, 4,000 to 6,000, but I can see this working.

"The awards are only ten days away. If you haven't already committed to a watching date, we would love it if you could come and share it with us."

A moment later, the call concluded, and J. said, "Beautifully done, my dear Em. Am I never to tell her that I believe that I have put the story together—that young Miss South Dakota was seduced and impregnated in her trailer by aging actor Damon Higgen? Even in the lobby poster of their movie, she looks so enamored, or is that great acting? Why else would my grandfather Jared James and Damon Higgen have a fight over her? It must have been pretty public to be in a newspaper. Why was the studio frantic to get her married? When I complete the chronology, I expect to establish that she had his baby, while married to Jared James Dunkin, and that baby would be my father, Jared Richard Dunkin. That would make us first cousins!"

"No, only one-half first cousins."

"You've thought about this?"

"It has been crossing my mind for a few days."

"What am I, in the middle of a fucking soap opera called 'Who's Your Granddaddy?'"

"How much does it matter? You said no babies."

"Would you be all right about it? Did you want any?"

"If I get to wanting them, I can always leave you. I've never been asked to stay."

"Only just *forever*."

*   *   *

"Wow, anguished, frantic sex is really something!"

"Awesome!"

*   *   *

"Hey, man, I'm calling you because I really need an intervention here. Where are you anyway? . . . The factory in Glendale? Working Saturday? We could meet for lunch halfway. Tam O'Shanter? . . . It doesn't matter how you're dressed, and they'll probably like that bitchin' bike so much, they'll park it by the door, like they would my Packard if I were in it . . . And hey, Ray, can we get Mark too? . . . No, no, it's not conflict of interest. It's not about those suit-happy cousins, so we can't get him to pay."

*   *   *

"Ooh, man. She dresses you cool," Mark said to Ray, whose black sweatshirt read, "You never see a motorcycle parked outside a psychiatrist's office."

Mark was ten minutes late, as he always was. Ray and J., who had pulled into the parking lot at the same time, as they often did, were seated in the middle room on a settle against the wall, already with drinks, when he arrived.

"How do you do that, man, always ten minutes late?" J. asked.

"A lawyer must survey the room for hostiles," Ray said.

J. admonished him, "When you're late, you have to sit in the dangerous position with your back to the room; you can't ever sit on the bench."

"I don't want to sit on the bench. I want to stay in private practice." Mark, looking somehow like a lawyer even in a hoodie, pulled out the rush-seated, straight-backed chair and threw himself into it. His spiky dark hair was considerably more disheveled than his barber intended.

Looking well-groomed in contrast, Ray set his bike helmet beside him on the floor and said, "He wears that shirt so he can put the hood up instead of the top up, in case he can't take the wind in the new convertible. How's it doing? Are you liking it any better?"

"Very Hollywood. I'm lovin' it. So why am I here on intervention? You want to marry this one? I've never heard you say that with any of the others. Ring and everything? I guess you've slept with her to know."

"In the biblical sense, a religious rite to know. But this is about who I am or may be."

"Are you kidding me? Your beloved grandfather, the late Jared James, our leader, fought what was almost a duel with notoriously wandering movie rogue Damon Higgen and put him in the hospital, and you didn't know about it? And are you seriously telling me that you couldn't count to nine months?"

"Are you seriously telling me that everybody knew but I? Why didn't you ever say anything?"

Ray interceded. "When it's in the newspapers, it's hard for things not to be known. And what did it matter? I never could see that Jared the Elder treated his sons any differently. I always suspected that you might not know, and if you did, you wouldn't have any reason to talk about it. What were we supposed to do? In kindergarten, I wouldn't have understood, and after that, I couldn't care less."

"Em didn't know either. Why would she? We're talking sixty-two years ago."

"How old is your grandmother anyway? She's still photographing great in our advertising. We flood her with white light, and she glows for our best wrinkle cream. If that ceases to work, we'll put her in radio advertising."

"Emmy hugged her and found out she was wearing Chanel No. 19 instead of Ingénue."

"Well, she was always loyal to your grandfather anyway. She always looked like a woman in love to me. So does Emmy, by the way. She's really great."

"Are you guys picking up here that Em and I are first cousins? What do we do? Can we get a license to marry? Do we have to expatriate, go to Mexico, or to Ireland with dual citizenship, given that we're both descendants of their famous actor? I saw a Mexican village on a catalog cover. I was ready to buy one of the houses until I saw it didn't have a garage and you couldn't drive on the street anyway. What do we do?"

"First, calm down," said Mark. "You're not pregnant, are you?"

"Last I checked, men don't get pregnant."

"You always said you weren't making babies because of your poor dissolved brother, God rest his strange soul," Ray said.

"You should go talk to your doctor," said Mark. "He will probably tell you that your brother's condition is not apt to happen again and that half-cousins are not like brother and sister. Let me check law before I commit. And don't you dare leave the posse and the country. America is your birth mother. And the old man doted on you."

"He told me he trusted my judgment, that I'd been recruiting executives for him since Cub Scouts."

"Your dad once told me that he wouldn't want to hire anyone who hadn't been in scouting. But you can't ask that when you're hiring. We miss him something terrible too—and your uncle— though the new owners are really working out. It's not like in the eighties when takeovers were death to companies, as we knew them. The other thing that's better now is that you don't have to have a license to wed, 'cause you don't have to wed, except to have community property."

"How did you find this grandfather stuff out now, anyway"?

"Scrapbooks. You show me yours, if I show you mine. I'm so afraid my grandmother isn't going to like Emmy. She's putting on too much warm hospitality. She's going to think Em made me see all this."

"Do you have a copy of your birth certificate? Call on Tuesday to get it; the office is closed Monday for Presidents Day."

"So what do you think, our candidate looking pretty presidential? Theirs is looking like a rock star, singing the same feel-good song."

*   *   *

"Two screenings tonight, six and nine. Burrito across the street between."

"Could we go to the Silver Spoon after? I really liked their Monte Cristo sandwich."

* * *

Over the scotch and Tanqueray on the rocks, Emmy said, "I liked *In Bruges*. It made me laugh."

"I laughed at *Fool's Gold.*"

"I can see the new ads in the Sunday paper tomorrow: 'Best Pictures of the Year. They made Em and J. laugh."

"No screenings tomorrow at the Guild. Arc Light or the Grove?"

"With or without knowing what's playing? I have to go to the antique book fair first tomorrow. Want to go along?"

* * *

"I'm more looking at than for. Sometimes I find great frameables though—maps and prints for the showroom. They can't be too rare because of price after a good frame. I once bought a Frank Lloyd Wright print from the first German folio that was piled in his studio when the gardener killed all those people. That's modern for you, but old enough to be antique. I paid 350 for it. It's so beautiful, I could never let it go. That's the danger here."

They had turned down Avenue of the Stars with almost no traffic. The sweep of driveway up to the Century Plaza Hotel was more lively. The fair was well attended.

J. was hooked almost immediately—maps and whaling prints, scrimshaw and old letters with the sprawling handwriting of seamen. He went from booth to booth discussing dates and historical events and places. The proprietors were all serious and kind and so very surprised when he returned to them and bought.

Presently Emmy was plucking at his sweater. "You must see this; you must buy this. Come and meet Leonard Fox from New York. He has a Benito, the illustrator who was the inspiration of Erte. It reminds me of the costumes Matisse designed for the ballet. The other person who has Benitos is your grandmother. They are with the Duquette mirror in the powder room where you don't go."

*　　*　　*

They were at her house Monday morning, up early enough for Emmy to get to the showroom and get her framing started. J. was apprehensive of the cat rubbing around his ankles. "It will be more days until my picture gears back up, if it does. I think I'll take some time to woo my grandmamma back. A good day for it. It's a postal holiday, and she will be bored without the mail and the catalogs. And she will be relieved that Nancy Reagan is okay and back home.

"The fashion print is a great entry, and I will ask her all about her picture part. And I shall not say a word about her wayward youth that screwed up my life."

"My dear love, she gave you life."

*　　*　　*

"Important anniversary! Two weeks!

"It's another important anniversary for me too, two weeks into the reentry to birth control pills. My doctor says they are effective after two weeks."

"You mean you started taking them again on that day?

"I'd have taken one at Clafoutis if I had had them in my big red handbag."

"Let's go back to bed."

"Let's go to Clafoutis. Pick me up at twelve thirty."

*　　*　　*

It was a misty rain, the kind that leaves you unsure of whether to turn on the wiper yet. It was wet enough, though, to send them up the inside narrow stairway instead of outside to the sidewalk. The same small hostess saw them emerge from the stairwell and led them to the back and asked, "Same table?" The waiter appeared with Lillet and scotch and asked which quiche and how J. wanted his omelet.

"I think the reel has been rewound, and this is where we came in. Is this where I tell you I'm going to seduce you?"

"No, that's an hour later."

"Is this then where I say let's get married?" J. produced a ring box.

"But, but, what's this?" She opened the box and found it fairly stuffed with a huge diamond of radiant clarity. "I know you're rich, but you shouldn't have spent it all. Can we do it?"

"Can we not?"

Chapter 5

"**B**ut what about babies?"
    "Isn't that why you're taking the pill?"
    "Let's give it a few more days. How did you know my size?"
    "I know your size. I am your size! And I've been alone in your house with your scrapbooks, your cat, and your jewelry."
    "It's sooo beautiful."
    "Have you ever been engaged before?
    "Oh, is that what it means? And I'm supposed to wear it all the time? Good thing it's for the left hand, or I couldn't raise my hand to eat. It's so great-looking. You have such great taste in diamonds."
    "I have great taste in women, but you have to say yes to keep it."
    "But we're cousins. We could go on like this forever, and no one would say anything."
    "It can be the longest engagement on record. I'm after a yes. You need to say it."
    She did and cried.

*   *   *

On Wednesday, they returned to the Palm for New York steak, charred rare, and a cappuccino. "This really is our anniversary, of our first time together," he said. "This is the night I started your seduction in the entry hall and the elevator and had you in my bed.

"Tomorrow is another Directors Guild screening. I know nothing about it, but you probably do. Afterward shall we share and go out with the bearded one with the blond mop? He called, and when I said we might, he asked if half of 'we' was my blond of two weeks ago. Hamburger Hamlet okay with you?"

"If you won't laugh when I want lobster bisque and a piece of their phenomenal chocolate cake."

* * *

The next night, when Emmy finally allowed her left hand to rest above the table, the eyes of the other couple were properly round, and the girlish squeal belied the blond's professional persona of someone rapidly rising in a production company.

"Oh, man, this is really rushing it," J.'s friend said. "I doubt you've known each other three weeks yet. That might not be long enough to know if she gets PMS. Do you guys know what you're doing?"

His companion interrupted. "As a girl speaking here, I think it's fabulous and a gorgeous headlight, if I've ever seen one, and I've seen too few. But don't you know you don't have to get married anymore? Most people wait to get engaged until they are sure and have given birth to the ring bearer and have a flower girl in preschool."

"Being sure is very good, and we are. We just haven't talked about where we're going on honeymoon yet. Actually, her parents are out of town, so I haven't asked her father for her hand yet. Haven't met him either."

"It seems that you have staked out the left hand anyway. Is that why you're having soup—you can't lift that hand?"

"Haven't you called them on their cell phone or e-mailed them yet?" the blond asked.

"We all promised not to bother them," Emmy said. "They are on the grand trip—England, where her family came from in 1630, and Ireland, where his father came from in the 1930s. I think they are at the Tate today. I made them pledge to see the Turners. Orient Express to Paris. I found her a vintage, black, satin cloche. Then it's on to Istanbul, Israel, Egypt, and North Africa and back to Spain on a small ship. They'll drive to Paris from there to fly home. Is that trip enough or what? They don't want to hear from us. Oh, and they went over on the QE2."

"Wow. What does he do for a living? I don't think he's in our industry, or he would be getting back after the strike."

"He makes buttons. I think the trip results from a contract with a cruise line to supply every traveler for years to come with a big round declaration of proud passengership."

"What about you, are you in the industry?"

"You see why I refused to share you with them on the night of the day we met," said J. "And to answer the inevitable next question: we met at voting. We've lived within shouting distance for all her life, but she didn't go to Hollywood High."

"It would have been much later anyway. And you and I didn't know each other there either; we met on a shoot."

"Yeah, the one where you wanted to shoot the director."

"I was aware of you in high school. I watched you run—swift—but you were a junior when I graduated."

"I certainly watched you too, big football star that you were. I bet you could have done that beard even then."

"So are you going to a viewing party for the Oscars, like we did last year at the Abbey?"

"We aren't," said Emmy. "We've invited his movie star grandmother to his big screen. And I was closer than shouting distance to you, J—I was at the Abbey that night last year. You must have been the big party having all the fun"

"It'll be fun at his house too. Join us and we'll call some others too."

"So who's going to win?"

"Hillary."

"No, no. I mean best picture. Director. Actress. Actor. Art director. Costume designer."

"I give you *Elizabeth* for it all."

"And you know it's not going to happen."

*   *   *

In the car, passing where Scandia used to be, she thanked him for not letting her identity be "granddaughter of." He thanked her for not saying that she bought his donuts when he told her his name was Dunkin.

"Well, I didn't think of that—only the yo-yos and a little later Slam Dunk. I hope it was all right to ask them to the Oscars."

*   *   *

Friday and Saturday were busy for Emmy. It wasn't sales but memo, renting out some semiserious jewelry and arranging the insurance.

Friday just after lunch, J. called to give her the list of people he had invited to the watching party; it was a short list, but he had arranged with his housekeeper to be there Saturday and Sunday and filled Emmy in what he had already done about food. She felt her busy-guilt rising, but he said that there wasn't anything she needed to do. She reminded him that for her, the next day's ceremony would start at three, with the arrival of the first long gown on the red carpet.

A young woman who was just leaving as Emmy closed her phone said that if she won, she was coming back for Lana Turner's prop ring from *The Three Musketeers*.

Emmy didn't know what she was up for and didn't want to ask. When she was gone, Emmy's assistant told her who that was and could not resist noting that she was gay.

*   *   *

77

The day was getting exciting, with only hours to go before the festivities.

At exactly noon the sun came out. At 12:50, the sky began to gray, and at 12:52, it began to rain. At 3:00, the determinedly cheerful announcers and interviewers came on the screen, out in the middle of tented-over, red-carpeted Hollywood Boulevard.

Emmy was cuddled deep in a big sofa, a lap robe over her knees and a cup of tea in her hands. She held the handle away and drank from the opposite side. J. called it Irish cup cuddling, from a time when it was the only way to keep warm.

George Clooney was the first ranking celebrity to arrive, moving from a limo to the protection of the tented street. He was full of cheer—maybe the Clark Gable of our time, or maybe not. Shortly after that the first red dress came on the screen.

The greetings of guests arriving at the Dunkin house at the other end of Hollywood Boulevard, the untented end up in the hills, were short as they settled down to watch their town torture itself with anxiety. Only the arrival of the Ingénue received their attention. Emmy thought that these friends from J.'s childhood must have met her many times before and yet were probably always this impressed. Presently J.'s grandmother was properly quiet as well, except to reiterate her hopes for eighty-three-year-old Ruby Dee, in her red satin dress, for best supporting actress. That perhaps she herself would be up for the award next year was unspoken.

Emmy wondered once again why God had given such nice warm clothes to men and had them stand by while near-naked women froze beside them, trying not to huddle or shiver. There's acting! The majority of them today were freezing in red dresses, bare to the nipple, often counter balanced by skirt volume, even trains, out in the middle where the carpet was dry.

Drinks were softly poured, the buffet quietly announced. There were cheers for the envelope openings and groans and protests as well.

Emmy held the remote and went to mute for commercials, at which time the room became a hubbub of comment, before quieting again for the return to the next category. The expensive advertising was having little impact on this audience.

With Ray and Mark, and Emmy knew not who else being part of the Ingénue cosmetics company, the interest in the makeup award was not surprising. The group cheered when Didier Lavergne and Jan Archibald won, and Emmy cheered with them, but her cheers were for candidate Marion Cotillard as Edith Piaf, under that makeup. And then Cotillard won for best actress. Emmy did not look at J. after that announcement, for he did so love the nominated golden *Elizabeth*.

Ruby Dee did not win. Ula Dunkin, though disappointed, was impressed with winner Tilda Swinton. She had never seen her before but declared her of great style.

They all cheered the honorary Oscar for Robert Boyle and his wonderful sets. Someone jotted down some of the names of his pictures, and someone declared him the next marathon after Elizabeth. They wanted to engrave what he said somewhere: "The moving image we all love."

Once when J. went to the kitchen for ice, Mark joined him. "Man, I don't know why I didn't pursue this the other day at lunch," said Mark. "It's become one of our best tools and the new plot line on the soaps: 'Who's your daddy?' and 'Whose daddy are you?' Conjecture, chronology, and gossip won't do. You gotta get DNA. Here, I wrote out for you what to do. You know it's male line, sons to fathers to fathers. Well, actually, women can trace the maternal line as well. Irish is fun—did you know that every fourteenth Irishman is related, back to an ancient, viral, and busy warlord?"

"So you could be my cousin?"

"I'd have to guess, who isn't, even through a busy, swashbuckling movie star!"

When channel 7 cut to the final commercial, there was a great buzz of happy and sad and then much attention to the big diamond the guests had been trying to see all evening. Congratulations were rowdy and raunchy and seemingly heartfelt.

The red-ponytailed Marina tried to gather up the Ingénue to take her home, but she was talking to a pretty dark-haired woman: she could see that the woman was sleeping on her right side, Ula said, and she must get a small, hard pillow and keep it above her ear to avoid those little lines that start at her age.

"Then you won't have to have the right eyelid done before both of them need it," she concluded. Then she settled down by Emmy with her vodka, ready to chat.

"It's strange to be here for a party. I've seen so many of them in this room. I think you like the house, don't you? It was my mother-in-law who did it first, you know. Mostly heavier pieces, though some of them are still here from her. Then, after me, J.'s mother worked with Gladys Belzer. Her style was perfect with the house.

"My father-in-law was named Jared too, and then there was my handsome husband Jared James, who often was called J. J., you know. Then my older boy was Jerry for Jared Richard, and now my precious grandson is only left with the initial J. Should you ever have a son, there is nothing left to call him.

"There is little of me still in the house, you know. I took it all with me, and my decorators all in turn added and adapted. It is really J.'s mother who has left her stamp here. You would have liked her. She was so pretty with that cosmetic-counter skin and beautiful smooth hair. There's a commercial now where they call that kind of hair 'polished.' Her hair looked polished, and she swung it down over the baby when she was feeding him—bottle, not beast, you know.

"She did so adore J. and went through so much to have him, after that poor ruined first son and all those miscarriages, you know. She was under a doctor's care for the whole pregnancy— went away to a clinic, in Laguna, I seem to remember. I'll never forget when she brought him home. He was so beautiful, prettier than even my two darling boys were.

"When I first saw him, Karen had just given him a bath, and that black hair was all sticking up in damp spikes, you know, for all the world, like he has it cut now. He looked at me as though he knew me, and then I was his forever after. She showed me all his little body parts, and he was perfect.

"I love having this chance to talk about him. I hope you will take wonderful care of him, in every way. You will meet my second boy's children some day too, you know. They are hurting so badly now. I am too. I don't know if it's worse to lose your parents or your sons. Sons, I think.

"I've been looking at your website, dear. I like what you do and the way you put up new things to see. I hope you don't mind that I had my framer do the Benito instead of yours. It was only so that it would match the ones I have."

"Oh, that's fine. They should match all together in the powder room. He was a fabulous illustrator. It's so happy making to see the well preserved originals."

"I, in turn was glad that you recognized them and got the additions."

Her messages and her vodka finished, Ula rose, almost gracefully, though that was a bit difficult for her, from a low, deep sofa. She slipped into the velvet coat proffered by J.—the coat matched her shoes, Emmy noticed—and sailed out.

*   *   *

"I thought they would never all leave. Into the elevator, my beautiful betrothed. This marks two weeks, and we have the safety measure of a few days on the pill. I shall fill you and spill out of you. I want to hear you scream."

He did.

A bit later, they awoke and watched some of the after-parties.

*   *   *

"I think it's time to go back to my house. My housekeeper says the cat is getting cranky and losing interest in food. It's nice to be missed that much. Thaibok is also Tyrant when he's like this, Tyrone when he's amorous, Tiger when he chases mice, and

Thai the rest of the time. Do you think the two of you will ever get to like each other?"

"He thinks he has 'Ti' for title. What's a Thaibok? It sounds Siamese."

"A fabric line developed by an American in Thailand, silky like he is."

"Now he's sulky. I'll bring him a treat when I bring the sweet and sour pork."

"Look out, he'll bite your hand. I'll make the tea and put a can of lychee nuts in the fridge. I stocked up when they had 'em at the 99 Cents Only Store."

*   *   *

It was a busy day, made busier by every customer and looker needing some Oscar talk.

At eleven in the morning, just as J. walked in, Emmy's sister called. J. stood and waited as she took the call.

"Hey, Peg o' my heart. What's up? Did it go your way? Are you still into George Clooney? What do you think of Xavier? . . . Yeah, I thought he was sexy, even paralyzed in the other movie we saw him in . . . Yes, I am . . . Yes, wait till you see it . . . I know I said that about diamonds, but wow! . . . Yes, I know it was fast . . . Yes . . . Yes, I know where they are at all times . . . Of course, but I'll be just as committed when they get back . . . Sure, I want you to meet him . . . Yeah, Wednesday's good for me, and no screening. Let me check with J. and call you back."

After hanging up, Emmy looked up to see J. in the doorway, carrying a folder of papers.

"Hey, Em! I think you bailed out without breakfast too, right? Let's run across the street for huevos rancheros, and I'll show you what I found. El Coyote is open on Monday, isn't it? But let me just show you this first."

On a glass display counter he ceremoniously presented an eight-by-ten of Ula and Damon in costume, beautifully lit, a studio portrait, signed by them both.

"Where did you get that? They shouldn't be looking at each other that way."

"But they're actors. What do you want? It's from a dealer on Hollywood Boulevard. He was glad of a customer. He was hard to get to, with a quarter mile of soggy red carpet being rolled up. Did you notice, though, on the TV, that the tenting came down last night? Let's blow this up really big and frame it for the bedroom wall. Do you think I could make love to you with our grandparents there?"

"Please, I have customers too." But a woman looking at a pair of candlesticks smiled and went right on contemplating them.

Putting the photo back in his folder, J. saw the display under it. "What's all this pretty stuff?"

"Those are buttons, from my dad's button company. I take orders for him, some pretty big ones from time to time. Mostly he sells through specialty and premium companies all over the world—conventions, seminars, parties, including political. Lately cruise lines have been great, for both the tie-tack things and the big round badges. Higgen Buttons."

"That's brilliant. Would he take a little order, like for our marathons?"

"The darling, he would do anything, anything for me."

"Great to be loved."

"Yes and yes." Then she directed her voice back toward the computer. "Scott, hold the fort." She knew he'd be glad to. He enjoyed the chance to talk to customers, especially interior designers.

Across the street, they sat at the round table in the near corner of the patio. J. ordered the eggs, but she asked for "enchilada Howard." Neither could resist the margaritas, which they ordered straight up with salt, or the guacamole and chips.

He spread out the new photos of movie star Damon Higgen, from the dealer of movie stills. In many, he was in costume. He was a swordsman in some and a pirate in brocades, braids, and ruffled cuffs in others, and in one glossy, he wore a white tie and tails. Damon was much younger in that last one, and Emmy said, "Ah, he looks so much like you."

"Everybody always said I looked like my grandfather—Jared James, that is. You don't suppose, in this ridiculously developing drama, that they could have been cousins too, do you?"

"You said every fourteenth Irishman is related."

"Our Damon is from Dublin, and the Jared whom I cherished as my great-grandfather moved from Limerick to Dublin as a child. The resemblance is surely the common black Irish—come, it is said, from Elizabeth's defeat of the Spanish Armada racking up on the Irish coast and the blue-eyed women wading out to meet 'em. Well, our connection is your grandfather seducing my sweet, young, innocent grandmother."

"Oh, yeah. I'll bet she waded out to meet him."

"I'm starting to be very grateful for the Midwest Norwegian quarter and for the half that is my mother's Swiss parents. I don't think the Swiss went anywhere, but the Vikings founded Dublin. What if that old warlord was a Viking? A from-Norway Viking?"

Emmy consulted the invisible chart she was building in her head. "Well, my mother's heritage is English from Colonial America, as well as German with Lithuanian and Hungarian farther back. Or is it further? Together we have eight grandparents, and we share only one. It doesn't sound so incestuous when you look at it that way.

"In my childhood neighborhood there was an artist who was married to his first cousin, and they had five children. Of course they all had funny hair. I still know one of them, and her children have funny hair too."

"Is that your entire research into related gene pools?"

"Your father and my father are possibly half-brothers who share two grandparents, and that would mean the poor dead brother of your dad was his half-brother, and they shared only your grandmother as parent. Is this the 'we had him last year' Hollywood father story?"

"No. It's the whom did we have last generation Hollywood father story."

"Only women can figure relationships. Guys can't do it. I remember my dad asking my mother, about someone in his own family, 'How is he related to me?' But it wasn't about your dad because I'm pretty sure she didn't know about that."

"I'm pretty sure he didn't either."

"And we can't even tell anyone."

"And I promised to your grandmother that we wouldn't even mention it to her again."

"In my history studies, my greatest interest was the movement of people on the earth. In that big game of musical chairs, they walked a while and stopped; some peeled off and stayed, and some walked on. Your Irish came from everywhere to Ireland and stayed and then came to America. Hers," he said, indicating the waitress in the huge pink skirt and embroidery-encrusted blouse, "walked over the Bering Straight when it was a land bridge, with no one there to meet them."

"Later they waded out to meet the Conquistadors."

"And do the greatest thing that anyone does with eggs and cactus."

"They are the best neighbor. Wait till green tamale time."

* * *

It was not until they were back at Stuff that J. asked her to go to the desert with him the next weekend, or sooner, for next week, Ula and grandson would be back to work, perhaps.

When he left, Emmy's assistant rose from his computer and approached her as she polished a glass.

"Emmy, you're entering a terrific new phase of life. He seems like a great guy. You're going to need some time and someone to do some of what you usually do, and I've wanted to talk to you before you realize this and go looking for someone from the outside.

"I'm a lot more capable than you have seen. You may have even forgotten that I graduated from the UCLA interior design program in addition to being a computer guy. I'd like to be promoted to a top spot and hire two younger, less expensive assistants. Everyone can do computers now and put stuff on the website. I think I can be good with customers."

"Show me—here comes one."

"Honey, you looked great last night," he said to the patron. "I saw you on the red carpet, and I was so pleased with you and our necklace. I hope you have a DVD to see yourself. Instead of just returning it, would you like to know a price?"

She would, and she bought it, in three payments.

"You're on," said Emmy. "What kind of money do you want? You can work the hire. I suppose they will both be gay."

"Not necessarily. Some straight women are terrific."

*   *   *

"I haven't been out to the desert in forever, only partway there, to my parents' house. May we please stop there? I have a key and know the alarm code. It's a great old Victorian on a big lot—palm trees, fruit. We can pick some oranges.

"They moved the factory out here to a complex of old freight stations when the Culver City rent began to eat profit. He is just so happy here."

*   *   *

The off-ramp ended at a tree-lined street, and she directed him left, under the freeway, almost to the slope into the foothills. There it was, a visitor from another time, visible from a distance at the end of a palm-lined drive.

The house was painted a teal blue with white trim. The trim was so abundant that the house read almost white. The white porch rail ran across the front and down the right side, forming a three-quarter circle at the corner.

"This is unreal," he said when they entered the house. "Look—the floor boards are even tapered to form a wheel at that corner. What do you know of the history of this thing?"

"That remains for my father to tell you, which he loves to do."

They wandered through, J. loving it, the huge kitchen best of all. He suspected that some partitions had come down to create its size. "Next time we bring the Packard that goes with it."

"Why do you like it so much? You're a modern person."

"Sure, but this was modern in its time, at least the latest thing, imported from *Meet Me in St. Louis*."

"'Meet me at the fair and don't tell me the lights are shiny anyplace but there,' except maybe Hollywood Boulevard."

"And maybe Las Vegas."

"It's so funny to be in this house without my parents. I'm really missing them, especially here at his desk. I don't know how you stand it without yours," Emmy said to J., but now she found that she was talking to the back of his head. She glanced back to the desk.

"Well, will you look at that? The man walked off with my favorite fountain pen, my mottled blue and white with the gold bands, much too feminine to even be sitting on a man's big old desk. I'll send him another one when they fly back here. Oh dear, I'm saying the wrong things. I can't even stretch my imagination to know how you feel."

She went to him, and he backed up and perched against the desk. She stood between his legs, their heads almost even.

"I've never felt this close before to another human, even you," he said.

"I never thought you could be as one with clothes on."

"My darling, we will take care of that later."

"We should push on now. A few oranges on the way out, and I'm taking back my pen. I'll wrap it in a baggie from the kitchen to not risk ink all over my bag."

*   *   *

"Wow, there's a lot more windmills than last time. I like the plain stems better than the lattice ones that look like cranes. The distant ones on the ridge look like hair on a dog's back. It's certainly the way to go. Why are we not doing wind power more?"

"But you just said we were doing more."

"I want more, more, more."

"Insatiable—I like that."

"Isn't there too much English country garden going on out here? It's like we came out to the desert because we liked it, so let's make it look more like Brentwood."

"I think I heard them say that—movie stars sometime in the late thirties. It's the lawns with their slowly turning sprinklers, changing the humidity among the roses, that get to me."

Even here he knew a great place for lunch, cool and dark, with great margaritas and enchiladas.

"I brought the Ingénue here. You know, she has a glow about her. I think she carries her own light. She was recognized and made a fuss over. Do I need to say that she liked the place?"

"It sounds like how Damon Higgen liked to go to his granddaughter's school plays. It was my sister Peg who was the actress, and he was very intent on her being good at it. Did I tell you that I had accepted a dinner invitation from her for tomorrow night but took a rain check on it?"

J. hadn't heard much about the sisters and asked. Peg had graduated from theater arts at UCLA and then thrown herself into the profession at least long enough to appear on a sitcom and meet a young advertising executive. She soon realized that babies were all she'd ever wanted anyway.

"I don't know that my grandfather favored any one of us— there were so many—but he seemed to like that one a lot. She was early with a great-grandson for him. And the other sister is a lawyer, married to a lawyer, juggling a job, two kids, a nanny, a boat, and a golden retriever in a townhouse in the marina.

"Damon must have known about you, his grandchild too, because he surely would have known your father was his if indeed he was. Do you suppose he ever somehow got to see you? There's too much we don't know, and that one person who knows is off-limits. Do you think she realizes we're snooping?"

Even this early in the year, the sun produced an unbearable glare as they stepped out of the restaurant.

"Will I like the house?" she asked.

"Yes, but it has no roses. I'm thinking about keeping it, if I don't have to sell it. Maybe I'll just give it to you, and then it couldn't be touched by my cousins . . . And there it is on that rocky rise of land."

"It looks like just a lot of clay jars shoved into the land. What am I looking at?"

"At the fantasy of a woman and her designers without a budget, reinventing domestic shelter."

They peered out at a series of squat towers, which looked to have been patted into shape by a potter and eroded by a century of wind-driven sand—pods on a rocky slope amid drifts of brilliant bougainvillea and a violet blooming grass.

"Why haven't I seen it in the magazines?"

"They can't get close enough. Did you see me turn off a beam down the road? The designers deserve to have it published later though. I'm not sure that the furnishing is complete, yet, but my parents were staying here. We'll go in the front door instead of the garage."

Emmy could see nothing that looked like a garage, nor anything that looked like a house, for that matter. The road had gradually become paved with narrow, long, squared stones with a drainage spine of small stones. The setback from the road warped and contoured in large gravel-like stones piled against clay walls that were never flat and never straight. It seemed at once a Santa Fe pueblo, a Moroccan village, a water-storage cistern in Israel, and the clay jars of the first impression.

"What a response to the desert! It is the desert!"

Then they stepped into the entry hall, a huge, empty clay jar with only a slot to enter and another to leave into the rest of the house, none of which they could see from this entry hall. The light came from above, spilling down the irregular walls that curved seamlessly down into the floor.

"Only once before have I been in a round room of utter stillness, at the Getty Villa. I feel desolate not to have known your mother."

The surprises continued. Nothing was regulation.

Boulders outcropped, carved stone candle niches were set into the clay walls, and fireplaces were holes or caves. Glass retracted, and there was no in-doors and no out-doors. There was nothing made of wood, no wooden sills, trims, cabinets, or doors. Only bathrooms and a few bedrooms had doors, steel on pivoting hinges. There was only an occasional wall to walk around. Ceilings stopped short of some walls, allowing light to flood to the floor. Walls were irregular and could go from polished smooth to gritty and pocked.

The kitchen seemed to be only a huge steel worktable, but a closer look revealed two walls of steel cabinets set into the clay. A mega television screen hung in a huge, round tower. There were no windows, no hardware, no light switches, no light fixtures, and no faucets. Water fell from wall projections controlled by foot pedals.

In some places trumpet-shaped funnels burrowed through thickened walls, high up for directed light.

"Where do you think a shaft of light will hit at noon on winter solstice?" Emmy asked.

"An icon will appear, of course, in shadow outline, only released at that angle of light, at that moment of the year. Everyone would have to pledge to be home to see it. Some of those trumpet tunnels have solar cells above for nightlights."

"Can you imagine some future archeologist even trying to visualize the scale of the occupants?"

"They will be more baffled by the stack of bathtubs that are all that remain of a ruined condominium high-rise."

A few banquettes proved sofa soft. For beds, there were platforms hanging from the ceiling by arm-thick ropes, allowing rugs to spread under them. Exemplary rugs were everywhere, and in one bedroom, a velvet wedding-tent hanging filled a wall.

The boulder outcrop from the inside spilled outside and contained water, a pool brimming to the top.

"Jared, son of genius, I think it is finished."

* * *

"I love stuff—objects, things. They are my life. But this! I could never imagine feeling so cleared, so soothed. No paintings, no sculptures, no toys on a coffee table. It's really being away. It is so wonderful! Do you think they ever wanted guests here? And look how we can plainly see the car, pulled into that glassed area, from the inside of the house."

"Well, why not? You pay so much for a car you like. No reason to stuff it away out of sight in a dirty little storage box called a garage. So they looked at their precious cars from the bedroom. And yes, there are guest pods. I think one of them was meant for me. I don't know that anyone else except the Grandloon has stayed here.

"And now if I could only remember what I know about turning on the lights, though it will be light in here as long as there's light in the sky. Is this modern?"

"No. It has no identity. Did you call ahead and have it cleaned?"

"Someone comes in routinely. Thank God they do and remembered the dog. I did call yesterday, though, which is why there is dinner in the fridge. Let us drink the sunset away."

"This is peace."

"I don't know what I believe. But I hope she is at peace too; I hope they are."

"You mostly speak of her, hardly ever of your father."

"She was more vocal, more colorful, but you sensed his power. He always seemed to lead with his shoulders, against the wheel maybe. All the time, he admired his hardworking, inventive, makeup artist-slash-businessman father without knowing his real father was a philandering, famous, old movie star."

"Your father is who raised you and loved you and loved your mother."

"Tomorrow I must do some work. I owe a newspaper an article about the historicity of some movie or other. I bought that skinny, shiny elegant new Mac, not to defile the look of the house."

"I didn't know you had other gainful employment. Can I read you? Do you get letters?"

"Of course you may, but none is here. I do get letters; occasionally I stir the ire of some movie nut to red-hot denouncement.

"Let's try to clap on some lights, fire up some candles, and eat in front of the TV. Big screen, big picture. But no, it's not Omar on the horizon. I have seen the lust with which you regard him. I couldn't bear to watch you watch him. Have you seen *Russian Ark*? I have it."

"Oh, how wonderful! I despaired. I thought I'd never get a chance to see it. They say it's like going to St. Petersburg and walking through the Hermitage."

"Without hurting your feet."

They sat entwined in one another as the handheld camera took them through that incredibly opulent, slightly shabby, remarkably gilded, grand museum. She told him about inlay and marquetry, lapis and malachite, and he told her about the purported sex life of Kathryn the Great and insisted that all the children of the last czar had perished with their parents.

They glided through a state ceremony in the throne room, danced through the ballroom, and swept down the grand staircase.

And then she laughed. "What if the cameraman had tripped on that last landing?"

"I think we'd be watching something else."

"Was this here, or did you bring it?"

"It was here, probably the last thing they watched, still in the player."

"Had they been to Russia?"

"Yeah, to the Hermitage. They must have loved this. They began traveling a bit after my brother died."

"Would you forgive me for a very out-of-line flash of intuition?"

"Is it in the form of a question?"

"Yes. Did she kill him?"

"Yes."

"You think she did or know she did?"

"I think I know she did."

"Oh! How?"

"Plastic bag when he was sick, sicker than ever. Poor thing. He was a miscarriage that got born. He'd been whimpering for a couple of months and sobbing and moaning for a couple of weeks. Somewhere in that time she thought he said 'Ma.' The doctors said he was mercifully on his way out. I was thinking about it a lot, the big plastic bag that she took with her sandwich when she went to sit by his bed. She'd been taking it a long time. Maybe against a time when his agony was unbearable."

"Did you ever talk about it?"

"No. Where did your flash come from?"

"Your grandmother knows."

"Did she say so? What did she say? Maybe she had been thinking about the bag too."

"She didn't, but it came to me. It may not be true, you know."

"It was at the Oscar party, wasn't it? What was she talking to you so long about?"

"About your mother, how she had been so careful and hospitalized during her pregnancy with you, so as not to abort—I mean not to miscarry—and how cute you were when she brought you home from where you were born. Laguna, wasn't it?"

"I thought it was Cedars-Sinai."

"Don't you people ever talk?"

"I guess not enough. Strangest thing—he was so small, but his penis was long, out of proportion. When I saw that, mine hadn't amounted to much yet."

"Did some remarkable catching up and surpassing, didn't it?"

"Hey, you've never complimented him before. He was wondering why you hadn't."

"He's lovely!"

"I wouldn't want to know what you are using for comparison and how early."

"Well, I was eleven, and I saw my father step out of the shower. He had the towel over his face, drying his hair, so I was able to back out and blush by myself in the hall. He looked a lot like you, but then he's probably your half-uncle."

"You sure you want the next movie?"

"It would have to be a pretty important one."

"I've been looking for it a long time, and here it is. Russian again, the Russian *Hamlet*, I hope without subtitles—like you could graduate from anywhere and not know the words."

*　*　*

He awoke when the night was at its blackest, aware that there was no sound at all. Then there was a crisp noise, the faint rustle of the down quilt. Emmy had intercepted an incoming moonbeam from the trumpet form in the ceiling and was playing with it in her fingers. The diamond flashed in the incoming beam and sparkled across the ceiling.

She laughed. "I know when you're awake; you couldn't fake the sound of your ragged purr, your night breathing, 'cause you have never heard it."

"How old are you anyway?"

"I'm six, and you're seven."

"You seem more mature than that. Let me see."

She was ready to prove it, awake in the night. He probed her appetite. He delivered a resounding slap to her presented bottom.

The sound produced a flood of light that revealed her face and its appalled expression of betrayal.

"I'm so sorry, my darling. We won't play that game. I wasn't sure. What can I do to get you back?"

"You could clap your own hands and turn off the damn lights."

Chapter 6

Each of the rooms in the old Hollywood house had visitation of sunlight sometime during the day. Now it was J.'s cluttered desk's midmorning turn to be spattered with shifting leaf shadows.

He had finished his article, begun in the desert, and reread it twice with some satisfaction. He printed it out and put it aside to line edit again before e-mailing it to the magazine and starting his notes for the next commitment.

By her strange intuition, his mother's house angel arrived just then with his third mug of coffee, and like a second cue on the set, the phone rang.

"Yeah, she took me out, never to forget that's she's an independent woman and doing very well, and it was leap-year day . . . What do you mean, prenup agreement? That's pretty cold. Ever the attorney, aren't you? . . . Not Em. Anyway, if this went bad, I'd give her everything and kill myself, dramatically. Look, should I be putting some stuff in her name where they can't get it, in case of need?

"Yeah, you know I have a will with a tidy sum left to the suing cousins to shame them if they drive me to suicide, and to my grandmother and the Motion Picture Home. You remember when the Directors Guild ran that trailer with Walter Matthau and Jack Lemmon urging us to take care of the Motion Picture

Home? I thought they were speaking to me . . . Yeah, I forgot—you have to go to regular theaters and pay to park.

"Yes, I got DNA stuff. As I thought it would be, there was his comb with hair in it, in a drawer where I guess no one had been. I suppose there are still papers and things to take care of in backs of drawers.

"Sure, we could all go out there sometime in the next couple of months before the air begins to burn. I know where there is good booze. There are a bunch of guest pods. You have to know this is not a house kind of house, though.

"Yeah, she liked it very much. She really got it. And you know, there are hardly any things in it, but she recognized the martini glasses. They came from her showroom—very expensive—and she knew who'd bought them, so she knew who the interior designer was. Hard to keep secrets in this town . . . Yeah, from me I guess it's easy.

"Emmy warmed to the subject. I think she's doing DNA for Christmas presents—her father, uncles, cousins, and me. She has her grandfather's hair in a locket with his picture. Everyone descended from an old warlord along with every fourteenth Irishman.

"Oh, and the birth certificates you suggested. I found his. It shows Ula Dunkin as his mother and Jared Dunkin as his father, but it would, because a woman's husband is assumed to be the father of her children . . . Yes, a naïve assumption . . . Now, now. Yours all look like you, only better.

"Mine's not there. What to do if it's in another place? Maybe Laguna? The Ingénue said something to Emmy that made her think it was a birthing center or something like that."

* * *

They had missed the screening of *The Vantage Point* but put it on a future list because they agreed that a Forest Whitaker picture should not go unseen. Saturday was the screening of *The Other Boleyn Girl*, a must-see because of Elizabeth. They went to the Silver Spoon afterward for the lemon rice soup, only on the Saturday menu. J. was loath to accept the historicity of the whole picture. "I've got to study for the Elizabeth marathon, so I'll get back to you on this one."

"There's some doubtful objects in there, so I better do some studying too."

"I know you know where your parents are. Do you think we should get hold of them to tell them about us? Or rather to ask for a blessing at the very least?"

"He won't mind if we wait. He is the dearest and sweetest of souls. When I was first driving, I took out the whole front right fender. When he came home and saw the car, I was in fresh tears, but he said only, 'I bet you won't do that again.'"

"You're really crazy about him, aren't you? A psychiatrist friend told me that any man would do well to check out a woman's relationship with her father. You never talk about your mother."

"She's okay now. We didn't get along very well in my growing-up years, but I can't remember why anymore. Him, I first crawled to, then toddled to, then ran to, and now turn to. He has a way of not dwelling on an event. He says to accept and move on. You get it solved faster that way.

"Once when I was little, my mother was sitting on his lap, and I wanted her to get off so I could be there. She said he belonged to her, and she had the ring to prove it. A few days later he came home with a little blue box with a tiny ring and tiny engraving: 'D. L. G.' for 'Daddy's little girl.' I still have the box addressed to 'M. E. H. From her Daddy.' The ring got off my little finger on a playground a lot later. I remember crying for it. He told me to accept its loss and move on. That it was gone had nothing to do with how much he loved me.

"That's what he's told me about business: accept and move on. Don't dwell and protest until you miss the chance to do something about it.

"Like my situation, his company is a continuation of the job he had in high school. Then he got a degree in business that made it go. He studied graphic design too. He really has some big clients. I think he's got the Democratic convention and the Army for recognition lapel pins. His sales skills are high, as is his intuition about choosing salesmen. I've learned so much from him.

"My mom has skills in business too. She runs a household like one. She ran the business in the beginning. I'm the one who looks the most like her. That might be part of why my dad is so good to me, not that he isn't to the others. I don't mind looking like her anymore. Now I think she looks like me. Yellow hair and the pale Lithuanian-blue eyes."

"And the legs?"

"Yeah, the legs. He says that's the first thing he saw as he was getting up from his drafting board. She came in about an order, and he hired her for his secretary so he could hold onto her until he could propose."

"Imagine getting turned on by a pair of legs."

"Isn't that shallow though? It's the you of you that I love, but to see you in that black underwear, I could melt. I get excited at the sight of your gym-hard arm muscle across a crowded room. Your arm touched mine getting on that elevator. Did you know it did?"

"Yes."

"Let's go home."

* * *

"This is a good Sunday. I'm glad we came to my house. It needed a little affection, and so did the cat. Were you surprised when he jumped up on the bed with you in it?"

"No, I thought he was coming to kick me out. He may be reconciled. He purred a little."

"What would you think of inviting the Ingénue over for dinner if she isn't all dated up? I see here the requested pan of enchiladas and the salad greens. You do great margaritas, and I have the straight-up martini glasses for them. She would recognize how beautiful they are. With any luck at all, Marina would offer to bring dessert."

"I like it. Shall I call her?"

"I'll call her, and you can work till they come. Do you know how to hook up to my printer?"

* * *

She didn't have any trouble with the five steps up to the front porch, and from inside, Emmy heard her giggle at the sound of the doorbell.

"Isn't this the neighborhood where J. went to grade school?" J.'s grandmother asked as she and Marina entered. "I even think I remember thinking this house was charming. I truly love the old Mission furniture and the nice brocades you've done it in."

She was dressed in a houndstooth check suit, its skirt short over credible legs in black stockings. She had a brilliant yellow scarf tied over her black cashmere turtleneck. Emmy recognized the suit as Chanel, vintage Chanel, and admired it aloud.

"Oh, my dear, I've been shopping in the back of my closet again. The new condo has even bigger closets, you know, so I won't ever have to give anything away."

"Oh, the more's the pity," Marina said, laughing. "I've acquired some nice scarves. That's about all that will fit me. You should have seen how I used one of them. You remember, in the desert, the guest pod where you have to step over a high-ish sill, the one with the bed supported on big fat poles stuck in the wall and ropes to the ceiling? Well. Ula was sitting on it with her feet drawn up, screaming and pointing. A lizard, a pretty big one, had gotten trapped in that jug of a room and was going round and round at the scooped-up edge, with one set of feet on the wall and one set on the floor. I was scurrying around too, trying to throw my scarf over him.

"Jerry came in at the ruckus and could hardly stop laughing long enough to throw one of those great big heather-colored towels over it and take it outside."

Ula shivered, remembering. "Those damn things can climb the walls, you know. My poor darling boy. That was probably his last good deed and his last big laugh. They all came in, and your Aunt Marta sat beside me, to calm me, with her arm across my shoulder, but she couldn't stop laughing. Dear God, so soon they were all four gone. We drove home, and they never made it."

"You never told me you were there then. Even when you went out there with me, you never mentioned it."

Marina, always so fast to protect her, didn't quite try to this time. "You people never talk," she said. "You just banter. Maybe she'll tell you about her first day on the set."

Marina had indeed rescued her, from explanation or apology, and freed Ula to chat about herself. "Well, I sailed onto that set and declared, 'I'll kill the first man who asks me if I'm ready for my close-up.'"

Laugher returned.

"Thank you for inviting Blaine tonight too. He has to go to a family dinner on Sundays. He's really a dear man. He lives right across the street, you know. He walks west to the light and then across and back east, clutching flowers for me. We wonder how many of those windows are looking down, waiting for him to come back. He has a timer now on his living room lamp that goes out at eleven."

It was not possible to keep Marina seated in the living room with her cocktail as a guest. She joined Emmy in the kitchen as soon as the hostess headed there. Emmy could not resist asking her whether they really had sex, the Ingénue and Blaine.

"All evidence indicates yes, and I've fixed him a few breakfasts. My boyfriend thinks it's heartening; he's happily looking forward to all those years of sex, a lot of it without worrying about birth control."

"Is yours a serious relationship? I'm realizing I don't know much about you."

"I know you guys don't talk about basic stuff, but I thought your gossip abilities were high. Well, my guy's a cop, a calendar cop, really built, as well as your J., but younger. We don't know yet how serious we are. I think he knows there's a lot of women out there, but he can't afford to strew child support across the city. I wear that newish hormone-dispensing circle thing and pray to God it works as well as they say it does. It's certainly comfortable. I don't even know it's there.

"The job with Ula is perfect. First, I like her. The things that come out of her mouth! She's been around in ways that I would never know. How else would I have ever met Nancy Reagan? Best, there's three hours a day to write. I'm not long out of a school, where they said I could write—that sounds more like permission than evaluation. Anyway, I'm doing a police novel, and boy, do I ever have research, my cop and his friends."

"It sounds as though you'll stay a while. J. could be worried about that. He adores her, and she's all of his family, though he's not all of hers."

"Yeah, them. They might not have had quite as good a mother as he did. Not that I didn't like Marta, but Karen was better at being filthy rich. One of J.'s Cub Scout buddies told me that when they heard about four-star generals and four-star hotels, they started rating moms, and Karen was an outstanding four-cookie mom."

"I wish I'd known her, though sometimes I feel like I do at J.'s house, with her taste and choices all around me. I like her style. I like yours too, those black velvet shirts you wear. Where in the world do you get them? This one tonight with that tiny braid and the great buttons?"

"These are Ula's choice. I think she has this style made. The other ones are from Citron, up on Montana in Brentwood, and she has pockets put into the side seams. It's important to have credit card, parking ticket, mints, cash, and Kleenex appear without fumbling in a bag. Wait till you see the one I wear when she is really finely dressed. It has little pleaty ruffles at the cuff and a satin stripe down the velvet pant leg. It's vaguely reminiscent of a tux. Pockets there too. I like the uniform thing. At least part of the time I don't have to think about what to wear.

"Let me tell you to feel comfortable in his house. If she's still hanging out there sometimes, she likes you. I know because I like you. You're straightforward and feisty. You speak cleverly, but I've not heard you say anything just because it seemed like something someone wanted to hear.

Marina checked the oven. "These are hot now. Where's a mitt? Wow, I saw these at Koontz Hardware, the twenty-five-dollar mitt, the red one with the yellow stripe! I'd have that if I had a kitchen."

Marina had brought a nice bottle of wine, and Emmy found a lime sorbet in her fridge as well as some fresh raspberries. She put the sorbet in little marble bowls that had become like blocks of ice in the freezer. A garnish of mint leaves produced something more special than she'd expected.

After dinner they stayed at the table in the cozy, book-lined dining room. Marina declared it to be the most expensive wall cover in the world. Emmy proudly pointed out the two shelves that contained books signed by their authors. She chose not to tell that they were mostly her grandfather's, rescued from being thrown away, though she often did tell this as a cautionary tale.

Emmy decided that this was the right time to give the Ingénue the new book on Tony Duquette that she had bought for her when she picked up her own copy for the showroom.

It was still shrink-wrapped, and no one offered her a tool to open it, so she could only ooh and aah over the fabulous room on the cover.

"Marina, be sure we don't walk away without it. I shall have it open on the coffee table and look at every picture in detail, even if J. stands there scowling."

"I read that the author, one of them, scowled over Duquette too until suddenly one day, she got his message," said Emmy. "She had just started an editing job at *House and Garden* when it stopped. That magazine was really the best; I'm going to keep the whole last year on a shelf as though they were books, forever.

"J., did my printer work? Do you have your column?"

"It did, and I do. I'll get you copies to read later. I've been reviewing obscure things and reissued films. I'm getting some interested reaction. This one is on the Russian *Hamlet*, and I could have done without the subtitles. It was surreal without them, like the recognition of an old dream. They changed it a bit. They never did say, 'Goodnight, sweet prince.'

"From the history point of view, I wanted to make the point that there were a couple of Hamlets before Shakespeare. He may have read them, or he may have heard the story when he was traveling with a theatrical company in Denmark, early in his career.

"One is about a Danish prince named Amleth who acted a mad scene to protect himself while he plotted to avenge his father's death. This took place in the ninth century and was written down in the twelfth in a history of the Danish realm. They believed then that if you killed a madman, his devil flew into you, so he was safe enough while he planned against his uncle. He got the uncle in a duel and lived to be king. It's not popular to doubt Shakespeare, but I swear it's a better plot. Common to all the plays is the prince's avenging of his father's death.

"If you thought great phrases like 'dead of night' and 'mind's eye' were original with Shakespeare, they're not. They're in that history."

His grandmother was sitting forward in her chair, and J. thought he must have her attention now because the topic was theater.

"Your column, dear—could you do one about the various Hamlets? John Gielgud was best, you know. Some thought Barrymore. Jared did his makeup at a time when he needed it most. Then there was our friend Olivier, and there was Burton, a very charming man, and I liked Gibson—at least the sets were the best, but I've never met him. There was also Kenneth Branagh—spectacular—but I really loved him the more as Henry V."

Emmy and Marina both rose and headed to the kitchen for a coffee refill. Marina muttered, "In this company you don't want to say 'avenging his father,' like George Bush having a war, do you?"

"No, you don't. Clinton or Obama?"

"I don't know, I don't know. I wish I liked one of them better than the other."

"It just has to be Hillary!"

Back in the dining room, J. and his grandmother were considering a *Hamlet* marathon. She would talk about the ones she knew, and someone would tape her. J. said that there was a play about the original Amleth. As he remembered it, it was called *Hour of Vengeance*, and he thought he knew where he could get it. Again they would tape it, all of them reading the parts.

* * *

"Leave the dishes and let's get to the bedroom TV. I set it to tape, but we can just make the start of it. It's *A Few Good Men*, Academy Award for Jack Nicholson."

"Marina and I did the dishes while the coffee was brewing. That woman is something else, and two do the work of three—or with her, maybe four."

"It's not on yet. I'll mute it till it starts. That bodyguard job is perfect for Marina, or she could be a cop like her guy."

"Bodyguard? You're kidding."

"The grandmother lady is pretty out there, pretty visual, and she could look like a ransom treasure in those commercials— thus, the red-haired lady with the gun who drives and takes care of the cars and is social secretary and shops and, on the housekeeper's day off, spells for her. From an old song, 'Plays alto and baritone and doubles on a clarinet.'"

"'And wears a size thirty-seven suit.' All that's in the title, isn't it?"

"How did you know that obscure old thing?"

"Maybe not so obscure. My mom uses it for anyone who is trying to be all things to all people or do extreme multitasking.

She is also fond of the lyric 'I've got a rose between my toes from walking barefoot through the hothouse to you, pretty baby.' But I don't know what that song means to her."

"I have another one: 'Will you still need me, will you still feed me, when I'm sixty-four?' Huh?"

"'Hold My Hand' . . . Anyway, Marina carries a gun? Really? I had no idea. Where does she keep it? Wow, I'm so naïve. I didn't pick up on that."

"I'm not sure where it is. Once she was in the parking garage getting into the trunk, and two big guys came up behind her and demanded her purse. She whirled around, gun trained on them, and told them to get out of this garage right now and go home and tell their mamas that they're sorry and won't ever do this again. I think she has a knife too, maybe in the cowboy boot, though I don't know how she gets that out in a hurry."

"Maybe she kicks out with it from the toe like Lotte Lenya in 'Mack the Knife.'"

"It's a good job for her, and she's saving money for maybe a motorcycle or a horse."

"And it gives her time to write that book."

"A book? Why wouldn't I know that? I guess everybody in town is writing a book. Women tell you things, don't they? Hang around my grandmother; she knows so much I want to know."

*   *   *

"I forgot what a good movie that was. Tom Cruise at his best. And I was looking at other things as well, like the backlit profiles and cinematography in general."

"I like Robert Osborn best. I want his job. I would have talked more about the history of Cuba and the American base and what else was going on in the world at the time of *A Few Good Men*. We don't get enough of what's going on."

"Like global warming."

"Did you hear what Cheney said about that? He said he's come to believe it's true, but he calls it 'spring.'"

"It would be fun to meet Marina's guy. Can we ask them out sometime?"

"Do you think he'd be overwhelmed by the Packard?"

"If he's got her, he's not overwhelmed by anything. It's I whom am overwhelmed by the Packard."

* * *

"Marina had told me about your house. I really liked seeing it, especially the library. We get called to a lot of houses, and I've come to believe there is less domestic abuse in houses with books. This is not scientific, you understand, just my observation."

He was good-looking, Marina's cop, with the sloping shoulders of a weight lifter, in a white sweater under a navy blazer. Emmy thought him very sure of himself, being so young in a snooty place.

To J. he said, "I see that your scotch and water is a different color here. As your passenger, I appreciated that you watered it before driving, but you know that you'll be all right with this one after you eat. I wish that women knew to drink carefully because it's different for them, even Marina."

"You are observant."

"Well, it's my profession."

"Mine too. Are you after being a detective? Is that what you would like to be?"

"No, the only thing I'd like better than being a police officer is being an actor. And for my first acting job, I'd be a cop on a cop show."

"Well, you do look the part. Do you two want to come to our *Hamlet* marathon?"

"Could you extend that invitation to the Elizabeth marathon that Marina told me about? I've always admired her and thought she had a lot to do with our law and order."

"Wow, that's what I think. Do you play handball?"

Chapter 7

Returning to the house after dinner, J. admitted that he hadn't thought much about security. There was an alarm system, and he usually remembered to set it, but the garage was equipped with just an opener, controlled remotely. The stories now about Beverly Hills citizens aghast at empty garages had gotten his attention.

"I guess we could track the Packard easily enough though," said the Beverly Hills cop, who had admired it in great detail earlier.

The house angel had set up the coffee and Baileys in the library, and J. lit the coal-grate fire, also remotely. Books on Tudor costuming had been shoved aside on the big ottoman to make room for the tray. Marina and her boyfriend thumbed through the books, their interest in Elizabeth piqued again, and they expressed their pleasure again with the invitation to the marathon.

*   *   *

"What about them together? What if we know they're serious before they do?"

"I've known her for several years now, and he is just what I'd choose for her. They've been together awhile. Evidently he can handle her."

"Did you ever wonder what she would be like in bed?"

"Of course. Great bottom, but I've never seen her legs. I speculate about every woman I see."

"Every one?"

"Well, not if it's too big a crowd of them, and I can't get around to 'em all."

"About me?"

"Especially you. I saw those legs, spread, in my bed. I speculated; then I invested."

"How about a return on your investment?"

"Show me your rosebud . . . You didn't think all this time that the Hearst character in *Citizen Kane* was nostalgically muttering about a sled named Rosebud, did you? He was thinking about his mistress, remembering her from the best perspective. Have you ever seen what I see? I'm getting a mirror."

"No, no, that's my grandmother's hand mirror."

"Oh yes, and when she bequeathed it to you, she put a spell on it so that no matter where she went, she would see what was reflected in it. Is that why you carry it in your overnight bag?"

The darling, she looked so embarrassed, so intrigued, so involved, so glazed in rapture.

*   *   *

"Welcome, dear friends and members of the Fictitious History and Film Buffs of Hollywood Hills, to the Elizabeth the First Marathon. Both the bar and kitchen refrigerators are full of beer of various persuasions, including Hollywood Blond and some English selections. A popcorn machine has been rented for the occasion. Fish and chips will be served between the two films.

"As it is our house, we get to talk about what intrigues us about this royal person. Royalty is what we came to this continent to get out from under, and later I want to talk about what this lady did to make that exodus a possibility.

"Remember that we are seeing into the Renaissance, the time of Leonardo and Michelangelo, who died in the sixth year of Elizabeth's reign, and—Em will tell you—of Cellini, who happens to be her favorite. He was born about the same time as Anne Boleyn and lived longer.

"Remember that Elizabeth came to the throne 343 years after Magna Carta first brought some small measure of freedom to England. This is the same length of time that separated the end of her reign and the end of World War II.

"I am totally interested in the historicity of the films and, by profession, watchful for every goof-up. Ms. M. E. Higgen, owner of a gorgeous showroom called Stuff, is, to no one's surprise, more interested in the stuff. And there she stands with the mike in hand. Can she do it? She has to have inherited some acting urges. Dear God, how I love that woman."

"First, it's his house, not ours, but he has given me this terrific diamond, and I'm led to believe the house comes with it later. I don't think I'll change much of the stuff. Some of it was chosen by the lovely Ingénue lady, Jared's grandmother, whom we are so pleased to have here with us tonight. But she was always way too pretty to play the role of Elizabeth.

"This is the first time we've blended our respective families and friends. My sisters and their husbands are here, and their kids are downstairs playing with yours in the care of the rent-a-nanny. My brilliant and knowledgeable showroom manager Scott Hamish is here and is going to run a short slideshow to begin this marathon. His two new assistants are here too. They also know their stuff.

"It would be wonderful if we could depend on the movies to give us accurate history. This seems to be harder for them than getting the sets and costumes right. The studios must have every book ever published as reference. There was one in 1938 titled

Shakespearian Costume for Stage and Screen. Preceding it, in 1796, was *A History of British Costume.* The portraits of the time are the best reference."

She had been standing beside him where he sat on his barstool, but now she pulled her stool away and out farther and handed him the mike. J. saw that she was wearing the lapel mike. Emmy climbed onto the stool and crossed her legs, one sandaled high heel over the rung. Those legs, those legs! And he realized that she was wearing the red sandals from the day they met.

The room darkened, and a portrait of Elizabeth came on a screen that had just been lowered. Scott was controlling the images from his laptop.

"Here is the lady herself, about ten years into her reign, still conservatively dressed. From a portrait in the National Portrait Gallery in London. My parents are traveling currently, and I've sent them there.

"Start noticing the ruffs and how often there are matching lace cuffs. Ruffs were called bands because they started as mere bands and then got much bigger than this. If you ever wondered about the derivation of 'stepped out of a bandbox,' it was about keeping these things clean and stiffened by starch and curling iron, in a bandbox. Here, in a later portrait, she is looking as though her head has been served up on a plate, so big is the ruff. And a third from 1592, her thirty-fourth year as queen. Note the ruff has become a winged collar. And another winged collar on the wife of James the First, to allow for extreme décolletage. And another on Mary, Queen of Scots, in her dramatic black and white. And don't give me any sympathy for her unless it's for her traitorous stupidity."

There were several more portraits with commentary about shoes and ribbons, farthingales, peasecod doublets, kirtles, and cloaks and then the portrait of Robert Dudley, Earl of Leicester.

"He was her cousin, childhood playmate, and close companion. Who's to say how close? She let him marry to end that speculation, for she was married to England as surely as a nun is married to Jesus Christ.

"In this first film we will see her as a newborn and then in a bright white lady's dress, aged three, as Dudley was also. If we could have seen him then too, we would have found him dressed like a miniature man, for there were no children's clothes. Here, instead of a ruff, he wears a falling collar and cuffs to match, and that's the order of the Garter around his neck.

"Here is another of Elizabeth's favorites and mine: Sir Walter Raleigh, in dramatic black and silver. Note the earring as befits a pirate. Watch for him in several of the films—though if you're Irish, as both J. and I are, we should hardly like Walter, who raped, pillaged and burned and became a landlord in Ireland.

"And here is the brilliant Francis Bacon in a long gown with ruff and cuff that makes you think they were keeping the velvet and satin clean. Did you ever see dress shields, and did they have them then? With a lower crown, the hat would look current today, and with a higher crown it would be like the hat we associate with the pilgrims, from less than twenty years after Elizabeth. This was a transition hat.

"As for the architectural contribution of the Tudors to the Renaissance, we have the innovation of the stairway built as case goods, as though it had been built in a cabinet shop and rolled in. Thus, a staircase. This is from the book *Steps and Stairways*, coauthored by one of my customers.

"Let's watch for these and other details, other stuff, in the films."

Yes, she could do it. She did! So prepared, so cool. He was glad he hadn't asked to edit or rehearse. And now there was applause, including from the Ingénue—in fact, she was leading it.

Someone said, "Awesome, the legs."

Another voice said, "First slideshow I ever saw that worked."

The room soon quieted, and *Anne of the Thousand Days* came on the screen.

When the lights came up after the film, J. took his mike. "Why do we applaud? The actors aren't here, and the film can't hear you, but wasn't it a fine one?

"Whenever I hear someone say, 'What a beautiful day,' I think, 'As Anne Boleyn said on Jane Seymour's wedding day.' And what did they say to little Elizabeth that day? Your mommy's lost her head, and you have a new mother?

"Henry was forty-five that year. He had been on the throne for twenty-seven years, with eleven years yet to go, and had grown quite used to ruling. And he had a talent for governing, as had his father before him. He would have been enraged that we came to know him by his wives and then by his daughter, the little red-haired three-year-old girl in the white dress who was destined to be the finest CEO in European history.

"But now I smell fish and chips, and I want a beer. Will you join me?"

It was a buffet, but of course, Ula sat on the sofa and waited for someone to bring food to her. It was Marina's beautiful cop who brought her a plate and napkin and asked which beer she wanted. Her request was for Chinese beer, and Emmy felt a certain surge of triumph at not being stumped. She opened it and delivered it.

"Get yours, dear, and come back and sit by me."

"Oh, you have a Norwegian beer," she said when Emmy returned. "I didn't know we made one. I guess it's God's gift to the whole world.

"An interesting footnote about the ruffs, dear. They still exist in the world, you know. The immigrant Lutheran pastors still wear them on occasion. I once asked a Danish pastor the irreverent question of how he kept it so snowy white clean. He had the grace, you know, to laugh and tell me that he sent it back to Denmark from time to time to be starched and—you got it right, dear—put into shape, you know, with a ruff iron like a curling iron. I guess he sent it in a bandbox.

"You did that so well, dear. Even boosting up to sit on the barstool was a difficult piece of business. I think you rehearsed that as well as the speaking part. Your timing is good, and your voice excellent. You might sit up a little straighter, you know, and there are some places where you could have paused a little. Never rush through material, even if you think they are not paying attention. Of course you know they are. When you get the video and screen it, you will see the parts that could have been just a little bit better.

"Are you Catholic, dear? Your grandfather was, you know, in a way. My Jared James was a Protestant. There are some of those in Ireland, you know. You know that he played tennis with your grandfather and any number of his sons—Jerry and Anders too, all in their white sweaters. They played at that club up on Mulholland near Damon's house, or at his house. I'm sure you know it well. I've never been there. I can't remember the actor/director who bought it. I guess it must have been inherited from Damon by the wife of the moment. You have so many aunts and uncles, dear. None of them are actors, are they?"

"Uncle Sean is. He's been on a TV hospital show for years. Sean Locke. He took his mother's maiden name, to stay out of comparison, I should think."

"Many do that. I think I know that your father is Patrick, and he kept the Higgen. You know, I'm sure I've met him, but never your mother. I think her last name was Remington—like the condo on Wilshire, where each unit has its own elevator—wasn't it? Was that her maiden name or the name of her first husband?"

"She wasn't married before. She was not long out of school when she met my father. She came to his factory, and I guess she never left, or so he says."

"I don't remember how old he is, but I could figure it out, you know, because he was just sixteen when J. was born. I think I thought about that at the time because Damon, almost a generation older than I, had a boy still in high school, when my boy had been to war and back and was giving me a grandbaby. I think that makes your father fifty-three, doesn't it?"

"Yes, he is, and in all that time he hasn't had a chance to travel much. This trip is really making up for it. They are out of communication, so they don't have to worry about anything. Of course, I have numbers where I could get to them at any time, and text to tell them things they have to see."

"This trip must be wonderful for your mother, dear, having started her family so soon, just like I did, you know, no time to be the pampered bride. And there I was taking care of adorable little Jerry."

"I wish I could ask you if he knew about his biological father."

"That's a phrase we hear so much now. It could be shortened to biodad. Or bioda, with the Irish *da* for dad. With the accent on the 'o,' it's a whole new word: bioda. We need some new words now, you know.

"In our Norwegian family we use the old-country word for father. It's *far*. Then *far far* is grandfather, your father's father. *Mor* is mother, and her mother is *mor mor* to you, and her father is *mor far*."

Emmy remarked, "In Irish *mor* is the word for big. My far has a cousin named Liam Mor, Big William."

"In Norway your husband is your man. If homosexuals marry, we need a word for that kind of marriage and for wife and husband.

"How do they decide who's who anyway? And who's mommy and who's daddy if they adopt or inseminate a rent-a-womb? And would the child know which was the bioda if one of them were it?

"I, for one, was glad when we could call them gay men. We needed a nice word, you know, but some people, Blaine for one, resent the loss of such a festive word for its real meaning. 'When Our Hearts Were Young and Gay' couldn't have been written now, you know. He promised me he would never say, 'I feel gay tonight,' even though it meant giving up a perfectly good word.?"

So obvious had it become that she was not going to answer that Emmy let into the conversation an eager young woman sitting on the rug in font of them.

"I'm in makeup at the studio. I worked for Anders once. We all liked him so much. I always wanted to tell you that. We could do anything. We could have made up even pretty you to play Elizabeth."

"Yes, I could even have been a Klingon for *Star Trek*."

"They told us in makeup school that aristocrats whitened their faces like Elizabeth did to further their pallor and distinguish themselves from the workers out in the sun."

"I guess my Jared and my Jerry knew that, though I didn't. I wonder if anyone knows why they ever wore powdered wigs, even two centuries after Elizabeth.

"I'm glad you liked him, my boy Anders. I liked him too. I always told him I did and would have baked cookies for the two of them even if they were the boys next door. I always found Jerry very smart and assumed he knew everything, if it were only by intuition. I miss him, miss them both so much!"

Then, like the gracious actress she was and knowing the young make-up artist would not know what to say, she fed her the next line by asking if she didn't think J. looked so much like Jerry.

"Yes, he does, maybe even more black Irish, but the voice that we heard tonight was like an actor's."

They were interrupted by another nearby voice as a stunt man asked Ula whether she had known Douglas Fairbanks.

"The son, you know, yes, I knew, but not the father. He died young, way before I came to town. She, Mary, was ten years younger than he, and I knew her when she was married to Buddy Rogers.

"I heard about a yearly tribute to Douglas senior on his birthday, some time in May at the Hollywood Cemetery. I heard they project one of his movies on Rudolph Valentino's mausoleum. You might want to go as the representative of your generation of the physically intrepid. Maybe he will be there. They say that Valentino has been seen."

J. was glad to take the mike again, before she got any further with her growing spiritualist beliefs, to introduce the next picture.

"The committee has chosen these first two films for their chronological order in Elizabeth's life, the first to present her mother and father, estranged though they became. If there had been a good *Richard III* available, they might have started with that to show you her grandfather, who took both the horse and the kingdom at Bosworth Field in 1485.

"This one shows the young Elizabeth, her girlhood, how smart she was when the object was to stay alive. They educated her, I think, just in case. I admire her enormously and have come to believe her love of country and the rule of law was the influence that gave us America.

"The committee has chosen the rest of the films, starting tomorrow morning, in the order of their production, for they all deal with many aspects of her life as prospective husbands come and go. Everybody is going to have a favorite Elizabeth. I'm torn among them—Bette Davis, Judi Dench, Cate Blanchett. Must I decide?"

Emmy was on her stool ready to speak. J. hoped she would be brief. And she was, saying only that when she thought of Elizabeth's stuff, she thought always of her pen and ink, with which she wrote a fine Italian hand and maybe the sonnets attributed to Shakespeare.

J. took the mike. "Coffee and dessert afterward, and we would like to return to the stools for a bull session with you in your various professions. And Chairman Alice will tell you the schedule then too.

"There will be coffee and croissants in the morning, and I happen to know the first film is the silent movie *Fire over England*, 1924, with Flora Robson. That was the year this house was built, two years after my immigrant predecessor came to town from the Irish stage with his makeup case in hand. It will be followed by the 1940 *Sea Hawk* with Errol Flynn and Robson again as Elizabeth, in matching cuff and huge ruff, the authenticity of which I question as not being in any of the portraits and being impossibly cumbersome for dinner or archery. And now, your young Elizabeth."

* * *

117

"Emmy, darlin', if you think you are tired now after this wonderful evening and two films, wait till tomorrow night after six films! But damn, it's fun. How fabulous is this to see the same material in the hands of so many different imaginations!

"And you, my dear, are very good, very smooth, but who's surprised? Did you know the whole thing was taped? That's Joe Silver. He's pro. He said he couldn't keep the camera off your legs. I think when you swung your foot a little, it did him in."

"Yeah."

"What did the Ingénue tell you this time?"

"When I started the paternity subject, she covered with chat and her new word, bioda for biological dad. I felt she was all but admitting that your father knew Damon Higgen was his father, though she still didn't say it. Why in the world would he have never told you that?"

J. did not know how to frame his answer and leave out the hurt—one grandfather pulled out from under him, another substituted, and now his father, not seeing that he could and should have trusted and told him. He spoke in some need to defend his father. "How do you say that? 'By the way, son, that terrific, big, handsome, rich guy you thought was your grandfather, well . . . And your sweet righteous grandmother, well . . . '"

"The Grandloon has told me again that she likes you very much, but that you are not for me. She intimated that some kind of spiritual guidance has told her that. Instead, she could have just said that we are cousins."

"It's half-cousins."

"Soul mates. Standing by the elevator, the other half of this lonely, only child, missing for thirty years."

"Bullshit!"

"Love."

"I love you too. We'd have been a different kind of playmates."

"Oh yeah. This is better."

* * *

"So that's what marathon means. I feel as though I just ran the twenty-six miles twice in the rain. Could we leave the litter and go to my house under the winter-weight quilt with the cat, and please leave me sleeping in the morning?"

"God! But it was great, seeing films about the same person's life piled on each other. Different makeup, hair, costuming, most notably ruffs—the interpretation of style of the time. Some of them failed completely to show the change over the years. I'm so sure it changed as fast as it does now."

"How about the Ingénue coming to the last day in that black, long velvet coat and ruff and cuff? Where did she get them?"

"Studio. She's got friends. Did you hear her say that she was Anne Boleyn had she lived? Do you think that any of those people will ever again say that Elizabeth didn't need to kill Mary, who was trying to kill her?"

"Why did Ula-Anne come without Blaine? Was it so she could flirt outrageously with her grandson's friends?"

"It would seem so."

"Everyone got on so well and opinioned endlessly."

"Opined."

"Yes, I know, but it's a dumb-sounding word, so I don't use it."

"The English language according to Mary Ellen Higgen?"

"Yes, it could use some help. And wasn't everyone just wonderful, bringing food, cleaning up, and filling out those cards, opinioning about this marathon and future ideas? The committee did a fabulous job, as though they were making a movie, which they usually are. I can't wait to read the cards, especially for everybody's favorite Elizabeth. Are they here, or did the committee chair take them?"

"Alice has them, probably reading herself to sleep with them. There must have been a lot of thank-yous to her. And there must have been something about how good you were."

"You were terrific. But is anyone surprised?"

"I thought we really had something good going together. I hope someone opines about that. Who was your favorite Elizabeth?"

"Emma Thompson."

"Cate Blanchett."

"Do you know she's in *Indiana Jones*?"

* * *

She awoke knowing it was late, guessing it was eight or maybe half after. The faint smell of coffee drifted from a thermos cup beside her.

What a guy to have sneaked that to her nightstand before going off to his first day back at work.

Overcome with contentment, she began to sing to herself, the only person she would ever allow to hear her. "I'm glad I waited for you . . ."

"I'm glad my heart waited too." He hadn't left. Oh dear, he had heard her. He came out of the bathroom, splashing cologne. His kiss was short because he was laughing and then holding her. "This is wonderful. Up to now I thought you were perfect, and now I know better. You're off-key!"

"What's key?"

"I bet you'll never know. This is why you weren't very excited about opera tickets."

"I like the sets and the costumes."

"You thought I had left, and your secret was safe. But I'm not due at the kick-off meeting until ten. We don't start shooting yet. Damn, that's my cell phone, and I'll have to take it. Probably change of venue or time."

He paused to listen after answering and then said, "Well, if it isn't the long-ago lawyer lady." He held the phone where Emmy could hear it.

"You remember that I started out in the attorney general's office, so you know who I still hang with."

"I think that would be with whom."

"Okay, grammar boy. Do you want a heads-up, or do you want to be right?" She didn't wait for a commitment but dived in, as though she didn't expect to hold his attention long. "You know how everyone in town can know gossip about you before you do, if in fact you ever do? You have no way of knowing how you smell or how you sound when you snore."

"Does this mean you miss me?"

"No, not you. Your body sometimes in the night and the condo maybe, the valet parking, but not you. Your snore isn't all that loud, though, and I hear you're still using that aftershave I found for you. Did the folks at Ingénue ever object to that conflict of interest? I go sniffing for it on other guys at parties.

"But listen, rumor has it that your cousins have grown tired of the wrongful death suit. They probably gave some thought to the possibility that Uncle Anders, whom I liked, by the way, may have been the navigator, and you could have countersued, arguing that he was the one at fault, Jerry not alone at the controls like little Johnny Kennedy was."

"Thanks, this is all good."

"Sure, that would be a relief. Of course, you are filthy rich, and money doesn't even mean that much to you anyway, anymore. But getting dragged through indictment and accusation of fraud and misappropriation of funds might get your attention, and the IRS might really be a bother in your life. Have you ever noticed that when you put the words "the" and 'IRS' together without a space, it spells 'theirs'? This isn't legal advice. This is just an old friend. And you are not all that bad, to have to go through something this serious that I know you didn't do. So today, go get yourself an attorney and a forensic accountant and start listing all your assets. I mean, move on this. Today!

"You'll be the boy in the dike. One thumb might do it now, but later the other thumb only works as far as you can reach, and you can use only one big toe and maybe your nose and . . . yeah, that too, yeah."

"Wow, and I've got a back-to-work meeting for my new picture today."

"Your picture, my ass. Are you still at that script thing? You must be making a fast thirty-five an hour by now!"

"Forty."

"Well, don't lazy out on this one. This is where I say goodbye. Goodbye once again."

J. found himself saying his thanks to no one; she'd already hung up.

Emmy sat up and pulled herself back against the pile of pillows, tugging the quilt to her chin. "Ooh, that sounded like 'goodbye forever.' Did she think you might get back together?"

"Aren't you just a woman though? Chewing over ex-lovers when we get warned of big troubles ahead."

And then the cell phone warbled again.

"Hi, Alice . . . Yeah, me too. Can hardly wait to see the feedback. But I'm employed now, so got to go. I'll text you Em's number right now. She's right here. Call her back now. She'll set something up."

As Emmy dived in her big bag beside the bed for her phone, he said, "Dinner tonight? Marina is off—her cop as well. Maybe your Scott too and Joe of the video. Not my grandmother though. She might not have the right costume for debriefings. She'd lecture. I do want to talk to her in depth sometime about our performance though."

Emmy stretched and responded. "Okay, dinner here, easy enough, now that I have my heart's desire, an almost full-time housekeeper, and I don't even live here anymore."

When Alice called, she sounded restive and worried. She was not back to work yet and had taken some time to organize and classify the file cards.

"Mostly they liked us; some loved. Different opinions of who was the best Elizabeth. One of them said that, like Hitchcock walking into his caricature, Cate Blanchett walked into his vision of Elizabeth. J.'s grandmother said, and I quote, 'Dears, that was good theater,' and she signed it in her full movie star name. Many wanted to come and play in your yard with your toys again."

"J. will be so pleased. He loves hosting and talking about film."

"You think?"

"I guess you would know that. Have you known him a long time?"

"Not before junior high—or middle school, as they call it now—like some of his friends. And no, I never slept with him, if that is a question you would like to ask and never would. No, Joe and I were an intimate item from sophomore year on. So I didn't know other guys. Still hardly do."

"Joe?"

"Joe Silver, the camera guy. We're divorced, but I kept the name Silver for the kids. Easier in school."

"I hear some pain in your voice. J. was hoping that you, as madam chairman, would round up folks for a debriefing dinner tonight at my house. Is that tough for you?"

"I welcome dinner out, since I'm not going to restaurants now after this whole damn long time out of work, McDonald's for kids excepted. The brats love having me home though. They were getting out of hand. That part's much better right now.

"My child-support fellow has come through so far, and I haven't been into capital yet at all. I have a big condo and three more in the same building. Those are paid for by others. They are called tenants. My oldest girl is in college on the fund set up for her at birth. She's at Woodbury University in Burbank, going for her degree in accounting, for the film industry of course. Good background for associate director. I didn't get much past second AD before the detour to acting. I got her a sweatshirt that says 'Accountancy, Accrual Profession.' So anyway, with that assistant director background, I should be able to round up these people of the committee. Where do you live?"

Emmy gave her the address along with parking suggestions.

"Well, there'll be one car less because I'll walk. I'm about three blocks from you, even closer to the life-giving pizza.

"Look, I wouldn't want you to think I've been out taking a poll, but we all think you are really good with Jared, much better than she-who-wanted-to-be-obeyed before you. Try as she might, she couldn't reshape him, and we couldn't think why she would want to.

"He was always a babe magnet—well, a people magnet. Where he sat was the good table. Even when he was fat in junior high, he just took his tray and glided into place, and everybody closed in around him, the in-kids anyway."

Emmy's voice was full of surprise. "J. was fat?"

"You should be glad. It's the only thing that keeps him humble. I don't think there's any need to mention that I told you. You'll see pictures someday anyway."

* * *

Everyone arrived on time, like a good committee at a business meeting.

Joe Silver ran a selection from his tapings, beginning with Scott's slideshow, and seemed smug with how smooth it was, pleased with J. and Emmy's commentary, and greatly pleasured by the repeated word "professional" from the committee.

Dinner was Emmy's grandmother's church-social goulash, well known by her housekeeper by now and called by her the slub-gum dish. It was served in bowls, and when they were finished with the meal, they all rose, mobilized by Alice, and deposited the empties on the kitchen counter. The table thus instantly cleared, Alice distributed a pack of cards to each member to read in turn.

"Here's a good one: 'You otta—o-t-t-a—be in pitchers, p-i-t-c-h-e-r-s.'"

"I like this one: 'Let's hear it for the committee.'"

"This person asks, 'Could we do *Hamlet*? I don't care what anybody says—I like Mel Gibson even better than Olivier.'"

"Here's another one that agrees, about Hamlet anyway, but likes the Russian one: 'In Russian, best.'"

"Here's a repeat of what somebody said in the audience: 'Only slideshow I ever saw that worked.'"

"'Encore, encore,' says this one. 'Had a great time.'"

It began to look as though the next marathon was established, and the suggestions for theme were many. The committee would be there, of course, when it was determined who wanted to be on it. The cards had some suggestions for members and for guests as well.

J., the history professional, made a strong case for the rulers of England. English history was such a neat package—confined to that island; borders geographically determined, more or less, from time to time; and with such whopping good stories.

This suggestion was seconded by several, and an argument ensued over whether they should start with the boy who pulled up the sword and would be King Arthur or with King Mark in the story of Tristan and Iseult, as in the recent movie *Tristan & Isolde*. Someone asked whether there was a version before this newer one because the new one forgot the better plot of legend and opera. J. noted that the Tristan actor of the new version was remodeling a house down the hill from him. It had been going on for more than one noisy year. J. digressed to describe the three hammer blows every morning at seven. He should have been called Tristram from the English anyway, J. said. But there had to be *Camelot*.

From Emmy came a long moan of appreciation. "Oh my God, the clothes, the wedding dress of cantaloupe seeds, the white-clad Vanessa against the white snow!"

Could they have both *Becket* and *The Lion in Winter* for Henry II? Then there would be Katharine Hepburn for Eleanor of Aquitaine as well. And did everybody know that Henry the Navigator was Eleanor's descendant and furthermore that Emmy had a costume sketch of her? It was not for sale. Was there anything for the much-later Duke of Windsor? Anything for Queen Anne? For Cromwell?

The documentary *Monarchy*, which had aired on public broadcasting and was available on DVD, was admired by some who had seen it, but none of them thought it could be considered a rival to their project.

The ratchety doorbell rang, and a beautiful, long-eyelashed, young boy arrived still in his white uniform from a karate class.

He cuddled up to Alice and from her encircling arm looked about for his father. They flashed twin grins. He soon joined the game and reminded them about William the Conqueror; he didn't know if there was a movie about him, but how about Robin Hood for King John? And was it the film with Errol Flynn or the more recent one with Sean Connery that featured both Richard and John? Then someone remembered Damon Higgen as the best Robin Hood ever but couldn't remember who had played King John.

There were those who preferred Robert Taylor and Elizabeth Taylor in *Ivanhoe.* That pleased Emmy because of the sets and George Sanders, the embodiment of cool.

"How shall we choose between Branagh and Olivier for Henry V?"

"If one of them has Henry IV or Henry VI in it, we won't have to."

They skipped about without any consideration to succession. Victoria was followed by *The Madness of King George*, and didn't he have a father and definitely a son in that picture? That would take care of two reigns if they didn't have a movie of their own. No one, not even J., could remember who followed George IV.

Marina's cop told about his mother, a history buff who had read about all the English rulers; she had a novel for each one in order on a shelf. Once, her overzealous sister had come to visit and cleaned the bookshelves, thoroughly, putting back books in any order. He said his aunt didn't know why his mother cried. This group groaned in understanding.

They all made notes, promised homework, and agreed on the next meeting. As Alice approached the front door with her sleepy son, Joe held it for her and offered a ride home.

"We'll walk."

"Ah, come on, babe. I know your G-spot."

"We'll just have to celibate tonight."

"You will, not I." And he went off down the front walk.

Emmy had heard but wished she hadn't and hoped the kid had not.

Chapter 8

When Emmy arrived at the showroom, the parking spaces off the alley had just been washed down. It was Miller's turn, and she had already done the sidewalk and patio and was just then coiling up the hose over an iron frame that had been a saddle holder in real life. Emmy wished she could find more of those hose holders. They sold well when she could find them. Perhaps they could be reproduced. She had never seen a better hose rack, fastened to the wall like that.

She pulled her car into her reserved space, one of the pleasures of ownership, and reached for the bakery box on the seat beside her. The doors were open as she approached the building, and she could smell Scott's fresh coffee and hear his music selection to start the day, a Stevie Nicks song, "After the Glitter Fades." There would be Peggy Lee, Amy Winehouse, Norah Jones, Bette Midler, and Streisand later. Her cell rang.

"Hey, babe. Where's the granola?" J. asked when she picked up.

"Pantry, bottom shelf. I came around by La Brea to stop at the La Brea Bakery for muffins. Too bad I can't share. I'll share my olive bread with you tonight though."

"The Grandloon has asked us to dinner for Wednesday or Thursday and asked if we could share some of our commentary. She thought maybe Scott and Joe could come and bring some segments. I don't know how they will react to her command

127

performance. Of course they do have a choice of nights. I guess they could say no. I don't guess that you'll say that, though it's always your privilege."

"I'm not that kind of a girl. I'll talk to Scott."

Scott was e-mailing a client the picture and price information for a more-than-precious putti garden sculpture when she asked him about the dinner. He hit send before he looked up to say good morning. "Sure, why not? I usually go to my mother's for dinner on Wednesday, but it's flexible, so it's up to Joe Silver. His ex is still crazy about him, isn't she? All those kids! If she took him back, I bet they'd have another one in a year."

"You're probably right. That was a beautiful kid, the karate kid. Do you think he might be gay?"

"Is there any doubt?"

"How will it be for him in the community, a slightly black, slightly Jewish kid with a somewhat Catholic, blond, sometimes-actress mom?"

"Flawless credentials, free pass to West Hollywood."

"Do they know?"

"He doesn't even know, and they will be the last to know. They have other kids, so they won't be bugging him for grandchildren. That used to be my mom's Wednesday night theme."

"Reconciled?"

"Close."

* * *

She answered the door herself in a floor-length dress that was just short of being a Tudor costume. She led Emmy to a sofa, and J. trailed behind.

"Come sit by me, dear. I've been looking at the Tony Duquette book, and I want you to see a picture of me in it. It was at the opening of his studio in West Hollywood, you know. I shall never forget that the valet at our car door was dressed in French, like Louis XIV, livery, breeches, and satin and lace. He couldn't keep a properly sober face when I told him he never looked lovelier. I told Oscar Levant that too. He was at a grand piano on the stair landing. There was, you know, a ballet commissioned for the evening, and the lead dancer almost died of happiness when Helen Hayes gave him her sweet, tiny, kid glove. I remember suggesting he keep it, you know, forever in the back of the drawer, behind the clean socks. I may have been disruptive, but they must have photographed me anyway. Here I am."

And there she was indeed, a beautiful, young star, glowing amid a circle of men in tails. Emmy was properly appreciative and then called their attention to a handsome man over near the margin. "Oh, look, there's my grandfather."

"And there's mine," said J., gesturing toward the man at the young actress's elbow. They both looked quickly at the Ingénue. Her face was unperturbed.

Joe and Scott arrived then, almost together. Drinks were served by the housekeeper. Marina joined them, in the ruffled black velvet with the jet buttons.

After dinner, it was she who served the coffee. The Ingénue added what must have been saccharin from a little silver box. Emmy silently identified the box as excellent, old and French, stopping just short of deciding how she would price it.

"Seventeenth-century," said J.'s grandmother, seeing her gaze, "with provenance. And now, my dears, while this young man sets up his computer, I have a few notes.

"First, you know you must recut the opening to a less specific audience, though I think I like that it is at your house. That room has seen a lot of film, you know. You might even say that. I think it adds a dimension of interest, as does the appearance of your committee. And of course they must get full credit in the titles, you know."

A screen came down in a place for perfect viewing from the table, leading the guests to believe that there had been many such conferences over coffee.

"Now, Jared, my dearest love, you know we must think of a good way to present your credentials as historian and screen buff. Emmy's are perfect as art historian and dealer, and how can we work Damon into her introduction?

"Now, my dear, your timing is almost flawless, but you must start talking, you know, while the camera is celebrating your legs.

"Let's look at the slideshow. It's very smooth, but you must have the Holbein portraits of Henry and Anne. We do need that reference to her parents. And I should like to see a few more objects from the time, in reference to your being a dealer of such things. You know, there are people who haven't even thought about the props on the screen and whether they are right or not.

"I think you can be quite critical about the lack of ruffs in the third picture. It's almost a signature of the time, and Elizabeth didn't get one until she was queen—as though it was a crown, wasn't it?"

* * *

They were almost down to the garage in the elevator before they exhaled, the four of them. Scott spoke on his first intake of breath. "Wow."

"Well, we have our director's notes," said Joe with a sigh.

"Wow," said J.

"Wow," echoed Emmy

"J., man, she has my phone number, my cell phone!" said Joe.

* * *

"Hi, J., this is Alice. Sorry to interrupt you at dinnertime. You weren't screwing yet, were you?"

"Is that 'yet' in the sense of still or already?"

"Whatever. Hold on to the phone in either case. The committee is already checking in with ideas and questions. Was there an English king in *Hamlet*? Somebody is remembering a movie about Roman rule of Britain, something about soldiers in a mist. He's not sure that it isn't just a book, or that it shows who they deposed. And who were Alfred and Harold anyway? You know, this idea is a lot more consuming than Good Queen Bess. That went fast and easy.

"Your good buddy Ray called and with some Hispanic pride made the point that Philip of Spain might have been the king of England except for bad luck and bad weather. He said you black Irish were the result of the Spanish Armada washed up on the west coast of Ireland."

"Well, I've got news for you. I'm probably related to every fourteenth Irishman by virtue, or lack of it, of an ancient and prolific warlord, pre-Armada. I understand DNA reports are showing that, and I shall have mine soon. He can be really glad that King Philip didn't make it. With the Spanish's distinct lack of governing talent, that would have been a bad glitch in the long march to personal freedom.

"And listen, you always know where to find anything. I need a forensic accountant. Where do you look for that?"

"I have no idea what that is, but I'll have one for you by Tuesday."

* * *

"Hi, J. This is Joe. Can I come over and talk to you?"

"Now?"

"Yeah."

"Sure, come have martinis and dinner with us. Your ex, Madam Chairman Alice, just called to say the committee is already working on the English rulers ideas. Shall I call her back and ask her for dinner too? We are at my house tonight. No cat."

"Thanks, but no thanks. May I take a rain check on that committee idea and come by myself? We're accepted separately by now, and even go separately to the same events, but I have something I want to run by you two."

* * *

J. touched the bedside lamp to low and pulled the quilt up. "You don't suppose that could happen, do you—my second-favorite fantasy, film critique? Joe sounded pretty positive, and he had already showed a proposal and a lot of his tape to his contacts. And wow, they're liking it! It's an obscure channel and not a fought-over time slot, but what a good way to start. And we thought we were just having a ball among ourselves, a bunch of film buffs rolling in happiness through comparing our beloved movies about the same character, the organized commentary because we're all that way in the business.

"But J., I get a little more commercial headed and I guess Joe does too. It could be owned by us, by the committee, and sold somewhere else later. Isn't that how your hero Ken Burns does it? I don't know the legalities of getting films to show in another context, but we can find out. Somebody better look into that before we all get too excited. We're using stills, a lot of 'em already in the public domain. We fill in much with pictures of stuff."

"Emmy, darling, this could be the winter of my content. Before you, scant days ago, I was discontent to despondent—family gone, finances muddled beyond my understanding, cousins mad at me, my work shut down by the strike. 'Out of the night that covers me, / Black as the pit from pole to pole . . .'" He paused dramatically, long enough for Emmy to intercede.

She obliged. "I thank whatever gods there be, / for my unconquerable soul."

"Are you sure it's unconquerable and not indomitable soul?"

"Not sure at all. I'd Google it if I could remember the poet's name. Is it possible he spent all day deciding between those very two words?"

"How do you know that old thing?"

"I'm educated too, you know."

"Yeah, I've wondered who taught you. I don't spend time on it, but I've wondered."

"I'm willing to tell you who taught me the poem. It was my father's for use when everything got tough, especially with number three, the drama princess."

"I think I'm going to like him. Where are they by now?"

"Their schedule says Italy, maybe Venice, working toward April in Paris. They're like kids who take off the year between high school and college."

"I want to take you to Venice someday. History stands still there. Today is the illusion. One of the things I collect besides Hollywood is Colonial American. I bought a small document signed by Governor John Winthrop and got interested in him. Did you know that his young son went traveling in maybe 1627 and was gone, and out of communication for eighteen months, all the way to Istanbul? On the way back he was quarantined on an island in sight of Venice and couldn't get a ship to England. No cell phone to call home. Finally, he got to Amsterdam, out of money, and had to pawn his trunk to get home, and only just in time to commit to the Puritan migration to Massachusetts."

Emmy's response surprised J. "The only thing I know about the son is the inventory of his first wife's trunk in a historic house in Ipswich, Massachusetts. I remember a red cloak. My mother's people came from there, and we went with her once to see their house."

"Do you in everything match my inquisitive soul? The Met has a room in the American wing that's patterned after a will inventory of household stuff from there. You don't suppose that very early Colonial time would play as a marathon, do you?"

"But J., the only film that comes to my mind is *The Scarlet Letter*. Do you suppose the committee would be interested in that time and place anyway? Puritans could sound dull, even if not to me, but then I know about the red cloak. How ever did you know all that Colonial history?"

"I'm educated too, you know. Augmented by reading catalogs of autographs for sale. I have some nice ones. I once tried for all the Colonial governors of Massachusetts. I missed the goal by one. I couldn't find the second one, Haynes, even in these last years when money wasn't an object."

* * *

"The Grandlady called and actually suggested that you lend your house to Marina and her guy on her day off."

"I think that's great. I had sort of mentioned my house to Marina."

"What if we borrow a house in the mountains for our five-week anniversary? The first weekend after it anyway."

"My little nephew has a soccer game that Saturday, the ninth. I thought you might like to go to that major sporting event."

"I hate soccer."

"I love soccer. I played in school. I was heavily left-footed. How can you hate soccer?"

"It's un-American."

"It isn't either. It's very popular here."

"Yeah, I know. The little bastards were even playing it on that Sunday that my dad evidently thought he could land in an empty school field, only it was full of little creeps kicking a ball."

*   *   *

"My friend says that March came in like a lamb, and the woods are beautiful. There's no TV though, so you can't watch Hillary. Isn't there something wrong here? You women always want the respect of not being called by your first names when the men are called by last names. And here are Hillary and Obama."

"She will win. She just has to. We just can't get your tired old war hero with the same old, same old."

"Just wait till that experienced old professional of mine gets to debate either of yours. He will shred them."

*   *   *

Every turn of the road offered more than the last, and the word "beautiful" was used and reused. The top was down until it became a little chilly. J. pulled onto a gravel shoulder and put the top up, which took only enough time to find that lips were warm still while noses were cold. Then it was cozy with the heat on.

"I love it here, but why are you borrowing a house when you have so many of your own?"

"Not all that many, but you haven't seen the big one up in the Bird Streets. They were living there, half moved in. She had just finished the redo and was starting on the home forty."

"That's the original pasture down by the river, isn't it? With the first one—room immigrant log cabin, with Kevin Costner in that great shirt."

"Yeah, and subsequent houses got bigger and bigger. This one has an office with an outside entry, and we just packed it full of their personal stuff and rented the rest semi furnished.

"We could go to Palm Springs next weekend. Grandloon and her Blaine are there now. I still have the house on a golf course that my parents had while that pod colony one was in progress. Help, I'm too rich. Maybe the cousins will take care of that. You're a much better cousin."

"Half-cousin."

"Have you looked into the law about that?"

"No. I don't want to know. I don't want anyone else to know."

"If no one at the wedding says they know a reason why these two should not be joined, then we're home free. You don't think my Grandloon would stand and denounce us, do you?"

"Yes."

"I wish we could do it now, even before your parents get back."

"I don't want to see a grown man cry over not being at his number one daughter's wedding. Why do you like this mountain house so much?"

"I don't know that I'd want to own it, but you'll see. It was in *Architectural Digest* for whatever that means to you."

"'Pends on the accessories."

"None. Unoccupied house theft is high. The furniture is all bolted down."

Indeed, when they arrived, she saw that it had all the charm of a great photo of a mountain cabin, but without the smoke from the rock chimney. J. had said that he had only to call ahead, and a cleaning person came by. This day someone had turned on a thermostat, and the room was warm. A fire had been laid, and J. started it up while Emmy put an old-fashioned percolator on a gas burner.

"Darling, this really is terrific. The chairs are great Craftsman, and the upholstery is a William Morris pattern— reproduced, of course. I've seen it on the rack at Pacific Design Center. It's perfect. The designer probably installed them permanently in place so that they wouldn't get moved around. With the old polished planks, the logs, the stones, and the firewood, the house hardly needs accessories. I just hope no one ever steals those knit bunk covers."

J., cradling his coffee cup, put his feet up on a rough wood table. Emmy laughed when he tried to shove it and it didn't budge.

"J., sweet, something I've been wondering about. If you like explaining movies so much, have even fantasized about movie critique, why didn't you do anything about it? You're really qualified, and your voice is so good."

"Don't know. Maybe I lack personal focus, but I'm really having a great time with the marathon idea."

"On the plains of hesitation / Bleach the bones / of countless millions, / Who have, on the dawn of victory, / Sat down to wait, / And died."

"What's that strange ditty from?"

"Over the door of the gym of Downey High School. A boy from there said it to me in college."

"So it was he who taught you? That's a rather rustic seduction line, isn't it? Did it work?"

"Oh, my! Is that why he said it?"

*　　*　　*

"Dinner tonight at the lodge, seduction by food and drink. Do you like venison?"

"From the pretty long-legged things we saw running across the road?"

"No, no. They don't make venison from locals; it's farmed in Montana. Come on. Let's go for a walk in the woods while there's sun."

And there was, backlighting trees and turning last autumn's leaves back to gold. They walked until the cabin was out of sight and then paralleled a small body of fast-flowing water. He said it was a stream; she said it was a river.

"Madam," he said, "I offer you sex in the woods." He shrugged out of his Peterman duster and spread it on the ground.

"I'll race you back to the cabin."

"No. I want it here, now."

"J., you're hurting my wrists. No, no!

"Then stop struggling."

She did.

Later, as they reached the cabin steps, J. turned her around by the shoulders. "I suppose you'll call the sheriff now. You did say no."

"I'm not that kind of a girl. I'm calling the fire department to put out where we smoldered the leaves."

*   *   *

"Now for the long drive back," she said. "It's a good time to talk, not that we aren't together all the time when we're not working."

"Hey, you're much better than the imaginary friend of my childhood. It was a boy. I don't remember when he disappeared, but one day I asked him something, and he didn't answer. Maybe he discovered girls then too."

"What was his name?"

"Jim. We called each other J."

"Mine was Janie, and I wouldn't let anyone sit on the sofa next to me because Janie was there. I wonder where she went when my baby sister arrived on the scene."

* * *

"Are you getting hungry, Em? There's a funny old steakhouse before we start over the hill."

"Is it shabby and expensive with buttoned red leather booths?"

"Does the one you're thinking of have huge baked potatoes with sour cream and chives? And you wouldn't see Debbie Reynolds at this one."

"Maybe not, unless she were going home to visit Burbank."

"I don't like this time of day, between early dusk and dinner smell. The day is closing, and I ask myself, did I get enough done, did I use it wisely? Today, yes."

"I don't know your next-week schedule. Are you going to be able to get on the accounting thing before you're really targeted?"

"You do that nicely, my love. It didn't even sound like nagging. I asked Madam-Knows-All-Alice if she knew any forensic accountants, and she said she'd never even heard of such a thing, but she would know a good one by Tuesday, the latest."

"That cute little curly-headed thing is a lot smarter than she looks, isn't she?"

"Oh yeah. She could do anything but hold onto Joe. They started way too early. It took him a lot of years and four kids to start wondering whether other white blonds would like him as well as Alice did. By the time he found out they did, she didn't.

"She always worked in entertainment, starting in school as a page at NBC. Her mother was the best kid sitter in town, and Alice always paid her going wages. She made good money too. She was a hot shot AD. Then one day she was producing a commercial, and the art director from New York was looking to cast a cute little blond thing. He couldn't find what he wanted and kept saying, 'Someone like the associate director.' That's how Alice became an actress for a while, with a sitcom part and then another, and put away a lot of money. She bought real estate.

I don't know if it's what influenced her, but I remember my mom always telling her that's 'where it's at.'"

"I suppose her mom will sit for her again when Alice gets a gig."

"Not an option. She got married and moved to Riverside."

"If the marathon were a go, Alice could produce it from home and earn a salary."

"Or a percentage."

"Which you might subsidize in the beginning. Then she could work from home."

"And home is big enough too. She bought an apartment building and converted pairs of units into condos—sold some, kept some."

"Maybe she can find you a forensic accountant. I guess your accountant doesn't know what hit him. How about your lawyer? Your friend from Hollywood High?"

"Can't. He heads up legal at Ingénue. I don't remember all I used to know about the deal. The Grandlady has half. My father and his brother were equal partners in the rest, and when they sold the business, they formed a corporation that held the stock that they kept and took in the payments and the rent of the land that they still owned, where some of the factories sit. Yeah, there's some more of my real estate, half of that land.

"They kept the little museum of Hollywood makeup—some great signed documents, masks, makeup kits from opera stars, photos, stuff, good stuff. It's near a park and well attended and managed by the corporation."

"Who manages the corporation?"

"There's a manager who was with them at Ingénue. There's an assistant and a secretary or two. They send money to my accountant, who sends it to my bank. It's way beyond adequate, and I haven't thought much about it. I never got involved or even interested in the business. In a way what I have now doesn't even seem like mine.

"I guess my cousins think I have more toys than they do. They say there's money missing, but I know my dad didn't do anything wrong."

"I'm thinking somebody did. Your accountant pays your bills and does your personal tax returns, doesn't he?"

"I bet your business head is thinking what he gets is rich."

"I think that's what the lawyer lady is thinking too. Your father was the one who made it into a major fortune, wasn't he?"

"Absolutely. Uncle Anders was a chemical engineer and makeup artist, like everybody was, and turned out a famous product, and Dad sold it big. He was a great guy, Anders. I used to like his kids too."

"Do you ever have a lot to focus on! And I don't suppose you can ask the Grandlady anything about the business. She is about as apt to answer as about your grandfather."

*　*　*

"Hi, J. I hope I haven't called you too early for a Tuesday morning, but I just found out that ex-husbands are good for something besides child support and filming movies.

"Joe has a relative's relative who is an accountant, a forensic one with some high-profile solutions to her credit. She's retired from the IRS and hangs with good connections. She's Jewish, which is important. You have to have a Jewish doctor, lawyer, and accountant. Other people are okay for anything else. I've heard that Irish lawyers are sometimes all right too.

"Anyway, here's her number. She's expecting your call."

*　*　*

"Of course I've heard of Ingénue. I have your lipstick in my purse and a lot of other stuff at home. The moisturizer is a miracle. I've watched the advertising that has those pretty young chicks and that great old lady.

"Yes, my Grandmom is still holding on as head icon."

"Your grandmother, you say. I'll be asking you a lot of questions then—especially, has she had much work done?"

"I don't think so, 'cause I don't remember her disappearing from my life long enough to have a recovery time, unless a vacation cruise wasn't. No, I believe they flood her with blazing white light from all directions."

"Maybe not enough under the chin. I thought I saw some telltale stiffness down from the earlobe."

"I guess we better crank up the wattage."

"I think we will get along."

"I think we shall."

"Okay, I like a man who knows 'shall' from 'will,' and maybe 'who' from 'whom,' as in who is doing what to whom."

* * *

"Alice baby, I love this gal. I took Emmy along 'cause she should know everything about my increasingly complicated life. She found the office way neat, devoid of toys and stuff. She wonders if you can trust anyone with piles of file folders for toys. But I think her wariness was because if it weren't for Emmy and the twenty years between the lady and me, I'd have attempted seduction."

"If you did, then the lady'd have a toy, a boy toy. Age is just a number."

"But when she is a hundred, I would only be eighty."

"I don't remember your being that good at math."

"As we were leaving, we picked up on what might be regarded as a toy, on a file cabinet by the door, a model of a BMW. We commented that it was like ours. She said a client had given it to her, as well as the full-scale one down in the parking garage."

"She must have done something right."

"Will I owe her a car's worth?"

"Is she taking you on? I guess part of her résumé is that she smells money with the fun of the chase. What did she tell you to do?"

"Get a big table and start putting things out, which brings me to my next question. Are you gainfully employed right now? I'd pay whatever you made as an AD, or whatever is right, to organize me. You could work when the kids are in school and take home work. Is it a possibility, your doing this and the marathon too?"

"It's a probability. Let me think. And I've been wondering how I could AD from home."

Chapter 9

"I thought this might be a good day to show you the Bird Streets house. We can take Alice with us to survey the stored stuff. My charming, tolerant tenant has asked us to a coffee."

"What does Alice do with the kids on Saturday?"

"It's Joe's weekend, and he's taking them to San Diego to the zoo."

"Great! Would you please take me there sometime? I love zoos, especially that one."

"You just squealed in delight. How old are you anyway?"

"Am I not six and you seven?"

"We could stay at that lovely old frump of a Hotel del Coronado, but the Del is for grown-ups."

"I grow up after gin on the rocks in the piano lounge."

"Been there, huh?"

"Yeah, loved it. Still do."

*   *   *

"Alice baby, I've got a zoo date with my lady. She squealed over Joe going there with the kids," J. said. "Em, I'd like to take you on a safari. Take a hot air balloon skimming over monkey-stuffed trees and, from a Land Rover, watch lions mating. They do it every fifteen minutes for a week or so. Then there are crocodiles—I have no idea how they do it, but they are delicious. Zebras are tough, and wait until you see an ostrich drumstick."

"When? I knew you'd been. I found a great-looking album embossed 'Safari.' The first photo is a plump kid reaching up to feed a giraffe. That boy needs to go to the gym."

"He did right after we got back, same one to which I still go. You have no idea of the viscosity of giraffe saliva. It's like maple syrup at the International House of Pancakes." He parked the car. "I'll go see when she wants us for coffee."

When he had gone off to his tenant, Alice seized the moment to comment. "Emmy, my dear, you did that so well, and now you are past that one, and you didn't hear it from others."

"Alice, my dear, forewarned is forearmed. He was a cute fat, though."

"Whatever shape, always cool."

* * *

When the tenant had left them alone, Emmy said, "She loved showing me the view and then wished she hadn't in case I should want you to move here and take the house back from her."

"Come on, J. and Em, out of the albums. Those aren't the books I'm looking for."

"You have to understand that Alice was the last one in senior accounting at Hollywood High. They had to keep the class open for her."

"Boy, was I ever glad I'd had that when I went back to UCLA for film school after NBC. I hope I know what I'm looking for here or know it when I see it."

J. had some idea of how various papers had been classified when they had been stacked away. His accountant had withdrawn much. He himself had looked for autographs. It occurred to him now that these were the only two women on earth whom he could tolerate running barefoot through his mother's things.

"There's nothing arranged for posterity here or hidden from it. They didn't know they didn't have thirty years to do it," he said. Threatened with a sniffle, J. turned away with his nose in a file folder, which proved to be the purchase papers for the plane. He showed the women.

"So your dad owned the plane, not with his brother. And his brother didn't have one?" said Emmy

"Not yet; he was going to. He had a bigger boat, big enough for all eight of us to go to Catalina for a week. Also a young guy teaching everybody to crew. I really liked the white sails against blue sky, but I didn't fall in love with it like Uncle Anders's family did. He had that Viking tilt of beard into the wind. It must have been his Norwegian name that did it.

"It's really a serious boat, oceangoing—and they did. The Grandlady refused the invitation when they went around South America and back, but they survived. And then it was a short hop, local flying, that was the killer. Grandmamma refused that too and survived, she and Marina."

Just then there was a delivery, two folding tables and cardboard file folders.

"Alice, dear old friend, who but you could get a Saturday delivery? Does this mean you'll take the job?"

"For today, tomorrow, and Monday anyhow. There's no way I'd let you sift through this again alone. And tomorrow I'd like to do it by myself, if you'll let me, and you should if you have decided to trust me to work through the tangle that is you. I'm a Virgo, you know, and you're not. Later we'll talk."

It was then that Emmy chose to go after sandwiches. She would take a little extra time to talk to Scott at the showroom, calling on her cell from the parking lot, and then pick up whatever everyone wanted. Both were noncommittal.

Taking Alice's sturdy box of a child-carrier car, she drove straight down Doheny to Ralph's on the Beverly corner where she often sat, like a second office, under the pine trees. If there was ever a pretty parking lot, she rewarded it with her patronage.

"Remember, Scott, eleven days to West Week. Is the new stuff all in and the fake candle window lighting all installed? Not that hordes of buyers are going to bail out of festivities at Pacific Design Center to come to us."

"You told me it took only one designer from Sacramento, doing a new ski lodge in Montana, to need a great Mexican food fix at El Coyote and see our fabulous window to buy yards and yards as well as eight amazingly expensive lanterns."

"Yeah, now I remember why we do it."

"It's almost all here. The newish girl with the Herman Miller 'M' tattooed on her wrist is doing well with us. She may even understand how important it is to be nice to customers. She does beautiful watercolors. I had three of them framed."

"You're pretty intuitive about people, aren't you? What do you think of Alice? J. is thinking of her for a personal manager."

"Alice Silver and gold. Do not hesitate."

$$* \quad * \quad *$$

"No preferences, guys. They're all rare roast beef on rye. The mustard and mayo are in those little impossible-to-open bags. Good luck. If you carry a Swiss army knife, then let me borrow it."

"We talked, but she's still going to get back to me on Monday," J. said, pointing to Alice. "In the interim, we're all going to the screening at six—you probably know what it is— and then we're going to the Silver Spoon for the Saturday special, the lemon rice soup. At least that's what I'm having after scotch. I don't know about you."

"Well, we are all in my car, so you are my prisoners." Alice had begun to segregate some items for perusal and now showed him a long thin black book. "Look at this. It looks a little like a bankbook, but none I've ever seen before. It could be just a notebook with some pretty hot plans in it, with reference to millions, but I don't know millions of what—square inches, dollars, or pesos."

J. took it in hand. "It looks old, kind of well rubbed. There's a crude number three on it. I wonder what number one and two looked like."

"It's already five fifteen. We better split for the screening. I'll keep a lookout for those books tomorrow. I guess J. still doesn't know what we're going to see?"

"Well, Alice, I surely didn't tell him. Was he always like this about film?"

"Maybe not before middle school."

* * *

"See you after. I'm not going to sit down front with you guys. Be careful—you could get absorbed into the screen, with no one able to get you out."

"Did you know there's a Down in Front Club? We're pretty dedicated. We don't even see that there's a rest of the audience."

"Yeah, but we see you, down there moving your heads from side to side, like you're at a tennis match, to see the whole width of the screen."

When J. saw that the movie was *10,000 BC*, he allowed himself one whisper: "This is prehistory; I'm history."

When the film ended and the lights went on, and they started up the aisle, there was Alice coming toward them, her hand linked with that of a bushy red-haired hulk of a man in a Directors Guild sweatshirt. "Look what followed me to a middle row. Can I keep him? He won't eat much."

"Of course he will. Why should tonight be different? How are you, man? It's been a long time. I want you to meet my lady, Emmy Higgen. Emmy, this is Jon 'The Bulk' Mason."

"Hey, would I be wrong to guess you went to Hollywood High?"

* * *

Jon Mason arrived first at the Silver Spoon, where he had staked out a big booth and thrown himself into it. "Man, that was great! I'm really into prehistory. Did anybody else read *The Time before History* by Colin Tudge? Wherever I am, I think about what it once was. On Wilshire Boulevard, I always see a line of woolly mammoths marching down the center of the street, following the yellow line. The Page Museum, full of their fossils, is the best thing we have in LA. The La Brea Tar Pits ooze right there at your feet, and they're still taking bones out of the tar. Geez. Anybody want to go there with me tomorrow to extend what we just saw?"

They all knew he meant Alice and let her answer. "May I take a rain check? I've got a gig tomorrow."

"Well, damn. I heard you were divorced while I was away, and this looked like a good way to get into your life."

"I'll give you my phone number."

"I've got it. Remember, I knew you both. I'm assuming it's the same place 'cause who would leave such a neat setup, except I guess Joe had to, poor guy."

Alice turned to J. "Your friend was never anything but blunt, was he?"

"He always regarded that as half his charm. But listen, Jon. You should see something that Emmy has in her showroom. It's a hand ax from 250,000 years ago. It's like a huge arrowhead, hand size, from before they had learned to bind a handle onto it, from when we were just getting used to standing upright."

"I always have a few of them," said Emmy. "They're like open stock. They keep popping to the surface of the North African desert. Little did the guy who made these know how good they would look on a coffee table."

"Where do you get 'em? I know you don't go to Africa after them yourself. I don't see you in your sexy boots jammed into the sand, waiting for a storm to uncover an ancient weapon."

"I buy them from the Hand Ax Club in Santa Monica. An artist's studio has beautiful drawer cases lined in felt and full of these things."

"Oh man. It's great to be back in a town that has everything."

* * *

"When your friend put Alice in her car, after that loud 'See you,' I heard him say in a near-whisper, 'Twenty minutes.'"

"You and your remarkable hearing! God, I hope he doesn't crush her. I'm glad we came to my house to receive this pretty thing. Look, it's full of Irish stuff, three different cheeses, wine, and for heaven's sake, two Waterford glasses. The tag says it's from Chateau Marmont with an invitation to the Saint Patrick's Day bash on Monday. I can only assume it's going to be a loud one, amplified and screaming into the night—a gift basket to every neighbor who ever complained. Their party sounds funnel up the hill, and if the neighbors are down there, they aren't up here."

"Can we go? I've a great green dress."

"Over a great body. Could I tell that if I were blind?" he asked, eyes closed, beginning his explorations.

*   *   *

It seemed silly to take a car to the valet at the party. They could almost see him from the back deck. They would have to take the car from Hollywood Boulevard, down Marmont Lane, then behind the hotel, around on Selma, and then right on Sunset to the block past the Liquor Locker to fetch up in front of the valet. With parking at such a premium, they fantasized that the valet would have to take the car all the way up to Hollywood Boulevard to park it, maybe in front of J.'s house.

So they elected to walk, stepping down a dark garden path and then accessing a neighbor's stairway of some three flights. They put Emmy's silver high-heeled sandals in J.'s pockets along with her silver mesh bag. She wore driving moccasins for the walk and J.'s Peterman duster over her beautiful green dress. They slipped and slid down the hill to the street, where they wrapped the mocs and flashlight in the duster and tucked the bundle under the stairs.

"You've done this before."

"Since childhood."

They walked down the sidewalk through the phalanx of flashes from paparazzi and fans and up the driveway to say their names over the guest list. J. saw hill people he knew.

"This is as good for meeting the neighbors as a good brush fire or protest meetings over zoning for nightclubs." He said hello and hello, though he couldn't remember any names, if he'd ever known them.

They were handed green champagne and presented with the hors d'oeuvres tray even before they reached the elevator. When its door opened into the crowed lobby, the first sight was the glamorous Ula, seated and somehow spotlighted, surrounded by beautifully dressed, slender young men. Her long green dress shimmered with a life of its own.

"Oh my God, I can see from here that the sequins are hand-sewn. Thousands!"

"Sequins or dollars?"

"Both."

Emmy thought J. then the most beautiful of the young men around his remarkable grandmother. She heard her introducing him as "my darling Jared," with no mention of his being her grandson. Emmy walked off onto the garden terrace to not break up the boy-girl ratio that Ula preferred.

Soon J. joined her at a table at the end of the hedged garden under the palm trees. Such a good party it was that food and drink reached them there.

"The Grandloon has asked that we take her home in an hour, which means that after a while, I'll have to leave you here with her to retrace our steps and get a car. I hope there's enough gas in the Packard. Her getting into that should make a satisfactory stir. I'll pick up the shoes and jacket on the way up. At least there is some time allowed for autographs."

"How did she know we were here?"

"Called to see if we had RSVPed. Marina brought her and left her here. I don't think she wanted another woman around. She's up to something."

They got caught up in the beat and watched the huge green shamrocks projected onto the hotel walls wrapping the terrace. "I wonder how the guests take to this. I think there's a shamrock projected through that window onto the wallpaper inside."

"Well, the guests were invited for the same reason we were, but with shorter to-go and probably didn't get a Patrick basket. You will be able to hear the drunken mumblings way into the night, but without complaint, 'cause you've been bought off. We used to call the police after one o'clock."

* * *

The Packard got enough attention for itself, but with the lady from the Ingénue commercials sailing down the cobbled driveway on the arm of one of the elegant young men, the gathered crowd behind the ropes began to cheer. At first keeping her eyes down shyly, she then looked up and did a grand wave to cries of "Ula, Ula" and "Ingénue, Ingénue," a mysterious spotlight upon her. As Emmy followed her, with people speculating as to her identity as well, she saw that the Ingénue had somehow slipped into long gloves for waving. Her graceful entry into the car was from years of practice with this old yellow Packard. With the door still open, she conceded to a few autographs.

Inside the car, J. said, "You can make arrangements for a flood of light on an old face but not the hands, but gloves will take care of old hands."

"Oh J., you're bad; she's fabulous."

"Was I really fabulous, dear? I got the part! It's not huge. It's mostly flashbacks, you know, but my character is the title. I have that role now, and I didn't even have to show them my bone density scan!

"And oh yes, dear, you were saying earlier about the dress. It is a wonder, a work of art. I haven't worn it before. I couldn't bear to even touch it. It was made in Palm Springs, you know, by a great artist who used to be up here with her wonderful little shop on the Sunset Strip. The final fitting was the same day my only two babies were dying in that accursed airplane."

* * *

"Do come up for a nightcap. They will leave the car right here, you know. It looks good with the building."

Inside she said, "Baileys Irish Cream, of course. A Guinness if you would prefer, but you know that doesn't go with that elegant suit. I know you don't think about that a lot, but you always look great."

They could hear that Marina was there, a television on in her room, but there were only three glasses next to the bottle of Baileys, so they did not expect to see her tonight.

"So do you, dear, look great, pretty and always well put together." She started to pour the drinks, her green-sequined arm moving like some dangerous serpent, catching lamplight and giving it back to the ceiling. Emmy felt a chill for the conversation to come.

"I've grown to like you, dear, but I still think you are not right for each other, too much alike perhaps, though laughing at the same things is really the clue, isn't it? I perceive that you do. It's going to be bitter for you when he doesn't want babies. You know about his brother, don't you?"

"Grandsweety, darling, I set great store by what you think. Would you like me to take her back to her house, get my ring back, and never see her again? Dear one, you must realize that I am irrevocably in love with this woman. Whether we baby or not is not about you, unless you are ready now to entertain some questions about who is your first son's father."

"My dear grandson, I would be quite foolish if I didn't know you were snooping around. DNA, for heaven's sake! Whom do you want to out? I just don't know everything you want to know. It's so tangled.

"I'm a mushroom, you know, kept in the dark and fed bullshit. You know, long ago I realized I wouldn't be able to tell what was the truth in what people presented, so I just decided to believe everything. I know other people in the public eye who do that too. We've talked about it, you know. One big star you would know said, 'If they lie to me, well, shame on them.'

"I know you think Damon was Jerry's biological father. We've been denying it a long time. Do you realize I would have lost my career? I always think of Loretta Young, you know, adopting her own daughter and having her ears flattened to not look like Clark Gable.

"We're so tolerant now, aren't we? The magazines reporting on who stole whose husband and is now pregnant with his triplets and who looks so chic in that high-waisted, flowered dress with the touch of grosgrain ribbon. They are thinking of getting married the next time she's expecting and will promise pictures—to the highest bidder, with proceeds to Indian, or rather Native American, children on the reservation."

Emmy felt called upon to respond. "I think from what I hear of Grandpa Damon, he would have been comfortable with that press. He was on stage from the time he was two with his father and mother and his aunt Mary. A lot of stories were printed about him. He told me some of them were true."

"I've always wondered how they got him to sign that contract with the morality clause. Did anyone ever count his children?"

"I have lots of aunts and uncles that I know of."

"When I think of him at all, it's as the Irish connection, the first of the wild bunch of you that I knew. There I was, the little Norwegian prairie girl dealing with the peat bog renegades from the Dublin stage."

"Yeah, Grandlady, and they fought over you—as in, had a fight that put Higgen in the hospital."

"Wherever did you hear a thing like that? It sounds so romantic."

"I have a master's in history and a background in research, and besides that, we found the clipping in Emmy's album."

"Well, boy doll, that did take a lot of education. You surely don't believe everything you read in the press, do you? For example, I happen to know it was a satin ribbon, not grosgrain."

"I suppose you'll sign a morality clause in this contract too, and then Blaine can't stay over."

"Jared!"

"Suppose when I get my corroborating DNA, we don't out you or even tell you, and you don't stand up at our wedding and say we can't get married because we're first cousins."

"If you were, and I'm only saying if, you would only share one grandparent in four, not two out of four. But maybe that's why I'm saying you're not right for each other. You're too much alike. You even look a little alike.

"I was remembering that lovely time in the long ago when we were all a close family and went to Ireland together. My J. J., your granddad, hadn't been back since he was six years old. Do you remember how he spoke Irish with the people coming out of the church where we camped on Saturday night, and you heard your ancestral language for the first time?

"J., would Emmy have loved this trip? It's not everyone's cup of tea to rent horse-drawn gypsy caravans and sleep in them in the field behind a new pub every night. We did a lot of walking beside the horses, especially on uphill roads.

"We had bicycles as well as lines of drying laundry hanging on the outside of the big, red-painted barrel of a wagon. You kids would grab bikes and take off up side roads, gone for hours, and join us later. Perfectly safe, it was impossible to get lost.

"You and your cousin Andrea, behind some hedgerow or other—you were her first, weren't you? And she, certainly your first cousin. When we got back, I took her to the gynecologist and got her some pills. I don't think her mother knew."

Her face was as sweet as strawberry shortcake and showed great surprise at J.'s explosion of laughter as he turned to Emmy, who was laughing too.

"If she holds this revenge out so long for her beloved litter, what is it like to be her enemy? I guess Andrea at least had a clue that you suspected that your grandbabies had gone behind an ancestral hedgerow and lost their virginity to one another. Like you, my darling grandmother, I admit nothing."

"Darlings, do have another Baileys."

*   *   *

The doorman was still on duty with a shamrock in his buttonhole and a hearty, fake brogue. "She's in fine condition tonight."

J. was not entirely sure if he meant the car or Ula, on whom he was known to dote. The green sequin dress had been enough to elicit devotion. As he held the door for Emmy, though distracted by her legs, he patted the car lovingly and declared it the "best that comes here."

"He meant your legs, babe," said J. as they drove away.

"I think he has it for Ula. Is he as cute as Blaine?"

"Blaine is about as distinguished as a man can look, which makes it funny when he clutches flowers for her. I wonder where he's gone off to tonight for this ethnic festivity. She probably told him she had to be alone for the ambush."

"Do you think she's speaking from notes? Is it scripted?"

"Sure, the giveaway was that she didn't say 'you know' as much as usual. We didn't read our lines right for her script, did we?"

"How do you spell passive-aggressive?"

"The old dear, what weapons did she have?"

"You mean besides gorgeous celebrity?"

"Yeah, besides that!"

Chapter 10

Emmy spent the first hour of that Thursday morning in her favorite parking lot under the pine trees, after she had picked up a breakfast roll and coffee at Ralph's. On her cell phone she managed to catch up on some calls that she hadn't gotten around to at the showroom.

She drove down Beverly Boulevard and found a good parking space in front of an antique store where she had an errand. She had been asked to evaluate a chair that her customer had seen there. It was a very nice one, and she was trying to think of it not as a lost sale, but as a favor to a good customer. From there it was a few minutes' straight shot down Beverly to her showroom, past Robertson and Cedars, but she pulled into a spot after La Cienega Boulevard.

"Hey, I'm parked in the second block east of La Cienega on Beverly Boulevard to call you because you just have to drive by Macy's window. Don't come down La Cienega. You have to be in the right lane going east on Beverly."

"As it happens, just after the gym, I went to my bank, the one with the good architecture near where I used to live, with the roof parking. So I'm in the first block south of Sunset on Doheny. That puts me right where you want me; that's not unusual. I suppose it's still an Irish window, though going green has a new meaning now. Your wish is my command. Why don't you get one of those hands-free things so you don't have to park to dial?"

"Should. But I'd probably park anyway. Maybe Scott will go to Radio Shack for me."

*   *   *

"Hey, white boy to scout! There I was in the display, chalk white mannequin in all black underwear. I was caught at the red light, so I got a good look at the Macy's window. I almost cracked up laughing."

"I'm sending our second man to photograph it. I'm at the showroom now."

"I'm headed to pick up that DVD on the British monarchy. I understand it's two volumes of hours and hours. I hope to God it doesn't negate our project. What about if we go to Palm Springs and hole up with it? Food delivery all weekend and just hang, taking notes the whole time."

"I'm in. I can't wait to hear whether you have invited Alice or Joe or both."

*   *   *

"Scott, are we ready enough for West Week that I can leave our empire to you this weekend and go off to Palm Springs to watch a video of the British monarchy?"

"Yes, we are, and I'm coming in Sunday, to go over the checklist and mop up. Listen, I've been thinking about the theme of the next marathon. I had a great time with Elizabeth and her stuff. I've been looking at a museum booklet about the Sutton Hoo ship burial find, on the coast of England from forever ago, way pre-William. I wish we had some of that stuff in the showroom. Great design and craftsmanship!

"I love this continuous thing from the ancients, but I got to thinking about something Jared said about the long march to freedom. It's through King John and Magna Carta, through

Queen Elizabeth. It really veers off, doesn't it, at King James? Not with his Bible, but with his son Charles and the hopelessness of those absolute, lawless reigns that drove worthy, enlightened protestors as settlers to the new world, and marching on and on to 1776.

"Then we gave it back—freedom—or exported it, rather, to become constitutional monarchies. Just something I've been thinking about."

"Wow and a half! That's heavy—and awesome!"

*   *   *

Emmy was fond of putting words to what she saw. "The hills are really greening up early, like a fresh coat of moss. They look so soft and faintly luminous. Look how the green coexists with purple as it climbs. The oak tree shadows aren't as black as they are in summer. A great California scene, great time of year to be out here. It shouldn't be this luscious before April."

Emmy had never able been able to sing them, but she could recognize almost every song she had ever heard, some even without the words. She didn't really know whether J. sang it well or not, but she knew "April in Paris."

"Alice, tell me if he's on key."

"Yeah, he is. Has he gotten around to telling you yet that he sang in Hollywood High musicals, some romantic leads?"

"J., will you sing to me in Paris?"

"I shall! How about a honeymoon of a different duet though? Promise me days in the room and nights out to late dinners. No museums until the second week."

"Cool it, guys. I've got a kid back here."

"But please, we can see the *Mona Lisa*?"

"Is the pope Catholic?"

Alice could not let that question go unanswered. "Maybe, but is our Archbishop Mahony? Can you imagine the altar off to the side? Can you imagine taking the sacrament without kneeling?"

J. could not leave that alone. "How can I imagine that the wafer is flesh and the wine is blood, anybody's?"

"Jared! This kid back here, I'm trying to raise him Catholic, even if I don't take him to mass tomorrow for Easter."

"Mom, I'm Jewish!"

"Only a quarter. You've had fractions in school. You know that one-half Catholic can trump one-quarter, unless you would like to devote Saturday morning to synagogue."

"How would he know what 'trump' means?"

"I do know. It's the guy on the TV with the funny hair who says, 'You're fired,' but that's not funny. It would hurt to get fired."

"Yeah."

"Yo."

"Yeah."

"J., this is the first time I've seen you clean-shaven in a long time. I'd almost forgotten how decent your chin is."

"Alice, I've never even seen his whole face before! J., why did you denude it?"

"If I get tan around my four-day growth, leaving white where it was, I have no options. So I can do it again in four days, if we want to."

"Well, it is a good chin, kind of John Travolta-like. I couldn't see before that it was cleft like cleavage, into baby bottom buns. I think I like it a lot, especially where there is a little line of hair you can't get out, a bit of a thong stuck in the crack."

"We're not listening back here."

"Breakfast, anyone? I see a Denny's.

*   *   *

Joe was finishing off his McDonald's breakfast sandwich in the parked car where J. had said to wait for him to arrive to open the mysterious gate. He couldn't see where it was but had to assume it was after a sharp left, almost like a parking stall between two rock cliffs. He had delivered his older son to the starting point of a weekend hike in the San Gabriel Mountains and was feeling expansive, full of well being from the softly green hills of early spring. He was ready to see this fabled house and work on a project close to his heart, especially since he was the one who had sold the project. He was looking forward to spending some time with his second son and working with his ex, Alice, who would have to be decent to him in this constant presence of others, if in fact she were speaking to him at all.

* * *

"Daryl, there's your dad, sitting in his car, trying to figure out where the gate is," said J. "Now watch how it's done. I make this turn as though I'm parking, and there's a half circle of rail around the car. It moves in a circle and turns up behind me, barring the next car, until I'm through it. Then it circles back. Later I'll draw it for you. It's easier to see on paper than in reality. It's inspired by a gate at a church in Ireland, a Catholic church. That one was meant to keep the cows out of the churchyard but let the people in."

Emmy was puzzled. "This isn't the way we came in before."

"No, the contractor just finished this one from my mom's drawing and sent me the code—and the bill."

"It's great that she got to exercise her talent in such an expensive art form. But she didn't get to see this one, this detail, this gate."

"She saw it all right. She was a visualizer, never surprised at how something came out."

* * *

The host announced that he was going into the pool to escape the shock and awe of new visitors.

"Oh, J., black trunks!"

"Yeah, I circled back to Macy's. Bought six of these and a whole new cycle of underwear, a dozen of each."

*   *   *

"So by now you have selected your sleep pods and, I'll bet, found the kid pod with the swinging rope ladder to the bunk bed."

He had not escaped the questions and enthusiasm for the house. They settled down on the big, plush sofa banquette in the huge, round, library-media room, the only room that was not flooded with light. J. was ready to slip the disc into the slot, but the guests demanded talk about the house.

Emmy had made a pot of coffee and brought it in with a soda for the karate kid, who had elected to stay with them to see the kings and the battles.

Joe demanded to know who had done what. "Where are the credits? We know your mom was cool and talented, but I didn't think she could do a set of plans."

"So true, and it really frustrated her. She did sketches and a lot of word pictures. She worked with a hot young architect named Marlon Bundy."

"Name sounds like the columns of killer ants from the movie with Charlton Heston. But he didn't come up with this eroded desert look, did he? Is this called modern?"

"I don't know what modern is anymore. I think my Mies Barcelona chairs are the greatest modern design on the planet. They were for an exhibition in 1929. Modern should be the most provocative concept, something that couldn't even have been done with last year's technology. Maybe Frank Gehry's Disney Hall is the description and the essence. Or is it a side step?

"Modern should be about progress on the way to better living. What's happened better than Neutra's steel-framed Lovell house that was built, I think, in 1927? Modern has become just another style when it used to be a religion."

Emmy contributed that it was indeed just another style name and remarked, "'Will madam have Tudor, California ranch, Greek, New England country house, or modern?' My Craftsman was the modern of its time, a milestone on the march from Victorian. Kitchens and baths are the real progress."

"Well, this complex of clay pods isn't going to influence anything except maybe pottery. It's a digression into fantasy."

"The interior design must have been Linda White. It's full of desert tribal reference, and I recognize some of the fabrics and stuff she got from me. Really so few objects and all museum-quality. She is a noted colorist. It's a good thing she liked terra cotta. Did you see over the dining table where there is a big circle of white painted in the terra cotta on the ceiling and it reflects like crazy? I don't know if the reference was intended, but it reminds me of the feeling of spiritual containment of the American Indian hut you can enter only from the hole in the top. Your dining room has that too, the white spot."

"Awesome, awesome—spiritual containment really is what the house feels like. It's so still and calm with that trickle sound from the pool! Says the mother of five noisy kids."

Emmy opined that this kid was pretty calm.

"Occasionally this one sits and contemplates his navel."

J. slipped the disc into the slot and dimmed the lights, and the monarchs of England burst onto the big screen and filled the room until lunch.

"Taking orders." Alice had menus in her hand. "How about Indian for Easter lunch and Thai for dinner? Neither of them Christian. I could get egg salad sandwiches from the Jewish deli."

"How did you do that? You've never even been here before."

"This is take-out/delivery city, and I have a computer and a telephone and a fax at my house. It is surely part of my job description to cater the set."

"Hey!" J. was jubilant. "You're taking on the job! Great!"

*   *   *

Joe was first to take his notes in hand. "As a cinematographer, I'm impressed. It's very beautiful with those

162

bursts of color, but I don't see that its existence is any threat to us. It's telling the same story, but we aren't coming from any reenactments of our own creation, only the movies of others, many others. And our story is about the movies made from the stories."

J. declared the reenactments a little thin. "They made do on occasion, with two close-up knights to depict an entire battle. I think this is a pretty good reference for us, but the historicity needs close checking. They spoke of Arthur, for instance, as an accepted historical character. I haven't heard that yet, that his existence has been proven. I thought I'd be the first to know. What do you think, Alice?"

"If I can't see James Franco as Tristan, I don't want to play. It's an awfully good story, isn't it, this first segment, right up to when Henry II came storming back across the channel? We must have *Camelot* whether Richard Burton's Arthur existed or not. Did anyone ever play Ethelred the Unready?"

"Emmy, was the stuff correct? You were scribbling a lot."

"Not very correct. They avoided certain close-ups of stuff opportunities. Ours will be strong in that area. The artifacts in an early ship burial will fill in a century or two.

"I was very interested in a certain story wrap. They referred to the early kings as chosen by the governed, and then the governed gave up liberties in favor of despots. Scott was talking about J. telling about the progress of liberty through Magna Carta. And then what? Elizabeth, yes, but not chosen, and after that, the progress of freedom is to America, for the chosen leaders that never happened fully in England. He thinks this whole thing is an American story right up to 1776, or maybe to the Constitutional Convention, crying out against hereditary leadership, or to the inauguration of Washington, or his farewell speech. As I recall, it had warnings about the dangers of loss of liberty in the future."

"Wooooo, chills up spine!" said Alice.

"Now that's important—timely too!" said J.

"The hell with artifacts, J. Your lady has a story mind."

"Would this mean we couldn't have *The Madness of King George*? It's my favorite, with the beautiful Prime Minister Pitt and his luminous eyes. I shall regret my proposal if we can't have him. Wasn't he the one who lost America? Another thing about this being an American story: did anyone think of William the Conqueror leaving from the very beach of our Normandy invasion of 1944? Didn't Daryl say that the other night?"

"Emmy, my dear betrothed, we thought you were just another pretty face." J. was jubilant over this turn of plot. "Let's make margaritas. Tequila is here, and I brought mix. After lunch, Emmy is to be rewarded for giving us purpose with her favorite Eleanor of Aquitaine, Queen of England, with Henry II's king. We better call Scott and let him know how much we like his idea."

"Having sold this thing, and given my cell number to Godmother Ingénue, I feel it's my place to remind you that it's still the goal to go with Elizabeth. Lots of work ahead, like do we pay residuals for *Shakespeare in Love* to get that fabulous moment of Judi Dench's Elizabeth, or is that a movie still or what? Et cetera, et cetera, et cetera."

J. smiled at the nod to Yul Brenner's "et cetera" line in *The King and I.*

Daryl Silver had been drawing on a notepad, and now he presented it, a credible sketch of William the Conqueror, outward bound from Normandy in 1066, and American soldier Bill in 1944, inward bound to a landing on Omaha Beach, with captions.

J. was impressed. "Hey, kid. That's good." Searching memories of childhood for things to say to kids, he exclaimed, "Last one in's a rotten egg!"

By the time J. had skinned out of the sweatpants that had been dampening over his trunks, Daryl was already running for the pool. The boy let out a curdling yell of alarm, as did J. right after him. The rest came running, and there was J., lifting a long, writhing snake on a pitchfork and throwing it over what he later described as a snake fence.

"Snakes. Why'd it have to be snakes?" screamed J.

Emmy replied, "Harrison Ford."

"Which one was that? What year?"

"*Raiders of the Lost Ark*, 1981."

All afternoon they were absorbed in the Middle Ages, but the late sun found them in the pool, J. and Joe chest-deep, sitting on rock ledges.

"Still heated for what they laughingly call winter out here. In summer you could get boiled, though construction marches on to get properties ready for fall use."

Joe needed to know how they got all the rocks under the water. "The pools I've seen with rocks around them look like they have petrified potatoes balancing on the edge."

"They over-dig the hole much bigger than the pool will be, with ledges way down that hold big boulders. Then they fill in around the boulders and spray the gunite around them. Then they plaster, usually black plaster. It makes the pool that teal-blue, mountain-lake color and adds five degrees to the temperature. I was out here with my mom in the heat. She directed the placing of rocks. Very big deal—cranes, sweating, swearing."

"Hey, it worked. Looks like a valley that happened to get filled with water. Man, would I ever like to film here, especially that grotto where you can pull yourself right out of the water into it. Looks to me like it was built for sexual liaison. Do you ever think about your parents doing it?"

"Yeah. You?"

"Yeah. You knew them—he was white; she's black. I always envisioned them in amorous entwinement that would look like a checkerboard. Those are the disadvantages of having a picture mind."

Emmy and Alice were lying like fish on a beach incline at the other end of the pool.

Alice looked in admiration across the long, long pool. "I love that you can walk into the water like at the ocean and then swim so far before you have to turn around. Not like the pool we had at our house, not like any pool except in a dream."

"We never had a pool at our house. We went up to my grandfather's, where my dad always watched over us, even after Peg was on the swim team at school. The pool was okay, but he lived high in the hills beyond the gas lines, and it wasn't ever heated, never warm enough until June. So much for movie star glamour."

"Ours came with the house when we moved there, and my mother fenced it in right away, or maybe fenced it out. I was three. Can you imagine the cruelty of taking their little Alice to a house on Wonderland Avenue? It wasn't so bad until I started kindergarten at Wonderland School. By third grade I was Allie and tried to tell them I was Sally."

Emmy gave voice to an idea she had often had. "Maybe the name should wait for the kid to choose. In J.'s family, though, it was a no-brainer. First-born boys were all Jared for maybe ten generations. Our family does a formula of ancestors. My name, Mary Ellen, is after my grandfather's grandmother. His aunt was also named for her, for her mother.

"He told me once that when he was a little tiny kid, he joined the family stage act with his father and mother and that aunt. He told about being so sad when she married and moved to America for early motion pictures. So he decided he would go to Hollywood someday too. She had died by the time he got here."

Alice asked whether Emmy had any idea whom she'd married.

"I don't remember. It must be in an album somewhere."

*　　*　　*

The Thai dinner was excellent after the whiskey sours and included Emmy's favorite sweet and sour pork. There was much discussion over whether this was the best or whether La Cienega's Asakuma Rice or Sunset Thai was best. Daryl, who had been watching the big television all afternoon, voted strongly for Kung Pao near the West Hollywood Whole Foods Market. He nodded off in exhaustion when he had hardly had time to evaluate this desert pad thai. Joe boosted him up the rope ladder to his top bunk.

* * *

"Let's stop at my dad's house on the way back and pick some oranges and whatever else is going to waste there."

"Let's look at albums to see if there's a picture of the Mary Ellen aunt you're named for. She'd be Patrick's great-aunt."

J., Emmy, and Alice soon determined that what was going to waste was three frozen dinners and some good gin, and then they moved to the albums.

* * *

It was at the beginning of the first album that Alice pulled from the deep bookshelf. "Oh my God, I swear I didn't know! But somehow I did! Did I see something at the Bird Streets house when I was going through things? I couldn't have known. Here, the wedding picture of Mary Ellen Higgen to Jared Dunkin, June 1915. J., this Jared is your great-grandfather, and Mary Higgen was your great-grandmother! And she was Emmy's grandfather's aunt and the sister of Em's great grandfather, who was Damon's father."

J. was overwhelmed with information. "'And the challis from the palace has the brew that's true.' Alice, how did you do that so fast? In fact, what did you say again?"

Emmy saw at once when she was needed.

"Jared, darling, the ninth or tenth Jared at least, you've admitted that we women are masters of relationships. You're the historian, but we remember the 'begots.' So let's look at this one. Mary and Damon's father were brother and sister. Their sons were, respectively, your grandfather Jared James and my grandfather Damon, so our grandfathers were first cousins. Their sons are your father Jerry and my father Patrick, second cousins, and their kids, you and I, are third cousins of old Hollywood. Big deal! Not as close as Franklin and Eleanor of New York."

"Masterful! Print the screen! I don't know how you do that or what you said, frankly, my dear."

* * *

"Well there, we've delivered our new manager to her brood. I hope I didn't keep you waiting too long in the car when I walked Alice to her door, but I had to say hello all around. Joe was there helping with last-minute homework. Their daughter Win, the accounting student and occasional child sitter, is developing into quite a beauty."

"I hope that strange ex-relationship doesn't get in the way of their working together. I don't know if I should have said it, but I showed her how to lock her door in your house, and she said, 'Like my ex would rape me. Big deal.' And I said, 'Sure and there you are the single mother of six instead of five."

"God knows she does it easily enough. Joe told me in all serious concern and some anger that his wife—not his ex-wife but his wife—was having an affair with Jon Mason . . . How about let's go to your modern-of-its-time Craftsman? It doesn't matter anymore where you are as long as you have your cell phone."

"Spoken like a true bachelor, and maybe as long as you have your car also and a gym bag with a change of black underwear, a razor, and a toothbrush."

* * *

"True bachelor indeed. Look what I found at my dentist's office this morning in an old magazine. There you are in a tux with a pretty girl as arm accessory. And captioned yet, 'Town's most eligible bachelor, cosmetic heir Jared Dunkin escorting Asia Pinta.' She's pretty, but you're gorgeous."

"It was a setup that worked. Haven't you seen her on the Ingénue commercials? New cosmetics to rival the Japanese lines. Brushed-on minerals. She refused to tell me what her real name was. You tore the clipping out and sneaked away?"

"I squealed and flashed my diamond and shared, even with the dentist. How could they refuse me the clipping?"

"You tiptoed out early this morning and left me sleeping."

"I thought about telling them I'd left you in my bed."

"I think that photo was at Sky Bar, and I haven't been back. I've been in your bed, or we in mine, ever since you voted for Hillary."

"You can't know that. Voting is private."

"Let's go to Sky Bar tonight, and you can tell me why she should be president, and I will tell you why she should not.

"Wait, I'm getting a call. Let me get this."

*   *   *

"All right, Grandstar, it's talk time. DNA is real science, and the only people left on earth not recognizing it as such were on the O. J. Simpson jury. The man was willing to give me only the short version on the phone. I have an appointment for next week to see the squiggles. Irrefutable bottom line, he affirmed that Damon Higgen is my father's father, that Damon Higgen is my grandfather."

He could hear that his grandmother, usually so smooth, was flustered. "Oh, dear me. Do we really have to believe it? Well, we really didn't talk about it. Really, how was I to know for sure? I didn't, you know, look pregnant when we married. The only thing was how we laughed when our premature baby was so handsome and fully formed. I just don't know what to say to you, except that you shouldn't mess with me. 'I'm older, and I have more insurance.'"

J. knew that was all the confession he would get and allowed himself to be warned off. "That was Kathy Bates in *Fried Green Tomatoes*, wasn't it? Do you know her? Is it true that they turned her away from the Roxbury when she came there after the awards with her brand-new Oscar in hand? It was for *Misery*, wasn't it? How long did that guy work there after that?"

"He shouldn't have messed with mature ladies. A friend of mine was stopped for speeding, and she told the officer she didn't have a driver's license—lost it for drunk driving—and no, she didn't have car registration because she stole the car and killed the driver, whose body was in the trunk. He called for his superior officer, who came with gun drawn. She immediately showed him her license and car registration, and he requested she open the trunk. She did—nothing in it. With her sweetest smile she said, 'I suppose he also told you I was speeding, but you already know what a liar he is.'"

"Very funny, and good for deflecting any further questions and conversation. Do you think I'll never bring it up again?

"That movie, the ultimate fan, capturing and holding the object of her affection—were you ever afraid of a stalker? Is that why Marina packs a gun?"

"I've had my share of affection, but gun? What gun?"

"The one that keeps me from worrying about you all the time."

"Oh, that gun!"

"Something else I'll bet you were afraid of—I bet you were afraid your son Jerry would find and fall for one of Damon's daughters. I bet you were relieved when he came home from the Vietnam War with a Swiss bride, my mother."

"Oh, so relieved and happy that he survived that horrible war, that both of them did, and that Jerry was stationed part of the time in Germany, visited Paris, and found the beautiful Karen behind the cosmetic counter in Gallery Lafayette. Even there he was always interested in Ingénue business, you know, checking out the displays. They just didn't know what they were displaying."

"And you all worried about my finding a Damon granddaughter."

"Well, we were all glad when the other two sisters got married."

"Who's we all? Does that mean my father too? He knew then who his real father was?"

"How do I know what anybody knew? Those beautiful Irish guys were always playing tennis together, you know. To my Jared James, his boys were always his boys, and I tried to be a good mother, you know, and mother-in-law."

"What about your mother-in-law?"

"Oh, Anne was always great. We got along fine."

"No wonder, she was closer to your age than to your father-in-law's. But I don't mean Anne. She was the third one, wasn't she? What about Mary? Isn't that the name of granddad's mother? What was her maiden name?"

"My goodness, I don't think I ever knew that. She died before I was born, when J. J. was only nine, you know, just after they built your house, when they'd been in Hollywood only two years."

"What if it was Higgen, Mary Higgen? What if she was Damon Higgen's beloved Aunt Mary Ellen?"

"Oh my God! Do you know this?"

"Yes!"

"Does that make J. J. and Damon cousins?"

"Yes, it does. Doesn't that make you the prettiest little ostrich in the Serengeti?"

"How can you tell me things like this over the phone?"

"I'll be at your place soon. I'm on the speaker in the car coming your way. I'm going west on that fast strip of Wilshire, past the Los Angeles Country Club."

"Well, you better hurry. You know that club doesn't allow show folk through there."

Chapter 11

"Come in, come in, my darling. See how fast I can make a cup of tea. Look at my new cups, or are they mugs? I just found them the most graceful things ever. We went to my framer and parked in the back, and a man there, you know, coming out of a back door, gave us two thumbs up. I asked him if they were for the car or for being able to get a Bentley into such a tight space. He said both and that we could come in the back way. Well, you know, it wasn't the back door to the framer at all but a terrific little shop called okay. It's been there for ten years next to my framer, and you know, I never noticed it before. Neither had Marina. I have to tell my shopper about it.

"These mugs were about four times as much as mugs usually are. I bought four dozen. That should cover my book club, don't you think? Maybe I should call for another couple of dozen. They are so much easier to handle than a cup and saucer."

They were beautiful. J. was learning not to think of expenditure with any relationship to his earned income, and he did not multiply well in his head. He was not sure how to get back into their phone conversation. He talked about the Palm Springs house, the retreat of the weekend, and the idea of an American story.

"My dear, I like it so much. It's absolutely a case of 'Why didn't I think of it?' Tell me what your staff of Joe and Scott thinks of it. You know, Ronnie would have loved it."

"The whole idea of it originated with Scott. Joe is enthusiastic and started thinking about American objects to photograph. The documents might be a cliché, or not. Joe's a funny guy. He's awfully good at what he does. He tries not to seem the intellectual he really is. We were talking about the cousin thing after we found the wedding picture of your father in-law, Jared, and his wife Mary. He was clearly bored, and we asked him how he figured out who were his cousins, and his reply was that his mother had told him which ones they were at family picnics."

"Well, you're certainly related to me. Our souls are connected."

"We're connected foot-to-foot?"

"No, silly boy, 'soul' with a 'u' in it."

"You're in my soul too, Grandestlady."

"Well, all this cousin, cousin, cousin thing. I'm bored too. Even if you were brother and sister, you could get yourselves spayed and neutered and live in unwedded, blissful, diamonded engagement forever and ever."

"Amen."

*   *   *

Emmy darling, there you are, all T and A and H and H, ready for Sky Bar. You have to be careful not to fall in the pool right there in the middle, 'cause they don't allow anyone not a guest at Mondrian to swim. I don't know how you get out of a pool without swimming."

"I understand T and A, but what's H and H?

"Hair and heels, long and high. And I'll tell you what the Grandloon said and what the DNA said, but you already know what that will be."

"And I'll tell you what came in over the weekend from my guy scavenging the garage sales."

*   *   *

173

They took the Packard, deciding that it would be fit for the scale of the hugely oversize door and the ordinary flowerpots, sized for the giant of the beanstalk.

"They make me feel like Lily Tomlin as Edith Ann. What a view! This really is special. Did you like the building when it had all those Agam colors on it? I had a customer, mostly for art glass, who had a huge Agam stainless steel sculpture in his garden, and he had to oil it down all the time with something that caught all the flying bugs. Very innovative, bug texture sculpture.

*   *   *

"Did the Ingénue really admit to family secrets, in actual straight talk, not banter talk and anecdote like always?"

"In the face of DNA evidence, it seemed she might have wanted to go all Simpson jury, or her second choice was to go Oz and say, 'You cursed brat, look what you've done. I'm melting. Melting.'"

"Oh no, she's no wicked witch, just a fabulous old celebrity, stuck with family promises to two, maybe three, dead generations. Didn't your family ever talk? I'm not used to that. My family is so open about everything."

"Did you phone home after we met to tell the family you had met the man you would marry?"

"Home wasn't home. I called Peg after lunch, from the showroom, not on my cell from the lady's room at the restaurant."

*   *   *

"You look really awesome in the tux. And 'awesome' is really the right word. I feel awe, as though I didn't know every bit of you without it."

"I shall be without it later tonight. You may want to reacquaint yourself with every bit of me."

"Yes, perhaps. But now I need to ask you, do you have a Patty Duke signature?"

"Yes! Did you actually get a Helen Keller signature from a yard sale?"

Emmy could hardly hold her pleasure in the telling. "Signed photo. It's in pencil, but it doesn't show; it's just engraved."

Jared was impressed, even excited. "You see, that's the essence of content, related to what she's known for, achievement in spite of her blindness. She couldn't have even heard anyone tell her the pencil wasn't taking. It can immediately be seen that the signer couldn't see! A gem, a gem and a half!

"By the way it's okay to fall in the pool. We have a room here tonight."

* * *

"What a really cool room. What delicious excess when we own two homes not a mile away. Wow, the view is great. It's mostly the same as from your house, but the framing makes it all different.

"This is our first hotel room. Where will the others be? Will the loving be different everywhere? You've never done that to me before. Nobody ever told me that loving would be as it is with you. I never even read anything that let me know how great, except that Romeo and Juliet were willing to die for it."

"And he only fucked her once."

"It's a classic. You don't say 'fuck' for classics."

"It's a fine old Anglo-Saxon word, standing for 'fornicating under consent of the king.' I wish to mutter other smutty words in the receptive, rosy sculpture of your ear."

"I feel you like you are part of me. It seems to start at the ankles. You inhabit me!"

"That's nothing like inhibit, is it?"

* * *

"This, our eighth-anniversary Tuesday lunch, can't linger. I have to get back to the showroom. West Week starts tomorrow. I'll be scarce until Friday morning."

"I think I'll make myself scarce too. I'll check on what's going on at the Bird Streets house. Alice sent for another three folding tables and has an appointment with the forensic accountant. Maybe by Friday I'll have something to tell. And I'm seeing my buds Thursday. Saturday is a committee meeting at my house. I think I'll have it catered by Pollo Loco."

With difficulty Emmy thought beyond West Week. "I'll call home and ask my house lady to make a vat of her famous chili. Have I told you that you can expect her homemade green corn tamales at Christmas? I don't know where she learned it, not exactly an Asian dish.

"Saturday you'll be missing *Horton Hears a Who* at 3:00, *Married Life* at 6:00, and *Meet the Browns* at 9:00."

J. feigned that he was appalled, betrayed. "What, do you write down the names of Directors Guild screenings in your day planner? You cheat!"

* * *

"My best West Week sale was a big order of lapel pins for my dad's company, for the next Rose Parade. Also good were some movie costumes and yards and yards of a fabric that is so inexpensive you could do a tent out of it. That one was an old client who was laughing because I'm not noted for inexpensive. The total take was not good, though. Sales are down. I might be scared if I didn't own the building and have two tenants."

"Stick with me, babe. You don't ever need to be scared."

Emmy laughingly accused him of being very MCP.

"I know PC . . ."

She translated. "You sounded male chauvinist pig."

"So?"

* * *

"It's kind of belated information, or no information at all. The buds found my dad's birth certificate, parents Ula and Jared James Dunkin, very much in order, except that he was a little heavy for a preemie, the birth weight not even fudged. Buds seem to know or thought they knew all along that Damon Higgen was Jared Richard's father. Old gossip that you never knew, although the neighbors always did.

"I wonder why the Grandloon let them name me Jared Damon Dunkin. It's almost like a hidden joke, the traditional naming method of a grandfather's name for a second name. I bet she giggled to herself when her daughter-in-law decided to name me after her favorite movie star."

"At Buckley there was a girl in our class whose mother threw herself off the Santa Monica pier when the girl was a few months old, so the girl grew up with her mother's sister, thinking that was her mother, and the sister's husband, her father. We all knew that, but nobody mentioned it. Turned out that the girl knew it from some time in grade school and never let on."

"My buds—and Marina's cop too—went looking for my birth certificate in Orange County but couldn't find it. It didn't turn up on the tables at the Bird Streets house either. I guess I don't exist. I've never needed it. My parents must have needed it for my passport, which I've simply kept renewing."

"J., the Saturday meeting was great, wasn't it? I've put those red sandals aside so that they won't scuff and then not match in the later part, when we re-cut the beginning. I'm pretty excited about it. The committee is really coming through with ideas and permissions and such."

"Good people all. Pros."

* * *

"You're thirteen minutes late to our anniversary lunch," J. said as he saw the top of her head crowning the rail wall surrounding the inner stairway from the parking lot below. "You should be spanked."

"Your place or mine?" she asked, sliding into the booth beside him.

"Ooh, I thought you weren't into any of that."

"Well, I'm not. I'm not that kind of a girl."

"I've heard you say that before. What kind of a girl are you?"

"I'm dependable."

"You are adorable."

"Adoring."

"Worth the wait."

"I'm usually punctual."

"Reliably orgasmic."

"Noisy?"

"Madam is a screamer."

"Appreciative."

"I thought it was your applause."

"Satisfied."

"Satisfying."

"Efficient."

"A talented girl, you."

"Organized."

"I'd say you're put together."

"Cool?"

"Any cooler, you'd be cold."

"Hot?"

"Enough to smolder leaves."

"Considerate."

"Dimpled."

"No! Where?"

"Butt!"

"Two?"

"Two of everything except the important part."

"Leggy."

"Those two too, oh yes!"

"Well dressed."

"Gorgeous."

"Admiring."

"Admirable!"

"Loving."

"Beloved."

"Uninhibited."

"Yes, you are!"

"Playful."

"You're childlike, not childish."

"Nice."

"Fabulous."

"Grateful."

"You're a Catholic girl."

"Agnostic . . . almost."

"Committed."

"Only to you."

"Happy?"

"I'm joyful."

"You're radiant."

"I'm pregnant!"

"*What?*"

"I went to my gynecologist to get that birth-control ring thingy implanted, and he said, 'Sweetie, too late!'"

"Wow!"

'Wow' upside down is Mom."

Just then the waiter appeared and asked if it would be the usual for Ms. Higgen and Mr. Dunkin.

"Make my scotch double."

"This lady isn't drinking."

* * *

At first J. couldn't find her. She was not answering her cell, and Scott didn't know where she was; she had not called into the showroom. When he called his house, there was only his own voice on the answering machine, and at her house there was only her voice. He went home, and there was no one there, only a note from the housekeeper saying that she had gone to the grocery store and asking whether dinner was going to be here or there, or were they going out?

Then he found Emmy at her house in the guest room, curled in a Craftsman bed, asleep, only hair showing, stringy on a tear-soaked pillow. The cat had pushed himself against her where a lap would have been were she sitting up.

He hadn't thought much about prayer since he was a child, but now he prayed for wisdom. He slipped out of his jacket, throwing it toward a chair, and then out of his shoes. He lifted the cover and curved himself into an S against her, spooning her as she began to awake, gulping tears. He patted her, a comforting pat, without the hint of arousal. He spoke about being one, from the ankles to the part in the hair at the mystical center at the top of the head. He'd heard of the name for this but could not remember it.

"We're in it together, but 'Houston, we've got a problem.'"

Emmy turned, and her tears now headed for J.'s shirt collar. There was something infinitely intimate about them running down his neck, and though she allowed herself a small laugh at his movie quote at a time like this, the tears did not stop.

The cat who had been curled was now crouched at the foot of the bed where the mattress met the oak footboard. He was hostile, snarling a threat at the interloper who must have hurt the lady at the center of his life.

J. searched for words for this failed dialog that must be reopened. "I think we changed political sides there for a minute. I, the conservative, took a very liberal position, questioning our wisdom and right to have this baby. You, my darling little liberal, went all conservative and wild mother about the right to life of this speck, potentially damaged by our doubly close relationship . . . Could we talk about the religion involved here? I've never heard from you on the subject."

A Kleenex or two later, she was able to speak, if haltingly. "What is there to say about religion? I'm like the captive who was told to hop on one foot and recite his entire religion. It took only one hop to say, 'Do as you would be done by, and all else is comment.' I do know, though, that a child who knows about the courage of David, the determination of Moses, and the gentleness of Jesus could never give them up.

"Are we obligated to pass them on, or are we obligated to leave our child with a clear, open mind for her first university class in comparative religions? And it's not a doubly close relationship anyway. You are so bad at the begots. Jared Dunkin and Mary Higgen aren't yours if Damon is yours . . . I've never asked you about religion either. I don't know if you believe in God."

"Well, who else made the trees? But I haven't prayed lately, until now."

"You have too. Whom do you think you are talking to when you're in a hurry in traffic, and you say, 'Come on, man, give me green lights'?"

"Surely not the main guy, if there is one."

"Surely then it's your guardian angel?"

"Is he the busy fellow who put you in that voting booth with your legs hanging out?"

"Do you suppose my guy and your guy negotiated? I like the song that says 'Because God made thee mine,' and besides, who do you suppose dropped this baby into me?"

J. raised his hand and said loudly, "I did!"

"Wouldn't you just love to know which time?"

He could feel her relaxing and his collar beginning to dry. "It's not really a decision yet. There are all those tests and sonogram pictures to go through before we know. We have some time. I did believe we were safe enough."

"Well. Beloved macho man, let me tell you what I once overheard at a shower: 'If your birth control method is 99 percent sure, that should give you one baby a year.'"

"I shouldn't have questioned whether you had forgotten to take any of the pills, and I didn't mean to sound as though I thought you were capable of skipping them on purpose."

"No, I'm just not that kind of a girl."

*   *   *

"Thank you, House Angel, Angela, gracias. Hold what you bought for dinner, and you know I like your pot roast better than anything, but I'm taking her to the Porterhouse Bistro tonight. Do you remember when I told you about it, the place that has the cotton candy with the light under it? My lady needs cotton candy."

*   *   *

"But J., seriously, how did you know I like cotton candy?" Emmy asked as they returned to his house. "I know I've never told you because if I had, I would have told you about walking with my daddy on the Venice Boardwalk when the fog suddenly rolled in with a wind behind it, and the cotton candy I was clutching in a paper cone went all over my hair. And if I had told you that, I would have remembered."

"I would know you would like cotton candy and hot dogs and frozen Snickers bars and vichyssoise and caviar and steak tartar and none of the flavored martinis." And then he sang, the lyrics not quite exact, "Getting to know you, getting to know all the new, wonderful things about you, getting to know what to say."

"Wow, J., I bet you are even on key."

"Wait, Emmy, we're going in the front door. Take these flowers. I'm sorry the stems are damp, but I had to put them in a wet towel, out here on the patio."

"It's like a bridal bouquet."

"You got it!"

He pulled her around, facing the thick old door, eighty-eight years away from a monastery, and stood beside her. "I, Jared Damon Dunkin, take thee, Mary Ellen Higgen, as my wife, my very life, to cherish through light and darkness, to protect, adore, to inhabit thee through all eternity, to bring you and the cat and all your amber and amethyst jewelry and crazy high heels to live here or where we mutually agree to be, from this day forward—forsaking all others, to love and cherish against anyone or anything that would try to break us asunder, forever and ever. Whatever I have, whatever I am, whatever I will have and will be, is yours. I thee wed."

Emmy was astonished and crying, and now it was her turn. "Jared, my darling, God made thee mine to love and cherish. I, Mary Ellen Higgen, promise to love and honor and live with thee, forsaking all others till the end of time. I plight thee my troth. Is that the same as I thee wed? Jared, how I love thee! And I *do* . . . Where did you get a ring?"

"It came in the Cracker Jack package with your engagement ring, and with it I am yours forever."

The kiss would have pleased any audience, had there been one.

*   *   *

"Hi, Emmy, it's Alice over at the Bird house today, working away at the elusive lives that were Karen and Jerry Dunkin."

"I'm so glad to talk to you, to thank you again for all the help when, as we liberated people now say, 'I moved in with my boyfriend.' Wait till my dad hears that one from my mouth.

"That his mother's closet and bath throw me into his is working out okay. I don't know if you saw it or not, but there's a mirrored octagonal room, and some of the sides have closets behind them. And it's kind of cozy to share the bathroom."

Alice's view of life came through as she replied. "Wait until you are diapering a baby on the granite counter between the bowls and among the Ingénue cosmetics and the Chanel No. 19."

Emmy paused for a moment and then hoped that her slow response didn't alert this sharp lady. "Well, I'm visualizing. I have helped with my sister's broods."

"It's not the same. You can't walk away . . . Listen, that accountant is here, and we've sifted through a lot of my presifts, and she very much needs to talk to J."

* * *

"Okay, J., here it is. I've done a little research before dropping this bombshell on you. It isn't all that hard to find just about anybody now. We found your adoption papers.

"No, no, I don't mean your father's. There was no need. A lady's husband is regarded as the father of her child. I mean *your* adoption papers. I didn't know if you knew you were adopted.

"Why are you happy dancing? And what do you mean, but you look like your father and you're fresh out of cousins?"

* * *

They talked about her joining him, but it did seem to be the kind of thing a man had to do alone.

It was a pleasant day for a drive. He headed down the 405, past the Assyrian ziggurat that had been a tire factory, now flying the war banners of a discount outlet. He passed the exit to Disneyland with a nod of his head to his boyhood and to the terrific people who had been his parents. There was a nod to Medieval Times too. He must take Emmy there for the horses, even if she had been to the show before, so that he could tell her the real story of the history depicted.

There was a subtle change now as the very landscape became affluent. He had always liked La Jolla, though he didn't know it well. He found the hospital with help from his Tom-Tom, which didn't provide any help with finding a parking spot.

At the main desk they said that Dr. McCarty was expecting him, and they alerted her that Mr. Dunkin was here. Later, he would always try to remember whether she was actually wearing the stethoscope badge of her profession around her neck when he met her, but he would remember well her white doctor coat with the red embroidery: Dr. Katleen McCarty, Chief of Pediatrics.

"Are you . . ."

"You weren't supposed to find me, ever. Yes, I'm Dr. McCarty, and you found me, and yes, I'm your mother, or I used to be."

"My God, if I'd met you at a party, I'd have hit on you."

"Well, you are a handsome hunk, and I might have followed you home. You look enough like your father and mine too for it not to have occurred to me who you were, and besides, I saw your picture on the cover of a magazine in my waiting room."

"You're my mom!"

"Wow," she said with some hint of sarcasm.

"Which," he said, "is 'Mom,' upside down."

"So it is, graphically speaking. Your adopted mom was pretty great. Best skin I ever saw. I spent a bit of time with her the year I was fifteen. Then I expelled you into her waiting arms. My mother was pretty devastated. She wanted you, but I've given her three others now, and you've given her ease and affluence and sent this daughter to Harvard Med."

"And my mom saved someone from a statutory rape charge."

"No, no. My deflowering penetrator was a sixteen-year-old boy at Beverly Hills High I was with for one macho prom night. It bothers me sometimes, but my therapist says it's all right.

"There is absolutely no record of him. That was part of the deal. So don't bother looking. Don't bother looking into the faces of all the fifty-three-year-old guys on the street. I don't know what he would look like now. You don't look that much like him anyway. That crazy chin was my father's."

"And nobody knows?"

"I don't think so. Let's think it through. Jerry and Karen, gone. Anders and Marta, gone. Pat, not telling."

"Who's Pat?"

"Ah, that's my mother. Her middle name's Patricia. I sometimes call her Pat. And the guy will never tell. His parents paid too much for the down payment, and then your Jerry and Karen took over paying. You're the most expensive little prince on the planet. The participating lawyers and doctors will be silent.

"I want this to be over again like I thought it already was over. This is our only meeting. There is not to be any Hollywood ending with a big family picnic in the park. My two daughters have a brother. They don't need you. And my husband has no need to hear about you. There is this one meeting, and it's over and out, so you better take notes. Ask me anything you want to know, and I may answer. Or not."

It was beginning to dawn on J. that he didn't like her. He wished he had a therapist along or at least his wool watch cap pulled way down over his ears. He felt a great need to throw her off-stride. "Well, I don't necessarily accept your terms, but do you know you look like Dr. Berber from Chickweed Lane?"

"You mean from the comic strip? Another son of mine says that too, but it doesn't appear in color, so you don't know if she has red hair. My son does."

He noted that she had good dialogue reflexes, including the recovery after her mention of Pat, who J. thought was probably the guy's mother, still surviving, a slender clue if he'd a mind to follow any.

"Those who know—do they include my grandmother, the Ingénue?"

"That was not the intention, but she looks pretty smart in those commercials."

"So you have followed us?"

"With that coverage, she'd be hard to escape. I did see your picture, their devoted son, at Jerry and Karen's funeral with the bereaved Ula."

"And you said to your husband, 'Look at that man with my father's chin, who maybe looks a little bit like our son, but with dark hair'?"

"Not, but actually you do. See." She produced a photo, a family, smiling parents, two pretty little girls, and the red-haired boy, the brother and sisters J. didn't have.

Where was that watch cap? Was she asking him politely not to shatter anything? "So what was the deal that sold me?"

"They wanted payment to stop when I was twenty-one but had to settle for payment until you were twenty-one. Harvard Med plus. That must be the sizable piece of change for which your accountant is looking. It's too late to return the merchandise for refund."

"Is this return policy in small print somewhere?"

"I don't know what you found when you found me way down the coast here. How did you?"

"I have friends in high places."

"Where? City Hall where the birth certificates are stored? Who was that cold-voiced bitch who called me to make this appointment?"

"That was my cold-voiced bitch, better than that I called."

"All right, what do you have to know?"

"I deserve to know what my biological heritage is. What about your mother Pat and your father with the chin? Where's the red hair from?"

"Her family is from Germany, three generations from Munich. Her maiden name was Meinhoff. Her mother's was Bear, or at least it was after immigration. The chin came from some Irish place, and his mother's name was more tribe than family name at immigration, maybe like Dr. Berber. It was Norge for Norwegian, three generations."

J. never imagined himself this far into the begots and did make notes for Emmy, who would probably chart it.

"And the biological father. You know the name; I don't. Any guess about heritage?"

"Definitely Irish. I thought his father and my dad were going to go at it in our living room. He seemed proud of his son that I was maybe the prettiest girl in the class."

She looked as though she might have said too much, or maybe his own thought was showing: run through the yearbook and segregate the Irish names.

"And his mother, did she come to your living room too?"

"No, no clue. I have an appointment now." She put out her hand. Long slender fingers, long thumb too. She had a firm

187

handshake, a firm hand with children too, he assumed. This was his one moment for a lifetime of touch.

Emmy had told him this was a condescending gesture, so he put his left hand over their clasped hands and waited for eye contact. "Katleen, we had a lot to lose, but now you do."

He made his way down the elevator and out the automatically opened door and threw himself into his car. His watch cap was in the glove compartment. He left it there. He would have liked to sit a minute, stunned in place, contemplating that being orphaned was not irrevocable, but not if she might be looking out the window. He did not look up at the building to see.

It was early for a bar, and it was a long trip home. He followed his Tom-Tom instructions to the main street where he remembered from a previous trip to La Jolla, a restaurant full of wooden chairs on wooden floor, smelling of orange muffins, with an ocean view. It was still there.

*   *   *

The view began to suffer from its sameness; the tea became insipid. There was scotch at home and the probability that Emmy was no longer a cousin. What would the Grandloon do with this information, should he choose to tell her?

In the car he remembered that there had been a buzz against his leg indicating a cell phone message, and now he retrieved it. "Hey man, what do you know about the two British tribal chieftains who tried to fight off the Roman invasion? Would they be English kings?

J would have thought that Katleen McCarty had delivered the rejection of the day, but then the police had rejected his car as well, thinking it had been parked overlong at their curb. Fortunately, the ticket had instructions for sending them an unreasonable amount of money. He did not have to appear, and they had been kind enough not to tow the car away. He pulled on the black watch cap and then felt the need for further enclosure and put the top up.

Chapter 12

Hey, babe, the good news is that I'm still Irish, even a little more so, I think. I was going to go home to a bottle of scotch, but I'm here across the street from you, going into El Coyote bar. What I need is you—and a bottle of scotch."

"Five minutes."

* * *

"This woman who agrees she's my mother says my father was a high school prom date, but of course that's a continuing cover-up, and this is the continuing soap opera of 'Who's Your Daddy?'

"It's hard to imagine my father philandering with somebody's babysitter—geez, my parents seemed so good together, so in love—but father has to be my father. I look too much like him, and the DNA shows Damon as my grandfather and so his father. Ula all but admits her fling with Damon. Big cheer for what a great guy J. J. was. She loves that they fought over her."

"Oh my, that's a lot of 'great guy' to accept her affair and her lover's son. Onto the generations and a big cheer for Karen Dunkin to go through such elaborate deception to get you from your Irish bio-mom. You're so fond of being Irish, but your Dunkin name is Scotch."

"There's a place where Ireland and Scotland are twenty miles apart. And history is long."

"That's more like swimming than wading."

"I'm guessing boats."

"That's just logistics. Anyway, what's she like, and how did you feel about her? How strange it must have been to touch your real mother. Did you have a sense of being part of her? Was there a family feeling? Did a bell sound?"

"Well, she's something else. Don't you read the literature? Guys don't tell how they feel. Anyway, you're my only reality to cling to, and I can't wait to do so."

* * *

At breakfast, meeting his birth mother was still the only topic except the decision about which cereal and whether there was any milk.

"Again about her office. What kind of a playpen did she have in it?"

"What kinds are there?"

"You'll find out, and they aren't modern and chic like you would like. I have to go looking for a black diaper bag with chrome buckles. There's a classic and very expensive baby carriage in which I'd like to indulge. It's more Packard than Lamborghini. And when she's out of it, it could just stand in the hall as sculpture."

"He. Or it can stand there as a threat."

"So we're already talking about more kids?"

"No. We're talking about no more kids. I want to take you traveling. You've hardly been anywhere. I could hold down one kid while you stare at Ghiberti's doors to the Baptistery but not two. I didn't avoid marriage all this time because I didn't want children. I was not married because I hadn't found you yet. Not wanting kids is another issue. Maybe they're okay. Maybe it was a lot about my brother."

"And now he's not your brother. She's not your mother. He might not be your father, and they're not your cousins, but she's your grandmother, by adoration. You have a whole new set of siblings you're not going to know. Maybe a whole new set of cousins, but blessings on us, I'm not one of them. This would never play on that soap opera, but it would still be called 'Who's Your Daddy?' Are you going to pursue this? Do you need to?"

"I want to run through the yearbook for the suspects, and then I have that DNA appointment that will show only what we know, that my adopted father and your father were half-brothers. Do I have that right? The DNA report assumes my father as my father and therefore Damon as my grandfather. Up to now I've been interested only in the convoluted relationships that made Lady Jane Gray think that she could be Queen of England."

*   *   *

The call was from Marina. "Get your asses over here. It's moving day, and she needs help, love, and attention."

"I must have been waiting for your summons, sitting here with my granola and second cup of coffee and reading about the children of the polygamous community who are in government custody. I'm yours till my DNA appointment on Tuesday morning."

"What's that, Department of National Anonymity?"

"Yeah. Need anything on the way?"

"We could use some of that anonymity. Some fans out front learned who's moving."

"Well, we always have a certain amount of anonymity along with us. Anything else?"

"Yeah. Donuts and cleaner's bags, a triple dozen of 'em at least. The long ones, the longest for long dresses, and some short ones too."

"You want the donuts assorted too?"

*   *   *

"Come on, bride darling, in gear. I got the summons. What the hell am I going to tell her that she doesn't already know? Or does she? . . . Well, aren't you awesome in blue jeans! I'm missing the legs, but I'm lovin' the butt."

In preparation for the move to the new condominium, Emmy's SUV from the showroom was at the curb. She handed J. the keys.

"This is a nice bonus of what yours is mine," said J. "It was great for bringing your stuff over to your new house. Pretty soon we will have to think about the household stuff you left behind and the household stuff at the Bird Streets storage. Your bungalow would be a great bed and breakfast the way it is if we knew anybody to run it. We could go there sometimes, on mini-vacation, except the cat would know we were cheating on him."

"Great, you're starting to think about the cat's feelings."

"A little displaced, I should think. He's a lot harder to find in this multistoried house. You call him, and he doesn't answer, just takes a message. Then you feel the step, step, step of him in the night when he comes to sleep with us, on your side, of course. I'm starting to like watching him when he jumps up too. He overjumps and sticks the landing like any other great gymnast. I've never had a cat. But I don't think I have this one either."

"Maybe we should get a dog sometime, all for you."

"Let's get a baby first."

"Oh, let's."

"Dear little budding mom, whom shall we tell and when?"

They were able to put off discussing that dilemma just then, for they had arrived at the donuts. They had gone down Crescent Heights and overshot Santa Monica Boulevard by one street to go around the block and fetch up properly at the entrance to the little strip mall. Most of the businesses had moved on already because Walgreens intended to build there. Rumor had it that the project was delayed when it was discovered that there had been a gas station on that corner.

"I'll do the cleaners, 'cause it's a funny request, and they know me," J. said. "You do the donuts of your choice, except that there has to be two chocolate with sprinkles for Ula."

When J. came out of the cleaners, there was Emmy hugging a small round man in sunglasses, across her box of donuts. "Hey, Marco, that's my new lady you're hugging."

"Yeah, and I'm kissing her too," he said as he did. "I should've thought of you two for each other a long time ago and introduced you."

"So what's happening to Marco's, with the best manicotti in town?"

"We'll keep making it here until they take down our building and then bail to the new place across the street."

"We'll be there."

"Yeah, you haven't yet. My manager said he saw you across the street, at Silver Spoon."

"Well, they have real booze, not just Italian grape juice."

"Try us for breakfast."

J. promised they would.

Chapter 13

The little strip mall's parking lot now provided convenient empty spaces in front of the empty storefronts and the three remaining businesses. The morning coffee klatch, the police officers, legendary consumers, and the locals who regarded it as breakfast stop were probably all hoping that the situation would remain the same with the donut shop.

The cleaner's bags and the pink box of donuts on the second seat, J. pulled Emmy's SUV out of its easy parking spot, onto Santa Monica Boulevard, and around the corner to Crescent Heights. The big vehicle had not gone two blocks when J. suddenly pulled it into a parking space at the curb.

"This is like coming out of the men's room dragging a trail of toilet paper off your heel."

J. laughed as he hurried out of the car to gather up a half block of cleaner's bags that had blown out of the backseat and out the open sunroof, connected by the tear line that held them together. Where they had been a neat package, they were now a messy, glacial pile under the now-closed roof.

"So you used to eat at Marco's? We might have met. I would have picked you up."

"Actually, I used to stop for a raised glazed donut and a French maple one. One morning this cute man was wandering in the parking lot, pushing up his sunglasses to dab at tears. His partner, his mama, had just died. I hugged him. He needed it so much. He told me his mama was an Italian war bride and had come back to America with her Japanese-American husband. He took off the sunglasses, so I could see his Japanese eyes. I don't know what his wife's heritage is."

"They always tell you things, don't they? Do you know about that Nisei regiment that he must have been with to be fighting in Italy? They were so brave that our other guys, out of admiration for them, would never let them buy their own drinks."

Emmy was impressed with the wide range of tidbit knowledge that J. had, though she could have told him things about the art of the Japanese Edo period that he surely didn't know.

* * *

Marina came to the door and looked disapprovingly at the armful of rumpled plastic bags. "You didn't have to mess 'em up like that. Can I assume they are clean and new?"

"Yes, I did, and you can. Assign us—what can we do, besides smoothing out these things?"

"Anything. It's the devil's own fun all down the line."

"It must be a battle if you are quoting Civil War generals. I'll take her a chocolate donut with sprinkles."

* * *

"Oh, my dear, that is so nice. I'll come out for a coffee with it."

She was well coordinated in camel and beige with some massive ivory jewelry, playing the part of a star, moving to a new condo. There were a number of unidentified people running about at the bidding of a pretty blond moving coordinator with a plan and a packet of different-colored stickers in hand.

"Do sit a moment, my dears, before you get started. I'm finding so many things I forgot I had, like this ivory. I hope you don't disapprove of my having it and, you know, wearing it. I must have tucked it away when someone did disapprove. I wouldn't buy it new now of course. That would just add, you know, to the demand of poachers, but it is so beautiful that it might be regarded as disrespectful if that poor old elephant died in vain."

Emmy was obviously impressed with the jewelry and admired it. "May I see the bracelet for its mark? I think I know it from its manufacture in a little hill town near Heidelberg. Yes, see, here's the mark. They have been doing it there for generations. They certainly outdid themselves with these pieces. I would guess from the early twenties. When they become body temperature, do you ever stop and wonder who warmed them before you?"

"My goodness. Aren't you a romantic!" the star said, taking the French maple donut. "I do have a slender bronze snake bracelet that leaves an indentation on my wrist, and I always wonder what other wrists it indented. Not many, I think, because it was found in a grave in a dig in Tripoli. Poor baby, maybe she only wore it that once. Thank God, you know, for modern medicine. We do have a better life span, unless we go out and get ourselves killed." She looked at the donut box. "I left the chocolate for Marina"

Emmy knew, for Marina appeared just then, joining them in the breakfast room, where the light was better than the entrance hall where she had let them in.

"Marina, wherever did you find chocolate velvet boot-cut jeans?"

"Her shopper, of course. Wait till you see the duster that goes with 'em, gauntlet cuffs with milk chocolate embroidery. I am so fine," she said, reaching for the chocolate donut, as Emmy knew she would. It was often her own party trick, to predict what guests would take, for people usually reached for the hors d'oeuvres and dessert that had a color relationship to what they were wearing.

"I'll put you two packing the American art glass," Marina said. "And I'll show you which crystal goes and which stays for the renter. The place will still be mighty presentable for them. The interior designer is working both sets with the moving coordinator, who will give you the right color stickers."

"Yes, you know, my decorator won't let me into my own new place until she's ready. We can't go there until there's music, flowers, and an ice bucket. She might let you in, but I'd rather you didn't see it half pulled together.

"Our own special beds have already been moved. And Her Imperial Designerness is sending us to a hotel, tonight and maybe tomorrow night. She will call when she's ready. Like all of them, she says it's my only chance to see my house the way other people will see it."

J. thought she was waiting for him to say it. He would have anyway. "Not a hotel, Grandmadre. You will come to us for however long you need to and want to. Mi casa es su casa."

"Well, it was anyway. It was mine for about twenty years, until we got smart enough to realize, you know, about the new thing called a condominium, with a gardener, a repairman, and a manager to get them for you—and a doorman and valet parking and a swimming pool, which we had never had. There's room for one, you know. Would you ever do one, Emmy?"

"Not till the children are bigger."

"Bigger than what?"

"Bigger than sometime in a perfect future, should we be so lucky."

"You know that I say you shouldn't do it, and don't ask me why again. How is your father? Does he know? Do your parents know about your engagement to my precious grandbaby?"

"Mom and Dad are in Paris by now, asking to be left alone unless we, or the business, really, really need them. Instead of a condo, they bailed out of their Hollywood house to a big old Victorian on the way to the desert. I think it gives them much more trouble than the one here ever did. I still love the

Hollywood house. I go by it every once in a while. Somebody is keeping it up nicely."

"There is just no telling, you know, which place you are going to love forever. My first apartment was on Doheny in the first block below Sunset, and I always bless it as I go by. It was so chic! The studio did it for me, all Merle Oberon modern, black-and-white checkerboard floors with those hairy, white, Greek throw rugs. Lots of white on white and a mirrored entry hall that reflected the crystal chandelier. I was so happy there, all fresh-faced from the prairie.

"I very early had what is now called a great rack. Well, you know, not quite an Arlene Dahl or a Loren or Dietrich, but really good. Did you ever see the photo of those two staring at each other's décolletage?

"I preened and smiled at myself in those mirrors. Once I double-bolted the door and let my robe slide to the floor. I stood there without anything on and did Betty Grable poses in those endless mirrors . . . Oh dear! There's a big moth. It must have come up in the elevator because they can't fly this high, you know. Please, somebody swat it . . . Well, you know, maybe it was more than once in front of the mirrors because I remember that the white fur chubby and the high heels were the best, even better than completely nude.

"Don't look so shocked, play-Jay of the Western world. You understand, don't you, Mary Ellen?"

"Oh, I love mirrors too. Oddly enough, there's a mirrored room off our closet."

"Yes. Isn't there though?"

Emmy, visualizing the Ingénue watching herself growing older in that maze of mirrors over the years, suppressed her giggle. "Did you know that the famous shot of Betty Grable looking over her shoulder was taken from the back because she was pregnant?"

"Well, I didn't know that. I told you I'm the last to hear the latest gossip. You certainly couldn't turn your back on a room full of mirrors. I was, really was, so lucky. As third runner-up to Miss America, I didn't have to come to town eating noodles and, you know, begging at casting offices. I would have done it though.

"I think the chandelier was mine, but I left it there because it was so right with the endless mirrors . . . Oh dear, there's another one, the biggest moth I've ever seen. Someone swat this one too. You don't think they were a couple, do you?"

J. obliged with the front section of the *New York Times.*

"Anyway, I like to think that chandelier's still there."

"And so, Grandstar, it's been your habit to leave some of your stuff everywhere you've been? Lots of good stuff at our house, lots here. Anything in South Dakota?"

"Dear boy, how did you know? There's a little rolltop desk, but my sister's daughter won't send it to me. But listen here, you wouldn't believe what I get for the rent of these condos, so well furnished. Marina's been putting them out on three-month leases, martini glasses and all. I even could almost live on it, you know, without all that other great money.

"Your cousin Andrea, yesterday, was so surprised to hear about my rentals. I don't think she has a great head for business. Their side was always the product. Blaine is helping them a bit. He's put some of their money out in real estate with a New York company at 10 percent interest. That's pretty good, isn't it?"

"A little bit too good, isn't it?"

"Oh, I'm sure it's okay. They get statements every month."

* * *

"Listen, babe. She's going to be with us for the weekend and maybe some more. I'm sorry, and I'm glad. But the Grandloon will not be able to resist directing you on Sunday when we cut the new introduction. There's no getting around it, and there's no putting it off; we're scheduled. Will you please take your cell to her powder room and alert Alice that the Ingénue will be with us? It's going to be a bumpy ride, as they say, but the Hollywood-smitten committee is going to love it. I've been assigned the final

stuff for packing, and it's the albums, and you better believe that
I shall peek."

* * *

The Ingénue, Emmy, and J. took the elevator to the garage to
avoid the fans out front at the street.

"I guess my young people with the autograph books are
going to a late dinner too. I hope you don't mind that Marina
took your name in vain and booked us a table at the Senora. I
know for a fact that they have gazpacho tonight, and we deserve
a good margarita. I construe it to be on the way home, you know,
but not quite. I suggest we take Wilshire to La Brea, and then
Second Street is right there. Marina will catch up to us by the
second drink."

* * *

Under the pretense of going to the men's room, J. managed
to head off the margarita for Emmy, substituting a virgin one. He
was sure his grandmother would pick up on her not drinking and
immediately think her pregnant. "The gazpacho's great, tastes
like Spain," he said when he returned. "Grandseñora, you were
with us, weren't you, in Madrid? We fell in love with gazpacho.
Had it in every bar in the country. Then a barman looked at us
with contempt for ordering it after September 1."

"I do remember that, J., and yes, it was Madrid, our last stop
on that trip. We had to get you back, you know, for the start of
school. And do you remember before that in Barcelona, how
with your high school Spanish, you could still understand the
lisp? And do you remember your father getting stuck in the
elevator because they turned off the electricity for Catalonian
Independence Day? He never would tell us how he got out."

"He went off on business alone a lot of times. We wouldn't
even have known where to find him. Maybe your mother knew,
but nobody tells me. Sometimes it's as though they think I'm

dumb, but I got very good grades when I went back to school for my bachelor's degree. It's like the way they are always saying President Bush is dumb, but his grades at Yale were higher than his opponent's. Oh, look, those little corn rolls. That's what I come here for."

"I ordered some to take home for tomorrow, lots, to go with the vat of chili," said J. "It's a workday with a bunch of us there to redo the Elizabeth beginning."

"Oh good, I'm glad to be there, you know. I have some ideas. And you look lovely, dear. Your fingernails are like those of a hand model."

"Why, thank you, Ula. Your beloved grandson sent me to my nail lady with a picture from the filming, to cut them to match. They had grown since then."

"That's my boy, pretending to make a living noticing details."

*　*　*

"My Grandloon didn't fuss all that much. Alice did a great job getting the house angel to do beds and towels and such."

"Do you suppose, my dear husband, that your Grandlady is impressed with my housewifery, which, in her book, means mobilizing others to do a great job?"

"You do get it! I do love thee!"

"You aren't going to count the ways, are you? Because I love thee more than Elizabeth Barrett loved Browning."

"I love thee more than Bogie loved Bacall."

"Well, I love thee more than Turner loved Garfield in *Postman.*"

"Oh no, not on the kitchen table! Angela would be devastated. I love you more than Abelard loved Eloise."

"As much as Cyrano loved Roxane?"

"More, more, much more even than William Holden loved Jennifer Jones 'high on a windy hill when the earth stood still.'"

"I love you more than Victoria loves David Beckham."

"I love you more than Beckham loves that Spice girl."

"I love you more than Elizabeth loved Hilton, Wilding, Todd, Fisher, Burton, and Warren. I love you more than Hepburn loved Tracy."

"And I love you more than Tracy loved Hepburn, and probably more often. It must have been hard to get out of the house . . . That's not a good one, I guess. Rumor is that that story was a cover-up for her liking girls."

"Then I love you more than Samson loved Delilah?"

"Do you love me more than Arthur loved Guinevere?"

"I do."

"Well, I love you more than Guinevere loved Lancelot."

"Oooh! You trumped my game. Go to sleep." Softly in the dark, Emmy heard J. singing the tune to Lancelot's song from *Camelot,* if not his words. "If I ever leave you, / It would never be enceinte. / No, not expecting, / You big with child. / I've seen you when pregnant, /And I must have been there."

Emmy feigned exasperation. "No fair, you know I can't sing back to you. Go to sleep."

*   *   *

Emmy had risen early, dressed as she had for her introduction on the barstool, and headed toward the kitchen. J., with his finger in the script and noting that neither his grandmother nor Marina was up yet, was now walking toward a raised voice.

It was Angela, her back to him, facing off to Emmy. "Telling what to do, my kitchen, bring you pots, pans. Tell how cook chili. Good Catholic girl think you marry 'cause you say so. Act like su casa. No priest, no people, no church, no familia, no God, his name in vain. I hear out there alone saying the words each other. You think you marry. He tell me leave flowers. I hear usted a porto en noche, ahora sick, soda crackers, having baby, J.'s baby. Big ring. No marry J."

J. looked at Emmy and saw wide eyes and open mouth; she was frozen, with her pretty fingernails on her deep chili pot.

"Well, Angela, you've learned a lot in those night school classes, and I've heard enough of it. Go and get your purse and bring me your keys and the house credit card."

Angela was sobbing now, and when she returned with bag, keys, and card, Emmy was choking back bewildered tears.

"You may come back on Monday for your things. Bring someone with you. You've gathered a lot over the years. Mrs. Silver will be here with you. I know you share an apartment, and it may not be your turn to use it, so here is two hundred dollars for dinner and a hotel room if you need it. Take your apartment keys and your car keys and hand me the rest and the card. I will have your last paycheck for you on Monday."

"But the years, the años, los años. You mama, you mama, missy Karen."

"Exactly, I couldn't have said it better myself." He closed the back door behind her.

J. enfolded Emmy in his arms, and she rested her tear-stained face against his sweater.

"I know, I know, she's been with us a long, long time. And I will supply her a credible letter, but she proved not to be with us. Good to know that now rather than later. We're probably safe to wait until Monday to change the locks. It happened, so let's absorb it and acknowledge it. There's no way back. The past is for the past. Put it in the past, and let's get on with solving the problem."

Twenty minutes later, Emmy's housekeeper from her bungalow was in her new kitchen, surveying the pots and pans and disputing the chili recipe.

* * *

"Well, my dears, I'm homeless, you know, out of my old condo. It's already leased, with my stuff in transit and the interior designer still on the new place. I've given her till Tuesday noon to pull it all together, and then I'm going to barge in whether she likes it or not."

Steadying herself, her hand on the back of a barstool, the Ingénue stood, unannounced, for her performance. "Well, fellow film buffs, I thought our hosts did a beautiful job with the new introduction. Personally, I liked the old one, fish and chips and all. I liked the idea that the committee was hovering there. I would, you know, so like to be on the committee. What does one have to do to get on it?

"Now, I have some ideas, mostly about the committee and the credits. I love talking heads. I thought the witnesses in Warren Beatty's *Reds* provided some of the great moments of modern filmmaking. I would like to see each of you identified by name in subtitle, and you would appear and say what it is you do in our beloved business. You won't say your own name because nobody can say their own name, you know. Alice would be first as chairman and then would tell us her profession. I think it's associate producer, or is it associate director, dear?

"Let's roll that right now, and then you can edit as you please. I like the way you are all dressed, for a work session, and each of you perched on a barstool, like the old *Dean Martin Show*. It is the same barstool, isn't it? It was here in the house, I should guess. Some of you with a foot on the floor, like a standing position but not so static."

There was no opposing opinion. J. remarked, "Alice Silver knows just how to do that, perching with a cowboy boot over a rung and at the same time showing her Levied butt, as cute as it was in high school."

"Is that you, Jared Dunkin, out there in the dark making a girl blush?"

Director Ula smiled in triumph for it was just what she wanted, this small woman caught in full length, tossing her mane of yellow curls before she declared her profession.

Mason was prepared for today with a limerick:
"When her boyfriend did not use Cialis,
An impatient young woman named Alice,

Used a dynamite stick for a phallus.
They found her vagina,
In South Carolina.
That's all, if you wish to see Alice."

"Does everybody get a limerick?" asked Alice as she slid off the barstool into the dark that covered her blush.

Next, the woman with the black sculptured hair and black leather pants declared herself a makeup artist. Emmy remembered her from that look at J. at the back-to-work party, as though she had owned him and would like to again.

She presented herself and her profession, and when Joe was through photographing her, she turned to the committee and nominated Ula as a member. Scott's look at her might have killed her if looks could.

"No, no, my dear," said Ula. "You mustn't decide that in front of me. Secret ballot, you know, so if I get blackballed, I won't know who it was."

When Joe proposed to photograph her, she said, "No, no, my dear, we would have to have my special Ingénue lighting, you know."

She took great care posing Joe Silver's handsome, dark face with the pale luminous eyes for his turn. Scott moved behind the camera and declared that now with the associate director and the camera director they were bracketed with silver directors.

J. was surprised to see during the lunch break that Emmy's housekeeper's husband, Ruben, had appeared and was set up and ready to be barman. J. remembered that there was a second room, now storage, that could make an apartment of the housekeeper's current single room. Reward from disaster. Things were looking up.

Eric Gomez was the first to speak out. Emmy thought of him as "BB," for bearded and burly, for she had yet to remember his name, only that he was an associate director. He clutched his martini and gave his opinion.

"It's going to be talking heads, but that woman really knows her stuff. Getting all of us nonactors to relax and think about our feet. What a girl, your grandmother! I'm getting pretty excited about this whole project."

*   *   *

"It's my thing, not her thing. What am I going to do?"

"You and I are going to blackball her in case no one else does."

As Emmy and J. stepped out of the elevator, the dinner smell was familiar: the leftover chili, now to be eaten over a grilled hamburger. Marina and the Ingénue were already seated at the old round table in the bay window corner of the kitchen.

"I know you like chili burgers and Mexican beer, but there are none of the little corn rolls left. You will probably like her cornbread, though. I always have."

"What's with her husband?"

"Newly out of work."

"Good. I mean, too bad but good."

"My dears, I like this very much. Marina, could we get our lady to do this with the flakes of chips and then the cheese on top, with that nice texture like tortilla soup? I'm not sure we have any dishes that can go back under the broiler. I did embrace this kind of food rather quickly, you know, so different from childhood. But you can still get herring and boiled potatoes at my house.

"People tease me about being a Norwegian farm girl, but you know we had a general store and a heating and downspout company in town. My father's brother had the dime store, the Chinese restaurant, and the movie theater. Our high school was rather large 'cause the farm kids came in to school on the big yellow buses. My oldest brother drove one once. We thought blue jeans were farmer clothes. I now know them for what they are, you know, the last surviving national costume in the world and now the global costume. Levi Strauss made as much visual difference as Alan Ladd, vulcanizing rubber. Did you know that the very first Levi's had rivets on the fly too? They got burning hot on guys around the campfire. Clutching their crotches did no good at all."

Sometimes when she was talking like this, her thoughts could be deflected, even channeled, if you hooked into her subject. J. tried. "Did you put your boys in Levi's right away?"

"Almost, right after baby-blue rompers. There's that laughing picture of your father in his first Levi's, so long they were turned up to his knees. Jerry grew so fast and went through sizes so fast that they were hardly worn when I put them on Anders two years later. Our darling boys, so different they were. Anders was born with my coloring, all blond, to go with his name, after my father you know, but I think the blue eyes were the Irish kind.

"My J. J. thought I was too thrifty sometimes. The Depression here in the movie business wasn't like in South Dakota. We got through it all right, you know, but you never really get over it. I have enough for my shopper to bring me Judith Leiber evening bags for every night of the decade, but I still worry about losing my job or getting another part, not getting my payments from the sale, not getting my condo rents or the interest on my money in the bank, or my investments not paying off. They say that when you get old, you have great anxiety about the social security check if it's an hour late. Add that to the Depression of my girlhood."

"Well, Grandsweety, bank interest is a justifiable anxiety, but you look pretty well fixed. I'm not expecting to take care of you."

"You don't remember bank interest. It was before you were born. We were getting 13 percent from the savings and loan, and the business has done so well in the hands of those three generations of brilliant men. The great expectations that women have for the magic effects of cosmetics make for some of the world's great fortunes, you know."

"But it's been you, in the ads, who has made the promises of beautiful skin, though yours was inherited from generations in a freezing cold, seaside village. Were you and they very disappointed when I showed no interest in the business?"

The Ingénue seemed uncomfortable that the conversation had taken that turn. "I don't know. I never heard my two boys say that. When they were little, I put them out on the hill to play in their miniature Levi's. Dr. Spock said that was the way you were supposed to do it. You know who he was, don't you? The oh-so-popular baby doctor whose book was in every household for two generations. The front of the book edge is always grubby from parents turning it frantically in the night for advice. The back half is less thumbed because new parents gain confidence."

J. did remember seeing just such a book. "I've seen it at our house and at the house where we used to vote, both thumbed as you say. But do you think they were disappointed?"

"Who, dear, about what?"

"Grand-queen-of-denial, I know that you know what I want to know. Was it a lack of interest from my generation that made them want to sell?"

"Maybe it was your cousin Tim's too-great interest after his law school education that made them, you know, want to sell while the value was astonishingly high. You never heard that from me, dear. Or just as likely, they had worked so hard that they wanted to play. And they did. They put on their designer jeans and their wildly expensive lizard boots and went out to play, and their toy killed them."

*   *   *

With Ula still a guest at their house, waiting for hers to be finished any minute, they planned to meet for their Tuesday lunch anyway. Emmy was there ahead of J. It was usually he who arrived first, a tradition not lost on the waiter. "You are expecting, aren't you?"

She hoped he didn't notice her bewildered pause—could she be showing already?—and the moment she understood his actual meaning. Yes, she was expecting a lunch companion. "I expect so. To those who expect, much is given."

"What is given would be that diamond. I forget from one week to the next how extraordinary and gorgeous it is."

"I'll wait to order till he gets here, ice tea in the meantime."

"You don't need to order. I know what you always have. You've changed men more than you've changed lunch."

She didn't know whether she felt indignant or not and was glad that J. chose that moment to appear. "Oh my God, the black watch cap from the glove compartment. What happened?"

"The DNA, my appointment! The good news is that I'm still Irish, now evidently over 50 percent Irish. Here's your father's pen and comb."

He dropped them onto the banquette beside her. "They finger him as the prom date from Beverly High!"

On a vast intake of breath, the implications swept her face. "My God, you're my brother?"

"In the soap opera called 'Who's Your Daddy?' I am now your half-brother."

"The baby!"

"In the soap opera called 'Who Gets Aborted?' he does, and I get a vasectomy."

"What if it's a girl?"

"Well, would that make it different? I can see the headlines now: 'Hollywood couple with female fetus jump to their deaths in each other's arms from the top of the hotel where they met last February, while her father was traveling, out of communication in Europe. There was no note and no known motive.'"

* * *

"Daddy, is that you?"

"That depends on whose daddy you want. Is that you, Peg? Baby, what's the matter?"

"Where are you anyway, Daddy?

"Your mom's in Paris, and I'm in Frankfurt."

"What's the matter? Why aren't you together? Is something wrong?"

"No, nothing like that. You Hollywood children always worry, don't you? Always afraid you could get a worse parent, one that one of your friends had used up."

"No, Daddy, what are you doing there? You'll joke about anything, won't you?"

"Your mom's found an apartment in Paris. A five-story walkup, but she says the view is great, worth it."

"But what are you doing there?"

"I came to buy a very sophisticated piece of equipment. I'm going back to Paris in a few minutes. I'm at the airport. Now tell me what's the matter. Is everyone okay?"

"It's Emmy, and I'm not really sure what's wrong. She was sobbing and kept saying, 'Daddy, Daddy, Daddy.' I'm pretty sure she's pregnant, but that shouldn't be a problem. She's engaged to a great guy with the biggest diamond I've ever seen, though they've said they wouldn't get married until you're home. His name is Jared Dunkin. They call him J. She said for me to call you, and you would know what it's about . . . Daddy, are you still there?"

"I'm still here, baby, but I'm fresh out of jokes."

* * *

"Yes, Emmy, Daddy told me to tell you again to stop crying and hold on till he gets here. He said, 'Don't do anything; don't think anything. Just hold on.' He was able to get a direct flight to LAX in half an hour. He must have paid a bundle for that, or maybe not; maybe it's standby. He said he didn't call Mom because she didn't know when he was coming back to Paris anyway. So come on to my house . . . It doesn't matter if you or he is here first, and yes, I have scotch for J. I'm calling little sister Zoe too. It's always good to have a lawyer in the house."

* * *

As Emmy's father came through the front door pulling his leather duffle bag, J. had the distinct feeling he had seen him before, though maybe just in the mirror. He felt it necessary to have the opening line, and so he rose and said, "Well, sir, you do look like your half-brother."

Emmy ran into her father's arms and was then at a loss as to whether she should offer an introduction. "Daddy, you even have a four-day beard like J.'s."

"Your mother liked it. I had no time to grow it for this occasion. Em, darling, you must have noticed some other resemblance before this. Peg, sweet, scotch for me too. And then, kinfolk, let's sit down by the fire and talk. First, J., how did you find out the two stories, the story of your father's parentage and the story of yours? We thought we had raked over all the tracks."

"Let me just say that you did a pretty good job."

"You're right to maintain a certain belligerence. I have a more important story to tell right now though. You know how they got me out of trouble when I was fifteen?"

"She was the fifteen-year-old. You were sixteen."

"By your birth, I was, yes, but that's not on any certificate, is it? I'm curious about how you found out these details, but you need to hear this more than I need to hear that."

"Simple math played a part, Patrick."

"Well, Jared Damon, I can tell you that life became sobering. I thought about all this on the plane and realized I couldn't tell you the story without details. My father was not without pride in my early version of his own philandering, and not without his observation that the girl was very pretty. Mother was appalled. I was put into a new school and got a summer and after-school job for a manufacturer of advertising specialties. I found I loved business and manufacturing and went for my MBA later. My BA graduation present was a warehouse building in the Hayden Tract on south La Cienega, event buttons for a start. I took an order on the phone, followed by a deposit check in the mail, for 'He's My Guy' on a big blue pin-on button. She said it was for her husband's birthday party. What a great deal! How good to be named Guy and be cared about and given a party with 133 people on his thirty-third birthday.

"I didn't have a whole lot of business yet, so they were ready, 150 of 'em, packaged under the counter, when she came in. What a beautiful woman she was. Lucky Guy, huh? But no. He was dead. And she wanted to know if she was in time to get her deposit back.

"Of course she could have her deposit back, I said, and my sympathy with it. She couldn't hold the tears, and I came around the counter and reached for her because she needed a hug so badly. I'll never forget the smell of her, the feel of her and the baby bump against me. That woman was your mother, and that bump was you, my darling daughter—you, Mary Ellen."

Chapter 14

There was a profound quiet around Peg's fireplace. Emmy and J. turned to face each other and could have lit the room with their glow as the first implications hit. Emmy was first to give voice to the relief. "Oh my God, I'm adopted too! *We're not related!*"

"My dear, beloved daughter number one. You and your J. are not biologically related, but you're not adopted. Your birth certificate says you're mine. City Hall, in its chivalry, assumes the birth mother's husband is the father of her child. And I am your father in all the important ways, and it is a pleasure to be so.

"Adored hostess and daughter number two, where is more scotch? And cherished daughter number three, young lawyer Zoe, get me a flight back to Paris. I've got some splainin' to do."

"Are you kidding, Daddy? After leaving my kids with my husband and schlepping across town, do you think I would leave the room for one moment of this family drama that snoopy I alone knew would be coming up someday?"

"You knew about Daddy and J. and didn't tell me?"

"No, Em, about Mom being married before; her last name on their wedding certificate was different from her father's, and the certificate was hidden away. It was like a story problem, solved by a scrap of obituary for a man with that last name, who had left behind a grieving wife by our mother's first name—and how many Letitias were there apt to be? The clipping wasn't dated, and I didn't chase it as hard as I could have. I guess I never thought of it being about you, except their wedding date and your birthday weren't nine months apart, and I'd never heard you were a preemie. And I'd never heard any of this about Daddy's early daddying that's got us a brother."

"And that's where I come in, bought and paid for by my parents, and I didn't know by whom else until yesterday. My DNA had confirmed that Damon Higgen was my grandfather, but I thought that was through my father Jerry; I thought he was conceived from a secret liaison of Ula and Damon when they did a picture together."

"Am I the only one in the room who doesn't understand any of this?" Peg asked.

Emmy undertook to explain these begots. "And in conclusion, this affects you, Peg, because you now have that brother you always wanted when you thought you were only getting another brother-in-law. Well, you're getting that too."

"And Daddy has a son."

"But, Peg o' my heart, I always had a son, knew about him, went to his USC graduation."

"I'm going to write a book, a novel about Hollywood titled *Who Knows What about Whom?* Or maybe *We Had Him Last Year.*

"What would you know, Peg? You went to Buckley."

"And that, my three little darling daughters, was a great idea. Van-delivered and supervised, how could you meet an older boy from Hollywood High? I guess I never thought about you not being blood-related to him, Emmy. I never even thought about you not being of my seed. I was there to sing to you in utero, there to see you, all yellow-haired and bloody, slip from your mother. I held you before she did and loved you as much as she ever did.

"Now, stop crying, Mary Ellen. This is turning out very well, except that I now must tell my wife about my teenage indiscretion."

"It's probably the lawyer raging in me," said Zoe, "but didn't Mom know you didn't have a dog in the race when you went to the USC and probably high school graduations?"

"With my cousin Jerry to see his son? No. And the crowds were too big to see me, and I left before Jerry and Karen went to be with their kid."

"Didn't Mom think that maybe Jerry Dunkin was your half-brother when I thought maybe?"

"You're too smart for the room."

"That's why you sent me to law school. But enough about me."

"It was the jar lids for Jerry's Ingénue cosmetics that sent you to law school. You've seen them pouring out of the factory for years."

J. slid to the front of the sofa and picked up his glass from the coffee table, where the heat of the fire had nearly melted the ice. "So, Patrick, you kept in touch with my dad all that time?"

"Why not? He was, after all, my cousin, second cousin, I think, from Da's aunt being married to his grandfather, or did you know that? There was always that persistent rumor that he was actually my half-brother and your biological uncle. But only Ula Dunkin knows for sure."

"Well, my grandmother Ula just doesn't tell anything for all the chatting she does, but she did say that baby Jerry was a bit heavy for a preemie, and she and my grandfather laughed about it."

"He still could have been her husband's if they didn't marry until after she was pregnant," said Emmy. "The studio would have fired her for that too. That's all different now. J. has a friend who says you don't have to get married until your oldest daughter is big enough to be the flower girl."

"Well, first daughter, maybe you're the one to write the definitive Hollywood novel. I have some clippings that would fuel the plot. My father and his cousin J. J. evidently had a big fight over Ula that landed Da in the hospital."

Emmy was quick to tell him, "We've found the clipping, and there is that DNA too, which is valid unless you are O. J. Simpson."

J. had still another question. "Did we ever meet in all those years, Patrick? You would know. I wouldn't."

"Easter egg hunt, tennis. Your game was not great, but Da and I went with Jerry to see you run and you were first-class. I miss Jerry, gone before he knew we hadn't covered all our tracks. You didn't take up his beloved tennis or, thank God, his flying. He's gone to his personal cloud and left the business in other hands, but the jar-cover orders are still coming in."

"Well, Patrick, my friends there in management know a good thing and what they are doing."

"I still have friends in high places. Jerry was telling me at lunch one day about the good life after selling that mega business. His only problem seemed to be what to do with all that money. He told me a few ideas about placing some of it offshore. Be assured that's not what I'm doing in Europe, but I do have to get back. We have to give some thought to what to tell whom and what to call each other."

The lawyer among them took the stand. "Well, Daddy, I for one have to tell my husband everything. He's the soul of legal discretion. I have even told him I find Brad Pitt wildly attractive."

"But little sis, have you seen James Franco? Devastating! He lives in J. and Em's neighborhood."

J. could not resist adding that the man was remodeling and noting again, "Someone pounds three nails every morning at seven and then leaves for the day. Em hasn't seen Franco yet, but I think I can keep her. As for what to call each other, Patrick, when you come back, and I can marry your daughter, you'll be able to call me son-in-law. We hope it's before we have a flower girl or a ring bearer. My grandmother will be there, and now I can tell her to stop telling us not to marry without telling us why."

*   *   *

"I love them as much as ever. My dad, poor baby, still has that explaining to do in Paris. I don't feel shattered. He was so sweet. But how good to get away to my grown-up life with you, now not related."

"That's not like not having relations, dear lady of my desire."

"We could hyphenate our name, Higgen-Dunkin."

"That's the short-story version of my life—first I was Higgen, and then very shortly thereafter, I was Dunkin. Then I was an orphaned only child, and now I'm unorphaned and brother to four sisters and two brothers."

"Halves, anyway."

"Six halves aren't like three wholes, are they? I can't help but remember what you said about your family being so open, no keeping secrets from each other. What do we tell our son?"

"We'll tell our *daughter* absolutely anything and everything. I'm having a genealogical chart embroidered on beige silk and hung in the hall. I've picked up new entries for it, maybe a whole bunch of nationalities. I'll get the courage to ask my mother about . . . about . . . her first husband."

"Can your mother sing?"

"Yes."

"Then we know that it was he who couldn't. And you know something else, that he was a great guy, because he had 133 friends. You might meet some of them someday, and you may have a lot of new cousins."

"You have no idea of the cousins you've picked up. I've never counted the descendants of old Damon. They are legion, and some of them don't talk about it."

"Or know it."

"Or have proof of it, until DNA now."

"Patrick certainly wasn't very interested in how Dr. Prom Date is doing now, was he?"

"He was probably pretty mad at her through the blackmail years."

"I don't think she held him down on that fateful night, do you? Maybe she waded out to meet him."

"He's, uh, built like you."

"Hey, babe. The word is 'hung.' My sweet, uninhibited darling who read Erica Jong, gone all prissy when it's about her daddy. Jerry was hung like that too and my grandfather J. J and I bet Damon too, a bit proud of his son's early prowess."

"You're more than just a tribe of black hair and blue eyes, aren't you?"

"Ask your ob-gyn how many weeks I can go on illustrating that point."

*　　*　　*

It was Ula on the telephone when Emmy answered. "Well, my dears, I'm calling to thank you again for your hospitality. It was lovely and cozy to spend three nights in my own old guest room. I like that you like the house, keep it so nicely, and treat it with the respect the old thing deserves. Don't bother thinking about the women before you. It's all yours now. I was amused that you didn't know that you had more operable closets behind the mirrored circle. That's how well they concealed the touch latches for me.

"Well, you know I'm nicely in now. It's fun to see what Linda did with my things here among the new pieces. I look forward to your seeing it. She is very good, you know."

"I would know from the things she buys from me."

"I told her about your wonderful cat. She also thought I should get one for the look of it, like an accessory, you know, as well as the comfort and body heat on a cold night. She said I mustn't buy it, though. It has to be a rescue cat. Where did you get yours, dear?"

"I wouldn't buy one either. Thaibok was a gift, so small he could have slept in a fleece-lined soup plate."

"Sounds like a Dadist object, with a fur-lined spoon. Bet the kitten was from a man, much better than candy and flowers . . . Hmm, you are without comment?" She paused long enough for an answer, but getting none, she proceeded. "Dear, is J. there? If he is, please put him on too. I want to tell a little story."

"Hey, Grandlovely, glad you are happily moved."

"Hi, beautiful boy. The move in was not without mishap though. Blaine took my jewelry to his safe while I was in transit, and he brought it back to me last night. The doorman phoned up, and Marina met him where his Bentley was pulled up to the door. He opened the trunk, and they took the two Louis Vuitton cases out. The doorman opened the door, you know, and Marina was wheeling in my cases. Blaine had brought me a gift, one of those shallow cases for rings, all done up in oxblood leather with beige satin lining and my initials on it. Or so he describes it. He fishes, you know, off Baja, and he brought me also a Saks bag with albacore tuna in it. He was getting the fish and the ring case out of the backseat when a man in a hoodie came from the shrubbery and grabbed them. He must have thought Blaine was a diamond merchant with a full case. Marina threw my cases into the open elevator, pressed our floor button, and whirled around with her gun drawn. Blaine had tripped the man with his cane, but he was scrambling up and ran like hell into the churchyard that we're next door to now, and she wasn't about to get trapped in there. He held onto the ring case but dropped the tuna sack on the sidewalk. But what I called for was to invite you to dinner."

J. made a guess. "Tuna?"

"Grilled."

*   *   *

"Em, darling, what'll we do for a housewarming gift for the Grandloon? Do we stop by your showroom and pick up something?"

"It's already here, boxed and wrapped. It's a bowl by a ceramist named Polia Pillin, from the late forties. I've always thought she out-threw and out-glazed Beatrice Wood. It has abstract figures on it, a lot of black, pink, and lavender and a shot of turquoise. Ula's interior designer was in the showroom and approved it."

"Hey, what a girl you are!"

219

*   *   *

She already knew the portrait-perfect place for herself and was sparkling in the floodlight.

"Oh, come in, my darlings. I'm all done up in my finest. I'm so glad I still have it. What would I have done? Go naked to the premier of my picture?"

The room was indeed beautiful, smelling of new things and perfect flowers. Emmy saw that that some of the French chairs were of the period, superb. The beautiful screens and the Chanel sofa had moved with her. There seemed to be more mirrors than in her last rooms. Emmy made a bet with herself that the Tony Duquette chandelier was in the new powder room. It was.

"My dear Grandrefugee, it's very beautiful. I thought that part of the reason for the move was so you could be on one level, but you still have two steps up to the living room."

"One would think that, of course, but if you fall in the living room, you know, and can't get up, then you just have to pull yourself along on your fanny and throw your feet over the steps. I call that bun walking. See where this place has those attenuated sculpture-like wands in the doorways to pull up on, or just use to self-propel going by? Fabulous touch, isn't it?"

"Awesome! They look like Giacometti but without human reference. Maybe like Diego Giacometti's sculpted furniture with the birds on the rung."

"Oh my dear, I have one of those from several places ago. I paid a bloody fortune for it."

"Grandhostess, Emmy said your bedroom is pure diva, diva, diva."

"Well, you know, sweet boy, you fellows like that in a woman's bower. My J. J. would have liked this one, to slip into my satin, lace, and chiffon for the opening scene. J. doesn't want to hear this, but I do talk to my husband, and I do hear him. Don't think I'm doing these houses only for myself."

Just then Marina entered with a tray of miniature kebobs and drinks, hers included. She curled in the corner of the sofa, one foot under her. "Good to have Chanel with us still. I'm grateful to have Louis Vuitton with us too. It could have gone the other way. I guess your grandmother told you about our adventure. You already knew I was armed, didn't you? But the bastard perp got the ring case just the same."

Ula could not resist comment. "And you with all that cop instruction in your bower."

"So she is full of innuendo tonight. Actually, madam, I'm pretty good on the shooting range. Can't shoot 'em in the back, though, when they are running away with your stuff. Don't shoot 'em in the chest when they have their hands up either, 'cause when the shirt comes down, its hole won't match the bullet hole in the body. You would have convicted yourself. The cops got here so fast that the cell phone was almost as good as a gun."

"Grandvictim, wandering your new digs, I counted four places at the table, one of them left-handed for Wonder Woman here, so I conclude that Blaine isn't coming to dinner."

"No, he said he could go some little time without albacore for dinner. He likes the new place though. Unlike some of my male guests, he doesn't long for the chiffon and satin to wear himself. I do want that ring case. Do you suppose the police will ever find it? I have enough really good rings to fill it."

"And another besides, I'd bet."

"Well, my dear boy, I've had some time to gather them. Em, dear, what are you going to wear to the premier of my movie? I can lend you some of my big bling."

"That's very kind of you, Ula, but in my showroom, I always have something spectacular enough for even such an exciting occasion as this. Some of it is on consignment, and I always hope I don't get stopped by someone such as that man with the ring case."

"But dear, your shop is in a very good location with all those restaurants around you. They say that 'eyes on the street' is the best protection. You know, you've told me what you would do for your building with a lot of money, but what would you do for yourself personally? You already have the most gorgeous ring I ever saw, to go with this nonsense of getting married."

"And he didn't even look that prosperous when he picked me up."

"Like Anne's boy George, going on his first date with Alana, calling for her in a beat-up old station wagon."

"Emmy, she means George Hamilton. I guess I'd forgotten you knew Anne Hamilton Spaulding, Grandstar."

"Darlings, I was so star struck, and she was friends with Gloria Swanson and Agnes Moorehead. I used to go to lunch with them. They were so outrageous and funny. Maybe I was too. But seriously, dear, how would you indulge yourself? And don't tell me all your chocolates would be Godiva."

"No, I'd still want a full box of See's, only caramels, milk chocolate. I've thought about it, though, and the one thing I know is that all my clothes would have pockets."

"J. probably thinks that's amusing, but I think it's extraordinarily perceptive. And you know, the other thing is to know exactly where they are for the smooth gesture of slipping your hands into them and controlling the skirt. I learned that from Josephine Baker, not that I was lucky enough to go to lunch with her. When I was newish in town, someone took me to see her when I scarcely knew who she was. It was on a Sunday morning in one of those glorious downtown theaters. We had good seats in a house you know that was so packed that aisle seats meant sitting on the floor in the aisle. I later saw film of her from earlier years, and she moved like fluid, as though she could bend anywhere you know, wet clay without an armature. Older but still that way, while singing she slipped her hands—no, thrust her hands—into the pockets of a blue taffeta dress and gave the skirt a life of its own. I've practiced, you know, in front of my surrounding mirrors and thought perhaps I could do it, if maybe not as well."

"Can one do that and carry a cell phone and the scissors you feel you must have with you at all times, to open new packaging that can't be opened without 'em?"

"Oh yes, dear, and maybe box cutters too."

*　　*　　*

"The doorman was as glad to see our Packard as he was to see us."

"That's because it's more Deco than we are."

"How much do you think he knows about architectural history in Los Angeles?"

"Are you telling me that he transferred jobs to be with the Grandstar, not the new grand building? He must have seen Bullocks Wilshire. The architects of your grandmother's condo building certainly did."

"Is that a building you want?"

"I already own it from seeing it—and its little brother, the black and gold one on Wilshire, second from the northeast corner at La Brea. It's sobbing to be taken care of. I own everything that I like."

"What else can I get you?"

"The Taj Mahal."

"I've never been there. But I've seen Hagia Sophia, and I'll keep it."

"I'll take the Pantheon."

"There's a small hotel in the mountains above Florence."

"I've seen Neutra's Lovell House now, and I'd keep it."

"I'd keep the Mies Farnsworth House."

"I want the bar in his Seagram Building."

"I think I want the new museum in Cincinnati."

"I'd like a new museum in Los Angeles."

"I just hope my Grandloon likes and keeps her new art deco building. Personally, I would not choose to live next to a graveyard, even such celebrity-studded grounds, or maybe especially."

"You didn't say anything about that to her?"

"No! Maybe all she's seen is the pretty little chapel on the street. She may not have been out on her balcony yet."

"You didn't tell her our story, did you?"

"No. She doesn't deserve information until she gives some."

"You didn't ask her to this next work session, did you?"

"No! I think she may be blackballed. I didn't know where to get black and white marbles, so I got yellow and purple jawbreakers. I give you at least four nos, me, Alice, Scott and Joe. It would even be safe for you to give me a yes,"

"I always give you a yes."

*　　*　　*

The work session of the committee had begun early and broken for the breakfast buffet, laid out on the huge old table and well tended by Ru and Ruben. J. was pouring himself a second coffee and was about to finish off his breakfast with a miniature pastry. He was overhearing in silent pain an appreciation of his grandmother. "She really knew what she was doing, posing everybody. That should read 'every body,' two words."

Another coffee was now coming out of the urn before him, and a low voice beside him said, "Be not dismayed, old friend. There must be something in her Ingénue contract that limits other appearances. Remember that this film buff is an attorney and where I work."

J.'s relief and gratitude to Mark were profound and unspoken.

"Joe, could we run those through again? Remember, we went into that without scripting, and some said what they do, and some didn't name their professions at all. And what is the name of the whole project? And are we to be full figure or heads? Should we be saying the names of any pictures we've worked on?"

Text flashed on the screen:

THE COMMITTEE
ALICE SILVER

There she was, bright and animated, the signature hair looking forever damp as though just now finger-combed from a fresh shampoo. A powerful, small woman making it believable when she said she was the chairman and in production management. J. thought he heard a sound from Joe, very like a moan.

HARRISON KAHN

He was highly believable as the film editor he identified himself to be, slight and leaning forward as though over the sprockets of an old Moviola. More usually he had been seen with one beautiful woman after another and, for the last two years, a beautiful wife.

JON MASON

"Sound," he said emphatically, as though his sound was never to be lost. He wore jeans, of course, and a plaid shirt with a highly detailed, expensive vest with a color relationship to his cowboy boots, the good ones, with the working heel. He was bearded now after returning from that gig that had kept him out of the country for the better part of a year. Jon Mason's live voice came out of the dark, over the video they were watching. "Hey, Jared, man, this is such rich shit. You gotta drag everybody's expertise in here. Like in the next project, Olivier's *Henry V*. The hair, man, the hair was everything. It was so silly-looking, it's what you remember, and Elra can address that hair on camera when that one comes up. My mom talks about that picture all the time. Joe, man, you're still all set up, aren't you? I want to go on camera and sound and do a rough idea I had."

"Yeah, Mason, I'm all set. Go, go, I'm rolling."

"When my mom's mom was just out of Hollywood High and in art school, fashion design, they went on a field trip with the interior design students, to see Olivier's *Henry V*. She even remembered that it was in a theater that is now a synagogue, the marble one near Crescent Heights on Beverly. She was blown away and scribbled her own sketchbook full of those stylized costumes by Matilda Etches. The hair, though, is the most memorable thing, like mushrooms.

"Later—and it wasn't much later—she and her boyfriend were in line at Schwab's on the Strip, there where Laemmle is now, celebrating his first civilian clothes, just bought at the men's store around that curve. They got to chatting with a woman in line, and it was Matilda Etches. They sat together, and then she invited them to her house for coffee. It was in that triangle where Sunset used to turn sooner around the old garden of Allah Hotel, leaving more land out in the middle. Mom's mom floated from Schwab's across the street to Etches's studio and never forgot a detail of it, including that dinner at Schwab's was an amazing sixty-seven cents each. Of course, that was without coffee. We don't pass that corner without hearing that there used to be a house there, with a garden full of tropical plants, and that later it was a nightclub called Pandora's Box. Hey, guys out there in the dark, whaddya think? Can we do more of that? *We are Hollywood*! Jared, man, whaddya think?"

"Hey, yeah. Much more of that! That'll go as is when that movie comes up in the next set. Much more of that. That's who we are! Joe, how soon can you play it back?"

"Instant, man, instant."

"Great!"

"As is."

"Redo Alice with more about her acting career and kids."

"And Harrison, more about the movies he's edited."

"That's so terrific."

"More of same."

"More about parents."

"Yes, 'cause we're second—and third-generation Hollywood."

"Fourth."

"We don't have to assign positions except chairman, do we?"

"Let's play."

"Yeah, more. Let's do it and see if we're hot. Elra, you're on."

She posed from the memory of where the Ingénue had placed her, and her sculptured hair sliced across her face just as it had, as though the script supervisor had pushed it there once more. Those leather pants made Emmy think of the "Highwayman" poem she had been obligated to learn somewhere in school, with the boots that fit with "never a wrinkle," "pistol butts a-twinkle," "under the jewelled sky."

"I'm Elra Janick. I'm a makeup artist like my mother before me, and like her, I've been on an Oscar-winning team. My dad is the advertising man responsible for the decades of cosmetic commercials featuring the opalescent glow of Ula Dunkin. I'm a movie buff, but before I know the plot or hear the dialogue, I'm deep into seeing the faces."

"Good, good, good! You'll have your thing talking about the white makeup of Elizabeth and the suntan of her adventurous men. Good, good!"

Emmy found herself thinking this might be about three "goods" too many from Jared to this woman who it seemed still lusted after him. *Just wait till she sees the pregnant bump yet to come*, Emmy thought.

Catlike, Elra slid off the stool and turned it over to the tall host of the back-to-work party where this project had been hatched.

He looked into the camera, blinked at the light, and announced that he was Latty Jenner, electrician to the studios. "When I was a little kid, I went to a presentation by a man from General Electric. He called two ladies to the stage and said he could turn their hats to the same color. He did. He turned out the light. All your art for a movie, I can undo in a moment. I have the *power*. In addition to all this, like everyone else in Hollywood, I'm writing a screenplay. It's about a . . . well, it's about half-done."

Applause followed, and Scott slipped behind the camera, allowing Joe to put himself before it. Joe tried to present himself the way Ula had positioned him for he had seen that it was to great advantage.

"I'm Joe Silver, a camera director and cameraman to this production. I'm a fan of directors and think the films belong to directors and the camera. If they are lucky, they have good writers and stories as well as sets and actors of quality, and herein, they all have the good fortune of the dynamic person that was Elizabeth I. If you have a favorite Elizabeth, remember that it may be because of the director."

He looked smooth in his ever-present camel-colored turtleneck sweater and spoke with an authoritative voice, as becomes a director. He didn't mention that another part of his expertise was selling this marathon project.

Marina's cop was next, the very figure of physical fitness, waiting confidently for his calendar photo. "I'm Shelly Neuburn, a Beverly Hills police officer and a dedicated fan of the film products of my native Hollywood. My mother is in wardrobe, and my father has the prop room. His mother was Jayne Raine, and yes, we have a copy of that film."

He had an air of no anxiety about whether his performance was liked but was gracious when it was. There were several requests to see the Jayne Raine movie with him. Marina brought him a cup of coffee.

Scott was last for the night, carefully dressed for his part. He wore jeans that Emmy knew had been shaped to him by the tailor at the cleaners. From a Clark Gable movie she remembered that his tie would be called "sincere," and she saw that he had bought himself Bruno Magli shoes with his raise.

"I'm Scott Hamash, showroom manager, computer dude, and movie buff. I am most interested in the set and the authenticity of the things there upon. On the screen, I see the table setting before I see who's eating and the piano before I see who's playing, with some interest in whether or not they are wearing the clothes from the time they are portraying. Some films do it so well that my role is simply appreciation. All those years they were able to have the most gorgeous, shiny, expensive reference books, and now they have the Internet for reference, and I have it to check up on them."

Joe's voice came out of the sudden dark. "It's a wrap for now and lookin' good! More people later. We are twelve members as of now. Leader man, come on down and we'll give you some house light."

Jared leaned on the stool and held an arm out for Em.

"We've got some decisions to make. I think we have decided that we're going to be successful at this and keep doing it. There were references in what was just recorded that speak of this specific series of Elizabeth. So do we want to do new bios each time, or what? That cool thing that Mason did is down the line for the next series. Think upon it."

Emmy felt the need to comment. "Jared, I want to say how much I liked it, though who's surprised that Hollywood kids are all actors and write their own great material? I especially liked the family connections to the film business."

"Yeah, Em." Said a voice from the committee.

"This is the creative committee for a project, but we are also close friends of long standing. I didn't tell Em that I was going to do this, but here we are together, and I want to tell you something about how it is with us. I think you knew things about me that I didn't know, maybe as early as grade school, or maybe you thought you knew and weren't sure. Now it's known from intense investigation and DNA that I was adopted. With my parents gone, I'm not telling a tale that would hurt them, and it's too late to ask them if they mind my telling.

"You know that Em and I are engaged. Here, baby, show 'em your ring. Catch the light and sparkle the ceiling. We've been going through the engagement thinking we might be closely related. A predecessor of Em's was married into the family I thought was mine. Guys, don't try to figure that out. Women may understand the begots, but men don't.

"My biological mother was s a high school girl knocked up on her first prom date. She doesn't want anything more to do with me because she doesn't want to have to tell her husband about her past or acknowledge a half-brother to her three kids. I didn't like her much, but I am grateful to her for not aborting me and for whatever she did to get me so well adopted. I don't need to like her. I have others to like."

Just then J. and Emmy were elbowed out of the light by Mark. "This is going to get maudlin, and I want to talk. I personally don't even remember all the rumors I've heard about you and yours from grade school on.

"Look, I don't want to be on your committee, but I want to be your lawyer. It's time to have a contract among you—'cause this is going to work, and a prenup saves steps. I want from each, in writing, your ideas and your thoughts on creative control, share of costs, share of profit, screen credit, voting for who's in and who's out, applying for inclusion, blackballing, responsibilities, and whether you want me for your lawyer. No need to sign it. You know my e-mail. You need Ray on this committee, and you need an accountant.

"No longer any need, though, to vote on your first applicant for inclusion on the committee because someone found a clause in the Ingénue contract about conflict of interest. The Diva regrets. She still has a command performance in her, though, Joe and Scott and Alice to dinner on Wednesday night to show her the introduction stuff you just did.

"Probably see most of you tomorrow at the seven o'clock screening at the Guild; I have a girlfriend member again."

* * *

From his seat in the back of the Guild Theater, ten minutes before the house lights went off with their precise timing, he came down to stand before them, back to the screen. "Man. I'm glad you're here. These are my crowd scenes. I haven't seen 'em folded into the movie before, and I'm pretty nervous."

He didn't seem nervous and never had, even at their first middle school dance. He wore a biker's leather jacket, J. thought a size larger than that last time they'd met for dinner at Hamburgeer Hamlet.

"Yeah, I knew it was yours; I even calendared it. Would not miss it."

"Be kind. My wife sent me down to you without her 'cause she's holding seats that are considerably better than yours. How do you see the whole screen from here? . . . Yeah, wife. The flower girl got old enough for the job. Just our parents and our kids. She said it was late for the white dress. We're pregnant again."

"Hey, double and triple congratulations."

"Thanks, man. Save the twenty-fifth—reception at our house." Now he did seem distracted and returned to his seat, less than ten minutes left now before his crowd scenes.

"Where's his helmet? What do you think she's wearing?"

"Well, you'll see. After we went to dinner with them, you said she dressed like Bette Midler playing Janice Joplin, remember? We should go to that reception. Their house is a really big bungalow up Gower in full view of the Hollywood sign. I think it's a size four, maybe even a five. They will probably go to the Silver Spoon after this."

"They're not actually on the bike, are they?"

"Probably."

"And the reception? Somebody will sing 'The Object of My Affection' from Streisand's pregnant bride scene in *Funny Girl*.

"No, saving it for you."

* * *

Indeed, they did come to the Silver Spoon. The roar of the bike could be heard above the animated conversation and ice in glasses.

"Good show, man, good show! Glad you're back!"

"Look, listen! This is why you need us on your committee. We could be as one entity. Don't you remember how she and I met? Through our parents, both sets of our parents, archivists in restoration and acquisitions!"

Chapter 15

The members of the command performance met beforehand for a drink and safety in numbers, with plans to drive to Ula's together. Marina had invited her cop too, who did not wish to brave an interrogation alone if he arrived before they did. He gallantly took the fold-down jump seat in the Packard. J. was the only one not apprehensive about her exclusion from the committee, flimsy though it might be. He knew her for a lady and an actress.

"Oh, welcome, my dears. My doorman says you all came in the Packard. It goes well with the building, doesn't it?

"I have a cat now who goes so well with the room. I asked my shopper to find me just, you know, a cat—any respectable creature would do—but she brought me the most beautiful cat I have ever seen. She is all white with amber eyes, or so I remember. She is, you know, in hiding. We know she's here because she eats, poops, and sheds. Blaine says a cat will hide for two weeks.

"Let me see your images right away, straight through, and then we'll have drinks while we see them again."

* * *

"I, for one, did not regret her regrets but thought we accepted them with proper regrets. As dutiful chairman, I took complete notes, and we will surely use some of her suggestions. She is sharp, if controlling. We should be able to smooth up and finish the committee intro at the next work session."

"Alice, where are our kids tonight?"

"Only just now do you think to ask after your kids?"

"Well, you always take care someway."

"Our little MBA candidate is studying tonight and volunteered to look out for the others. The rest is pizza."

"From Raffallo's still?"

"Yes."

"Is Gloria still there?"

"You know she is; she told me you were there last night."

"Old haunts are the best haunts."

*   *   *

"My Garmin Nuvi got me to your house. I just don't know where the in is. Well, there you are. I see your head and cell phone behind a pile of rocks."

"Hey, that's not a pile of rocks; that's my house. Sharp turn to your right and sharp turn to your left."

"I haven't been out here to Palm Springs since I was working on a forensic thing for Sinatra, and my god, he's been dead for ten years."

"Here, let me take your bag. We put you in one of the more nearly conventional rooms. Em is on her way in, about seven minutes away, with tacos, pastry, and Starbucks. Want a seven-minute tour?"

"I need a two-year education. I don't get it, but I get it. Was your mom a genius or a madwoman? They must have pitched out all directions except how to throw a pot on a wheel."

"We thought this a good weekend to be out here. It's going to get hot soon enough. Now, in May, ceiling fans take care of it without the AC. And the pool's great."

Em came in a different way and appeared suddenly around a thick wall, announcing food, not sure if it was breakfast or lunch.

"We are so glad you could come this weekend. We are going fast with this project; it's sort of written itself. We're going to need some creative accounting."

"I don't know if you want it to be creative. Jared's mother was pretty good at that, or so I'm beginning to believe. Did you ever go to Switzerland with them? Germany? Belize? Did your mother have dual citizenship? Later about all that."

"Shall we run through a rough overview—the introduction, the committee, et cetera? See if you have any interest in this thing?"

"No, Jared, I really need to run through the soap opera that is you two. Remember, I found that alternate mother, and I haven't fit it all together yet."

"I haven't come to terms with what to tell whom and why. Em says she's going to have our genealogical chart committed to embroidery, framed and hanging."

"Charming. Who's your father?"

"She didn't tell me. Wouldn't."

"I couldn't get that either, but she exonerated Jared Richard Dunkin and said enough that I have a list of candidates."

"Yeah, I did that too, but now, I have the DNA report."

"Well, that means that you knew one or more possibilities to get the mouth swab or an object he used. Do you want to tell me or pay my fee while I figure it out? Because I can, you know. It's impossible to hide from a determined IRS agent, or a former one."

There was no holding back anything from this determined accountant. And when they were through, she congratulated them on their impending wedding and declared her mouth was sealed.

"Poor babies, you must have been in agony."

"Pool?"

"You just want to see if my legs are anywhere as good as hers. Well, they're not."

She walked down the beach entry, plunged in, and swam the long length, strongly. J. knew she would.

"Woo, is this a slot in the Grand Canyon, or is it a crevasse filled with spring runoff?"

"When does a crevice become a crevasse, I've always wondered."

"I'll get back to you."

Em had noticed that the accountant had her laptop with her and would probably have that information for them before sunset.

J. was now demanding that they address the second order of business: drink, get takeout, and watch the movie or watch and go out to their favorite Mexican restaurant. The guest was not slow to vote her preference and asked what drink mixes they had for her to make cocktails.

"And for takeout, how does the guy know where to ring the bell?"

"Been here before. Thai food okay?

"Very."

"Sweet and sour pork, pad Thai, Mongolian beef with green onions, California roll . . ."

"Shrimp, honey walnut maybe, and brown rice, and I brought some crackers with red caviar and that great homemade cream cheese from Tatiana's. It's in your fridge. And I'll make whiskey sours?"

Emmy looked pleased. "Everything is accounted for!"

The media room was a tower and, in plan, a spiral, so that most of the circle was lined with sofa. J. found himself caring very much what this woman thought of their film.

The caviar had all but disappeared, the screen had filled with the committee members identifying themselves, and J. had spoken when the Thai food arrived. The light was on only long enough for the cartons to be opened, and then Em was on the screen. She felt a great need for a drink, but of course, she didn't indulge.

The introduction slid into the movie, and *Anne of the Thousand Days* began. "Love this movie," their guest said in the dark.

When they had passed that first look at the toddler Elizabeth, red hair, in a gleaming white dress, J. proposed to stop the movie, for there was little more of her in it, and they had all seen it before. Two women's voices said no. And the guest asked if they were equipped to pause when she asked him to.

They were, and she did, and he did. She asked for that pause in the trial scene, and the picture stood before them like a still photo. "That's my father, a stalwart breed, a working actor. You have seen him hundreds of times and not remembered him once. He's gay. I grew up with him and his partner."

"Where's your mom?"

"Split."

"So your soap opera isn't 'Who Is Your Daddy?' but 'Who Are?'"

"You got that right. So where's the film?"

The lights were on long enough for a Baileys Irish Cream to appear along with the rest of the movie.

*   *   *

"As an accountant, I'm always trying to figure out why. Why is this the most fascinating character in history except maybe Lincoln?"

"As an historian, I'm always trying to answer stuff like that. What's the commonality in those two? Is it leaping ego? There was a lot of that in others too, not so interesting."

"They were both masters of PR, and judging by the attendance at exhibits of each at the Huntington, they still have fans."

"Is it genuine love of country? What about the current set of political candidates? We've got a proven love of country in one of them. He'll kill 'em in debate."

"I don't like anyone. Next! Send in another set of résumés. I'm going swimming. We address the mysteriously missing money in the morning."

In the morning she was up before they were. They heard her in the pool. The smell of coffee brought her out of the crevasse in the rocks, stretching and toweling. "Nice to have money, and I flat-out love the way they spent it. I'm closing in on the way they saved it though.

"By the way, I really do like your project. I'll write you a proposal. You do that personal sponsorship very well. You're pretty people. Ever tempted by the actor business?"

"No, you?"

His compliment got half a smile and a no.

"Nor I," said Em. "In plays at Buckley, I always wanted to stage 'em, not be in 'em."

"And there was the teacher wanting to use the inherited acting ability of the famous Damon Higgen. So who's your daddy?"

"Always and forever Patrick Higgen!"

"Hero worship. I like that in a woman. Does she feel that way about you too, J.?"

"Of course."

"Well, I wish I knew more about the alternate Dunkin parents. It's somewhere in that damn corporation they formed after the sale. Did you know that that fool accountant who manages for you is new? He's what we in the IRS called a UP, which stands for 'unqualified practitioner.' Ula Dunkin doesn't use him, does she?"

"Her half is way separate from ours. Remember, she already had her money with the death of my grandfather. I'm not even sure when my father and uncle got their money. They were spending pretty well while their father was still alive and after he retired."

"Eventually, I will know everything, and you may not love it . . . Tell me about the ubiquitous actress lady, aging so beautifully on every little screen in the known world. Is it a job or family loyalty?"

"She's paid the going rate for legends and will go on and on, even if they have to spackle her. She loves the role and the extra money with which she can buy up the rest of Wilshire Boulevard.

"She's in charge. She's no dummy, but she has experts for everything. The business manager is 'Bizman.' The nurse who comes by three times a week is 'Wren' for registered nurse. Her interior designer, who brings flowers twice a week and sometimes French chairs of the period, is 'Idee.'

"Let's see, her physiotherapist is 'Fizz,' and her personal trainer is 'Petey.' Her investment advisor is Irv, which may actually be his name, not short for anything. She listens to Blaine but does not do anything he suggests, no investments anyway. And the doorman, with whom she plays Ethel Barrymore, is called 'Darling'—not 'My Darling,' just 'Darling.'

"Marina holds it all together. You would never call her by a nickname though. Emmy is 'My dear,' and I'm called 'Adored baby boy' and other such things. For me she is the passive-aggressive 'Grandloon,' though I do not say this to her face. I adore her and consider it a great privilege to be hers, even if I'm not. She may know everything you need to know or nothing at all."

*　　*　　*

"Will you two be staying over? I'll be going back directly after the late lunch at the Mexican restaurant that you claim has the best margaritas in any town, where we'll have some more time to talk."

"Yeah, here only till after lunch tomorrow. Em has to get back."

"Tuesday, first thing, I have to look in on the preview of an auction, Charlton Heston costumes and the golden tablets," Emmy explained. "I'm starting to do a business in beautiful costumes in cases that swing out from the wall to see both sides. Moses anyone? What I really need to get back for, or stay for at this TV, is the last night of *Dancing with the Stars*. I'm betting on Kristi Yamaguchi to win."

"You may be right, but I question whether gymnasts and ice stars are not already dancers."

*   *   *

"Well, she's not all bad. I don't think her fathers gave her any architectural background, but she seemed to dig the house. She made a couple of efforts at word descriptions. And no contempt. That's always good. I guess we can invite her again. I wonder how Philip Johnson chose houseguests for weekends in that pristine box of his in Connecticut. They would have to pledge not to litter the Sunday paper. It's my favorite house in the world, but I'm not sure I could live in it or, rather, live up to it."

"Dear one, you could hire someone to follow you for pickup of shed shorts and socks, notes and scripts. And for picking up after me too, I guess, though I'm four stars neater than you are. If you love that house so, why don't we search out ubertalent and build?"

"I guess this one will do for the state of some art or other, for now."

"Yes, but it's not in Hollywood."

"Waking up this morning, I was doing some thinking, and there is something missing from my monologue, something I need to say about motion pictures: We are the only species with stories. It's one of the great gifts that evolution or creation gave us, separate from other species.

"Your beautiful pale-eyed Malamute dog may joy in the snow when you take him to Big Bear, but his mother wasn't able to put in with his instinct the story of how she was on the winning team in the Iditarod three years ago.

"There were stories in prehistory, oral when we started to talk and written when we learned to mark letters on a clay tablet. There were cave paintings and sculptures, telling a story. There was myth, then history. In our need for story, we began making it up, and it was called fiction. We acted it out, and it was called theater.

"We drew, and we painted and cartooned. *Dennis the Menace* is a short story a day. We got the camera and photographed pictures to become history, and then we began to move those pictures to fulfill the insatiable need for story and the child's constant question: 'And then what happened, Daddy?' And when you're through with the story, he demands, 'Again.' And don't we too? Have you seen *Casablanca* yet this year or a *Hamlet*, a *Carousel*, or any of the many Elizabeth I films?

"Lately they fulfill the need for story faster and faster—consider movies with staccato cuts like a handheld camera in an earthquake."

"Jared, my dear love, there's your thesis for your PhD."

"Hot damn, maybe so."

"A little art history wouldn't hurt. Also, I think it's a book, a picture book with the progression of civilizations through their primitive periods, their high periods, and their dissolution and their own storytelling in pictures, the descent into sentimentality, et cetera.

"On a parallel tangent: Remember last week when I absented myself for an afternoon to hear a friend's presentation of art to a gathering of mostly Jungian shrinks? It was like a thesis, hitting on the importance of the unconscious among other themes. One thing I took away with me that I had all but forgotten from school was the importance of *contrapposto*, that wonderful moment in the progression of sculpture when the statue was no longer static and frontal. Its weight and balance was now shifted to one foot, giving it the visual potential of continuing to move. Paintings, too, started to look moving, natural, and on and on to the motion picture.

"And remember the remarkable ability of humans for storytelling, that we can think of the next thing we are going to say while we're still talking."

"Great, I don't know where that works with what I want to say, but it's in."

"Wow, I'm liking it. Do you want to write now or swim?"

"You know what I want to do."

* * *

"Mom, Mom, Mom! No, I don't want to Skype. I need to hold you tight. I'll play with Peg's kids until she gets you back to her house from the airport. I want to be there when you get there. Are you okay? Are you sure you're okay?"

* * *

"J., darling, shall you be going with me? I can't see how this drama plays out."

"I think I shall if only because I don't want you to be driving in the dark in a heightened emotional state. Tears flood visibility.

"It's going to be hard for me for a while to remember who is related to whom and how, maybe even why, but does it matter?"

* * *

"I like your mom, starting with how much she looks like you, so much so it's hard to see room for you to look like your bio father at all."

"She says I do—the pale-blue eyes, moons on all my fingernails, and his sister's legs. She says she doesn't think about him much to remember him. They hadn't been married long, though they had grown up as neighbors. It was tender of you to go off and watch a movie with Daddy and host Gary."

"It worked. I didn't have to have a serious conversation with Patrick. I'm not ready, and he was jet-lagged."

"Mom was a little hesitant about talking about falling into Daddy's arms so soon after the death of her husband. She found herself sobbing her grief against the chest of the most beautiful young man she had ever seen. She said it's known that a woman is never so vulnerable and sexually needy as when her husband dies. From the funeral to the nearest pickup bar, it's said. She has read a novel about that—a great movie if anyone had the courage to try it. To make the movie, I mean, how would you pitch that?"

241

"The low budget it would take, maybe? We have a lot of good cemeteries here to choose among, and a bar is an inexpensive set. Did she love him? That didn't seem to bother Patrick."

"Well, I think she was all prepared for that question. She said of course she did. She went on a bit about the expectation that they would marry, about the two families and the Lithuanian mothers—new immigrants, friends, and he much older, graduating from college when she was going to her first dance in junior high. Oh J., I know his parents! When my mom took us to her parents' house, to the Remingtons', their neighbors were often there, my other bio-grandparents, as it turns out. They had to act like just neighbors, Mr. and Mrs. Lucas, when they saw me and not hug like grandparents do. How awful for them."

"You have to go and see them, and you have to invite them to the wedding. How old do you think they are? They have to hold our baby! Will he have Lithuanian eyes?"

"My God! I'm not Irish anymore. Will you still love me?"

"Will you still need me? Will you still feed me?"

"Oh yes. Always. I love that song. Could we have that at our wedding? Could we have the Lauritz Melchior recording of 'Because'? He was Damon's neighbor on Mulholland Drive, and he used to play it for us."

"You can have anything you want, except him in person. He died, when I was about three years old, I think."

"How ever would you have remembered that?"

"He made five movies, that's why, and I was jealous of his voice."

"I wouldn't have known that he was better than anyone else if they hadn't told me. So you can sing to me."

"Oh, how we danced on the night we were wed."

"So where shall we have our wedding? And soon, before I blimp up."

*　　*　　*

Around her favorite tree, the air had that look of palest violet that in a few days would turn to a crowd of bloom on the bare branches. Emmy parked her car in her reserved space behind Stuff. She pushed open the iron gate to her courtyard and gasped in pleasure at the sight of the jacaranda tree and in gratitude to whomever had brought jacarandas up from Mexico.

On the way back from the desert, in some warmer spots, its blooming was a little further along. J. had been reminded of seeing Nairobi full of such trees, blooming in October.

"Hey, Em!" Scott handed her the phone. "For you."

"Oh my goodness, yes," she said after answering. "I'm thrilled that you remember me. That was the day I delivered that fabulous jewelry chest. We met in the bathroom of our client's new house. I remember our telling her together what to do to neutralize her overly pink tiles without replacing them. We agreed that aubergine would do the trick. I said an aubergine folding screen and you said an aubergine velvet robe . . . Yes, I saw on the news the gorgeous pink wedding dress you did for her. What, no aubergine? Loving the tableware you're doing and your house that I saw pictured in one of the magazines . . . What, you were in when I wasn't here? I'm so, so sorry to have missed you! What is it you're looking for now? . . . Oh! Oh my goodness, what a remarkable gift! I'm overwhelmed! I shall be there . . . Goodbye."

Scott came back to the counter to wrap a customer's purchase and could see that she indeed was overwhelmed when she told him about the call. "You are kidding me—the dresses for the wedding? By Vera Wang?" he exclaimed.

"His grandmother said she would fund anything I wanted as long as it all had pockets."

*　　*　　*

"Daddy, remember when I was a little girl and planted my first garden under that jacaranda tree at the old house, and one morning the tree had begun to shed, and I thought my planted flowers had come up and bloomed in the night?"

"Yes."

"That's why your yard there is full of jacarandas, isn't it? Because of me."

"Yes."

"It would be a perfect setting for a bride in that color, wouldn't it?"

"Yes."

"How about we have our wedding at your house?"

"Yes."

"How about the trees? Will they still be in bloom in three weeks?"

"Yes."

"How do you know?"

"I'll hold 'em back."

"You can't do that."

"I'd do anything for you."

"J. and I are paying for the wedding."

"No, I always buy weddings for my girls, but you better hurry along before you start to bloom too."

"Oh dear, how did you know?"

"I guess. And I hug."

"That and Peg told you."

"That too."

*   *   *

"Hey, baby daughter! It's been only ten minutes. So is this the same telephone conversation or a new one?"

"It's not exactly a continuation of the last one, more like an alternate. This must be what marriage is like. Jared has a whole different idea of a place for the wedding. He wants it to be in the room where we met. I was voting for Hillary in the hotel ballroom. He wasn't. Daddy, did you know he's a Republican?

He may have even booked the room already. I'm okay about it. Our friends won't have to travel so far, though you will."

"That works. From the upstairs ballroom you can still see jacarandas. Do I have your leave to call Jared, and then I'll call there for the rehearsal dinner in the restaurant? And on another note, is it going to break your heart when Hillary doesn't win?"

"But Daddy, she will! J.'s grandmother says that Obama keeps calling for change, change, change, and if she were there, she'd give him change. She'd throw a handful of pennies at him."

"So that lovely old lady plans to go to the inauguration, does she?"

Chapter 16

J. had begun to realize that he could indulge himself in most anything he wanted, but he added the rationalization that the sports car he had been driving these past two years was not much of a family car. This new Aston Martin had surely the best smell in the world after newly sawn wood, mowed grass, and freshly showered woman. They took it on its maiden outing to the friends' wedding reception up Gower, in full view of the Hollywood sign, hoping the parking valet would not administer the first scratch. Em thought seeing it driven off might be like leaving a firstborn for the first day of kindergarten. The parker, experienced and cool about cars and probably seldom impressed, smiled in pleasure at being 007 for three blocks. He returned it in apparently pristine condition.

"Great wedding—or rather, delayed reception. Maybe delayed wedding too, by the age of their children. Are they in the swing of our marathon project or what? Did those clothes look Elizabethan to you?"

"It's called vintage by us, purveyors of stuff, but I didn't know it was available from much before the twenties of the recent century."

"Weren't those reenactors' costumes?"

"It was a reenactment anyway."

"Like my Grandloon, they have friends at the studios."

"J., I do really love their house. It's my favorite kind, with the pop-up roof for the second story opening to a sleeping porch, and the color job is terrific—khaki and grayed teal, with a crazy little trim shot of plum and terra cotta. It's very knowing. Someone did a very good job. It's nowhere as rumpled as they are. I hope she knows what the little table we brought is."

"What would *Antiques Roadshow* say it is?"

"Stickley."

"Wow. That's one of the basic food groups—Chippendale, Sheraton, Hepplewhite, Stickley, Maloof, Eames, and Mies, isn't it?"

"How did you know all that?"

"It's history now. You give the best gifts in town."

"I have a lot of stuff."

*   *   *

"Have you thought about the fact that we'll get a lot of loot?"

"When I've moved in the rest of the household goods, it's going to be more than 'plenty of plenty.'"

"And that's aplenty for me," sang J., channeling *Show Boat.*

"Really, the guest list has burgeoned exponentially. I swear you have everyone on it except maybe your barber and the waiter at Clafoutis. How about your gym mates at Crunch and your marshal arts class and your entire graduating class from Hollywood High?"

"Damn, how could I have been so forgetful? Maybe I still can add 'em. The invitations haven't gone out yet, have they?"

"Scott's doing them. His graphic design is really good. The envelopes are mostly addressed."

"My god, I didn't think of it before: whose daughter is marrying whose son?"

"How about this?" she said as she scribbled on an envelope:

You are invited to attend
as
Mary Ellen Higgen
and
Jared Damon Dunkin
are joined in matrimony
as
Mr. and Mrs. Jared Higgen-Dunkin

"Is it too much 'as'?" J. wondered. "It solves a lot of problems. And shall we say, 'in the room where they met'?"

She conceded, "Maybe we need 'daughter of M&M Patrick Higgen' and 'son of the late M&M Jared Richard Dunkin.'"

"What if we told the truth and said 'daughter of the late Guy Lucas and Letitia Remington Lucas Higgen' and 'son of Patrick Higgen and Dr. Katleen McCarty.'"

"Now, Jared the twenty-third, that ought to confuse our friends. Where would they send the gifts? Are you trying for the whole cast of your soap opera, *All My Parents*?"

"Okay, but what about gifts? We don't need them, but I don't think you can even say 'no gifts' on an invitation. That's rude but practical or practically rude."

"Why don't we register at some hot places on Rodeo? Then when guests go there, they can be handed a pretty little note that suggests a contribution to Union Rescue Mission instead."

"Yeah, Tiffany on Rodeo would be lovin' it."

"And the truth is that part of me wants some gifts."

"And the truth is that you're crazed over merchandise."

"Things are my thing."

* * *

J. had given his grandmother a shiny new cell phone and lessons on how to use it and had programmed his own number into it.

248

"My darling boy, I am so excited," she said when she called. "It's going to be at the ArcLight. Isn't that fitting, so close to the Palladium of my youth? You have no idea how wonderful Stan Kenton was—and Jimmie Dorsey and Tommy Dorsey too. I was too late in town for Glen Miller. Did I think I'd still be doing it all these years later, or rather be doing it again? The answer is yes.

"I'm sure your pretty lady knows what to wear. Does she have something reasonably spectacular but not spectacular enough to outshine this diva? I don't know who will escort me to the premier. Blaine is away, crewing on the ship of friends, going around the world. What would you think of it being your newly divorced cousin? Andrea and Tim and spouses will be there too. How is that going to work?"

"Hey, Grandwonderful, I'm civil. I never threatened to sue the Anders three."

* * *

Out there along the dark fence beyond the red carpet, they could hear the whispering in loud hisses. Emmy was delighted to be the subject of speculation. "I can hear people saying, 'Who are they?' and once I heard someone say something about my coat."

"Well, it is the wildest thing I've ever seen. Where did you get it? I've never seen that in your closet."

"Afghanistan. It walked into the showroom with some other ethnic costume things, and I squirreled it away, totally in love with it. But damn, it's heavy, all these little shields like tiny tuna can tops sewn on and then this chain fringe."

"You light up a sparkle on the ceiling of the canopy. Even more than the paparazzi flash."

Just then Jared heard his name called and turned, expecting to see a friend, but he did not. So he did the smile and wave that was customary in his native village. "That must be from when I was enlisted as escort about town to those little cosmetic queens."

Andrea, separated from him by their grandmother, swung around to look and lay a fog of displeasure over the procession. She brightened for the cries of "Ingénue, Ingénue!" and then did a little smiling at the crowd herself.

Emmy thought her a good-looking woman, dark and tall with that nice skin they all pretended came from their bottles and jars. She looked a bit like J., as did her brothers, in spite of the many degrees more of genetic separation beyond what they knew existed. They seemed stolid and a bit uncomfortable. Her husband was blond like her father had been. Tim's wife was trophy blond.

In whispered aside, Emmy asked J., "Do we invite them to our wedding?"

"What gift do you think they would bring?"

"Something edible and deadly?"

*   *   *

"Inside the theater, Em and J. were seated at Ula's left, the cousins at her right. The lights and the camera found her in the audience, and she displayed no signs of anxiety. Her fingers were crossed, though, when she put her hand on J.'s knee and said, "I'll have to go home with the fella I came in with."

"That doesn't muck up the Chateau Marmont celebration afterward, but we'll park at home and climb down the incline. If I can't get near you, do remember that I will have known you were brilliant, and I adore you."

"Of course. Our souls have been together in other incarnations and will be again. I love what dear Emmy is wearing and her taste in men."

*   *   *

"Grandmegastar, you got up early, didn't you, to see the paper and field the calls? Your line's been busy for an hour . . . I knew you'd be brilliant, and you were brilliant. The *Times* said you were brilliant too, mentioned that Oscar word, and printed your picture on the Calendar section, front page. The *Hollywood Reporter* will be loving you. We're proud, proud, proud—so happy for you we cried. Yes, we will come for dinner. I thought you'd never ask."

*　*　*

She was dressed in the most unlikely of garments—a bias-cut gown in white satin, floor-length, and in the back a bit longer.

"Are you Barrymore or Harlow tonight, Granddame?"

"Presently you shall see."

Marina was in black pants and boots with a white top that had the look of a military uniform, or so J. thought, or maybe the uniform of a lion tamer.

Her martini half down the swoop of Baccarat crystal, Ula rose in full dramatic intention, satin pulling diagonally across the curves that were remarkably still rather like they once had been. She glided to the bedroom door and disappeared. Then she glided back, and when she was well into the room, they saw that she was trailed by a white cat, as beautiful as a cat could be. A large cat was she, the coat short and dense, the tail high.

"She came out of hiding on the tenth day. We are absolutely devoted to one another. Her name is Harlow. I wrote a poem about her:

She's a perfect cat,

She's where I'm at."

Ula sat on a French chair, and the cat executed one of those perfect gymnast's jumps and landed on her lap to be stroked. She looked around with amber eyes.

"She is very vocal. She says 'Hello.' She can't manage her Ls, so it sounds more like 'Herro,' you know, but she only uses

251

it appropriately, like first thing in the morning. She's working on her name, 'Harrow.' At night, she even sleeps on my stomach."

"Isn't she heavy?"

"Heck no, mister, she ain't heavy. She's my cat."

Dinner was announced.

* * *

"That last session of the committee picked off a lot of the problems, but there are two more permissions to go. Also, we have to get back into our narrative to pronounce Robson as 'rob' instead of 'robe' the way we were doing it. I can't understand how this many detail-oriented types overlooked that mispronunciation. Flora Robson—Dame Flora Robson, that is. I looked at her bio to be sure. What a girl, pages of credit. She played Elizabeth again, at the other end of her career, 1970, at the Edinburgh Festival."

* * *

"Too much for Saturday. What would be better than a cool movie on a hot afternoon? Let's go to the four o'clock screening at the DGA."

"It's *Chronicles of Narnia*. It'll be full of screaming kids. Will you be okay with that?"

"Maybe I better get used to it."

* * *

"Thanks for picking me up at the showroom. I did owe my business that three hours of attention."

"Hey, look—the sky over the hills is smoky. Flip on the radio. Let's not go in until we know what it is."

"Oh no, the back lot at Universal. That burns jobs."

* * *

It was Sunday morning, and they sat with the *Times*.

"Yves Saint Laurent died. He was only seventy-two. I thought he was an outstanding genius, but I was also mad at him for designing a cigarette."

"The fire's under control."

"Look at the fabulous photo of a street full of jacarandas."

"Does the caption say anything about the anger against them for the mess they make?"

"I don't want to hear it."

"Do you want to hear this one about gay marriage?"

"Are they getting it?"

"Doesn't look like it. I'm not threatened by it, but it sure needs some other vocabulary. You need to know which it is when a guy talks about his wife."

"Scott says both men call themselves husbands."

"Yeah, you ask a guy if he's married. He says yes, and you have to ask, 'To a husband or a wife?'"

"The worst thing in the paper is the news that Hillary seems to be losing. How could that be?"

"It must be an Irish name, O'Bama. Get used to it—he's your candidate. But we're going to beat him."

*   *   *

"I usually love Wednesdays, unassociated with either weekend, but this one could have never come. Hillary Clinton is going to Diane Feinstein's house in DC tonight to concede to Obama."

"Now he will be your candidate, and you will have to cry again when he has to concede to us. Could we just chuck the whole campaign and go get married before we get involved with them?"

"Yes, 'the days dwindle down to a precious few,' and we could elope if it were not for Linda and Heather White, that mother and daughter partnership so deeply involved in the design of the wedding. And Alice too, with so much completed.

Would it have been gauche to say on the invitations that it's catered by Wolfgang Puck and designed by White Interiors, with gowns by Vera, jewels on loan from Stuff, and groomsmen from Hollywood High? We could have done it like screen credits."

"Look, my Dr. Berber is in the comics today. I swear she's a redhead."

"The first lesbian weddings are tomorrow. Do you think there will be any bride figures left for our cake in three days?"

"Is everything under control?"

"I doubt it."

"My Grandloon said she was coming over today. What part does she play?"

"She plays the scribe. Her handwriting is beautiful. The prairie school evidently insisted. She said it was called the Palmer Method, but she learned a fine Italian hand too. That's what Elizabeth wrote. Before art school, I thought it meant that everything the Italians did was fine."

"Invitations long out, what's she going to do?"

"Double-check the guest list returns. And I have something to show her."

*　*　*

Emmy had had no intention of going back to the showroom after she had turned the whole thing over to Scott on Saturday.

But his Sunday text message had sounded, if text messages can sound like anything, frantic for her to meet him at the showroom. He was not given to panic, so she went immediately, only to find him purring over an object that had come in on Saturday. It was the most beautiful piece of lace she had ever seen, handmade, a square of it, with tiny pearl strands braided into the edge like fringe.

"This will be fixed with pins into your hair under the veil. I took a photo of it and e-mailed it to Vera, who says yes."

"Hey, I told you to take over, but this is ridiculous."

"The pearls can be combed into your hair."

* * *

As Emmy returned home, Marina was just arriving as well, carrying a pink box. "Ula passed up three other donut shops but then fell for the one still leftover on your near corner. Could not resist. Is there coffee going?"

"Ruanna has just put up a pot."

"But you call your housekeeper Ru."

"Yeah, and her husband is Ruben. J. calls them the Rus."

"I'm in the market for a pair of couple names in my book. Would it be okay to use those?"

"I can't think why not if they aren't the bad guys or they don't get killed or have the same last name, though you will be tempted by theirs; it's Ruiz. We'll ask them. They might like it— or not. How's your book coming?"

"Momentarily bogged. My advisors on legal and police stuff have left me dangling on a plot point I got myself into. Hey, Ru brew is really good."

Marina watched in amusement as Emmy held off until Ula had selected her choice from the donut box before she swept up a French Maple donut, a generational alpha struggle that only a writer, or shrink, would love or notice at all.

"Alice set you up with the list and return cards on this table," Emmy said to Ula. "It looks like a good turnout. We can give them a final count tomorrow. Is this all really happening?"

* * *

"I want to share something with you all, down in the mirror closet, but wait while I see if the coast is clear."

* * *

The octagonal room of mirrors was full of the four women and their thousand reflections.

"My dear, the lace is exquisite!"

Emmy pinned it lovingly back on a quilt square and put it back in a closet, out of the cat's reach.

Marina protested, "You broke up our reflection and diminished us by at least a hundred."

Ula appeared to have forgotten how wonderful the room was with all its lights on. "Why have I never done this again? I must have a room like this in, you know, my next condo. See, they are not all full hanging depth—here is a place for purses and belts, and look here, how perfect for her pretty amber strands and those ethnic necklaces. Most of this closet is under the front patio, and two of the deeper closets have vaults with fur safes. Is there still a fur safe, dear, or in fact any furs?"

"I don't know. I didn't think all of the mirrored doors could open. I think that one opposite the entry door is stationary and must be back to the retaining wall that holds the hill."

"Oh yes, they all open. You have to fool around with those two to find it, a little trip catch, hidden here at the top. Yes, yes, I can find this one."

The cat began to yowl outside the door, excluded from the activity.

"Let him in, dear, and see if he sees his reflection."

He came in and went right to his chosen work of rubbing ankles, ignoring the thousands of cats that had come in with him.

"Some just can't see themselves," said Alice with an acid tongue.

"I think it's been a while since it was opened. What is this, that talk show host Geraldo with the empty prohibition safe? There, it's coming now, and I think my hand remembers where the light switch is . . . Look, the fur safe is still here. What if there are still some furs in it? I think I remember the combination 'cause it's my high school telephone number."

There was a little garden chair beside the safe, and Ula perched on it, reveling in the full drama of being a safecracker. She pulled off a handful of rings and put them in Marina's outstretched palm. Ready to work now, she bent to it, rolling the dial back and forth, listening for clicks. She pressed the handle at last, and the heavy door began to move.

Ula pushed it open. There were no furs. There were, instead, small wooden crates, one of them open—and therein, gold coins.

Ula picked up a handful. "Oh my God in Heaven! Is this a Swiss bank account?"

Marina slipped Ula's rings into her pocket and grabbed Alice by the wrist. "Let's get out of here. They might have to kill us. You go get J., and I'll stand guard and not let anyone in."

Emmy was wide-eyed. "Good Lord, Ula, this looks like the backup storage for Disney's Pirates of the Caribbean ride. Are they real? They look real to me. You don't suppose that's what's in all these other little crates too, do you?" She hefted a box. "The weight's the same!"

She suddenly needed to sit down. Looking about the blearily lit little room, she saw another of the garden chairs propped against the wall and a folding table as well. Even in shock, she was able to identify them as authentic French café furniture, in good condition, nicely aged, and she wondered if there was more.

"How do you get stuff like this into the house? It doesn't come UPS, does it? I think that's a one-ounce gold coin, and gold is more than a thousand dollars an ounce. My God, Ula, let's make necklaces."

The Ingénue had begun to laugh. "A much prettier thing to do with it. My dear, I've begun to know you as a practical girl. I bought some gold, you know. The seller brought it to me, you know, at the bank safe deposit box, a lot smaller backup storage than this. It was a while ago. It's nice to hear it's gone up that much. The first gold I had, except my grandmother's watch and chain, you know, was a little bracelet. It was thirty-five dollars an ounce then. I remember things like that very well."

J. was going over bar stock with Ruben, and it was not easy for Alice to get his attention without sounding urgent. She wasn't sure whether to tell him it was his grandmother or Emmy who needed to see him. Alice settled for both.

Jared bounded in, ready for broken pipes, dangling wires, or mouse infestation. He found instead his two most beloved ladies giggling and sifting gold coins through their fingers.

"J., come in and see what Ula found in my closet!"

"Ah, dear Grandboy, do join us. Look what's in the fur safe. Trinkets, dear boy doll, possibly your lost mother's lost money. I found it, but—and I know you don't like to hear me say things like this—but I was, you know, guided. It's clearly a wedding present from your parents. They bless your union.

"Behind this other door, you know, is probably your Aunt Marta's lost money. She just didn't have a big, hidden, fur safe dug into a hill to put it in. I remember that the combination is the same except for the last number, my uncle's telephone."

This house, with its thick walls, had always been a very quiet one. A loud television in one room did not disrupt the others— indeed, was scarcely heard. Today, however, loud laughter, perhaps traveling through some forgotten vent, filled the kitchen, pantry, laundry room, and entry hall, causing Ruanna and Ruben to smile, probably about weddings in general.

J. pulled out his cell phone as he said, "Got to get my accountant." He went through to the bedroom for reception.

She answered in her crisp business voice on the third ring. "Does everything you want come to you? I'm on Sunset just about to turn down Doheny to my office. Is this your karma or mine because you need me? I swung into an empty parking space to answer this. I'll pull a U now and come back to you."

* * *

"Wow, it's beautiful, isn't it? It never corrodes. Gold coins and bars—everything I do is the symbol of this, and I never get to see it. I had found some of the missing money in Switzerland and the Cayman Islands, no big-deal amount, but substantial. We have to get it declared though and pay the fines. There is an amnesty, and there are people going to jail. There is so much of it you have to wonder how Switzerland can survive. That was a Swiss bankbook, by the way, at the Bird house, starting with a child's savings account. I guess Karen was always good at putting money away.

"Not knowing you have money there is a pretty good excuse. I have also found, though, that the IRS was already paid tax on a great deal of money. Had no idea where it was. It is my belief that this pretty stuff is all free and clear of them.

"This was not a dummy move, you know. Not even naïve, considering all the fine, old, trusted financial institutions now circling the drain. I have no idea how much your parents knew or how they knew it, J., but I get a picture of pretty smart cookies with a distinguished mattress. Gold's not tumbling like interest has and will.

"I'll find all that convoluted paper trail you know. When are you going to tell the Anders cousins you call the 'Anderthree'?"

"You bad grandbaby. You know that sounds like Neanderthal when you say it, and you know better. They are just concerned about a great deal of money."

"And chose me as the target without conferring, not that I would have known what to say. After we're sure that there is a Marta stash, I'll call a my-attorney, their-attorney meeting and hand them a few boxes and suggest they come after the rest."

"In my accounting profession, we always say you never know anyone until you've shared an inheritance with them. And it's late to ask, and I don't know if it's my business, but I think it is, if only as the bridesmaid I am honored to be, on our short acquaintance. Have you two been to an attorney for a prenup?"

"I thought we should. I wouldn't want him to take my bungalow and the cat."

J. seemed not his playful self as he responded. "I, however, think no. If this woman to whom I am addicted left me, I would do a reverse Omar Sharif and walk away without water, into the burning Arabian Desert, into the blazing, blinding sun, and die, face down in the broiling sand, maybe even the quicksand."

Emmy was quick to explain. "We saw *Lawrence of Arabia* the other night, clear through the intermission to the exit music."

*   *   *

The group found that the kitchen table, to the despair of the housekeeper, was the best office and conference room. Plans and lists were spread there.

"Alice, have you any idea where the bachelor party is? Did Joe say?"

"He wouldn't, and he didn't, and I don't see him all that much. And children of divorce don't carry tales or messages either."

"I hope they don't do that naked girl thing for the party. I hope they don't do anything to embarrass him. Maybe Joe will take care of him or maybe Mason."

"Jared has seldom needed taking care of. Emmy, your guy's a nonrighteous, self-designated driver kind of guy, more apt to drag some other drunk home."

"I haven't seen Mason in a while, not at the last work session. How is he?"

"Heavy."

Emmy was uncomfortable with her vision of a crushed Alice and hastened to offer her another cup of coffee.

"Yeah, I'll grab it. She makes good coffee. What else is there to tell about your Ruanna?"

"What can I tell you? She went to Hollywood High, at least for her senior year, fresh from Burma. Her father was a gemologist there, and her mother, a doctor. Here, they are not. She speaks English and cleans as though she thinks it fun."

"Works for me. I hired a security company to guard your house during the wedding. There's a brand of scum that watches the newspapers for weddings and funerals. When everyone is out of the house, they swoop in. Let's extend 'em until you and J. get back. Not that just anyone could find the stash! Did he get the combination from his diva grandmother?"

Emmy was never sure how much she should share with Alice, but this information seemed all right. "Yes, she volunteered it, so he didn't have to ask anything like 'how do I get in there after you're gone?' She wants to come over, though, and be the one to dramatically open the safe for the Anders cousins." Emmy wondered if Alice hoped to be there for that scene too.

"So you've also seen how tender he is about never mentioning anything about her age, never saying 'in your time,' and never saying a word about inheriting anything from her, because that would mean she could die."

"Yes, I have thought about it. Once she was going on to me about how everyone, absolutely everyone, is compelled to say something that sets her aside as being aged. I hope I never have and won't. J. must have realized that ubiquitous prejudice and now seeks to ease it."

"I've noticed how he takes her elbow on stairs and hands her in and out of cars as though she were his date, not a less-able grandmother."

"Marina told me about a woman at the Ingénue's condo once, J.'s date. She came out of the powder room laughing in delight over the crazy Tony Duquette chandelier. She goes, 'There's something J. won't want to inherit.' Marina said he took her home early and never called her again."

"Was Marina reminding you he had a life before you?"

"Maybe just reminding me to be nice to his grandmother."

"Well, you are, and she likes you."

"Oh, is that why she doesn't want me to marry him?"

"Another day with return cards, after deadline. You can't tell 'em the offer's over. Alice, Alice, Alice, who are all these people? Why would they come to see me sacrificed at the altar? They must have heard about the Vera Wang dresses. Do you like your dress? It's Ray, in his best man role, who directs the guy's suits, isn't it? Daddy's too?" Yes, I love my dress. What is not to love? Ray should be able to do his part in this show; he runs that whole huge company now, you know. It was the right decision that he shouldn't be on the committee. He's not in the movie industry, and he's totally busy with Ingénue, but he has always had Jared's back—and J., his—since kindergarten. Emmy, did you know that J. is godfather to Ray's three boys? It's all three because it's official, real godfathership, legal guardianship if anything happened to the parents. See what you could be getting into? Cute, though, aren't they? Especially the little guy who acts as ring bearer, with the over-the-calf, white wool socks and knee pants.

"Those two have been like brothers. My best school memory of them is of them leaving after the graduation at Hollywood Bowl. They were waving their diplomas from a motorcycle, with the wind plucking at their caps and billowing their gowns. I don't remember who was driving, but I remember them threading through the cars in that huge parking lot and yelling something I couldn't hear."

"Are the socks on your checklist? It looks pretty detailed to me. I like all the check marks. Really, really, how are we doing?"

"We are really, really doing very well. Linda and Heather are doing most of everything and doing it so, so well. Did you know that they go downtown to the flower market in the very, very early morning? And your mother is great. I like Tish a lot. Do you realize she and the Granddame are the only ones we are not costuming for this production?"

"Wait till you see what the Ingénue sent over—bejeweled and pearled swirls that are put on with combs just above the ears. I've never seen anything so fabulous. They go so well with the bit of lace head cover, all under the veil. Is this happening to me?"

"For something new, you could tuck a gold coin into your bra. And your dress is way beyond great! Our dresses too, and all of them with Empire waists, so who would notice if any of us were carrying? My personal gratitude that they are pale celadon and not Alice blue, but you would never do that.

"Your bridesmaids in stair-step order puts me at the end, where I can watch my girls, who are excited out of their minds to be flower girls, so that's perfect. You will be able to visualize and adjust at the rehearsal tomorrow night."

* * *

She wasn't sure she could push through that vastness of smiling faces, but then she saw Jared, beaming at a great distance, in that unfamiliar James Bond tuxedo. She proceeded forward with her father, who handed her over to J.

Only slightly louder than a whisper, J. said, "Brava, Vera. What color is this?"

"Margarita? Moonstone?"

"Dear God, you and the dress are fabulous."

"It's got pockets."

"Who's got the ring?"

"The kid."

"Are those pearl gills?"

"Yes."

"Where did the preacher's ruff come from?

"The Grandnorweigen."

"Laundered and shipped from Norway?"

"Hush and listen so you know what you're getting into."

"You, babe."

"Shush."

* * *

"Was that Four Seasons breakfast just the best you've ever had?"

"I rather liked the cornflakes and milk the first time we ever slept together. All I longed for came true, sleeping on the wet spot, with you snoring gently in my arms."

"Do I snore? You never said."

"The operative word is gently."

"I want to remember everything about the wedding. Mostly I remember the smell of flowers."

"You get that at a funeral too."

"But here the faces were smiling, yours best. What did you think when the doors burst open and the bride march began?"

"She's not big or fat or wide."

"What else?"

"I have paid the price in goats, and there is her father bringing my woman to me. He will throw her at my feet and hold her down in front of my hut, while I break the hymen."

"Joe did say you should have a glass wrapped in a napkin, to step on."

"Well, we did have a chuppah."

"I thought it was a baldachino."

"You're way too educated to keep barefoot and pregnant in the suburbs."

"Oh! Lean over and look out my window. I think we might be over South Dakota by now."

"Have I told you my pledge that you will always have the window seat? And as much gold as you want?"

"Was that before you knew there was gold in them there closets?"

"Yep!"

"Are you worried about it being there alone?"

"Nope."

She kicked off her shoes. "Do you want the paper slippers too? All the benefits of flying first-class, and you may always have flown that way. I would have liked a gin on the rocks. Do you realize that water on the rocks looks the same? This is terrific."

"Scotch, no paper shoes."

"Tell me about the wedding before I came in. Did you think about turning and running?"

"Couldn't. Ray was holding onto me. When your side saw me appear on stage, there was this great sucking sound and whispers of 'Patrick.' Then there was the same sound when my side saw Patrick. Apparently, they saw the resemblance. They probably were explaining to each other that you didn't marry till you were thirty 'cause you were looking and waiting for someone like your father. 'Wow,' they said, 'she sure found him.'"

"And we won't tell 'em that you found me in the wrong booth. It looks different out my window now. What's after South Dakota?"

"Does it look like a blue state or a red state?"

"It's all cloud bank and brilliant blue sky, but I think they are all red states out here. But we Democrats are still going to win. I know we are".

"Of course not."

Neither was going to make a dangerous subject of this.

Emmy slipped out of the paper shoes and stretched. "I love flying. Best thing about it is settling down by the window with my gin on the rocks and a book. But I can't have my Tanqueray this time, and I don't need a book."

"And you won't be able to raise a pint in a London pub either. I think they have lime without the margarita."

"I was so proud. I didn't even feel like upchucking. I hate it when the bride barfs. And you, you darling, quietly arranged for something nonalcoholic for me in the color of everyone else's drinks. Vera arranged high-waisted for all of us. I think Peg might be pregnant again. Close cousins would be great."

"If they don't want to marry . . . Joe, by the way, called and asked Vera's studio to put aside some of the bridesmaids' fabric, for maybe sleeves and a train or fuller back skirt in case Alice should marry again—and he didn't mean some other guy. He is so in love with her still."

Emmy did not look surprised. "And she is so mad at him still."

"She's doing a great job for us. I don't know who did what for the wedding, but I'm pretty impressed with us."

"I can't wait to see the pictures. Will we still be in a daze when we get back? What was the wildest thing for you?"

J. did not need much time to think that over. "After the reception line while the big room was being converted magically to a dining room, and everyone was seated, and Ray and Peg led us up onto a round platform and told us to stand still. The curtain opened, and I still didn't realize we were standing as the bridal figures on a big cake replica. The laughing and applause were not exactly for us. They were more for the wedding planner. I'm not even sure when I caught on. Am I ever to know who did it to me?"

"No!"

Chapter 17

It had begun to feel like a very long trip. J. had bestowed his admiration on the well-designed, little toilet compartment with all the needed fixtures in such cozy, small space. He had often thought he would like that little pod with an adjacent stainless steel shower in his own house. He had read his carry-on book until he drowsed off, and then he had slept fitfully until roused by a slight turbulence. The space around him was now littered with magazines. He segregated three to show Emmy whenever she awoke. They included pieces written by reviewers who thought highly of the Grandloon and her movie, and in one, Em's spectacular Afghan coat from the premiere glistened at the margin. Next to him, Emmy stirred awake, and if she had been snoring, it was gentle enough to be covered by the plane's roar.

"Well, good morning, love."

"Are we there yet?"

"No, we're at an intersection of gray cloud banks and white cloud banks."

"Oh, to be in England when the lilacs are in bloom."

"I bet you didn't know you can rent a room and stay a few days at Hampton Court."

"Oh heaven! The golden rain will be in bloom on the arbor! I'm so glad you are planning this part of it."

"Okay, how much gold rain do you want? I happen to have a bunch of it."

Presently the pilot made an announcement, and Emmy glued herself to the window. "Oh my God! It really is that green. We're low enough to see rivers and mountains. How beautiful is this? Are you feeling a strong genetic pull?"

"Almost strong enough to bring the plane down at Shannon, and I've been here before, but I'm more Irish now. You have tears in your eyes too."

"I'm crying over my lost Irishness. I miss it."

"I had a long talk with your mother. We are going where her father's family came from—Taunton until 1520 and then Dedham."

"Uh, that's Constable country!"

"I was intrigued right away with that date. Why did they move right then to East Anglia, hotbed of political and religious reform? Martin Luther had just thrown the inkwell, and it was only a few years before Henry became Protestant, if for other than religious zeal. It was eight years before Elizabeth came to the throne.

"And there you are, the very heritage of English freedom, moving to the New World with the great migration of Governor John Winthrop. I'm surprised that they have never made a movie about him. I've waited and waited. I have a document signed by him and no movie actor to go with him for my collection of paired signatures. Look at me, married to a woman whose ancestors came to Massachusetts with him, my hero. How come we never had the chat I had with your mother?"

"We did talk about the time I went with my family to see the old houses in New England, but I was only interested in the stuff there."

"Wow and a half. This is the very embodiment of our next marathon, the part with the holes in the movie sequences."

Jared began tapping notes into his phone. "Demi Moore was in a Puritan film."

"It was Hawthorne, wasn't it?"

"You must have been paying attention in English literature. And how did I find a woman who doesn't run from the words 'history' and 'literature'?"

"*Barry Lyndon* was much later, wasn't it?"

"Yes, remember the costumes?"

"I'd still like to go to Stourhead."

"What's Stourhead?"

"Where they filmed *Barry Lyndon*. That garden is maybe the most famous one in the world."

"Sold! England is yours."

"Funny to have this English chat over Ireland, where they behaved so badly. That first look at Ireland as she materialized out of the surf, so saturated green! No wonder they call her Emerald."

It was then that J. determined to buy her a seriously big ring, an emerald to compensate for her lost Irishness. It must be an important thing for the right ring finger to balance the diamond on the left.

"I do know something else about Mom's father's family, the first ones in Massachusetts. I looked it all up again when I lost my Irish part. Their name was Reed, and there were three daughters, Martha, Margaret, and Elizabeth. It was Martha who married Daniel Epps and named her daughter Elizabeth. Margaret's married name was Lake, and the other sister married John Winthrop Junior. It's Elizabeth Epps who's my ancestor. Funny, she named her son James, the name of the king they had just fled. Her brother Daniel was in the first graduating class from Harvard! It was only the red cloak I told you about that I was interested in when we were there.

"Now that's all I remember about it, and it wasn't reinforced by art history, given that it was a particularly dreary time for paintings. They brought no Holbeins, and I doubt they even knew what glorious paint had been applied in Italy for several hundred years."

J. looked smug, for she had hit his special knowledge.

"Actually, as a young man, Winthrop the younger had gone traveling. Remember? We talked once before about how he went as far as Istanbul, Constantinople then. Coming back, he spent some time in Italy, doing business in old documents, maybe drawings too. He was an amazing man and smart enough to marry into your family. He would be a great movie. Did you know he went to college in Ireland, at Trinity in Dublin? I've always thought they sent him there to scout about settling, before they determined to go to America. He was once shipwrecked on the west coast of Ireland and had to hitch his way back to Dublin. Seriously, what a guy, what a movie!"

Emmy was remembering that teenage trip with her family. "Did I mention before that his papers are in an old filing cabinet in the Ipswich Library?"

"Aren't you becoming valuable! I did not know that. How could I have missed it? Take me there!"

"The total rest of what I know is that they took three hundred years to get to California."

"Bride, darling, you are from the very stream of the narrative of our county's freedom."

"I miss the Irish emigrant that I thought I was. I know more about your grandfather than you do, and I know it only took him the time of an ocean liner and a train to get to California."

"Maybe sometime I'll take Patrick to lunch and talk to him."

"Idiot, he's your father."

"He's your daddy."

*   *   *

"English food doesn't have the best reputation, but this is great."

"The linenfold paneling is even greater. You have no idea how wonderful it is to me to see the real thing in this terrific old hotel."

"There's older and more wonderful. Tomorrow and the next day, more great old stuff. I thought we'd start the morning with a city tour on a double-decker bus to get the feel of what you want to see, as well as what you have to see."

"You mean like the red buses for tourists on Hollywood Boulevard?"

"The same, a working prototype."

* * *

"J., do you think that Shakespeare really was in this very room?"

"I believe he even wrote here, his revisionist history in favor of the Tudors."

"I think I'm voting for Paul Scofield's *A Man for All Seasons* for Henry VIII. He was still a beautiful golden hunk then. I was really jazzed to see his armor, a giant for his time. And wasn't it amazing to actually be in the Tower of London?"

"A good point about the armor, my sweet. You're not just another gorgeous blond."

"That was so funny when I was sketching that ancient gun, and the guard approached me: 'You wouldn't be after stealing our weaponry design, would you?'"

"The stuff of the time is such good connective tissue, that armor so obviously from his younger days as depicted in that movie. I did a Ken Burns on the armor photo and shot from the feet up to head. I'm e-mailing some of my production to Joe tonight. Photography is not my thing, but I may have some lucky breaks, and at worst, when Joe comes over, he will have mine as historical and detail reference. We had a teaching session, and he gave me a bunch of tips."

* * *

"It's a really good zoo. I liked the canal boats winding through the flight cage, designed by Princess Margaret's husband."

"A guy's gotta have a profession."

"The San Diego Zoo's better all around."

"Probably," J. conceded, "but they couldn't come up with lunch in a fine old dining room like this one. You don't suppose the fish came from the canal, do you?"

"Our wedding dinner came off so well. It really was amazing how fast they got rid of the chairs in rows and got them around tables."

"I wasn't surprised that it all came off so well. My great surprise was how happy a man could be—I mean, how overcome—from lifting a veil."

"For me it was you in the ubertailored 007 tux and the pale, pale, pale-blue shirt. It was my something blue. When the dancing got going and you took your coat off, the shirt looked painted on. With the flap front of no buttons over that gym-honed body, it was the fit over the fit. Can you die of happy?"

"I thought I might!"

"How did you know what to get and where to get it?"

"Ms. Wang told me the tailor, and Joe said not a white shirt because of flaring the photos. Ula's shopper sent me to Anto in Beverly Hills for the shirt. It took a long time, but I started ordering right after the diamond. I ordered a second shirt for our anniversary party and then four more because the minimum order is six."

"You're so sure, aren't you?"

"Yes. You?"

"Yes."

* * *

"Of course we will go to see Leonardo's *Madonna of the Rocks*. Or is it on the rocks?"

"That one's in the museum on Trafalgar Square. There's another one in the Uffizi, in different colors. If a fabric comes in the same pattern but different colors, we call it colorways."

"I know you think Leonardo was the greatest brain ever put in human skull, but he never did anything."

"He just wasn't good at closure. Your Shakespeare was. Then again, he never left anything in his hand or published, but you are so sure he wrote it all."

"And at that table where you sat."

*　*　*

"It's awesome to walk where Elizabeth walked."

"In her long reign she walked almost everywhere, at her hosts' expense. I have a place to go tomorrow where she stopped at least once. I don't know where she was going, but we are going to Stonehenge and Stourhead, and it's on our way. We have a B&B near the garden. I've been advised to get there before it opens in the morning, and the B&B promised an early B."

*　*　*

"It's a handsome old house, isn't it? There was no family to inherit it, and it's on the National Trust. A whole lot of remodeling went on here, but there's an upstairs gallery, unchanged since Bess visited. That's a lot of gravel to crunch up to the door."

"How does a guy know things like that, anyway?"

"I have a consultant, a master's in history, and more important, Google."

They walked into a large, light-filled reception addition, almost a glass house. It was full of summer bloom in urns and pots. J. took a brochure from an iron stand by the door and put it in her hand.

Em glanced and gasped. "Is this the Vyne? This is my mother's grandmother's maiden name, right here on the cover. I haven't thought of this place for ages! Oh my, my, my!" She began crying. "I don't know much about it. I never even thought about it being real and here, and I never thought that I would ever see it."

J. already knew about it though. "It came into your extended family after the English Civil War. When your immigrant

273

ancestor came to America, his first cousin stayed and sided with the Parliamentary army and Cromwell. His lawyer son became speaker of the House of Commons under the second Cromwell and was able to buy this house."

"And Cromwell was a hero here and a beast in Ireland. How did you know all this?"

"Your mom, and besides that, the house has a website. I know, therefore, where there is a portrait of the owner's grandfather, who is also your ancestor."

"Mrs. Higgen-Dunkin, good morning. I'm the curator, and I'm given to eavesdropping."

They looked up to see a nice-looking man in a well tailored suit with, Emmy noted, a hand-stitched lapel.

"Your husband has it about right. Welcome. And would you sign the guestbook with some whimsy about being the American cousin? We haven't had one for some time. It was a presidential candidate's wife the last time—Democrat, I think.

"We were so pleased when your husband e-mailed us you were coming. Do walk about. We close for lunch, but for tea, there are buns and cakes for sale in the coach house."

*   *   *

"It's truly awesome, in the old sense of the word, overwhelming and high on the world-class, astonishing, must-see list. But when you've seen it, you've seen it. I'm told it's at its best in this low, late afternoon sun. Even your little point-and-shoot images will probably come out great."

"Have I failed to show you what's already in my little point-and-shoot? My Leica point-and-shoot? You think you can get through art history without taking pictures and classes in the same? I even had some classes with Julius Shulman, the iconic photographer of your beloved modern."

"Madam, my apologies. Let me see whatcha got! . . . Um, that is good, but of course it's the photogenic Stonehenge."

*   *   *

"I hope this is as good as it looked on the website. I think it's the next village."

The GPS announced, "One-point-four miles, turn left."

"We've been well informed by madam so far."

"Recalculating. Three miles turn right."

A disobedient driver, J. explained to the British voice that he knew that, but he wanted to go through the village.

*   *   *

"Amazing in the rain! The lake! Oh my God. Do you think it will photograph still? My last shots were silhouettes of umbrellas. This one will be a beautiful blur at least. See, it is a beautiful blur. It's so gorgeous here, glorious!" Em put her retracted Leica back in her pocket.

"Is that why you're shivering? Or is it this cold marble bench we're sitting on? Stand up and let me put my Peterman duster under us. I'm remembering doing that sometime before."

"Is that when we conceived?"

"Because I forced you? That would be great here, with everybody gone home out of the rain. It's early for tea. Let's make a run for it."

*   *   *

"You are right on time for tea. Usually honeymooners are late, if they come down at all."

J., who seldom or never looked embarrassed, did. "I thought that, given our ages, you might have thought we had been married for ten years."

The lady smiled a British smile and reached across the beautifully laid tea table. The silver service, Em noted, was probably Adams and very good; the china cups were translucent; and the platter, Wedgwood, was filled with tea cakes with pale celadon frosting—the color of Emmy's bridesmaids' dresses. In the lady's hand was a manila envelope, which she handed to them.

It was too early for the bill. When they opened it, they found a shiny color photo fresh from a computer printer. At first it seemed to be an image of the plaster figures from a wedding cake, but it was instead J. and Emmy, smug-faced and very happy, standing still on the top of a huge cake replica.

"How did you do that?"

"I'm computer-literate, even skilled. I would have to guess you left home before seeing any photos, including this one on the cover of a magazine. Privacy is old-fashioned. The object of that Twitter nonsense is to be so boring that no one cares. You may ask how another Hollywood couple withheld their babies' pictures for later sale, and I just wouldn't know . . . Do have a cake. Did I get the bridesmaid dress color right?"

"I think you are saying there are more pictures. Is that true? May we see?"

"Yes, of course, after tea. Now tell me about yourselves."

J. admitted to himself that he was beginning to feel trapped. It must be the fussy table and its fussy things before him when it was getting on toward time for a man's scotch. "Well, for openers, we are Los Angeles, not Hollywood."

"Forgive me. All the articles say you live in the Hollywood Hills and identify you as Mary Ellen Higgen, granddaughter of Damon Higgen, and Jared Dunkin, heir to the Ingénue cosmetic fortune. What is it you do in Los Angeles, young man?"

"Madam, where is your scotch, and do you have any American ice cubes?" He steamed off in the indicated direction.

Emmy didn't know whether to laugh, apologize for him or defend him. She did none of it. "May I tell you what I do in Los Angeles? I have a showroom mostly for interior designers, where I attempt to have things as beautiful as these items on your tea table. It's all I can do to keep from turning over the saucer and picking up the silver to look for the marks."

"Tomorrow I'll show you what's for sale. Did you perhaps know Jones/Hutchinson in Los Angeles on Robertson Boulevard?

* * *

J. was on possibly his third scotch as they put on their coats for the eight o'clock dinner reservation already made for them. It was Em's first chance to wear her new London coat of butter-soft, nearly rumpled leather, like an Italian handbag. It was topstitched and embroidered on the cuffs in a color that upon close examination was pink. She had fallen for it and decided to buy it in spite of the price. She had said she could live in it, and he had said there were people who lived in houses that cost less. When she had proffered her credit card, he had pushed it away and presented his. Now he nodded at it in a way that Em took for appreciation, though he went on to speak instead of their hostess at the B&B.

"Who is she anyway? And for that matter, who am I? Heir to a cosmetic fortune, grandson of a star, closet grandson of another star, history buff, film buff, and occasional script supervisor when I want to be. What the hell is all that?" He softened then and said, "But I'm husband to the beautiful Mary Ellen."

"She said there was a decisive battle somewhere near here. Her husband would know, and he will be home late tonight. He travels a lot, setting up computers. She said he's redheaded and has to have a full beard because a stubble like yours, which she likes a lot, would look like a rash on him."

"They all talk to you, don't they? Can we go down now? There's time to see the wedding pictures again."

* * *

"Wow, this is very, very good," J. said.

"Yeah, our hostess said this chef went to Paris, got his Cordon Bleu degree and the tall funny hat, and then came back to his hometown to do this amazing restaurant."

"We do fall into good stuff."

"Let me tell you how good is good. I doubt you ever noticed a place called Jones/Hutchinson on what I think of as upper Robertson. They were a great resource for interior designers, a little more country than those antiques that I have, but reliably good quality. Hutchinson had a great eye for special things, like old tools and toys. They stockpiled in a barn in England all year and came here for two months every year. They had a half of an old house in this town. Would you care to guess who their friend, gatherer, and stockpiler was?"

"Could it possibly be a woman who also runs a bed and breakfast?"

"What a dream we walked into, or did you know? I couldn't put it past you."

"Not! 'Of all the gin joints in the world . . .'"

"Be still a minute. I'm eavesdropping."

"Aye, many's the night I've cried after ya," said a woman at the next table.

"Ah, lass, I didn't know. Why did ya not tell me?"

Just then another course was delivered with accompanying sound that covered the conversation of the couple at the next table.

*   *   *

"We are in England when the lilacs are in bloom. I never heard that they were even headier at night. And the gravel is crunchier. There, now that we are on concrete, I can eavesdrop again. I overheard them in the restaurant, that couple ahead of us. I think they're going where we're going."

"But Em of the big ears, they're not talking. They're just walking along, holding hands."

*   *   *

"Well, Higgen-Dunkins, this would be a good time to Skype your grandmother if you've a mind to. My husband is home and, to no one's surprise, in the computer room. We used to call it the library. The books are still there. They take the wall space, but the new paperless society takes the whole rest of the room."

*   *   *

"So Grandmum, Emmy is going to walk you through the garden with our photos, not sorted or edited."

"It's way more gorgeous even than the pictures in your book, though there wasn't a peacock near the bridge like that cover shot. We've always seen the bridge from the side, but when you're there, walking toward it, you can see the most wonderful thing. The perfect lawn goes right over the bridge. I thought I had never seen anything as beautiful. We can't do it justice with our shots, but we can show them to you now. Our host here is a genius with the computer. I'll introduce you to him, and you will see that he doesn't look anything at all like a geek, and here is our hostess too."

The Ingénue sat regally in Marina's desk chair, seeming to be waiting to be told that the camera was rolling. It was evident, at least to J., that she had been briefed about the small monitor in the corner of her screen where her own image appeared and was careful not to look at it. She had made sure that her ringed hands were positioned.

Her better side turned slightly to the screen, she acknowledged the introduction and then could not hold back from comment on the hosts' good English skin. She continued, "My dear, you're very nice-looking, but you know you should pluck those eyebrows a bit more, higher on the outer arch. And you, dear"—she was flirting now—"there's just nothing a handsome man can do about having red hair."

The photos were on now. "This was first thing in the morning. Our tickets, through the kindness of these hosts, let us in an hour before opening without another soul around except for one black-clad man on the other side of the lake reflecting into it when the path took him close to the water. At that moment, it was the only way you could see where the grass ended and the water began. Green into green and the smell of the dew! The rhododendrons are amazing. Remember that detail was wrong in the movie *Barry Lyndon* with Ryan O'Neal. They hadn't been planted that early, in the mid-eighteenth century. You can't fault them for not tearing them out for the authenticity of the movie though.

"Here we are at the far end of the lake, and here is the Tudor-style garden pavilion. The umbrellas went up, and we fled to the Greek temple."

"My dears, your pictures are very good!"

The cat, with her own sense of time, chose that moment to make a graceful landing beside her lady and preen in the warmth of the light. They could actually hear her purring.

Later Emmy asked J. if he could tell for sure which of them was purring. It had been noted that, with the white cat in residence, the Ingénue now was more often dressed in white. Today she wore a nubby, white, vintage Chanel suit. She must have been shopping in her closet again.

When they had rung off, the hostess, with her British reserve down, all but gushed. "That was great theater."

*   *   *

"There now, our men off to see a battlefield and the guests off to the garden except for that one couple, whom you must have seen at the tavern last night. You'd think they would be down by now. Only young couples and ancient ones come down later than this: 'Uncle Fred and Aunty Mable / Fainted at the breakfast table. / Children, let that be a warning, / Never do it in the morning.'"

She heard them on the stairs just then and gave instructions in the kitchen for their breakfast. She greeted them and said to Em, "Take your mug of tea, dear, and we'll go to the barn."

"He was an old dear, Hutchinson was," she said as they walked to the barn. "We were very good friends. He was often in my kitchen, as well as my barn. Jones was a sweet man too, but not funny. I miss them horribly. Jones lives in London with his sister, and Hutchinson's now a year dead. I heard their final sale was quickly over. When he was here last, he knew he was on his way out. He said he didn't mind, that he had done everything he ever wanted to and slept with everyone he ever wanted to sleep with. I would have thought it was just Jones, but from here he traveled with a lady, to Italy mostly. Belated gossip, isn't it?"

"Gossip is good anytime. I remember them well. They are missed by their interior designer customers. Designers could always depend on Jones/Hutchinson to have English writing boxes, apothecary jars, chests, and good iron stuff, all in usable condition. I think I'm going to see that in your barn. Imagine my finding you. It's surreal!"

Emmy's excitement built as her hostess wiggled an elaborate, long, old key into an ancient lock. She saw, though, that a modern key in a modern lock and a ritual pressing of buttons to turn an alarm to green followed it.

"If this barn were in Los Angeles, I would wish I had it for my house."

The door creaked open, and a flood of lights went on. It was hard for Emmy to remember the buyer's code, to curb enthusiasm to keep prices down.

"Start telling me prices—for instance, this platter."

"I know that you know it's Wedgwood and unusual in this size. Start taking your notes."

"I will. I want that one for myself."

"Good choice. It's still wholesale."

*   *   *

"I do love a professional," said the hostess, "your beautiful list with the inventory numbers in neat rows, your warehouse address, shop address, telephones, faxes, cells, e-mails, and the names of your staff. And thank you for your home address as well."

"Someone should playfully publish new personal address books with a space for a land line, his and her cell phones, his and her business phones and faxes, e-mail addresses, websites, and maybe the vacation house number, though the cells would probably cover that."

"My husband will tell you that can be done electronically in your cell phone. Your vacation house is in the desert, is it not?"

"Yes, how did you know that?"

"He can find out anything. It's the geek game; they look up even things they don't care if they ever know or not. But I know you're pregnant, and he doesn't know it."

"What makes you think that?"

"I'm a mum. Of five boys."

"Where are they?"

"An Englishman will give 'em to ya, but then he'll wrest them out of your arms and send them off to proper schools."

*　　*　　*

"Wherever did you get your discerning eye?" asked Emmy.

"I've studied a bit, but best was traveling with my uncle, an important dealer, starting when I was twelve. His personal collection specialty was a French ware, a bright, deep yellow with black pattern. We perfected the act. I would poke around for it so that he wouldn't appear interested, and then I'd coax for it for my dolls. He would give in reluctantly."

"That's reminding me of a collector who spots a rare Ming bowl. There is a cat drinking out of it. He negotiates to buy the cat and suggests that the cat should have its familiar bowl to take along. The dealer says 'of course' and reaches behind the counter for its ordinary plastic bowl and says, 'Here it is.' He sold more cats that way."

"That way you could let your old mother cat have all the litters she'd a mind to, as long as she'd let them foster out."

"I think I know that yellow ware. Is it Cray? And not always with the black pattern? I had some. I sold it very well."

"That's fine, as long as you bought it well."

"My partner had gotten it in Laguna from Carl Yeakel. Was it maybe from you?"

"Why, yes, I think that was my uncle's. That was Yeakel's own collection and must have been sold after he died, as I sold my uncle's Cray to Yeakel. My, we are a tight little society! See anything more you like? You've taken a lot of notes."

"Well, I have to buy well. Let's start talking about a price if I buy both whole lists."

* * *

"You will reach our friends' little hotel near Chatsworth in plenty of time to get ready for dinner. You'll find her cooking very good for an English woman. Fortunately, she learned it in Italy.

"Have a look at the Grinling Gibbons carving for me. I run over to Chatsworth to see it every few years. Don't miss Longleat. It has some semblance left to the old formal gardens from before Capability Brown re-landscaped all of England. And Haddon Hall had the advantage of belonging to a family that had another grand house and let that one go fallow, so it never got remodeled out of its original Tudorness."

"Don't bypass Sissinghurst," said their red-haired host. "We know that your Elizabeth was there with her posse in 1573. It's fifty miles south of London. Call around though. I think the family is in residence; Nicolson is writing a book about the place."

Their hostess had yet another poem to share now: "'Buried in time and sleep, / So drowsy overgrown, / That here the moss is green upon the stone / And lichen stains the keep.' But remember, my dears, there has been a lot of gardening since Sackville-West wrote that."

J. was always impressed with a history buff who knew something he didn't and asked how the hosts knew the date of Elizabeth's progress to Sissinghurst.

"Oh, I'm there from time to time," said the husband. "I installed their computer system. I have some renown for being able to hide wires in old piles. In the pipe soon is a charger that has no wire connection to it. What will there be following that?"

"We will Skype, and you will be back to see us. And tomorrow I shall Skype your Scott and let him know the damage you have done."

Chapter 18

"This may be the very spot where Simon de Montfort stood to see the deployment of the troops of his student, the prince who became Edward I. He found it good and is said to have said, 'I taught him that.' I doubt there has been a movie on either one of them, but they were both important in the progression of freedom. De Montfort added what was to become the House of Commons. This is the site of the battle. Edward won, in 1265, in August, I think, and saved his father, Henry III. With your ancestor clocked in near here in 1268, you have to wonder if he was here for the battle or stood here later with his son and told him about de Montfort, when it was still news."

It was the perfect time of day for their photos to turn out well, with the sun glowing across the green field of summer. The pact was that Joe Silver would come and shoot anything that wasn't first-class. No falling in love with their own work if it didn't work.

"This is going to have to be one of those segments when we vamp and tap dance to cover the lack of a movie. There's great stuff in the museum from the thirteenth century. Oh my God, do recall the studio research of the twelfth century that gave you *Becket*."

"I thought Burton gave us *Becket*."

"Yeah, and Peter O'Toole took him away."

"And look who got the Oscar."

Em didn't remember but guessed Burton. J. confirmed his memory that it was and asked her if she had a favorite scene.

"The horse galloping away on the beach with the purple cloak billowing behind him. You?"

"Canterbury Cathedral. The assassination."

"Do we have to choose between *Becket* and *Lion in Winter* for Henry II?"

"Couldn't."

It was such a great picnic spot that they thought to go down to a pub and get sandwiches. The pub turned out to be so directly out of set-design research, and the barman out of central casting, that they settled down by the small fire still picturesquely burning in June. They lifted several pints, hers ginger beer, with their sandwiches.

"What," she asked him, "did you like best at Chatsworth?"

"That would have to be the orangery and the glass house against the wall, with the duke owners living there. I wonder who the little kid was, peering out the window. Contrary to your family branch at the Vyne, they kept having descendants."

"Like our hostess with the eyebrows that need arching, I fairly worshipped the Grinling Gibbons carving. I loved being there because I've read so much about Bess of Hardwick, who built it."

"It was vastly remodeled by others after her, unlike Haddon Hall. What did you like best there?"

"Oh, no contest, the great hall with the trestle table on the raised dais at the end. "I wanted to say, 'I've seen this movie.'"

"You did say, 'I've seen this movie.' I think I saw it too, but it had huge mastiff dogs lying around on the bone-strewn floor. My best thing was the chapel with the demons and hellfire murals that either didn't get painted over by Puritans or the Church of England or that were revealed when their whitewash was recently removed. My pictures of it are good. I could make posters for the nursery."

"No way. You'll just have to suffer through the cute stuff, which you can paint over later. Little girls like pink until they're eleven."

"You should know with all that experience with my sisters. Are you going to want to know what we're having before he's born?"

"She."

"He."

"She."

"He!"

J. channeled *Carousel* and sang, "You can have fun with a son, but you've gotta be a father to a girl." He continued from later in the same show, singing now, "I've never known how to make money, but I'll try! By God, I'll try!"

"We're headed for Stratford. We should be quoting Shakespeare, not American show tunes." But still she followed his lead, quoting from that American show tune, though speaking, never singing: "'Brush up your Shakespeare; start quoting him now. Brush up your Shakespeare, and the women you will wow.' That's a decent rhyme, but from *Kiss Me, Kate* is the best worst rhyme in the English language: 'If your blond won't respond when you flatter 'er, / Tell 'er what Tony told Cleopatterer.'"

J. inquired after the best good rhymes.

Emmy was sorry she couldn't sing it, but she answered anyway: "'A tinkling piano in the next apartment, / These something words / That tell you what my heart meant.' We could listen to Ella Fitzgerald singing 'These Foolish Things' on YouTube to find out what the real word was instead of 'something.' But I do love 'apartment' and 'heart meant.'"

"Any Shakespeare rhymes?"

"Later."

*   *   *

"My family lived here in Taunton from 1268 to 1520."

"Oh?" said the woman tending the desk of the historical society.

J. bought the tickcts, and they went into the cavernous, small museum, smelling faintly of all the years it had been there. There was little from before mid-sixteenth century, a marble mantle piece, some weapons, a very early kettle, all duly photographed. The brochure of the town included an ancient map that showed the castle had been there even before 1268.

*   *   *

Camera in hand, J. directed Em, "Move a little to your right and stand and look at the gate. Now walk a little way and stop, a little way and stop. Go through the gate doing that, and I will shoot each time. This will be so much fun to show our son."

"Daughter. Maybe we can come back when she's a toddler, on our way to Ireland. I could hold her hand, and you could do the same shots."

"Great! He will love having those pictures of the castle where his ancestor rode through that thick, stone gateway. God, I love history. I hope he does too."

"Just wait until Daddy tells you all he knows about your Irish."

"Will that include my maternal grandfather, Dr. Berber's father, too?"

*   *   *

"We've been together for months, but this really is different," J. declared.

"You mean there's no Salisbury Cathedral in Los Angeles?"

"I mean a honeymoon is a time to get to know each other in a neutral place, to be having a great time when you find out that I throw my clothes on the floor."

"I think it's erotic to have a man's pants on the floor beside my bed. And look what happened when you put your shoes under my bed."

"Who could wonder why I am so fucking addicted to you? And I don't mean just addicted to fucking you. I mean sublimely, irrevocably, terminally, happily addicted to you."

"Likewise, I'm sure," she said, imitating Judy Holliday's voice from *Born Yesterday*.

"Bitch, sweet bitch."

*   *   *

"Oh my God! Oh my God! To have been standing in Shakespeare's house. Did you love the rock floors? And he climbed that little stairway."

"I, on the other hand, was more jazzed by the tavern in London where he worked and talked to other guys to get some of his plots, and drove returning sailors crazy with his questions. Such a shame that I'll never have his signature to put with an actor who played him for my pairs collection, being that there are only six in existence, or is it that there are only six for Button Gwinnett?"

Emmy knew only that this was not the name of any major painter from her art history and had to ask, "That's not Brad Pitt getting younger instead of older, is it?"

"No, good try, but it's a signer of the Declaration of Independence. There are collectors of the signers, but only six can have all of them. That means only six mega-funded guys can achieve it."

"You're a mega-funded guy."

"I guess I am, but which of those guys, whoever they are, would give up the ultimate mass signature collection? It's not on my longing list anyway, to own them. I have some signers, hoping they turn up in movies."

"There's a good painting of a bunch of them, not great, but good."

"Then there's that film of the same usual suspects framing the Constitution. That's a good end for our film—King Arthur to President Washington."

"Can we make any kind of case for Shakespeare in the march to freedom?"

"Well, dear blond, he killed a helluva lot of English kings."

*   *   *

"Do you think she will actually send you those two volumes of the complete works of Shakespeare? The one of them that she said was out to mend, you can only hope it will be a good mend. They look so great. I hope it's not a bait and switch. The illustrations are so good that the books could be dismantled and framed for sale. Please don't faint. I would never do it."

"I'm glad to have heard that promise. For a minute there I thought I'd have to watch you constantly, but what's so bad about that?"

"You should save the mailing label or receipt because who would believe that those big red leather books came from the Chaucer Head Bookshop in Stratford upon Avon? Almost too pat."

"You do believe he wrote all that stuff himself, don't you? We haven't talked much about it, and this is important!"

"I've heard the list of candidates, and I can't buy any of them."

"You do believe, don't you, that his was the greatest brain ever enclosed in human skull?"

"Leonardo!"

*   *   *

"Okay. If you'll take me to Kew Gardens for the glass house, I'll take you to Trafalgar Square to see Leonardo's *Madonna of the Rocks*. I thought I had seen that painting in the Uffizi in Florence."

"You did. As in the fabric business, we call that 'in a different colorway.' He was nothing if not an experimenter."

"Will you go with me to the tailor for the second fitting?"

"Are they put off by your black underwear?"

"No. That underwear is very conservative, like my politics, which they might be put off by, or more grammatically, by which they might be put off."

"Isn't 'off' that kind of a word too?"

"Who's grading?"

"Will you go with me to Liberty department store to get some gifts to take home with us?"

"Do we have to go home?"

"Yes, you have to share your gold stash."

J. looked distressed. "I don't even think about the gold."

"Then why the song you were singing in the shower today? 'I've got silver, and I've got gold, gold in the noonday sun.'"

"What are the words to your shower hum when I'm not in with you?" He hummed the tune he'd heard.

"Oh, they are 'Lie closer, my dear.' It's from the old *Moulin Rouge*. 'These thirty-nine years on the banks of the Seine,' I sing in my head."

"Well, thank God it isn't the alternate words to that tune: 'I worry and wonder.' We seem to have so little to worry about. Wonder, maybe."

*   *   *

"What did you think of me when we met?"

"What could a girl want? Well spoken, well rounded, well funded, well endowed, well muscled, well educated."

"I wasn't even well dressed. That was the only thing you could know about me. I mean even before hello, at the elevator."

"You were standing in my personal space, and I wasn't even uncomfortable about it."

"I must have exuded essence of Patrick. When did you see the resemblance?"

"You were so familiar. I thought that was what love was."

"Getting familiar was what I had in mind."

"You really know how to rush a girl."

"You weren't all that easy. But really, when did you see the resemblance?"

"Only when I knew he was your biodad. Even then, I didn't fully see it until the wedding when you were both dressed alike.

291

You walked alike and danced alike. I was fighting hysterical laughter. You probably looked that much like your Jerry dad too, given that he was Patrick's brother."

"Half-brother."

"Yes, half-brother. If you had been wearing the same aftershave and smelled alike, I would have lost it."

"I danced with your mother. I wonder how she is doing about all this. She looks like you. I think I like her better than you do."

"I might be growing up. I'm starting to like her too."

"When did you know I had bucks?"

"Well, your car. I knew what you had paid for it, same as mine. So I knew I wouldn't have to feed you at my house."

"I guess you've done some feeding . . ."

"More than once—this is Hollywood. No, this is London. That's Hollywood. And the car was above the pay scale for a script supervisor. So I thought you must be supervising your own screenplay."

"What did Dunkin mean to you?"

"Yo-yos and donuts. Second, bagpipes and plaid. I always wanted the patent royalties on plaid."

"If you get that, I want checkered."

"Umbrella might be good here."

"What wonderful thing can I buy you with my royalties for checkerboard?"

"I'd like a margarita, but I'd settle for two tacos . . . My dear new husband, I think you want to know if I can handle being rich. You know those things I just bought at the B&B barn? I really took a flyer by acquiring such a big lot when business is slow, but I now know I'm not going to starve."

* * *

J. wasn't always willing to drive on the wrong side of the road at night to unknown places. He gave the turbaned cab driver an address. It was a tiny place, the trail of light beaming out across the dark neighborhood.

"This, my beloved, may be the only Mexican restaurant in England."

* * *

"Hey, boss lady. This is Miller from the showroom. Scott said it would be all right to call you. I just couldn't wait for an e-mail answer or not . . . Yeah, yeah, yeah. Everything is fine, selling stuff. Your daddy came by to check us out, and so did that curly blond woman . . . Yeah, Alice.

"We printed out a lot of your photos, you piggin' out over the stuff in the sun and the rain at the flea market . . . I wish I knew how to say this in a dramatic pitch, so you would say yes, but we just gotta start a genuine blog. I just hope you know what a blog is. The first thing could be video of you shopping, and Scott or I would do a voice-over about some of the stuff and what you're doing—the shopping, I mean, not that other good stuff. I don't know if I'd be shopping on my honeymoon, but that coat is worth the trip. We'd only show the stuff when we know what it is. And that terrific stuff from that terrific barn. It'd be great for business. The blog could just be updated every week, with you on it. It's such a great world, so much to talk about, trends and color and accessories, exhibits, and fabrics and for the English segment, the difference between Sheraton, Hepplewhite and Chippendale and paintings and artists!"

"Yes."

"Wow, I got it, and I don't know what to do with it."

"Bye."

J., who had been listening only to silence, inquired, "Who was that? Everything okay?"

"The newish employee at the showroom, the girl with the tattoo. All's well."

* * *

"I love Constable, love Constable country! I love that we came from here, before he painted it, but I can't think it looked very different. The church was here. I loved his painting of it way before I knew my ancestors were baptized in it."

"It's funny, you raised semi-Irish Catholic visiting East Anglia, the hotbed of Puritan protest, and part of you was part of it."

After a pause she replied, "That's democracy."

They walked the countryside.

"I feel good here. It's so beautiful. If I hadn't known Constable paintings, I might think I was having a magic race memory."

"I saw the Constable show at the Huntington. Didn't I see your picture, barefoot and pregnant in front of one of his pretty country cottages?"

"That was your sister Peg."

*   *   *

"Is it just that we're so steeped in her? I see Elizabeth all over town. Like the boat—I heard it bumping the stone wall where they took her to the tower, and I saw her at the far end of the golden rain arbor here at Hampton Court."

"It must have been a reenactor. Was that rain even here for her reign?"

"I think what I saw was Judi Dench from my memory bank."

"Her father moved his business to the country too and remodeled an old house, this one. He also was a good administrator, you know. It's a shame he has to be remembered for his efforts to get a male heir."

"Yeah, for some guys that's easy."

"Running a country, it has to be in wedlock to count. If he'd been really smart, he'd have padded Katherine's clothes and sent her away for months to come back with one of his bastard redheaded babies."

"Please, you're getting emotionally involved with the kings of England."

"But what an heir he fathered!"

"Girls sometimes turn out well. I read that Denmark changed its constitution not so long ago, so that the oldest, boy or girl, gets to be the monarch."

"You can have fun with a son, but you gotta be a father to a girl!"

"Don't worry; you'll be great at it."

* * *

"Elizabeth is still admired here, isn't she? Liz I that is. I think they like this Liz II also, but no one thinks she's a reincarnation of the first one. Margaret Thatcher, maybe."

"The First made a tremendous difference in the world, didn't she? I still don't have a clear picture of how you'll handle her in the new project or which film version of her you'll use, but she is the pivot, isn't she? I look forward to seeing how you'll handle the abrupt change in the English language after her."

"Yeah, like a week from Shakespeare to Milton. I'm mulling theories."

"Do you have to substantiate with other authorities?"

"I'm mulling that too. I just don't know. Robert Osborne never recites a bibliography. I saw an article last month with pictures of party guests, and the caption listed 'Ken Burns, historian.' I don't think I've heard him recite bibliography either. I might have thought 'documentary filmmaker.'"

"I might have thought, 'Ken Burns, hero.'"

"That too."

* * *

"This, our last shot at the British Museum. Before you go off and look at your paintings, come see something with me."

The room was full of tables covered by raised blue velvet curtains that appeared propped up in the center and then sloped down on either side of the tables.

"It looks like an architectural model of a housing development, being fumigated."

"How did you know?"

J. had to part several pairs of curtains before he found it, neatly glassed and framed. "Here, look at this. It's a letter from Elizabeth to Essex. It was lost for all those years. Guess where they found it."

"Couldn't begin to. Where?"

"Here in the museum in a filing cabinet. I think I remember it was in 1948."

"Fabulous! Look at her fine Italian hand! We can insert that with that film. Can you get a picture?"

"Not allowed to take one, but I can buy it and, thus, permission. I'd like to stay here and list and deal. Can I meet you at the door we came in, at closing time?"

*   *   *

"What are you going to say when you are asked if you saw the queen?

"I could say I saw the movie."

*   *   *

"Last venue. What'll it be? Victoria and Albert Museum or John Soane's house?"

"They're both on my must list."

"Well, which one would our son rather see when we come back?"

"Let's leave Victoria and Albert for our daughter then. I have a customer who says no one should build a house without seeing Soane's house first. She says it answers the two designer's questions: why, and why not?"

"Why? Are we building a house? We already have six."

"What?"

"Our house, your two houses, the Sierra Towers condo, the desert two, and the Bird Streets house, and then there's the boat that Mason lives on and you haven't even seen."

"Not only will I not starve; I won't be homeless."

*　*　*

"This is all amazing. Let's be sure to own the book when we get back, if for the light alone. Look how it comes in at the base of that little dome. Hennessey-and-somebody should have the book. I don't want to carry that big thing."

"If only for the collections of stuff, the way Soane housed things. I love, love, love it. And it's Hennessey and Ingalls."

"I always think, 'Hennessey Tennessee tootled the flute, and the music was simply grand.' Look down here where the paintings are almost on top of each other. Look what I found here."

In full drama, J. pulled aside a blue velvet curtain on a rod, like those in the document room in the British Museum, and there was a large watercolor painting.

"Oh my God, a Turner, up close and personal! This is a life-changing moment!"

*　*　*

"I feel like I'm doing pretty well. I haven't upchucked lately, and I was even looking forward to this airplane breakfast. As soon as we get back, I'll check in with the obstetrician. It's the same guy who was my gynecologist—g-y-n, now OB. You'll like him. He's gentle. He won't hurt fathers. Do you think the British perambulator will come in time for the baby?"

"I doubt it. I think you're supposed to order it right after the engagement ring."

*   *   *

"Hi, home. We're on the ground. What are you doing there, Alice?"

"Petting the cat. He's still mad as hell, and you can't even give him a treat 'cause he'll only eat that loud crunchy dry food. I shall try to tell him Em is home.

"I wanted to intercept you when you got down. Your grandmother's in the hospital. She's just fine now, no danger. She thought she was having heart troubles, which she was, and she called 911. It was not a heart attack. Anyway, she has a pacemaker now. She's at Cedars. It's on your way home."

*   *   *

"Em, this is what I want to do. Drop me off at Cedars, and you go home. Alice is there. Ruben is there for the luggage. Let's call again for soup to be ready for you, a cover-up for soda crackers if you should need 'em. I know you're tired. You need to get right to bed. You don't need a hospital scene. The Grandloon won't mind being alone with just me."

*   *   *

"Lady darling, if I had been in town, Marina would have called me, and I would have been here as soon as you were. Tell me how you are."

"Marina called me." It was Ray's voice. J. turned to see him emerging from the bathroom. "I don't live as close as you do, so she was already on her way from ER to surgery, and they wouldn't even let me hold her hand until after. Your girl cousin was here for a while then too."

"He came to protect his investment, to see that they didn't cut anything photographable from me. It really wasn't terrible, and I was awake the whole time. And now I'm battery-operated and should be good for many more Ingénue gigs."

"I don't know how to tell you this, beautiful lady, but I've always loved you almost as much as J. does, at least from kindergarten on."

"Well, my dears, I just have to tell you my story, and you know I'm not one to moan about such things. I woke up about four, lying on my side, head buried in pillow, and thought, *My dear Lord, I've smothered myself.* I jumped up and ran, not that I jump and run anymore, but I at least hurried for the balcony door, you know, and took big breaths and then two aspirin in case it was a heart attack, but I didn't have any of those symptoms that, you know, they tell you about. I was suffused in heat like a sauna.

"I went back to bed and tested for stroke—you know, arms out straight, and you see if the left one drifts down. None of that, but I began to see extravagant purple and gold behind my closed eyes, and then I saw it, very spectacular, with my eyes wide open. Then I realized I had almost no pulse.

"I dialed 911 and yelled to Marina to be sure the paramedics could get in. In about three minutes my room was full of these gorgeous young men, and Marina was handing them my insurance cards. They called my doctor at the hospital, and he sent me another gorgeous young man, about twelve years old with a crooked smile like Dennis Morgan, and he was in scrubs putting in my battery. You wouldn't remember Dennis Morgan."

"*Kitty Foyle* with Ginger Rogers, Irish tenor with crooked smile. 'My desert is calling. Oh, come there with me.'"

"I loved him, and I love this young doctor for fixing where my electrical system had gone completely to hell. Did you know your heart has electricity as well as plumbing? All those cards and posters about heart attack and stroke, but nothing about this. You could die of not knowing. Why don't they warn about it? . . . And how is Em doing? Is she past the throwing-up stage?"

J. attempted to keep the surprise from his face. "I sent her home. How did you know?"

"Have you ever noticed I'm smart? And besides, my friend at her gynecologist's office saw her reading the baby magazines.

Do you know which kind it is? I do. I'm a sponge for gossip, but no one can ever squeeze it out of me."

"But you just dribbled some on me."

"Well, you know, I don't know much now that you don't. How do you like Patrick?"

"I'll take him to lunch sometime."

Ray was rising to leave. "Congratulations, man. Am I the godfather?"

"You are! Granddarling, you know I'm godfather to his kids too, right?"

"Yes, well, don't all four of you go flying together."

* * *

"Hi, sweet babe. Move it over. You've got the whole bed. Mm, you smell good. You showered instead of falling right to sleep. I envy you that sleep thing you do. Head hits pillow, and sleep and deep breathing come right away, while I stare at the ceiling."

"Maybe if you were to close your eyes."

"Oh, what a concept! That's how you do it. My grandmother is going to be fine. Poor dear, she had to go through it all alone and sign stuff herself, with all those people around her. Hospitals are fussy about whom they let in, relatives only. Maybe we should get some kind of legal document drawn up so that Marina can sign and be with her. Did you know that Marina sleeps in clothes so she can hit the ground running? Ula should have some button that allows her to get right through to Marina."

"She would have waited as long to squeeze it as she did to yell."

"After she was in her room, Blaine called and wanted to come, but she told him the studio wouldn't be able to get hair and makeup done in time. She was fussing because they took away her pearl gray silk satin pajamas, but they were the old ones with the crossed tennis rackets embroidered on the lapel. That had to have been for Grandpa, and he's been gone for twenty-one years.

She did say she has newer ones, all pearl gray, a clean set every night. Good thing she has so much laundry money . . . Hey, the cat's not here with us. Have you seen him?"

"He was lashing his tail and telling me off while Ruanna unpacked, and then he peed in my suitcase. I told him off, and he's sulking."

"I wonder what Grandloon's white cat will tell her. She's probably under the sofa singing, 'It's so easy to leave me, all alone with my memories.' Ray was with Grandloon as soon as she was in her room. He stayed all day until I got there, and Marina had just gone down to dinner. Cedars has a credible restaurant, you know, beyond that grand piano in the lobby."

"That's so good. You can have dinner while I'm in labor with our daughter."

"Son."

"Daughter."

"Son."

"D."

"S."

"Her."

"Him."

"She."

"He!"

301

Chapter 19

"Hey, leader man. Welcome back. How do you ask how it was when you are asking about a honeymoon?"

"Assume great."

"We have clues. We posted the photos you e-mailed in the proper places."

Joe flipped on a series of rigged work lights, flooding a wall apportioned off with stretched string as a giant storyboard of sticky notes and push-pinned photos and clippings.

"Man, it's rough still, waiting for your fine-tune. We did it from Winston Churchill. You could have done the chronology from memory, but it does no harm for a lot of us to know more about what we're doing and what these figures did. I'm hooked on Henry V right now myself. I have to tell you, we're all pretty excited about this project, even enamored."

"Yeah, I do see some problem areas. You haven't dealt with the second Arthur. You need a lot more space for the three Edwards in a row. We should mark century breaks. A helpful gimmick to start remembering dates is to get a key one in each century. I've always used Henry IV as a pivot. He came to the throne in the century break of 1400. Em's pivot date is 1500, the birth of Cellini. Of course that was in Italy and of no use to us. She had to go see Italian painters when we were in London."

"How's your other lady this morning?"

"I'm on call to pick her up. She says she gets to stay for their delicious gourmet lunch. They haven't been doing pacemakers all that long. She'd have died."

"Well, we were all doing prayers or meditations or whatever we do after Alice got Marina's cell call."

"Thanks. Something worked."

"Yep. Modern medicine."

"A lot of time was poured in here. You and everybody working?"

"I'm holding my breath on a pilot. I'm okay. I put bucks aside. I've got child support. Everybody's starting to get good work now, or some work anyway, but we're all behind this. Latty's dog got a lead part in a commercial, and his wife's working. And so on.

"When we printed out your photos, we thought we knew where some of them belonged. You'll stare. Is that rock rubble really Hadrian's Wall? I didn't know any survived."

"Quite a bit of it, enough to be of interest to tourists. We stayed at Hadrian's Wall Inn. The Roman emperor was an absentee landlord. How do we cover that? I've got to sort out Marcus Aurelius here too. Doesn't that recent Arthur film have some Romans in it?"

*   *   *

"Hey, Scott, look who just came in the back door!"

"Hey, hey, there she is, Sadie, Sadie, married lady."

"Hey, Miller. Hey, Scott. Hey, everybody. I'm lovin' the blog!"

Scott came around the counter, dropping a dust rag as he moved toward Em and enveloped her in a bear hug.

"Don't tell me we've lost the dusting lady."

"You know I'm a Virgo for detail."

Young Miller, with her blog a success, ventured a cheek kiss for the boss. "Could we sit with it and talk about what worked or could be better?"

"Yes, but maybe not today. Is anybody looking at it?"

"Yes, they are."

"Come on, Scott, grab your notes, and let's go across for enchilada Howard. You have no idea how famishing it is to be without Mexican food."

This early, the opening time of eleven-thirty, the table she regarded as hers was crouching empty in its corner of the patio. The waitress, billowy of skirt and bosom, delivered margaritas almost as soon as they were seated. With practiced eye she saw the new wedding band and knew why her customer had been missing. "Where on honeymoon?"

"England."

"Beautiful man! Macho!"

"The country's not bad either."

The margaritas were doubles, a recent innovation of management, and Scott would have to get into the second drink as well, to avoid any speculation about pregnancy as a reason for Em's not drinking. She was glad not to be blimped up so soon after the wedding. Her girlfriends all said that not telling people too early would make the waiting feel shorter.

She wondered whether poor Scott would be able to function the rest of the day. She had seen the new guy manning the computer.

She ordered a diet Coke with lots of ice. "It's so hot today after a cool London," she said to explain.

Scott took a large gulp of his drink and spread some papers between them. "You can see how business is down the first half of this year from the same time last year, but we're not suffering yet. If Obama gets in, it's bound to get better. If it's the Republicans, it'll be the same old, same old.

"That line of nubby silks had hardly any orders, and they were going to take it away from us. I suppose they think that someone in Pacific Design Center could do better, though it's not exactly crowded over there. But they saw the blog and left the fabric line for another chance. Then look what I did—155 yards for padded walls in a screening room, the pretty amber color. Some folks still have money out there. And yes, it's proforma.

I got the payment with the order. The check cleared, and I sent some to the factory."

"As I recall, that's the one called 'umber amber.' I don't know the blog rules. Could we say something about it with the designer's name?" Emmy asked, all PR-brained. She put her lips to the rim on her glass, clearing the salt and leaving a lipstick trace, and poured some of her drink into Scott's as he looked away for the next papers. "J. says Obama's a dangerous man."

"Not nearly so dangerous as Harry Truman was."

* * *

They assured J. that they were not new at this rodeo and would keep her hidden until he called to say that he was there waiting. The coordination worked well. A nurse wheeled Ula through the door, Marina beside her, as J. pulled to the curb.

"Hey, Granddiva!" He immediately stepped out of the car and put his arms around her. "I wonder if you know how grateful I am you made it, dear lady."

"A sentiment I share, dear boy!"

Now there were photoflashes and calls. "Ula Dunkin!" "Ula Brenholm!" "Ingénue!" "Be well!" "Loved your movie!" "You'll win the Oscar!" "I use your moisturizer!"

"I always thought Ingénue moisturizer sounded like a naughty story."

"You're just a bad lady. I knew some of them would be here, so I thought the Packard would add to the scene."

"It could only have been more dramatic if you had hired a driver in an appropriate cap and had swept me, aging cougar, into the backseat, you unidentified, beautiful young man."

"I could continue my status as unidentified."

"Oh my goodness, I didn't think that mattered to you. I've seen your picture on the cover of a magazine, and you could have been an actor if you had wanted, to you know. You certainly have enough inheritance of it."

He pulled out of the covered parking into the double street enveloped by the north and south wings of the hospital, the curious and the well-wishers surrounding them there too. Ula smiled and waved.

"I'm waving back here too," said Marina, "to see if anyone might think I'm somebody too. So far I've had several waves back."

"Well, Marina, you're pretty. You could be in pictures."

"Yeah, I use Ingénue cosmetics, and you dress me cute. But I vant to vrite."

"I vant to criticize. Ven can I read it?"

"Soon, J., but don't hurt me."

"And Grandlady, Grandmadre, what do you mean about my acting heritage? Is that from you?"

"Well, sweet darling, besides that, my husband J. J., your granddaddy, was the son of Damon Higgen's Aunt Mary. They were on the Dublin stage together in a family act. So your new married name of Higgen-Dunkin comes round again with your great-grandmother Mary Higgen Dunkin."

"Don't make my head swim when I'm driving, Lady. Are we ever going to straight-talk?"

"No."

She was digging in her metallic gray bag, so big, J. thought, that she might have the gray satin pajamas in it if Marina had not been carrying a paper bag that said "patient's belongings" on it.

"I'm so grateful here. Is there something I can endow? I wish I could have bought them the grand piano. I didn't hear it as we were leaving. Marina, don't they play it all the time? I should think it would have a comfort factor in the night as well as day. I could hire four or five shifts of really great players. Musicians, you know, always need a gig.

"Listen, children, I could support a closed-circuit TV to patients' rooms. They could request tunes. The pianist could even say something about the piece—if from a show, who wrote it, and even why and, you know, when."

She began to hum "Let Me Entertain You" and drowsed off, tired, into a nap. The only sounds were traffic and the huff of the Packard, all down La Cienega Boulevard. At the right turn onto Wilshire Boulevard, the driver of a BMW lay on his horn when he thought the big yellow car didn't make that turn tight enough or fast enough.

The passenger roused to murmur, "Idiot, what does he do with the UPS truck?"

"J., would that be the same as he does with FedEx?" asked Marina.

"Or the Brinks truck?"

"The city bus?"

"A gas-delivery tanker truck?"

"A car carrier?"

"Not a car carrier; it corners better."

Ula napped until just after the tree-shaded median strip at the Beverly Wilshire Hotel, her hand still in her bag on a mirror rather larger than purse size. "I have to see what saving my life did to my décolletage. I hope this swelling isn't here forever. How could I go on advertising Ingénue décolletage cream? You know, if you hold your shoulders back taut in the bright white light, you can get away with it. Shoulders forward, and your chest falls into puckers and folds. Puckers and folds—that's from a poem my mother used to say to me while she did my hair. It's an epic-length piece in which young lovers are cruelly separated, and she gets herself to a nunnery. Oh so many years later, he finds her. She's the Mother Superior by now, and she says, 'My time halts but hurriedly. State the cause why you seek me.' He wouldn't have recognized her either. 'Your face, ah, your face, like a curtain let fall by a hand that's grown weary, into puckers and folds.' I was, you know, always terrified of puckers and folds.

"Mother delivered it very well. She had had elocution lessons, you know, and had seen the Chautauqua when it came to town. I was the last of her multitudinous brood, the last chance to fiddle, you know, with daughter hair, and she sent me off to school looking like, well, you know, looking like Miss South Dakota.

"We're passing my country club. I belong to it as Mrs. Jared James Dunkin, cosmetic fortune heiress; I'm not regarded as show folk there. Blaine likes to come here for a drink, sometimes even for dinner. He thinks it's funny to talk about show business in the rather quiet dinning room. I tell him he's going to get me kicked out.

"Did you ever hear about the time Esther Williams attended an event here in black satin pants and was asked to leave? She protested they were by a great designer, but they sent her home to put on a skirt."

"The Magic Castle does that too. I warned Emmy in time, and she found the most rustling taffeta in town, long and full."

"I like that girl. Wasn't she beautiful in the wedding dress with pockets?"

"Yes!" said J. and Marina in unison.

"You'll come to me soon to tell me all about the honeymoon."

"No, not all."

J. was making his left turn to the Ingénue's building to the evident pleasure of the doorman, who was proudly holding a wheelchair for her. He insisted on leaving his post to take her up to her own door, as though no one could do it as well.

"Thank you, darling boy," she said, ensuring his continuing devotion.

Behind the door, Miss Harlow the cat was screaming accusations of desertion.

"Marina, I think I'll nap in my clothes. I'm not to raise my elbow higher than my nipples. Is that today's nipples or where they should be and were, before the weary hand? I'm too tired for any elbow raising now. Thank you for the stylish lift, Grandbaby."

J. went to the kitchen and requisitioned two cups of coffee from the housekeeper, who was worried for she too had not heard the drama in the night. She had waked only when the entry hall was full of paramedics.

Presently Marina joined him. "Hey, coffee at the coffee table. And aren't we grateful to be here with her dozing in her bedroom? It could have gone the other way, you know. I feel terrible that I didn't hear her sooner, grateful that I did when I did. She's promised to alert me right away now for anything. While she was at Cedars, Alice found me someone—big bearded guy—to install some electronics, like a baby monitor, so I can hear her snore, I guess."

"Heavy snoring?"

"Not apnea, no. Not much louder than the purr of the cat, who is, as we speak, stretched out on the diva from navel to knee in a purring storm. How did Em's cat respond to getting her back?"

"Scolded during unpacking and then peed in her suitcase."

"You have discovered the true origins of the term 'pissed off.'"

"An excellent phrase. How's your novel coming?"

"Well enough. Living with this fabulous creature, this darling old devil, I must constantly resist writing her in. You couldn't make up the things she says. Real life is so much better'n fiction."

"What does *better'n* mean?"

"It rhymes with 'veteran,' meaning 'better than,' in the English subdialect that includes my favorite question: 'maskoos callin?' That means 'may I ask who's calling?' A more famous exchange is 'jeet?' where the answer is 'no, jew?' And that means 'did you eat?' and 'no, did you?' If you said 'it be better'n,' it would be jive. You speak jive, don't you?"

"Not well enough to interpret in *Airplane*."

"You're good. You always get it. I failed to ask about your project. How's it doing upon reentry? What are you anyway, documentarian, producer, historian?"

"I wish I knew. At a garden party once, there was this big wicker chair full of a man in a white suit with the biggest flash of sapphire you ever saw on his pudgy hand. I said, 'You look interesting; what do you do?' I figured he was, like, a choreographer who hadn't danced in thirty years, and he replied, not without pride, 'I am the heir to the Doris Duke fortune.'"

"Oh yeah, the butler. I remember."

"He couldn't even have that job anymore, and I wanted to say, 'Hey, man, is that all there is?'"

"Poor thing, but you could have been an actor. I just heard that, not an hour ago."

"As though it were the only thing a man would want to be, if he could. Maybe I could have been one of those angry boyfriends with the five o'clock shadows on a soap opera."

"Well, you're barely shaven, and you are a soap opera."

"You're in one too, growing up cute, hot, and cool. I guess you were already that when you came to us. The Grandloon threatened me with excommunication, disinheritance, and worse, dismemberment if I put a move on you."

"She didn't know yet that my paycheck bought my abject loyalty, even against her oh-so-attractive RTC grandson."

"RTC?

"Randy tomcat."

"You noticed. I took care of the issue though. I dreamed about you, and you weren't that good!"

"Check with my calendar cop."

"See how easy it was to get your attention, to get you to boast about your sexual prowess? Don't you think the rest would have been as easy?"

"No! Go home. Bad boy."

*   *   *

From the cars at his curb, he knew who was there for this opening of the rest of the wedding presents. They were all assembled, drinks in hand. Em's mother put down her Boodles Gin on the rocks and came to J. for a proper hug.

"Here's that man who makes my daughter so happy. And do you really think that gives you leave to pat me on the butt?"

"Dear lady who gave me her beautiful daughter, do you not know an Irish kiss when you feel one?"

"My dear new son, I've been pinched repeatedly by your grandfather, seduced by your biological father, and Irish-kissed by a vast selection of cousins you haven't met yet. Kiss the cousins all. You're welcome as the flowers in May. Come get your drink. We have determined that you will be the one to open the first package. It's addressed just to you, with no confession of the giver."

J. tore off the green ribbon and pushed it under the coffee table and then removed the paper. He pulled from the box a handsome bag, dark olive canvas with leather trim and strap. Attached was a tag: "Dude's Diaper Bag." He opened the flap, which pulled up a cardboard cutout of a cat and triggered some hidden device that asked a tinny question: "Who let the cat out?"

"Well, my darlings," said Emmy, "now that the cat is out of the bag, we're so glad to share with you that we're expecting. I'm expecting a girl, and J.'s expecting a boy named Jared."

* * *

"Man, we have got the Google going and have a list of English monarchs from Offa, who reigned till 796, up to Edward, Harold, and Edgar of 1066. And there is another film we're now pursuing: *Alfred the Great*, MGM, 1969. I could've read all night for that."

"Well, Joe, you could've read all night 'cause you don't have a woman telling you to turn off the light."

"Yeah, and it's killing me to work with her. That little rear end, after five kids, still as cute as it was in high school. She walks as though she had a fence around her, and I can't get near her. Is she really having it with Mason, that scratchy beard and all that weight? He might hurt her."

"Would that be worse than the way you hurt her?"

"That stings."

"Well, we're all equal friends to both of you. You're both equal friends to all of us. It's hard."

"Never thought of it that way. Hey, I have Warren Beatty's *Reds* for you to look at, the witnesses we all remembered admiring. They all come into the right side of the frame and never fill half of it. It's what makes it work, keeping their status as observers. Oh, and hey, I have one image of Emmy, kind of curled into the frame as though to fill half of it without trimming off any head the way a Gucci billboard does. She looks great. We have to plan so as to cut all of her stuff before she pods out."

"Everybody knows?"

"Sure. We're an ant colony. Everything is known all down the column."

* * *

"Hey, man, out here in the dark. What, if anything is this committee going to do with the mess that was left in England after the English Civil War? The restoration of son of Charles and trying to turn England back into a Catholic country?"

"What's wrong with a Catholic country?"

"Come on, Alice, everything! That's the point of what we're doing here in this whole project. A country can't be Catholic, but a person can. It's okay to be Catholic in this country, or to be anything or nothing."

"Hey, another member out here in the dark. All that doesn't matter. Our freedom had already turned its path to the New World. Let 'em stew."

"How long and strong are we going to be," asked Mason, "about Roger Williams? Without him and his separation of church and state we mighta hada all been Puritans? Though we at Plymouth had some modicum of toleration. Yeah, we were *Mayflower*. So are many, many. One Thanksgiving my mother had seven descendants of the *Mayflower* at her Thanksgiving table and didn't even know they were, until she got to boasting about her own Plymouth heritage."

"Until a certain movie about a slave ship, I didn't know, and now when you talk *Mayflower*, I can say that we came over on the *Amistad*."

"Cool, Joe, then your roots got intertwined."

"One of my girls was in one of those classes where they talk about their heritages. When asked hers, she answered, 'Baptist, Jewish, and Catholic.'"

"Mason out here sounding off again about Roger Williams. Remember the prosperity of Rhode Island when he let in Jewish merchants, honoring his own dedication to separating worship and government."

"Hey, and Jewish accountants." came the voice of the accountant who had dropped in on this work session to see what was going on with her new client.

"When we get to him, let's not forget to credit also that ancient king who was smart enough to let in the Jewish merchants,"

"What about Viking raiders? Does Kirk Douglas or Ernest Borgnine grunt anything about taking the longboat to England?"

"I'll rent and listen."

"I have to have Vikings for the art history. Their jewelry was terrific. It seems, though, that it was at its best in the second century, and we're talking maybe ninth. Good stuff there preserved in a bog, even cloth."

"Did everybody see the broach of Alfred the Great on the Royals' website?"

"Hey, this is getting awesome!"

"Does anyone remember Mel Gibson's *Braveheart* well enough to know if it specifically identified the English king?"

"Hey, that's my favorite movie," said Elra. "I'll watch it tonight. I get to see my best scene—those bare, winter-white legs, a whole line of 'em, knees pumping across the battlefield. There's a makeup comment. The highlanders denuded and painted themselves blue and psyched themselves to a rage to go into battle. I'll be in touch with notes."

*   *   *

"Darling boy, I'm on my new cell phone. Shall I learn to text?"

"No!"

"I don't drive very often, daytime only. I wouldn't text and drive."

"You could drive your driver crazy. At least when you're on your phone, she knows what you're plotting."

"I just called to share. We, Blaine and I, watched an old John Wayne movie last night. Wasn't that a fine figure of a man though? Nice straight shoulders, you know, and small tight buns. As good as he looked in a leather vest, he was even better in a tuxedo, you know. I even saw him in tails once. I knew him, of course. After he died, I was on a panel at that giant book club, you know, with the music and the lunch, at the Beverly Hilton, I think. It was after that pretty little book I did, you know, *Star Beauty.* Wayne's widow lady was there with her book about him. I loved telling her that I found him so beautiful in tails. I'm supposed to know what's beautiful, you know. When he was away once, they lost their house in a fire, and he sent some extravagant piece of jewelry with a note that said, 'To Pilar, the girl who has nothing.' There was a football player with a book there too, Matuszak, I think, *Cruisin' with the Tooz.* I have it in the library. I also have a wall of signed books. He called me 'little buddy.' No one had ever called me 'little buddy' before and maybe not since. Anyway, in the movie, Wayne stood fiddling with the ties on a saddle for the longest time. That was to give him something to do while he delivered a lot of necessary dialogue. It gave me time to look at the saddle and think about its development from early, early. Then thinking about the John Wayne statue on Wilshire just east of La Cienega, I was remembering, you know, the equestrian statue on Capitol Hill from Roman times. Whatever was that saddle like?"

"The development of horse and saddle along with law and order: brilliant, dear lady. When we were in Westminster Abbey, we saw a brass plaque on the wall that told readers that above them on the beam were the saddle and shield of Henry V. I bet I can get a photo."

"Brilliant, dear Grandbaby."

"How are you, and what's happening at your house? Have you been out on the town yet?"

"Well, I may go out this week. My movie is playing in Westwood. I can almost see the marquee from here. I'm not on it, but Blaine says I'm on the poster."

"The reviewers are glowing for you. I'm sure you have a clipping service, but I'm clipping too. It's scrapbook time."

"Thank you, darling baby. Bye for now."

* * *

"Hello, is this Larry Edmunds Bookshop on Hollywood Boulevard? Do you have lobby cards and posters of current movies?"

"Is this Jared Dunkin, the collector on the hill-end of my Hollywood Boulevard? I have half a dozen of each, and would I ever like to have them signed!"

"Sounds okay to me. Send me all six, and I'll send you back five with her signature as 'The Ingénue, Ula Dunkin.' Good to hear she's that popular."

"Sending tomorrow."

"Oh, also while I have you, I need a signature of the guy who played Geronimo. Is it Chuck Connors? 'Cause I have a penciled signature from Geronimo himself."

"I think that's worth about seven thousand bucks now, from a recent catalog. Did you know that he sat in the prison yard and did that rectangle with his block-lettered name in it for a dime? Where did you get it?"

"Well, there was this old tattered scrapbook at the flea market in London. They wanted five pounds for it, but I got it for four. Is this a markup or what?"

"Good. And yes, four pounds is quite a markup over a dime.

*   *   *

"Hey, babe. Can you get away for an early bookstore trip and dinner at Musso and Frank, and then we can go to the nine o'clock screening? I'll pick you up at five."

"You must mean Edmunds. What if I meet you there at five-thirty? Miller can give me a ride up if you'll take me down to the showroom in the morning."

"A deal. Where do you want breakfast?"

*   *   *

"How about the Grill for the best French toast on earth?

"The classic answer is 'no one ever goes there anymore; it's too crowded.'"

"Let's be brave and shoulder in."

*   *   *

"Wow, so good. We should send Ruanna here for breakfast to see if she could duplicate it. And the pressed coffee too—could not resist this one stimulant to start the day. It was good last night getting that ride with Miller. We got a chance to talk about the blog. It got off to such a good start, and we have to keep up the momentum, changing it once a week. Maybe it should be once a month. Miller's going to be really good at it. Can't wait for the English stuff to come in. May I use your flea market photos? I wonder if it would be a good idea to show your Geronimo. It could be a cautionary tale about throwing out old paper, or about throwing it out before offering it to you first. The coffee—I'm going on and on.

"Oh my God! I feel something—a flutter! She's kicking me! It's started! It's so faint. She's really in there. I can just barely feel her inside. I don't know if you can feel her from the outside yet. Here, put your hand here and press a bit. Oh, this is the most exciting thing ever! Except for when you put her there."

"I can't feel him yet. Lucky little Jared, higher up than big Jared ever got. What did it feel like, like God jump-started him with a stroke of lightning? I didn't hear any thunder, but your face—the look on your face. Dear glowing one! This is real!"

* * *

"Omg. What a great day. English B&B shipment & perambulator arrived. Making pink pillow. Mom & Daddy coming to dinner."

"Great. Blue pillow. When you text, I miss your happy voice."

Chapter 20

"Hey, Granddarling. How goes all at your house? Caught you on Jay Leno last night. We thought you were great. Thanks for the plug for our Elizabeth project. Leno liked you. At first he was going gentle with you, but you kept with him. He really went for that. I've seen him a couple of times at our mechanic. He's buddies with the Motorman, from the Sunday morning radio show. Leno is a car buff and drives, among others, a Stanley Steamer that can catch fire up there on the freeway, but he says you don't stop—you just go faster so the wind will put it out. He called our Packard a yellow boxcar. But listen here, you have a new picture you haven't told us about yet? What's a grandson for?"

"Oh, baby darling, I just signed it, you know, and I'm so nervous about it. I've passed the usual health quiz. They didn't seem all that worried that I was, you know, battery-operated. How will I come out on the rest of the gig? It's a comedy, you know!"

"You'll be terrific. You are a funny lady."

"Even sometimes by intention. But for comedy you gotta not laugh, you know. I can't always manage that. I thought I'd break apart when Anders' children came, you know, for the gold. That sounds like an Olympic team on the ice rink. If I had looked at your calm face when I turned from opening their safe, I would have lost it entirely. I about did, you know, when you told Tim to pick up one of the bars, and he couldn't. How did you know about that?"

"Google. The slick sides on that heavy slope-sided bar make your hand slide off. Harder for a thief."

"So tell me, they have come and taken it all away?"

"Yes, you are a funny lady. You saw that my so-sharp forensic accountant had had her lawyer draw up that sort of storage lease that holds the landlord unaccountable. And you were there when Tim slid the bar to the front of the shelf to pick it up. She made them all three sign for that and for the coins they all took. I saw you being careful not to catch her eye.

"Isn't it sad, we cousins estranged? We four played up and down these stairs and even in those mirrored closets. Remember how you saw to it that we couldn't get locked in with those inside latches and showed us how to hit them? That didn't stop us from imprisoning a visitor and laughing to hear him try to get out. Kids are so cruel!"

"People are cruel, dear one. We are, you know, compelled to it, as self-preservation."

"I don't think I can buy that. I've never known you to be cruel. Well, maybe a string of broken hearts left behind."

"Maybe the doorman, but he didn't get left behind."

* * *

Em hoped it was not to be one of those long speeches of gratitude that cools the gravy and maybe even the bowl of steaming mashed potatoes. The beautifully browned turkey would hold its interior temperature for only a little rhetoric.

"Our deep thanks to thee or these who giveth this woman, for allowing the interruption of the Higgen tradition so that the newly Higgen-Dunkins may host. What a year this has been since my grandmother and I sat, along with the tonight-absent Blaine, in a restaurant for the festive meal of gratitude. I now know what gratitude is. Let us eat."

Em felt gratitude that J. had not counted the ways—or expressed his bitter disappointment over the so-recent election. She further hoped that no one would mention Sarah Palin or Hillary. A while into the meal her father was compelled to hope aloud that the country had made the right decisions. Ula said that she had every faith in her country, that it would recover.

The passing of replenished gravy boats deflected the moment. Em was grateful for their arrival, as well as that Ruanna and Ruben had no American schoolchild sentimentality for Pilgrims trudging through the snow that would have led them to be elsewhere on Thanksgiving. Those poor Plymouth men in their white stockings and cold legs. She set to wondering when long pants had been invented. In a David painting? Maybe Napoleonic? She would Google that later.

There were several more speeches, the last one J.'s with the champagne, which they all doubted had been present in the Plymouth colony. J. included his gratitude that his grandmother was well.

"Well, I'm battery-operated now, you know. That's why J. calls me Grandenergizerbunny."

"I'm very uninformed about what causes an electrical heart disconnect."

"Well, Patrick, so am I. I asked my doctor, and he said, 'A-G-E.' I was trying to think what that stood for, maybe accelerated genetic energy or arthritic something or other, when I realized he was spelling. And you know, that's the best pumpkin pie I've ever tasted."

Em was gratified, for she had spent most of Wednesday on it. Scott's instructions had been to follow the recipe on the can but to separate the eggs and fold in the whipped whites. "No milk," he had admonished. "It turns it that baby shit color."

* * *

"Seriously, J., don't you want to know? How could they not have had long pants in all those millennia? That's as ridiculous as how long it took to put wheels on luggage. It makes no sense. Why wasn't Blaine here tonight? You did invite him, didn't you?"

"His estranged daughter called him, and he gets to see his grandchild for the first time."

"It was a great dinner. You do love hosting, don't you? Next year there will be two more high chairs, for Peg's baby and our daughter."

"Our son. The long pants came after the time of our second project. Everybody, all the guys, had white knit legs during that Constitution summer."

"They must have looked like a birch forest when they all stood up."

*　　*　　*

"Oh my God! Elizabeth is ready to run. And they have scheduled a date!"

*　　*　　*

"The Grandbunny's scenes are shooting. Would you like to waddle onto the set and watch?"

*　　*　　*

"Wouldn't it be funny if the hospital called to ask our decision about circumcision and that's how we found out it's a boy?"

"But I've just picked up the pink cushion from my drapery workroom. One of my suppliers does the prettiest pink silk you ever saw."

"Blue!"

*　　*　　*

Emmy shifted her considerable bulk, looking in vain for a comfortable position.

"Hey, mother of the pod people. Is he trying to get out yet? Pecking at the shell?"

"Poor baby, is that all you had for pets, Easter chicks? Didn't your dog have puppies? Didn't you ever see a bitch in labor?"

"I think I'm going to."

"Not today."

"Sit up, sweet stuff, for this cup of tea, and then you can decide between reading the two comic sections in this Sunday paper or listening to our review."

"Oh my God, so soon? Quick! I can't stand it! It just started last night—in a blaze of gorgeous, I might add."

"It's so East Coast, the morning-after reviews. The guy had to have watched all those hours, with the advance tape too. Be ready. Here it is."

Elizabeth the Glorious has been dead for more than three hundred years, but her fan base is legion. We hunger for the latest gossip about her. And it has come along in movie after movie over the years, the first a silent movie from 1924. How she would have loved film. Her PR ran to portraits, controlled, edited to exude power and opulence. Not just for her own pleasure did seed pearls cascade down her velvet sleeve.

A pleasant, good-looking couple host the movies, one after the other, beginning with the future queen as a newborn and then as a red-haired toddler on her mother's execution day. It also happens to be her father's wedding day. Henry VIII was an outstanding executive, a successful king, but unfortunately as remembered for his marriages and their culminations as his daughter is remembered for resisting marriage altogether.

"Jared, darling, this is flat-out wonderful. Here, let me see how it looks. My God, it's the whole page, almost, except for the mattress ad." She was sitting up now, holding the earthenware tea mug with the carved face on the side.

J. could scarce control his elation. "My whole life is passing before me. I remember when we bought that mug at the Renaissance Fair."

"Where's yours?"

"Broken."

"Beyond repair?"

"Yes. Beyond landfill."

"Read!"

The producers, M. E. and Jared Higgen-Dunkin sit or perch on or stand against the barstool from the old Dean Martin and Glen Campbell shows, and it works as well for them. Yes, she's the granddaughter of Damon Higgen, and his grandmother is Ula Ingénue Dunkin. The current generation does not fail us. She is an art historian and he a historian. They praise and critique, telling us what in these films is accurate and what is not, in events and in objects presented by Hollywood. They are backed by an entourage of Hollywood pros—music, costume, makeup, hair, lights, camera, and action—credited as "The Committee." This project is no camel. It's a horse of a different color.

"Hey, babe. I look up to see your happy-dance face, and it isn't there. You're squinching. What's the matter?"

"Take the paper with you to read in the car, alert Ruben, and call the doctor."

*   *   *

323

"Hey, there's a grand piano down in the lobby, and it's piped into the television. You can request numbers, and he will play your requests. I called and asked for my favorite, 'These Foolish Things Remind Me of You.' What he said then went out over all the hospital's televisions. He said, 'This is from upstairs in maternity, the labor room. I bet you are reminded of him, aren't you, sweetie? Call down when it arrives. I've got some baby songs.' Then he sang the whole song. I heard laughing."

"Gee, that's a great idea. I wonder who thought of it and maybe endowed it."

"It is a great idea. Where were you? Did you get some breakfast?"

"I was downstairs in a hall, near the piano actually, but I missed the personal drama. There's a food station in that hall; I found it when the Grandloon was here to get battery-operated. I got a huge and terrific cinnamon bun, then and now. Do you want some of it?"

"Oh, please no. Don't talk dirty. I could upchuck on you. The pressure is terrible, and there's no turning back."

"My baby is havin' a baby."

"Wish you could share this part too."

"What we learned in those classes? Is this where the heavy breathing starts?"

A woman entered, and he could see that she was a no-nonsense type. Her hair hung in one long ponytail over her left shoulder, and a stethoscope swung against pale-violet scrubs that were printed with what appeared to be images of Winnie the Pooh. "My name is Jane, and I have heard all the heavy breathing jokes and jokes about what happened nine months ago that have ever been delivered."

"And you do delivery jokes too."

"I doubt Mary Ellen is going to listen to any jokes 'cause it's getting serious. She's doing well. Stick with her. There's coffee over there when you're through with your Starbucks."

Just then, Emmy's cell phone rang, and it was a marketing call, offering free delivery for something. They didn't listen to find out what.

"Here, please take her new cell phone away with you," said the nurse. "She has some serious concentrating to do. So far she's called her office twice and called home once. And of course, she's called her mother."

"It was Daddy actually."

"We should have heard out that phone call about free delivery. We could have saved $10,000."

"She says you live on the hill behind Chateau Marmont," Jane remarked. "I used to live in a sweet little tile-roofed house on that street, backed up to the hill. I sold it well and bought two down on the flats near here, one for my mom. Great babysitting after my divorce. Do the guys coming off their early morning shift at the Chateau still clang their salvaged empty bottles in the dark in wire shopping carts?"

*   *   *

She had been going to this doctor for the last five or six years, always noticing his beautiful brown eyes and hoping that the lady in the picture frame on his desk really appreciated him. His funny little pointed beard was covered now with a surgical mask, isolating the brown eyes that swam above her. His voice was kindly and enthusiastic. "You've got a fine baby boy, dear. His little baby parts and his little boy parts are all there and beautiful. There's only one thing, dear: he's red-headed."

*   *   *

"Oh, look at him, J. He's you in a different colorway."

*   *   *

J. was all but running beside the gurney taking her to her room. She had seen his eyes in ecstasy before, but now they shone with extra stars, like the white painted bursts of glamorous light created by the great story illustrators in old magazines.

* * *

"Em, darling, look at him, look at him, my son!"

"J., my beloved, look at him! Look what we did! He's gorgeous, beyond gorgeous."

"He can keep his hat on, but the red eyebrows are always going to be a giveaway."

"I think it's adorable, and not just red-gold. It's carrots and mahogany like the blue-eyed imps in Irish travel brochures."

"Think when he's grown-up, the chest hair!"

"Oh my God, as long and thick as yours!"

"And under his arms, a red wire tangle. And think of his arms and legs when we go surfing at Venice Beach."

"You can have fun with a son, but you would have had to be a father to a girl, right?"

"Aw, you've got no girl. Are you okay with it?"

"Wasn't it a son I wanted? I had no idea they were so cute. I bought some blue things in case."

* * *

Over the heads of the other cooing observers at the window of the nursery—Em's mother and lawyer sister and the vastly swollen sister Peg—J. and Patrick exchanged their first conspiratorial acknowledgment of the red hair, a contribution of Dr. Prom Date McCarty.

* * *

"I hope he likes it here, his room all yellow and pale green like what he sees out his window."

"Good man! He prevented you from going to the inauguration."

"But this is great. I can feed him while we watch. Maybe he won't cry."

"Why would he? He has it made. Look at his round cheek with your round breast. What a shot!"

J. was kissing them as the big Lincoln rolled onto the screen with the new president and his wife.

"Isn't that charming, the way they are getting out of the car and walking beside it? And I love what she's wearing."

"Well, you know I'm terrified with that big cloak of office he's wearing."

"J., don't worry. It's going to be all right, even great."

*   *   *

"I'm telling you, Granddarling, you can have any ringtone you want. Scott does all that tech stuff for her. When March comes, she'll have 'The winds of March that make my heart a dancer.' Is there any memorable music in your new picture? Seriously, I know it was you who rang your piano player and told him to do 'Baby makes three; we're so happy in our new Aston Martin.'"

"Well, J. sweetheart, 'silver' is two syllables, and you know that doesn't scan, so I couldn't say 'so happy in our silver Aston Martin.' Or bctter, you would like a solid gold Cadillac? We saw that play in London with Margaret Rutherford. Did I ever tell you that story? J. J. was such a fan of hers, you know. He sent her a note saying that he had always loved her and asking, could we come backstage? I think she knew who we were, maybe at least when she opened the door. She said, 'One often hears that one is liked, but to be loved is so special!' Her husband Stringer was there, and we four sat in big, deep, broken-down, chintz chairs and drank warm gin. We struggled to our feet when she wanted to toast. 'To your president, and to our little queen, and to our Beatles, so like your astronauts, are they not?'' Comedians never laugh, you know, but I was afraid J. J. would spray gin out his nose.

"I think I'm funny in this movie. Nobody laughs while the camera is rolling, you know. After the take the director with a totally somber face says, 'Very funny, Ula, very funny.' I wish you were there to tell me."

"I'm involved in this daddy role. I'm loving it."

"Em is deep in the mommy role too, isn't she? They are beautiful together. He looks so much like you. I saw you almost that early. The way he moves his legs like he's running in place, you did that too. Your father didn't do that."

"Hmm."

"Now, now, J., whatever you believe is all right with me."

"I asked her what extravagant gift I could bring her to celebrate this miracle. She said a nursing bra."

"Oh, and I bet you knew where to get that."

"I didn't think Frederick's of Hollywood or Trashy Lingerie would have them, so I begged Alice to shop for me, and I bought Em a perfectly huge and wonderful emerald ring to commemorate the birth of Jared Patrick Higgen-Dunkin."

"And did you take about a dozen gold coins with you and put the rest on your credit card?"

"That's dramatic. I'm sorry I only thought about the credit card. Wow, did she deserve extravagant. She was so gallant! When she slipped Em out of her hospital gown and into her own nightie, the nurse said, 'Uh, sexy nightie—you'll be back here.' Em had the grace to laugh."

"She was laughing because she knew she'd never come near you again."

"That much agony is a serious design flaw. Women have not evolved as well as men."

"In the movies, even if there is a blizzard out, the man always leaves the cabin. You darlings now stay and help, though. J. J. always stayed in the waiting room. That was at the old Cedars of Lebanon, where Scientology is now."

"I sneaked out a few times. Ray and Joe came by, Joe citing his superior experience."

"We go through all that and then have to worry about those sons going to war because that's how you guys have evolved."

"I'm terribly aware of that, shepherding this project. When you trace it straight through like this, you become painfully aware of the constant state of war, from prehistory to right now. I hope those struggles for freedom and liberty come through well in our hands."

"I only hope we can keep our freedoms now. I'm really worried, J., about a free society, not about your second project. You are getting great reviews on Elizabeth."

"We have to keep it good for little Jared Patrick Higgen-Dunkin."

"I see him in the schoolyard being called Jarick."

"What schoolyard do you see him in? Gardner Street, Le Conte, and Hollywood High?"

"I'm sorry, J. baby, whatever you believe in, like maybe the public school system, you have to send him to private school."

"I've been thinking about school again, for my PhD."

Chapter 21

The neighbors hadn't said much yet about the cars of the committee that were taking up the curbside parking for what might have been half a block on other streets. This hillside however, offered no street down for so far that it became a huge block. When first there, Em had discovered that, her legs trembling when she walked around the block and finally reached the house and a cup of tea.

This was a fully attended meeting, everyone with a folder of notes.

"Thanks for the state of the committee report, Alice. It does feel as though we're doing pretty well. We are all involved enough in motion pictures to be able to work like this in bits and pieces, out of context. Skipping ahead of the time line, I want to draw attention to *Plymouth Adventure* with Spencer Tracy as the master of the *Mayflower*. I don't know how I missed this. I didn't know it existed. Watch the clothes for long pants. They're probably not there yet. Em has a fixation about it. She thinks she may have pinned down their first appearance to 1810, almost two hundred years after this. That would answer when, but she wants to know why.

"We need to get out the Mayflower Compact and read it again. It was pretty important even though Plymouth was outside the mainstream of development. There is popcorn in honor of it. Joe, go."

The room darkened, and Joe asked their indulgence while he showed them something else first. It was the Ingénue, dressed in white, nose to nose with her white cat, who was stretched out from the piano top to her *adorata* on the piano bench. "I don't know what they called her in her former life," said Ula, "but her name is Miss Harlow now, and we belong to each other. Harlow is a rescue cat."

"Wow, that's nice."

"It's a current series gig I got—celebs and rescue animals. They plan to do a calendar too. The Ingénue instructed me about the right angle. She said, 'Careful, the asshole on a paper-white cat is so obvious.' My client thinks this turned out real well, sans asshole, with the black piano and the dark background. Before this I didn't even know she had a piano."

"And the Grandmadre plays it too, boogie and ragtime. And she sings. That's how I learned the old songs. They left their big piano here and downsized to a new baby grand when they downsized to a condo. Em says her grandmother moved to Oregon, so she had to learn the old songs from Ella Fitzgerald."

"Patrick's mom is with the Shakespeare Festival in Ashland, isn't she?"

"How'd you know that, Mason?"

"An acting year there. Let's get on with Spencer Tracy. He's better than I was."

"Hey, Mason. This is Latty out here in the dark. We saw you and thought you were very good."

* * *

"I saw one pair of cut-offs that looked like they were made of sail cloth."

"There were a lot of bare legs."

"Historically speaking, there is nothing to indicate that the Tracy character was hitting on the passenger and that this made

331

her kill herself. Her husband's notes say simply that when he returned to the ship, his wife had drowned."

"I liked the way the film handled the compact, and you can segue into its importance. Would it be worth telling about the *Mayflower*'s other influence on the future country, about how they were eager to wash clothes after the long, stinky voyage, but it was the Sabbath, so they stayed on board and washed on Monday? Monday washday ever after."

"How could that relate to freedom? There was no freedom connected to washday until the washer and dryer."

"I hope you can all stay for two more films after Ruben's tacos."

Em had replaced the previous table with a huge, rough, old country table with heavy legs. She joyed in the price. Before her, it simply hadn't found anyone with space enough for it. It accommodated the entire committee, on benches and circus chairs, for she had not yet found the proper chairs. With the table she had acquired two very old and high monastery doors that she had tucked away pending some remodeling.

On the table now, three big platters, her new old Wedgwood and two terra cotta, were piled with the ground beef, chili, guacamole, salsa, sour cream, and lettuce to fill the stack of handmade tortillas. Em was well pleased with this new specialty of a house that was beginning to feel like hers.

The baby was removed from her lap, screaming in protest, by the nanny, a pretty blond girl from South Dakota, awed to find herself in Hollywood and living on Hollywood Boulevard. With the expertise of a practiced older sister, she cooed, "Dear little darling, trying to turn his sweet face the color of his pretty hair."

Jared Patrick was mollified and carried off to his blue bassinet, still in his parents' room.

"That's my boy, paying attention to pretty women."

"I love the real Indian mocs you found for him. May I ask where, since it's obvious I shall be shoeing another one pretty soon?" asked the frazzled mother of the flower girl and the ring bearer from the size four or five bungalow on Gower.

"I got another pair for my sister Peg's new cutie and another one for good measure. You shall have it. The Huron Indian tribe makes them. They are right for the style of your wonderful Craftsman house, built when we were romanticizing the American Indian. I saw that you had Hiawatha bookends. Great touch."

"Came with the house. My grandfather made them. He taught shop in high school."

"Hollywood High?"

"Wasn't here then, was it? It's an art deco building. But where did you find the shoes?"

"My wife haunts the catalogs," said J. "Too big with child to go shopping, she did all of Christmas that way. Incoming boxes every day, to the showroom too, where they got wrapped."

Taco shells now filled, every head was tipped left, save that of the left-handed Jon Mason. He was biting the right end of his taco. Scott was unable to resist the symmetry and the exception to it and jumped up with his camera. Before the coffee and flan dessert, he ran to the computer workstation he had set up for Em and returned with an adjusted print that showed the identical margarita glasses and the choreographed line of the committee, with the dissenting Mason.

*   *   *

"We won't find it difficult to remember what his first television-viewing experience was. We can tell him it was his great-grandmother, competing at the Golden Globes. It's getting close. You can hear the party prep sounds down at the Chateau Marmont. On the off chance she wins, I'll go down for a little while. You okay with that?"

"Sure. And we'll stay here. I haven't been out yet, and standing at a party is not a great idea. I almost wish it were supporting actress. Don't you think she would have a better chance at that than lead?"

"I don't remember that there is a supporting actress category for a comedy or musical. That's what she's up for, best actress in a comedy or musical."

"Do you know for sure that's the party she's going to? Who can ever forget the night Kathy Bates, clutching the Oscar she had just won, was turned away from a party?"

"I know where she's going. They will let her in. I talked to her. Marina said she was nervous; she said she wasn't. I told her to break a leg, and she said, 'I take my Boniva pill for bone density every month. I won't.'"

*　*　*

"J., bring your beer and come quick."

"She won't be first. She explained that there's a rhythm to arrival, after some comparison and before any boredom."

A bright and excited interviewer, herself in a beautiful, low, long dress, was trying not to ask the same question over and over. Down the line they could see the Ingénue coming now into camera range where the details could be seen, one of which was that she was accompanied by cousin Peter, He was quite good-looking, Em had to admit.

"Oh my God, J., look at her! It's a beaded duster coat, white of course. It looks like it's over a floor-length, white cashmere sweater. Where would you even get anything like that?"

The cuffs were like gauntlet gloves sliced into for an extra fullness, with bead strings hanging like western fringe on the outside seam, elbow to wrist. The big collar was turned up around the head, on which she wore a white beaded cap that resembled a pilot's helmet, the flaps hanging loose, each culminating in a cascade of beads, ending in what appeared to be a huge diamond that hit each knee as she walked.

"J., darling, that's the most beautiful thing I've ever seen. It's Vanessa Redgrave in *Camelot*. It's Lindbergh in the *Spirit of St. Louis*. It's Gloria Swanson in the twenties. It's Amelia Earhart in heaven. And Ula won't be frozen like the rest."

"What a girl! If you can't out-décolletage 'em, make 'em look as though they have forgotten some of their clothes. Whose line is that again—'I'm older, and I've got more insurance'?"

"What a waste. They've already voted."

"What do you mean? She's going for the next role."

Nor was Peter without decoration. Out from under his tuxedo shirt collar hung a gold coin mounted, medal-like, on a striped ribbon.

The greeter said that he would be able to know the value of it on any day. "Yes," said Peter, "any morning on that website."

"And you, Ula Dunkin, Ingénue, are simply gorgeous. One almost wishes you could carry your Miss Harlow as an accessory."

"Well, Em, that woman apparently has heard both of Ula's commercials, and Peter always did have the best Halloween costumes. I just hope he can get her in there gracefully."

"And up there gracefully if she wins."

"And that too."

It seemed a long wait until they saw her at her table, surrounded by attractive young men. They thought she might be a little disappointed that some of them were not in tuxes and bow ties, but in business suits, dark of course.

The suspense was unbearable when her category of nominees was read. Jared Patrick's fussing went unheeded. The moment came for the envelope to be opened. It was Ula!

She reached the stage quite smoothly, borne along on the applause. "My beautiful darlings, every one. Thank you for your votes. You in the industry of the press, in your symbiotic relationship with our industry, give us the reviews we cherish and then reward us with this beautiful event besides. Thank you, every one of you. Margaret Rutherford once told me, 'It's nice to be liked, but to be loved is so special.' If we are lucky, your reviews show that you like us, but this celebration feels beyond that, like love. And I certainly love you." Then she went on to love her director, producer, writer, and everyone else—especially makeup (which got a good laugh)—and her family, "that handsome brood of grown-up grandchildren."

"She nailed it, quoted a then-functioning actress older than she, and made it off on time, clutching the spoils. I think I better go get into my tux and blue shirt now."

"Pumps too. You're barefoot."

*   *   *

"Well, my dearest love, I have enrolled. I want to do my dissertation on how theater and literature have treated my new favorite hero, England's Henry II, married to your favorite, Eleanor of Aquitaine, whom he stole right out of her husband's castle. Did that have anything to do with his inventing the jury system? How much do you suppose she had to do with governing?"

"Much!"

"It's your turn too. Do you want to go for your master's?"

"Yes. I shall write my thesis on pants."

*   *   *

Alice was in the middle of gathering papers, requested by the accountant for year-end reports. Deeply involved, she took the call anyway. She confirmed that she was the producer but noted that she thought they should speak to Jared Dunkin (she didn't like that Higgen hyphen). "Jared, it's the *LA Times*. Calendar section. They have that taco photo, and they want to talk to you."

*   *   *

"Hi, Grandwinner. Yes, I saw the taco photo and liked it. Nothing compared to your PR, and there are more of us . . . Yes, he rules the house. Did I do that too? . . . Yes, I know how to change him, but he has to want to change . . . Yes, the Redman laughs all the time . . . Yes, I carried him in that sling thing on my chest. He seemed to like Manet best. Emmy is teaching him to read. She saw somewhere an article, 'Your Baby Can Read.' She holds up flash cards while she says the words: 'Mama,' 'Dada,' 'cat.'

"Yes, he said 'cat' first. He's past Ula. I never thought of it before, but that sounds like a baby's first cry . . . You're right, I haven't heard a lot of baby's first cries. That's okay, but I sure like this one."

*   *   *

"I dropped by my showroom. Something's come up. I need to talk to you. The building next door. I've always reminded the owner to let me have first refusal. I didn't think it would be this fast or when business is down."

"Hey, terrific. I have the money. What are the terms?"

"Well, I can start paying you back almost right away."

"I don't mean that, silly ass. I mean, what are *his* terms?"

*   *   *

"I've never liked the roofline—on either building, actually."

"I've been thinking about it. Wouldn't it make sense to have a second and maybe a third story? Maybe some of it could be a production studio for our film business. The neighbors up here are looking funny at us, and I heard someone mutter the 'z' word. But Beverly is zoned for most anything we could want, isn't it? You can have your tearoom with tinkling cups and lady sandwiches, and we could do a playroom for the Redman."

"Parking is the big zoning issue."

"That couldn't stop us. There's underground. It would be unprecedented to do a nice one."

"They won't let you light it very well."

"We'll have a nice, dimly lit one. I—I mean, we—own a building with decent parking garage under. It's a neat one by Craig Ellwood."

"Can we get him for this one?"

"No, he's dead now—the other building's a midcentury modern. My mom wasn't emotionally involved with their stuff. She liked that building, though, if none of their furniture. Well, there was that Eames lounge chair, rosewood. We lose the people but not their stuff."

"I think the Soane house has some theme we need to remember. Could you pick up the book we didn't get yet? Maybe call Book Soup to see if they have it. They better have everything 'cause pretty soon they're going to be the last bookstore on earth."

*   *   *

"Winning the Golden Globe doesn't always mean the Oscar. That really great PR lady, Randy Chasen, has taken me on and pretends to think I might win. It's your turn to escort if I'm nominated, Jared. Would you mind, Emmy?"

"Why would I mind? I get to watch you get cold, out there at the other end of our street. I was just remembering the Sharon Stone Golden Globe for *Casino* but not the Oscar again."

*   *   *

"For best performance by a supporting actress," said the presenter before listing all the nominees. "And now the envelope please."

The camera found Ula in the audience a moment later, J. holding her hand, as she gave her performance of brave defeat and of appreciation for the winner, when she would have cheerfully killed her.

*   *   *

"I know we have to get really serious on this opening now, but I have a present for you." Elra was wearing her leather pants again tonight, and she swung her stylized haircut forward as she slid out of her chair. She presented J. with a paper roll that he undid for all to see. It was a big paper bag-brown poster with black silhouettes of Stonehenge and, in big letters, "Give Me That Old-Time Religion."

"Great, great, great. Could we use it?"

"Hey Mason, not separating church and state leads to human sacrifice?"

"OK Latty. Post it as a warning."

"But you have a calendar now."

"Does yours have summer solstice?"

"Let's get rolling on what we got," requested J.

"Joe, you're on."

"I'll be going to England to pick up the shots we need, a lot of them to background the spoken critique. I think it's pretty much decided that it all has to be motion, when possible. Sometimes the landscape with a blowing daisy is enough. We've been studying the prevailing horticulture for historical timing. For instance, early England was covered with pine, and then oak took over. That's how you can date the deluge that cut off England as an island. You'll see if the filmmakers took that much caution. It might look more like California live oak in Bronson Canyon.

"Some of J. and Em's shots are pretty good; some are just good scouting shots. They're in here pending replacement. J.'s final beginning is final if it's final. Music too."

J. had been filmed with the barstool as on all the finished segments. They had all decided that since it had been referenced in the review in the *Times*, the stool was still in. On the screen, he stood against it, chatting easily from a teleprompter. "Why this peninsula, this farthest projection from the continent, save for one large island between it and the far-off, watery end of the world? Its isolated geography contains its story. A human skull at least 250,000 years old confirms the characters, the costumes, the animal skins, the tools, rough flint. Newcomers brought agriculture, polished their flint, and made pottery, without a wheel. Copper and tin pulled from the earth combined for the Bronze Age, usually said to be 1000 BC to 400 BC.

"Less than nine thousand years ago, while pyramids were being built in far-off Egypt, some movement of earth sank the plain between England and Holland a few hundred feet. The ocean rushed to the North Sea. The Straits of Dover and the English Channel now further isolated the peninsula, as an island. Invaders still came, sometimes to plunder, more often to stay in this favored spot of undefended villages and farms. Bronze gave way to iron. Belgic tribes arrived with chariots and horsemen. Caesar had heard of them settling in the lowlands; he had heard that inland peoples were aboriginal and that the island was strange and monstrous, on the ultimate fringes of the world.

In August of 55 BC he made an unsuccessful attempt to invade and returned the following year with eight hundred ships. The defenders and the sea prevailed, and Britain went almost one hundred years without Roman invasion, unexpected when it did come. After years of fierce and determined revolt, the subjugation was complete except in the north, and Britannia became one of the forty-five provinces of Rome.

"And so it remained, with the Roman talent for planning, governance, roads, and warm baths and tolerance of religions, for four hundred years, until the Roman life became a country villa style, the towns decaying. Hadrian came himself in 122 to organize against northern tribes, and his wall was five years in the making. It was repaired by Emperor Severus in 208, and there was peace for another hundred years.

"Inroads of barbarian invasion began against the Roman Empire, on the continent. Legions in England were called home. Saxons from Germany rowed long boats against new British shore fortifications. Picts and Scots pressed from the North. No Roman coins minted after 400 have ever been found in England.

"The long, dark night of the Saxon invasion was upon Britain, its citizens butchered, enslaved, or withdrawn to the mountain fastness. There were last battles against the Barbarians, who fought with sword and ax and spear and wore little armor. A small force of Roman cavalry moving from place to place against them could have proved invincible. There is chronicled a remarkable leader in twelve such battles. The last of these battles, at Mount Badon, can be dated with some certainty as between 490 and 503. Was this Arthur Pendragon?"

Joe did not stop for comment but rolled right into the beginning credits of *Knights of the Round Table*, with Robert Taylor and Ava Gardner and Mel Ferrer as Arthur. Joe then paused when the film ended. "We really had to have that one for its old-time religion, Stonehenge, implying Druids and prehistory, and for the shots of Hadrian's Wall, though we will have some of that in the current era, in the background to J.'s commentary. I almost felt that the movie was saying the end of the Romans was good, when J. just told us it couldn't have been worse. Its references to Christianity were important. It gave at least ten good laws to start with."

"We have chosen to put Em's stuff-commentary between the two pictures," J. rose to say. "We're trying to justify using two Arthurs when we can't be sure there was even one. But I believe. My wife can't buy that any woman would prefer Lancelot to Arthur. Her favorite scene in all of picturedom comes up next when Burton's Arthur meets Redgrave's Gwen in the snow on the way to Camelot."

Joe now began recording Emmy's introduction to *Camelot*.

"We visualistas only care about stuff. I'm thinking *Camelot*'s castles look Norman, which was years ahead of them, perhaps 500. Hard to authenticate the stuff in a myth when you can't pin the myth, but there are beautiful objects in museums from anytime King Arthur could have been, the sixth century perhaps. I'd like to have some of these in my showroom."

The screen was filled and refilled with containers and implements and jewelry. "And for this next picture, *Camelot*, I care not about authenticity. Think opulent creativity."

The barstool on the screen was now occupied by Elra Janick, who expressed enthusiasm for the makeup in *Camelot*, and then by Marina's cop, who told of seeing the costumes in storage when he was a little boy; he never forgot the long-trained wedding dress of sewn-together pumpkin seeds. "Kid's memory. I'm pretty sure it was from *Camelot*. We'll know when we see the picture now."

When *Camelot* had played out on the screen, the floor was opened to comments, and Jon Mason stood. "Working the sound on this, I'd heard the intro before, which gave me time to think about it. It needs to bracket our contention. We say that at last personal freedom and our country work because of no hereditary leadership, or as you have said, 'no magic blood.' The other point is that there is no state religion; no religion tells the government what to do, and the government doesn't tell the church. The Constitution has that to protect religion, doesn't it? Romans seemed okay on religion. Arthur was practicing his, and it looked like everybody else was too. It looked as though his leadership rested in the magic blood as well as the sword of his father. So how 'brave new world' was he in the return to hereditary governance?"

"Good, good, good! We better return to that one."

* * *

"I think using two films for some and none for others works. We have to have *The Lion in Winter*. Henry II is really important. Two of his successor sons are in *Lion* except that they are each important in freedom-path terms—Runnymede, for God's sake."

"Then there's Henry V with Olivier in the bangs and wild costumes, with that personal committee story about 'em."

"The Branagh one is necessary too. The speech is so great. Listen, we have to talk about Shakespeare somewhere here. He might be the most important member of the committee."

"At least son Henry VI contributed nothing to warrant a Shakespeare play or a movie. They carried him to the battlefield, where he sat under a tree and watched. So much for the magic blood theory that sent them scurrying for some kin or other when the king died."

"But seriously, what could they do? There was no system to hang on while they found a next leader. Vice president was a far-out concept still."

"The religion part gets really hot with Paul Scofield in *A Man for All Seasons*, but should we be using Charles Laughton's *Private Life of Henry VIII*? It's black-and-white, of course. We have to look at them all to see which best depict inherited power and church and state."

"It's going to be a blast to see this stuff all together, running on, one great color explosion after the other. Some black-and-white, like we did for Elizabeth, has to be okay. Otherwise, the choices would seem fake, as though the priority was color and not idea."

"Hey, here's a thought. I went to a science fiction convention recently, and there was this midcentury scientists flick called *The Time Travelers*. They get stuck in time and are condemned to relive, to go round and round. At the end they reprise the whole film, a few frames for each scene, and then do it again with fewer, and at last with just one frame each. It was perfect for that, and it would be a smash for this."

"Yeah, I've seen that—much impressed. The guy who did it lives on our hill. You pass his house to get up here. If we need permission, you don't have far to go for it."

*   *   *

"Yes, dear Grandlady, we've seen that one too. It was hard to choose just the two we did. Emmy loved Sean Connery, once again Arthur, more than Richard Gere playing Lancelot. And the Disneyfied castle was hard for her to take, as well as the Viking funeral pyre floating in the lake, when the Vikings didn't arrive until 800. But who's counting?"

"Count yourself lucky, Grandbaby, you know, that she likes older men, with your being seven years older than she. J. J. was ten years older than I. I liked that then, but now I adore those young men. I wish they would, you know, make another

Elizabeth film when she was old and cast me. I would have executed Essex and sobbed about it, but then there were all those other young men."

"Damon Higgen was twenty years older than you."

"Now, now, Grandpuppy, you weren't going to do that."

"If the studio thought you were the right costars, and it was a very good picture . . ."

"Oh."

"Em's favorite castle was in Mel Gibson's *Hamlet.*"

*　　*　　*

"Grandstar, you'll never believe this one: Alice is going with him to England. What a guy! He shamed her into it. How could she let their personal relationship get in the way of company business? He needed really good management to handle appointments and permissions and such, he explained. It will be two rooms all the way. He promises it will be businesslike. The kids will stay at our house. Em's mostly home even now in Jarick's second year, and Ruben will pick up for school and lessons. Alice will Skype with the kids regularly."

"What a guy indeed, that beautiful, pale-eyed fast-talker. I give him a week to seduction."

"Well, we need that filming now. We're almost finished, and we know exactly what we do need. That she knows the project as producer will keep the cost down."

"What does your hot-shot accountant say to that?"

"She said, 'Take two gold coins and call me in the morning.'"

*　　*　　*

J. picked up his cell phone to call his friend's wife. "Hey, Mrs. Jade Tree Queen. You better get on down here. That big house on Selma is getting serious about the remodel, and they are starting to take out that whole block of jade tree hedge."

"Oh my God! I would not have known without you. He's home today, writing on his screenplay, so we'll be there soon, with clipper and buckets. Our backyard's almost a good enough source by now, but not quite. I think I better start my own hedge in the front, behind the azaleas. Thank you, thank you."

"There's another good stand in my doctor's parking lot—a kind of red border around the leaf."

"Great. I'll be asking you that address."

* * *

"Hey, babe, what's up?"

"I'm in the car. Scott's taking me to Cedars. Grab my little Louis Vuitton, all packed, over by the Barcelona chairs, and come on down."

* * *

This time Jane was wearing yellow scrubs, printed with smiley-faced hearts, and it was a girl, which J. and Emmy had let themselves learn in advance. They still had not decided on a name.

"Hey, she's prettier than Elizabeth, newborn in *Anne of the Thousand Days*."

"I'm willing to bet that's the only other newborn girl you have ever seen. And how they ever managed to get a just-born actress for that elaborate scene, I'll never know."

"A red haired new born yet. This one could do that part, except she's almost as beautiful as her mama."

"If only we had a naming system for girls like you all do for boys, she would be named for my mother. Peg already used that though. Maybe we should take Peg's name, Margaret, or your mother's."

"I loved her, but I don't really like the name Karen, or did you mean Katleen? The little red-haired girl from Peanuts never had a name, did she?"

"Kaitlin?"

"Sounds like an abbreviation for Catalina."

"Chloe?"

"Not an Ingénue fragrance."

"Roberta?"

"After my ruined brother? No."

"Geraldine for your father or Patricia for your father?"

"No forms of male names."

"Briana?"

"A favorite cheese."

"Fiona?"

"Hmm."

"Cliona?"

"That's one of the three Great Waves of Ireland."

"No, I mean, look what your grandma sent! It's a tiny knit pilot's helmet like her Golden Globe one. 'Cliona' is written on a tag."

"That's an Irish lady who knits for her, only she calls her Knit Lady or Nitlay. Those great little boy sweaters are from her, only called Rory after another of the Great Waves."

"Did you tell the waiter at Clafoutis that we won't be in this week and it's a girl?"

Chapter 22

"Okay, all, we would like to introduce Cliona Amelia Higgen-Dunkin."

The nanny appeared with the sweet bundle in her aviatrix helmet. She took well to the applause. Three women asked to hold her, and though it was too early for smiling, she seemed happily disposed to the baby talk. Jared Patrick, the Redman, was allowed in for a few minutes too, and he loudly announced that his sister's name was Ona and spelled it: "O-n-a." Then, in his miniature blue jeans and Rory sweater, he clambered up the back of his father's chair and stuck his look-alike face over the shoulder of the original.

"From the 'Teach Your Baby to Read' program, this is what we get, an editor. Flash cards for Cliona start next week."

"Man, we didn't know you this early. First time I saw you, you were maybe three years older than he is, and the kindergarten teacher was pulling you down off the windowsill, where you were presenting a part of your anatomy she would probably have liked to whack."

*   *   *

"So here is the finished product, pending your final okay. Over the coming days and nights at our house, there will be an almost constant buffet. We counted toilets—we think there are ten. We'll break only for some sleep. There are beds and sofas, and I see some sleeping bags. Call home if you have to.

"Alice has taken the liberty of furnishing steno notebooks with your names on them. It's for her convenience. We know you are all educated note-takers. I am wondering if you are all thinking as I am, that we should identify the members of the committee as before, that nice presentation of each of us on a barstool with a personal tale to tell. What we didn't have last time was a name for the group of us. My grandmother has been scolding me about that ever since. Scott has come up with this."

Joe flashed a logo on the screen, a pale-blue horse silhouette, behind it a splendid camel, the words "COMMITTEE PRODUCTIONS" below the images.

"Yes!"

"Yes!"

"A horse of a different color!"

"Yes!"

"A horse by a committee!"

"Go for it!"

* * *

"J., I think you've done it. I got a lot of happy calls. How about lunch tomorrow at the Tam? . . . Yeah, just you and I, just Ray and J. from Hollywood High."

J. arrived first from his morning class at USC in his Levis and pullover sweater, a particularly nice one from his grandmother's knitting lady. Ray was in a business suit, also a particularly nice one, custom from Rodeo Drive, it seemed to J., who was already seated at a small table with his scotch. "Man, I didn't even know they had two-person oak tables, back in this side room. Anyway, everybody I know about is okay. And how are the rest of them?"

"As far as I know, good. Let's get everybody together here next week. Mason and Joe and Alice and Latty have all called me to express great happiness and expectations." J. paused and then said quietly, "This is like girl gossip, but what do you think about Joe and Alice? Is that ever going to work again? When they got back from England, with great stuff, by the way, their daughter asked, 'Did you sleep with Daddy?' and she said no."

"I think he's playing it right; maybe she'll ask him. But listen, I've got something to talk about. The Ingénue is very hot right now, on all those talk shows and that rescue cat commercial and the awards, but . . ."

"You're not planning to boot her, are you?"

"God no, I'm no fool. We will prop her and patch her as long as we can, but if anything happens to her, I can't just go to black. I need transitions and related product. We've done a bit of that. I'm sure you remember your bachelor days of escorting the lovely airheads with perfect skin we used in our advertising. I particularly remember a funny little creature named Asia photographed with you at some promotion party."

"Where do you find them?"

"We don't. They are self-screening, like the president of the United States. I didn't turn him up to vote for. He decided he wanted it, and it's beginning to scare me wondering what he wants it for."

"You too?"

"So what about your beautiful new daughter and her baby skin? We'd intimate you can keep baby skin all your life, showing her in her Amelia helmet with her great-grandmother in her beaded Golden Globe award helmet, face to face. We'd shoot at your house." Ray paused for breath, but not for long. "The new fragrance would be called Cliona, for one of the three Great Waves of Ireland, the native land of our noble founder, your great-grandfather and the father-in-law to the Ingénue. Patrick Higgen of Higgen Buttons, in a slow business cycle right now, could handle the container. Rory would be the men's cologne, and it would be packaged in Waterford with a cut glass wave, boosting the gross national product of a naïve place that is in gross national trouble from thinking prosperity is selling houses to each other, when they should have known better after studying Econ 101 in high school. Or they might have remembered once before, putting it all in potatoes."

"My daughter, responsible for all that when she is only just now able to hold her head up?"

"You named her."

"Her name is Ona."

"Yes, I heard about that."

"If you know everything that goes on in my house, what did I have for breakfast?"

"Well, it's a school day. You probably grabbed a granola bar with your thermos of coffee for the car."

"Damn you! What about your daughter?"

"Mary?"

"You guys say, 'Mary, Mother of God,' don't you? We could probably work something up for Easter, like a sacred heart container."

* * *

"Hey Babbydaddy, I do so hope it happens. I just love the continuance of the family, me her daddy's Grandmama with his sweet girl child. Maybe we should do a Cliona baby powder as well and lotion, a gift set. I guess by now Ray has talked to you about it. It can film at your house where the grand piano is grander. I want Joe to shoot it."

"My dear Grandglobewinner, yes I had lunch with Ray, and I don't know what I think of it. Em doesn't either. At first I thought she was going to clutch the baby to her and run screaming from the house. Now she just stares at me."

"We're not asking her to be Shirley Temple or Judy Garland."

"She probably will inherit Em's nonsinging voice anyway, though she seems to be cooing in key." said her father

"Shirley did all right, about my age, you know. Remember, she was a US ambassador to one of those G countries. And I plan to use Cliona perfume as my personal scent."

"I can't say that she always smells all that good."

"Think about it. For the family and the business."

"Family connection? Truth in advertising and DNA?"

"DNA, schmeeNA! Shut up and inherit."

After that dramatic line J. expected her to shut down the phone, like strutting from the stage, the proper diva. Instead she was all purring again.

"Marina's cop came for dinner last night, very enthusiastic about your *Freedom Road in the Movies*. I asked him about the George Washington voice that I recommended. He said yes, very good."

"Yes, thank you for that actor. We all thought he was perfect for that important speech. He probably sounds five times better than George did. How did you know him, Grandcasting director.?"

"He's also a director. We were traveling with a Directors Guild group—don't ask me how we qualified—so we didn't, you know, know everybody," said Ula. "We were traveling on the Finnish airline, and it happened when we first started out in Helsinki and were standing in line at the airport—I remember for sure where I first heard Alan's great voice. Someone asked where the others were, and from behind us someone answered, 'I just saw them disappear into Finn Air.' That was Alan. After that trip we all started meeting for Chinese dinner downtown, and also he turned up in my French class. We've seen him through a second marriage and a lot of interesting women. They follow the voice until he is, you know, tired of them."

"I remember that trip. I was about fifteen and thought I should go along."

"It wasn't very long after that nuclear plant accident, and we wouldn't have taken you. We spent a good amount of time in Russia, and the Russians didn't really like it that we were there. There was a certain element of danger. That's probably what kept that group of us together. They've all been very kind to me since J. J. died. That was almost his last trip. I hope Reagan and the wall and the Soviet collapse will always be part of your memory."

"Absolutely, and I hope the country will remember it too. I can only hope our memory of 9/11 stays fresh as well, without it being reinforced by another incident. I think we make the point of how attractive is the separation of church from state."

"Marina's cop says that what Ken Burns did for Lincoln, you are doing for Washington and the Constitution."

"Good man. Let her not get tired of him."

* * *

"Hey, Ula. This is Emmy. I have everything under control on this job site and have time for a telephone call. I wanted to tell you how much we enjoyed dinner at your house last night. We were so pleased to share our building plans with you. How well you read those plans! I studied blueprint reading at UCLA, and I still I can't always tell at what I'm looking . . ."

"Well, dear, you will know by the time the building is finished, and you will have leftover, unused expertise. Your means of getting to upper floors seems very creative."

"Yes, I love that stairway and elevator best of all."

"So true, if you have ever seen the Bradbury Building, it is forever in your vocabulary, but this is more modern ironwork."

"The treads will be onyx, transmitting the light. I like the way the stairs and the elevator are part of the same tower. The success is dependent on it being acceptable, if not downright fun, to go upstairs. All that modern glass is for my husband."

"Now, it's important for tenants to like it."

"Yes. Just this morning I got another tenant—a pillow lady—and I was able to catch the architect just in time to have him put a drop shaft from her second floor space to a waiting car below. It's a perfect meld with my showroom 'cause I'll show some of her pillows."

"And it's all solar heating? I hear so much about that now."

"Oh, yes. The solar will be state-of-the-art, combined with skylights positioned to let in light without sun to fade stuff. The onyx panels around the edge, set in the floor, are somewhat experimental, but I believe in them.

"I had hoped to see Blaine at your house. I've never met him."

"Well, little Mrs. Higgen-Dunkin, you are insulated from the latest gossip. I couldn't say anything in front of the other guests last night. Blaine has left town, and I am surely the only one who knows where he is in the wake of a man named Madoff who made off with a lot of people's money. He got none of mine because I don't listen, but Jared's three cousins are bereft and probably thanking God for gold. I can only hope that they got straightened out with the offshore and Swiss accounts when J. did. Those orange jumpsuits are so unbecoming. They don't tell me everything. I'm just not sure how long Blaine's been gone now, except I can say what current events were in the news the last time he called before leaving because he told me the comedy writers feared layoffs as two thousand Tiger Woods jokes wrote themselves, and his mistresses were unionizing. Then Blaine rang off without really saying goodbye. I don't think he's coming back."

"I guess I was too busy being pregnant to know about all these other things."

* * *

"Hey, Granddarling, we caught your talk show interview. We thought you were terrific. I still think *The View* was the best ever, though. They seemed to like you so much, and they weren't condescending just because you weren't born when they were."

"I love the *View* ladies. I get up early to watch them. I didn't feel old among them."

"That's early? This interviewer last night thought you were cool, and he was playing for it. Can't blame him—you are cool!

Are you having fun, a lot of it? You sound sniffley. Has the Icelandic eruption cloud reached Westwood?"

"Well, this morning wasn't nice, and I guess I was a bit tearful. Where are you anyway?"

"Just coming from school. Saw your call and pulled into the loading turnoff of the museum on Wilshire."

"How many museums are there on Wilshire?"

"An uncounted number. This is County, near that forest of old street lamps. Can you rustle me up some lunch if I come by? You can dilute my scotch for driving."

"You are so precise and careful about some things, and then you drive like a bat out of hell."

"I'll be there in seventeen minutes."

"That's what I mean."

The drive through Beverly Hills was relatively full of green lights and without many shopping ladies slowly turning right. He chortled at the long stretch of country club without stops and the canyon of condos moving smoothly.

"Okay, lady darling. What's the matter?"

"Well, I went to my breakfast book club this morning."

"And the bacon wasn't crisp enough?"

"It was just right and in the quiche. Afterward these three ladies came over and cuddled up at the table across from me. I was about to suggest to the one in the purple suit that she should use a serum under her makeup when she said to me, 'I just wish that I could be as fabulous as you when I'm as old as you.' I had this sudden memory of Richard Pryor in a movie playing a blind man, and someone said, 'Black like you.' He looked astonished and said, 'What? I'm black?' So I said, 'What? I'm old?' They laughed too much, and their spokes hole said, 'See, didn't I tell you?'"

They went away, and I went home and took two aspirin and a nap and cried a little. And maybe a little because Blaine's gone. My sex life may be over."

"Poor dear! You're not a naïve little May wine, we concede. You are vintage. How could she expect to be fabulous later if she isn't fabulous now? They don't have a chance."

"You do help, dear Grandbabydoll. Your lunch is a ham and cheese, in the George Foreman."

"Give me a hug and come dance with me. What's on the gramophone?"

"You are so bad."

*   *   *

The museum loading zone proved to be an excellent spot to pull into to use the phone, and J. stopped there the next day as well. "Hey, babe, what are you doing this very moment?"

"I'm standing in my closet in my underwear shopping for clothes to wear in Palm Springs."

"Perfect! Put the cat out and close the bedroom door. Then take off the rest of your clothes and bend over, facing away from the door, which I shall burst through in fifteen minutes."

The cat was yelling in protest outside the closed door when he arrived, but Em was lying in bed, the quilt pulled to her ears, her arms out with the morning paper. She proved to be without clothes, and when it was over, they read the paper together.

"Hollywood on Hollywood," read the headline on the front page of the Calendar section, to be laminated, framed, and hung in the front hall. They would be preserving the other page too, with both pictures and text by a reviewer who loved the committee camel, the concept, and this marathon movie about movies.

*   *   *

J. was on his cell phone. "It's astonishingly fortuitous that it's going to be running on Memorial Day weekend, especially this year when—you hate to say it, but when there will be fewer people out using up their gas money. Maybe they will be staying home, watching us.

"We will have more or less continuous food. Short-order and buffet and chowder, chili, vichyssoise, and gazpacho. And booze.

355

Em found a vast flock of rough marble bowls at Berbere Imports. They are from somewhere in the Middle East, used for kneading small bread loaves. After being in the fridge for a while, they stay super cold for hours."

"As your accountant I am pleased to tell you that you can afford the air conditioning."

"Yes, it will be getting hot by then, but we are well ac-ed. Bring your bathing suit for morning and night swimming. I don't think you explored all the property. There are small, smooth sleeping pods with mini bathrooms nestled into the rocks. You can't get to 'em except by ladder through a hole in the top. Sometimes we think she must have thought to run a hotel if all else failed."

"Is the gold home alone?"

"Alice hired armed guards for home. You and so few other people know why. Ruben and Ruanna will be with us there, along with the nanny, and we are hiring one of her friends as well."

"Live-in audience."

"Sure, the whole committee. My grandmother is coming and bringing an old Western movie star she met at the studio. Alice and Joe will be there with all their children together. Both declined to bring a date. Joe is getting to be a famous cinematographer, you know."

"You lucked out!"

"It's not tax time, so perhaps you can stay a long time. You are probably in desperate need of a rest. Would you want to bring your fathers and/or a date?"

"No."

"I've hired a couple of young guy lifeguards. There will be all those children, Em's sisters, and her parents. Oh, and Em has an actor uncle who'll be here."

"Like he's not your uncle too."

"I'm not used to his being my uncle too. I've never even met him. Scott and Miller from her showroom and blog will be there too, just through Monday. The actor who did Washington's voice and one of my USC professors are coming as well. We are importing an audience and expect rapt attention unless you can present a certificate that you have seen this film or that—because how many times can you see *Camelot*?"

"With Burton? At least three more times, this year."

"And *Becket* with Burton?"

"Three. Your cousins coming?"

"They got an announcement postcard like a thousand other intimate friends we and the committee have."

"I wonder how I knew that. Your dentist?"

"Damn, I forgot him."

* * *

When all the guests had left, the compound was strangely quiet, if anything could be quiet with the Redman in residence. That he could take a nap had not occurred to him, as it had to his sleepy parents.

"Was it good for you?"

"If I smoked, I'd have a cigarette now."

"While it's fresh, what did you like best?"

"Same as always—you the actor playing the scholar and your very real and deep scholarship that chains the whole of it together. What I loved about the whole project was coming around the curve and down a little rise on Sunset where Tower Records used to be and seeing the huge billboard: 'Out of the Dark Past, See Your Path to Individual Liberties,' with the silhouette of Stonehenge against a dark orange sky and that unfurled sproketed roll of film that loops toward you. Reminded me of the 'ribbon of moonlight looping the purple moor.' It was a life high!"

"How will we know how well watched we were? Best, as always, I liked your legs. They have such authority."

Ruanna worked on a vichyssoise stain in an oriental rug, a Bokhara, and there was a distant whir of vacuum cleaner. There was an occasional plop of an object added to a pile of the forgotten belongings, to be taken back to town. Little Jarick could be heard as a succession of fire engine, train, and airplane sounds, and the nannies were giggling, probably over the cool young lifeguards.

There had been no drownings, no electrocutions, no upset stomachs, and no quarrels. Euphoria set in, and the Higgen-Dunkins went to sleep on a hanging sofa, J. feeling secure that he had been the only one to see Alice and Joe behind the boulders at the far end of the pool.

* * *

"We could stop at Daddy's on the way home."

"Why? Is there some fruit on the trees? Isn't it early for that?"

"We could gather up some orange blossoms for Alice and Joe. I just hope that he realized in advance this was to be the weekend of his success and brought protection. She fertilizes so easily."

"And you don't?"

"I do—I did before I said, 'I do.'"

"English is such a great language. Anyway, they do terrific kids. The older boy is a great *Big Lebowski* fan and even bowls. He and Joe go bowling together, and Joe is such a fan of Roger Deakins, the cinematographer of the Dude movie. Did you know there was a Lebowski festival, and they are going to it this year?"

"The second son will be a great fan of dudes too."

"Yeah, where better than in Hollywood or, better yet, West Hollywood?"

"Does Joe talk about it? Does he know the kid is gay?"

"Pretty inescapable knowledge by now. I suppose by the time he's grown, he'll be allowed to marry."

"But not if you're voting. Does this digression have anything to do with whether we're stopping or not? Daddy and the Redman get on so well."

"He bought him a soccer ball. That doesn't mean he has to play soccer, does it?

"It's our individual liberty to play what we want to."

"Tennis is nice, and they have those cool little white sweaters."

"Would I find it in the attic, that cool little white sweater Patrick wore in that famous photo at Grandpa Higgen's egg roll?"

"I don't know, but that's another place to look for papers and photos."

"Daddy, we're in the car but past your stop and are bopping on home. We have learned to take advantage of when the babies are asleep. It will be nice to get them into their own beds. They smell so delicious when they're asleep . . . So you hung over my crib and breathed me, huh? I think I must have known that. Love you so much . . . You watch my blog? I didn't know that. Yes, the baby furniture one was fun. I really do believe in the furniture clear to the floor with no room for monsters. You can open drawers and see they're not there . . . Yes, Miller does those. Funny little thing, isn't she? So talented. She pulls her weight . . . No, we don't know what project is next for the camel. J. says, with the soap operas phasing out, he would still like to do one. You know *All My Children*? Well, he wants to do one like that, a Hollywood story called *All My Parents* . . . Yes . . . Yes . . . Bye, Daddy."

"Why did you tell him that?"

"I lost my head when he was expressing so much pride in you."

"Oh."

*   *   *

"Are you getting a bushel of calls, boy doll?"

"Hey, Grandvintage, we really are, a lot more than for Elizabeth. Maybe because there was more viewing time invested. For Elizabeth, it tended to be like voting for best actress in a drama about a queen. We didn't tally, but my sense was that it was essentially even. This one had challenges for each one of our theories about what was a step to personal freedom. One caller didn't notice that it was all rulers and wanted to know where Robin Hood was. Em took the call and said she would have missed him too if it could have been Sean Connery. The caller said it should have been Damon Higgen. He really was the best of them, wasn't he?"

"Dear boy, what are you asking?"

"Who, me?"

"Do you mean 'who, I?' or 'who am I?'"

"No, it's too late if you have answers to that. I know who I am."

"It's so good to know now that you are a very talented filmmaker, isn't it? It takes a while to find yourself."

"And who ever looked as hard as I did? And you, my love, how come so long between parts?"

"I was busy, and then I was doing Marina's job."

"I guess I was learning, and then I was doing Alice's job."

"You stayed over D-day at the Springs, didn't you? I hope it's not forgotten. Sixty-six years."

"And you were Miss South Dakota at that time, waiting for the boys to come home."

"Yes, and some didn't."

*　　*　　*

"Ladies and gentlemen of the committee, I don't know about you, but this is my idea of heaven, deciding on an idea for which film to make instead of pounding on doors with a beloved film you wish you could make a deal for, before someone's stolen it."

*　　*　　*

"I thought she was pretty cute, sitting with the top of her little baby buns visible in the bunched-up white blanket. But when she bubbled, 'Ulala' for Ula, I thought Joe would spray gin out his nose. She got her first audience laugh. She may be hooked."

"Yeah, earlier in her lineage, she would have joined the act on the Dublin stage. And there would have been no mom strong enough to say no. That's my line in this drama."

"Ray says she could prevent another potato famine."

"No."

*   *   *

"I think she's a ham. She always knows where the camera is. You will have taught her to read soon. She could choose her own scripts."

"Ona is going to be able to be what she wants to be when she's grown and educated. She might even be a doctor."

"You mean like Dr. Berber in the funny papers?"

"With a stethoscope and a white lab coat."

"With her name embroidered on the pocket?"

"In red thread."

*   *   *

"Is she upset by kids yelling, 'Ulala, Ulala' at her in the street?"

"I don't think so, and neither is the producer."

"Your Grandloon is really fabulous and so funny in that role. How do they dare base a series on those vintage silver ladies? What if they lost one?"

"They would have to go find her. Or do you mean by death? They would have to have an alternate script for each of those possibilities, ready to go at a moment's notice."

"Sounds heartless."

"Isn't."

*   *   *

They had been in Paris for a week and were not entirely restive to get home to the children. Em was beside herself over everything French, maybe most over the bakery that made clafoutis, or the Hall of Mirrors, or the Opera House, or the Mansard roofs, or the *Mona Lisa*, or the Impressionists, or just being there.

On the returning flight, as they passed over the Great Plains, she was still working from memory in her sketchbook.

*   *   *

It was the first Tuesday home. It had been a cool summer, more like spring all year. The global warming jokes were tired. The carefully tended median in the Sunset Strip at Sunset Plaza, however, was full of flowers appropriate to the calendar season.

The meeting for lunch was well timed, and a quick cell phone call confirmed that Em was heading down the drive in her car to park behind the shops just as J. made his left turn. He found a space soon enough that he was able to catch up with her at the base of the stairs. They kissed for they had been apart for four hours.

Going up the short flights of stairs and broad landings beside her deprived him of the remembered pleasure of seeing the slight tightening of calf muscles as she climbed those stairs.

The waiter was apologetic when they entered—the machine was down, and they had no way to accept credit cards. Together J. and Emmy found that they had enough cash.

"We are open for breakfast now."

"He might get up for that sometime. The usual please."

"We're out of Lillet."

"House white wine then, reluctantly"

"Breakfast is served until twelve."

"Sometimes he gets up before that."

"But quiche and omelets are breakfast items only now. We don't have them for lunch."

"It's the end of an era."

*   *   *

"J., my darlin', I'm lovin' this building. They took the paper off the skylights, and that sawtooth form is fabulous. The whole place is glowing. The quartz treads are going in as we speak."

"Sometimes fulfillment looks like what you dreamed."

"We'll come back after lunch to see them before they put the construction paper over 'em for protection until we open. See you there."

The traffic seemed heavy for a Tuesday. J. had to wait through a second light cycle to make his left from Fairfax to Beverly. It was a favored route for the long, long fence around CBS. The bougainvillea covering the fence was in full bloom in every color it came in, a block of brilliant stripes.

It was early enough that J. found a parking space, if only in the outskirts of the El Coyote lot. During his childhood, for that every-Sunday brunch, there had always been a choice of parking close to the restaurant, though the regulars had started filling in the lot by the eleven-thirty opening.

The El Coyote smell reached him at half a block out as he walked the sidewalk toward the squat white restaurant that must have been a house before the thirties, when it began delivering this smell over its part of the neighborhood. The smell never quite reached across the street, so Emmy's tearoom wouldn't have the Mexican restaurant fragrance. She was probably going to spray it with Ingénue's Cliona.

Approaching the building, he remembered his father and his grandfather before him, reciting from Omar Khayyam in this very spot:

Wake, for lo,
The sun has scattered into flight,
The stars before it

From the field of night.
The tavern door is open wide.
Why waits the weary traveler outside?
He was looking forward to reciting that ancient poem here to Redman Jarick.

Before he reached the canopy, J. became aware of the tied-up traffic, the pink skirt of the waitress at the open door, the knot of people and police down the block at the corner, and the wail of a departing ambulance.

The distressed waitress looked even more distressed when she saw him. She waved him past her, pointing. "Your lady, in the crosswalk," she said.

A woman standing at the corner holding a blanket seemed to recognize him as the husband. "She was conscious; she said she was meeting you. She might have a concussion, though, besides a broken leg, 'cause she also said, 'I make a good living.'"

"Let me guess—did you put that blanket under her head and ask if she were comfortable?"

"How did you know that?"

"Where did they take her?"

"I heard the driver say Cedars."

Scott had just crossed the street and circled around the crowd. "Let's go. Where's your car? I'll drive so you can run in while I park."

"You'll be without a car."

"They have cabs in LA now."

* * *

"She's going up to her room, and when they get her into bed, you can go up and continue to hold her hand. We have to keep you waiting some more. There's more coffee. The leg is badly fractured, so she'll be here a few days. She is lucky the injuries weren't more extensive. The police report says that the driver in the second lane ran a red light even though the driver in the first lane, which your wife had just passed in front of, was stopped. So I guess they apprehended him."

"Yes, I saw the son of a bitch leaning on his car with cops all around him."

"He's probably lucky you didn't go kill him."

"Yeah, not in front of the cops. Please, I've got kids."

"And the rest of the news—the baby's okay."

"What?"

"You didn't know she was pregnant?"

"Oh my God! The third wave!"

*   *   *

Ona could not quite understand that her mommy was not at home, that she would be gone for a few days without having said goodbye. On the other hand, when J. told his children that their mother would come home in a cast, Redman understood all too well that she was hurt and erupted in yells and tears.

*   *   *

It was the third day. J. parked in the next-door office-building tower, which always had a spot, even if it were at the top. In Cedars' South Tower, he hauled his big bouquet of yellow roses up the elevator off the piano lobby and dropped it at the nurse's station.

He pushed open the door and flung back the curtain. "Hey, babe, we've made it!" He was waving the *Hollywood Reporter* from that day's mail. "Look at the headline: 'Broken, one of the two best legs in Hollywood.'"